"When you care to read the very best, the name of Barbara Delinsky should come immediately to mind."
—*Rave Reviews*

"One of this generation's most gifted writers of contemporary women's fiction."
—*Affaire de Coeur*

Dear Reader,

Thank you for joining us to celebrate Harlequin's 50th anniversary! 1999 is also an anniversary year for Harlequin Intrigue—our 15th. For fifteen years we've dedicated ourselves to bringing you the best in steamy romance and heart-stopping suspense. We're thrilled to present a Barbara Delinsky Intrigue title in this unique Harlequin anniversary edition.

We're also pleased to have this opportunity to bring you a very special story from up-and-coming Intrigue author Amanda Stevens. Since her first Intrigue novel appeared in 1996, Amanda has gone on to write eight more Intrigue titles. *Her Secret Past* is a spine-tingling tale of amnesia, murder, treachery, family ties and, above all, a love once lost but never forgotten.

We hope you enjoy *Her Secret Past*, and many more Harlequin romances in the years to come! Happy 50th anniversary, Harlequin!

Sincerely,

The Editors
Harlequin Intrigue

HARLEQUIN CELEBRATES

FIVE DECADES OF ROMANCE

LIMITED COLLECTOR'S EDITION 2 IN 1

BARBARA DELINSKY

THREATS AND PROMISES

AMANDA STEVENS
HER SECRET PAST

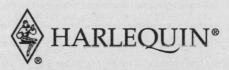

HARLEQUIN®

TORONTO • NEW YORK • LONDON
AMSTERDAM • PARIS • SYDNEY • HAMBURG
STOCKHOLM • ATHENS • TOKYO • MILAN • MADRID
PRAGUE • WARSAW • BUDAPEST • AUCKLAND

ISBN 0-373-83411-X

HARLEQUIN 50th ANNIVERSARY LIMITED COLLECTOR'S EDITION VOLUME 3

Copyright © 1999 by Harlequin Books S.A.

The publisher acknowledges the copyright holders of the individual works as follows:

THREATS AND PROMISES
Copyright © 1986 by Barbara Delinsky

HER SECRET PAST
Copyright © 1999 by Marilyn Medlock Amann

This edition published by arrangement with Harlequin Books S.A.

® and TM are trademarks of the publisher. Trademarks indicated with ® are registered in the United States Patent and Trademark Office, the Canadian Trade Marks Office and in other countries.

Visit us at www.romance.net

Printed in U.S.A.

Table of Contents

Threats and Promises
Barbara Delinsky

Prologue

The dark of night lay thick in the garden of the lavish Hollywood Hills estate where two shadowed figures conversed in low tones. Both were men. One was tall, broad and physical; the other was smooth, arrogant and cerebral.

"Are you sure? Absolutely sure?" the smooth one demanded, sounding less smooth than usual as his eyes pierced the darkness to head mercilessly at his companion.

"She wasn't in that car," the tall one insisted quietly.

"You said she was. I buried her."

"You buried ashes of what we thought was her. We were wrong."

The smooth one's nostrils flared, but he kept his voice low. "And how can you be sure it wasn't her?"

"One of our men heard talk around the coroner's office. There was no evidence of a body, charred or otherwise. A burned purse and shoes, but no body. Unofficially, of course. Officially, at least as far as the heat's concerned, she's dead."

The arrogant one cursed under his breath. He pulled a pack of cigarettes from his pocket and barely had time to raise one to his mouth when the underling snapped a match with his thumbnail and lit it.

"No body," he muttered, squaring his shoulders. "So she got away."

The physical one had enough sense to keep still. He knew what was to come, knew he had his work cut out for him.

"I want her found," the smooth one growled. "I want her found *now*."

Still the physical one remained silent.

"She didn't have any family, at least none she ever told me about. She wasn't in touch with anyone else, and her friends were mine." A long drag on the cigarette momentarily brightened its glowing red tip. "She must have had help." Smoke curled out with the words and dissipated into the air. "New identity, new location, money.... Damn it," he gritted out as the wheels of his mind turned, "she sold the jewels. There wasn't any burglary. The bitch took the jewels herself and sold them!"

"I'll find her."

"Damn right you will. Half a million in diamonds and rubies, not to mention another hundred thou in furs—no woman can steal like that from me!"

"Do you want me to bring her back?"

The tall man's boss pondered that as he stroked the closely shaved skin above his lip. When he spoke, his voice was low once more and as dark as the night. "She's a thief. And a traitor. I've given her a funeral fit for a queen. I won't suffer the embarrassment of having her materialize from the grave." He paused for a moment before continuing smoothly, arrogantly, cerebrally, in his own perverted way. "She's dead. That's how I want her. Make her squirm first. Let her know that I know what she's done. Get the jewels and whatever else you can from her. Then see that she's buried, this time with an unmarked stone."

Tossing the cigarette to the grass, he ground it out beneath the sole of his imported leather shoe. Then he straightened his silk evening jacket, thrust out his chin and walked calmly, coolly, back toward the house.

Chapter One

Lauren Stevenson looked at herself in the mirror. And looked. And looked. "It doesn't matter how long I stand here," she said breathlessly. "I still can't believe it's me!"

Richard Bowen grinned at her reflection. "It's you, and if I do say so myself, it's smashing."

She slanted him a shy glance. In the weeks during which she'd come to know this man, she'd grown perfectly comfortable with him as her doctor. But she couldn't ignore the fact that he was attractive; hence his compliment was that much more weighty. "I'll bet you say that to all the women you've worked on."

"Not necessarily. Some only look good. Some only look better than they did before. For that matter," he added with a wink, "some looked better before the surgery."

"You don't tell them that, do you?" she chided.

"Are you kidding? If it's vanity that's brought them down here, I'm not about to make an enemy for life. But it wasn't vanity that brought you here, Lauren Stevenson, was it?"

She shook her head. "It was sheer necessity." Once again she eyed herself in the mirror. "I'm amazed, though. I knew there'd be an improvement..." She faltered. Narcissism was foreign to her nature. Her cheeks grew red, her voice humble. "I didn't expect half this,"

Richard's laugh was filled with intense satisfaction. "Cases like yours are the most gratifying. You had the makings of a real beauty when you walked in here. All it took was a little rearranging."

Very lightly, she ran her fingertips down her straight nose, then along her newly reformed jawline. "More than a little." Her hand fell to graze her hip as she turned back to Richard. "And I've put on ten pounds in as many weeks. Funny, but I would have thought that having my jaws banded together and drinking through a straw would make me lose weight."

"You couldn't afford to have that happen, which was why I put you on a high-calorie liquid diet. And now that you can take in solids, I want you to follow the regimen I gave you to the letter. You could still use another five pounds on that slender frame of yours, which means you'll have to work at eating. Remember, you'll be able to chew just a little at a time until the muscles of your jaws regain their strength. How's it been since we removed the bands?"

"A little sore, but okay."

"It's only been three days. The soreness will ease off. You're talking well. In some cases we have to bring in a speech therapist, but I don't think you have to worry about that." He rose from where he'd been perched on the corner of his desk. A soft breeze wafted from the open window behind him, bringing with it the gentle rustle of palms and the fragile essence of frangipani blossoms. "So what do you think? Are you ready to go home?"

Her sigh was a teasing one, and her eyes twinkled. "I don't know. Ten weeks in the Bahamas...body wraps, massages, manicures...sun and sand and sipping all kinds of goodies through straws.... It's not a bad life."

"But the best is ahead. When does your plane leave?"

"In two hours."

"Nervous?"

"About my debut?" She sent him a helpless look of apology. "A little."

"Will someone be meeting you when you land in Boston?"

"Uh-huh. Beth."

He squinted and raised a finger, trying to keep names straight. "Your business partner, right?"

Lauren smiled. "Right. She's dying to show me everything she's done since I've been gone. She rented the spot we wanted in the Marketplace, and from what she writes, the renovations are nearly done. We've got prints and frames on order and have been in close contact with the artists we'll be representing, so it's just a question of getting everything framed and on display."

"For what it's worth, Lauren, you strike me as a patient but determined woman. I'm sure you'll be successful." He threw a gentle arm over her shoulders as she started for the door. "You'll drop me a line and let me know how things are going?"

"Uh-huh."

"And you've got the name I gave you of the specialist in Boston in case you have a problem?"

"Uh-huh."

"And you'll be sure to eat—and eat well?"

"I'll try."

Releasing her shoulder, he turned to study her face a final time. His gaze took in the symmetry of her nose, the graceful line of her jaw and the now-perfect alignment of her chin before coming to rest with warmth on her pale gray eyes. "Smashing, Lauren. I'm telling you, you look smashing."

"Thank you. Thank you for everything, Richard."

"My pleasure, sweet lady." He gave her hand a tight go-get-'em squeeze, then turned back to his office. The last thing Lauren heard him say was a smug but thoroughly endearing "Good work, Richard. You done us proud this time."

Laughing softly, she retrieved her suitcase from the reception area and headed for the airport.

"YOU...LOOK...*smashing!*" was the first thing Beth Lavin could manage to say through her astonishment when, after Lauren had grinned at her for a full minute, she finally realized that it was indeed Lauren Stevenson who stood before her.

The two women hugged each other, and Lauren laughed. "You sound like my doctor."

"Well, he's right!" Beth's eyes were wide. Hands on Lauren's shoulders, she shifted her friend first to one side, then the next. "I don't believe it! Your profile is gorgeous, and you've filled out, and your eyes look huge and wide-set, and you had your hair cut...."

In a self-conscious gesture, one of pure habit, Lauren threaded her fingers into the hair above her ear to draw the thick chestnut fall forward. Then she caught herself. With a concerted effort, she completed the backward swing, letting her hair swirl gently around her ears so that her face was free of the cover she'd hid behind for years. "I really look okay?" There was honest anxiety in her voice.

"You have to ask?"

Lauren gave an awkward half shrug. "I look at myself in the mirror and see a new person, but in my mind I'm the way I've always been."

"I'm no psychologist, but I'd say that's normal." Beth's expression brimmed with excitement and the touch of mischief Lauren knew so well. "A different person—think of the possibilities! What if you were to bump into someone you'd known before, someone like Rafe Johnson—"

"Macho Rafe?"

"Macho Rafe, who would never have thought to look at

either of us, but all of a sudden he sees this gorgeous woman and makes his play. You could string him along, then reveal your true identity and cut him off dead. Ah, the satisfaction!''

''You're awful, Beth.''

But Beth was staring at her again, this time with a touch of awe. ''Maybe…. God, you look marvelous,'' she said, moments before her face twisted in mock horror. ''And *I'm* going to look positively plain next to you!''

''Fat chance, Beth Lavin.'' Lauren hooked her elbow through her friend's and started them both toward the baggage pickup. She knew that Beth was attractive; she also knew that Beth had worn her dark brown hair in the same long, straight hairstyle for fifteen years and that her clothes—the round-collared blouse, wraparound skirt and flat leather sandals she wore now being a case in point— were as down-country as Lauren's own had always been. ''Neither one of us is going to look plain by the time we're ready to open that shop. I learned a lot down there, Beth. There were seminars on hairstyling and makeup and dressing for success. I took tons of notes—''

''You would.''

''So would you, so don't give me that,'' Lauren teased gently. ''Tell me, what's the latest with the shop?''

Beth took a deep breath. ''I finally got the ad to look the way I wanted it. It'll appear in the next issue of *Boston*. The workmen should be done in another day or two—which is good, because the prints have started arriving. Not to mention the order forms, sales slips and stationery. And the frames and hooks, wire and labels. I've got everything stashed in my apartment.''

''How *is* the apartment?''

''I like it. It's compact and within easy walking distance of the shop. Beacon Hill is exciting.'' Beth paused to ogle her friend again. ''I can't believe you!''

"In another minute I'm going to put a bag over my head."

"Don't you dare. I'm thoroughly enjoying riding on your coattails. For that matter, I still wish you'd let me take a bigger apartment so we could room together."

"Rooming together *and* working together, we'd get on each other's nerves in no time. Besides, you want the city, while I want the country. Lots of room, wide-open spaces, trees, peace and quiet."

"You're thinking of that farmhouse."

"Uh-huh."

"You'll be isolated!"

"In Lincoln?" Lauren crinkled her nose. "Nah. I'll only have three acres. When the trees are bare, I'll be able to see neighbors on either side. And the commute will be little more than half an hour."

"But that farmhouse is a wreck!"

"It's simply in need of loving."

"Tell me you've already put in an offer."

Lauren grinned. "I've already put in an offer." At Beth's moan, Lauren delivered an affectionate nudge to her ribs. "When I couldn't get the place out of my mind, I called the realtor. The purchase agreement is ready and waiting to be signed."

"Lauren, Lauren, Lauren, what am I going to do with you?"

Lauren's eyes twinkled. "You're going to put me up at your place tonight. Then, tomorrow morning, you're going to take me on a grand tour of our pride and joy. After that we are both going shopping on Newbury Street."

"Oh?"

"Uh-huh."

"Could be expensive."

"That's right," Lauren agreed remorselessly.

Beth hunched up her shoulders and gave a naughty

chuckle. "I love it, I love it." Then she abruptly narrowed her eyes and flattened her voice to a newspaper-headline drone. "Country bumpkins take city by storm. Effect transformation reminiscent of Clark Kent."

"Clark Kent?" was Lauren's wincing echo.

"Or Wonder Woman, or whomever. Of course, you know we're both a little crazy, don't you?"

"We're twenty-nine. We deserve it."

"I'll tell that to the creditors when they come calling."

Lauren Stevenson wasn't worried about the creditors. She wasn't a spendthrift, but she'd finally come to the realization that life was too short to be lived in a cocoon of timidity. Thanks to her saving prudently and the legacy she'd received when her brother had died nearly a year ago, Lauren had enough money to buy and renovate the farmhouse, pay what little wasn't covered by insurance for the corrective surgery she'd had, get a wardrobe befitting the new Lauren and establish the business.

"Here we go," she said as her luggage appeared on the revolving carousel. "Did you drive over or take a cab?"

"I drove. Your poor car was so glad to see me, I swear it got all choked up."

Lauren grunted. "Must need an oil change. On second thought, it needs to get out of the city. See, *it* wants to live in the country, too."

They left the enclosure of the terminal and headed for the parking lot. "Will you be driving north this weekend?" Beth ventured.

"To see my parents? I guess I'd better."

"I'd think you'd be excited—the new you and all."

Lauren grimaced. "You know my parents. For ultraliberals, they're as narrow as a pair of shoelaces. They didn't see the need for facial reconstruction. They thought I was just fine before."

"But medically, you were suffering!"

"I know that and you know that, and one part of them must know it, too. They're both brilliant, albeit locked in their ivory towers. I think they associate plastic surgery with vanity alone, and vanity isn't high on their list of admired traits. They said they loved me the way I was, and I'm sure they did, because that's what being a parent is all about. But let me tell you, I feel so much better now, even aside from the medical issue, I'm not sure they'd understand."

"Of course they would."

Lauren didn't argue further. Her trepidation about seeing her parents went far beyond the reconstructive surgery she'd had. She was starting a new life, and much of that life was being underwritten by her brother's bequest. Her parents resented that. Brad had been estranged from the family for eleven years preceding his death. Colin and Nadine Stevenson had neither forgotten nor forgiven what they'd considered to be their only son's abdication from the throne of the literati.

Lauren sighed. "Well, whatever the case may be, I'll see them this weekend. It may be the last time I'll be able to in a while." Lips toying with a smile, she darted a knowing glance at Beth. "I have a feeling that the next few weeks are going to be hectic."

"Hectic" was putting it mildly, though the pace was interlaced with such excitement that Lauren wouldn't have dreamed of complaining. With the completion of the redecoration of the shop, she and Beth began transferring things from Beth's apartment. Prints were framed and hung on the walls. Large art folders, filled with a myriad of additional prints and silk screens, were set in open cases on the floor for easy browsing. Vees of mat board in an endless assortment of colors were placed on Plexiglas stands atop the large butcher-block checkout counter, behind which were systematically arranged frame-corner samples, each attached to the wall with Velcro to facilitate their removal and replacement. Bolts of hand-screened fabric were attractively displayed beside bins containing unstained-wood frame kits; matching pillows were suspended from the ceiling like bananas from a tree.

Lauren signed the agreement on the farmhouse in Lincoln and, since it was already vacant, moved in a short week later. Her enthusiasm wasn't the slightest bit dampened when she saw at firsthand the amount of renovation the place would need. She had only to stand on her front porch and look across the lush yard to the forested growth surrounding her, or to smell the roses that climbed the porch-side trellis, or to listen to the birds as they whistled their spring mating ritual, to know that she'd made the right decision.

And, more than anything, she had only to look in the mirror to realize that she'd truly begun a new life.

In keeping with that new life, she and Beth did go shopping. They bought chic slacks, skirts, bright summer sweaters and lightweight dresses. They bought shoes and costume jewelry to coordinate with the outfits, all the while feeling slightly irresponsible yet enjoying every minute of it. Neither of them had been irresponsible before in their lives, but now they had earned the luxury.

Three weeks after Lauren returned from the Bahamas, the print-and-frame shop opened. It was the second week of June, and the fair-weather influx of visitors to the Marketplace kept a steady stream of shoppers circulating. With sales brisk, Lauren and Beth were ecstatic, so much so that on the first Friday night after closing, they took themselves to nearby Houlihan's to celebrate.

"If business continues this way, we'll have to hire someone to help," Lauren suggested. They were sitting at the crowded bar nursing cool drinks while they waited for their table.

"Tell me about it," Beth complained, but in delight. "There isn't enough time during the day to do bookkeeping, so I've been taking care of it at night. And you're going to need time to work with printmakers and the framer."

"I'll call the museum. Maybe they'll know of someone who'd be interested. If not, we can advertise in the newspaper."

In slow amazement, Beth shook her head. "I can't believe how good things were this week. We really lucked out with the location. There are people all over the place."

"Summer's always a busy season, what with tourists in the city. The Fanueil Hall is one of *the* spots to see."

"Wintertime's supposedly as good. At least, that's what Tom next door—you know, at the sports shop—told me."

Lauren's lips twitched mischievously. "So you've befriended Tom, have you? See what a new hairdo and clothes can do?"

Raking a hand through wavy black hair that had newly been cut to shoulder length, Beth wiggled her brows. "Look who's talking. That guy over there hasn't taken his eyes off you since we walked in."

"He's probably in a drunken stupor and I just happened into his line of vision."

"That's a crazy thing to say. You don't believe how good you look!"

Beth was right. Lauren had been accustomed to being practically invisible where men were concerned, and old habits die hard. Now she dared a quick glance in the mirror behind the bar to remind herself of the woman she'd become. Even her smart cotton sundress of crimson and cream was an eye-catcher.

With a conspiratorial glimmer in her eyes, she turned

again to Beth. "Tell me about him. I don't want to be obvious and stare."

Beth had no such qualms, but she spoke in little more than a whisper. "He's of medium height and build and is wearing a brown suit. His hair's dark, a little too short. He's got aviator-style glasses—must be an affectation, since they don't go with the rest of him." Her voice suddenly frosted. "Oops, there's a wedding band." She instantly swiveled in her seat and stared straight ahead. "Forget him. He'd only be trouble."

Lauren grinned. "Forgotten."

"Doesn't it bother you? I mean, I'm sure he'd make a play for you if you flirted a little, and the bum's married."

Shrugging with her eyebrows alone, Lauren took a sip of her drink. "I think you're making too much of it. I was probably right the first time. He's probably in a fog."

Beth grew more thoughtful. "We're going to have to do something about this situation."

"What situation?"

"Our love lives."

"What love lives?"

"That's the point. They're nonexistent. We have to meet guys."

"We have. There's Tom from the sports shop, and Anthony from the music store across the way, and Peter, who sells those super hand-painted sweatshirts, and your neighbors, those three bachelors... We could always reconsider and go to one of their parties."

Beth snorted. "We'd probably get high just walking into the room. I'm sure they're on something. Whenever I run into them, they seem off the wall. I'm telling you, we were smart to chicken out last time. We're so naive that the place could be raided and everyone would run out through the back and leave us holding the bag."

"Hmm. Maybe we'd meet a cute cop."

"I don't know, Lauren. I still think you should have gone out with that guy who came in on Wednesday."

"He was a total stranger, just browsing around."

"He was nice enough. And he did ask you out for drinks. For that matter, the fellow who came in this morning was even nicer and better-looking."

"He was a pest—trying to be so nonchalant about asking where I come from and where I live and, by the way, what my astrological sign is. I don't know what my astrological sign is. I've never been into that."

"You're scared."

Lauren hesitated for only a minute. "Yup."

"But why? You've dated before."

"That was different."

"You're right. This is supposed to be a new life you're leading!"

"On the outside it is. On the inside, well, I guess it'll take me a little longer to catch up. I don't know, Beth. Those guys seemed so…fast. So slick and sophisticated."

"You look slick and sophisticated."

"*Look*, not *am*. You know me as well as anyone does. I've lived a pretty sedate life. What dates I had were with quiet men, more serious, bookish types."

"Bo-ring."

"Maybe. But I'm not a swinger."

"Maybe you're gonna have to learn."

The hostess called their table then, but Beth picked up the conversation the instant they were seated in the glass-domed room just below street level. "Maybe we should try a singles bar, or a dating service."

"If we didn't have the guts to go to your neighbors' party, we'd never have the guts to go to a singles bar. And blind dates give me the willies."

"Blind dates gave the 'old' you the willies. The 'new' you doesn't have anything to worry about. Besides, it's not really a blind date if you go through a dating service. You get to express your preferences and pick through the possibilities.''

"Just like they get to pick through us. Uh-uh, Beth. I don't really think I'm up for that.''

"Well, we have to do something. Here we are, two wonderful women who are bright and available, and we should be having dinner with two equally as captivating men.''

"Maybe we should put an ad in the paper,'' Lauren joked, then promptly scowled. "Only problem is that we're cowards. All talk, no action.'' Her eyes grew dreamy. "They say that good things come to those who wait. I'm more than willing to wait if one day some gorgeous guy who is bright and available and gentle and easygoing will walk up to me and introduce himself.''

"According to women's lib,'' Beth offered tongue-in-cheek, "we shouldn't have to sit back and wait. We can take the bull by the horns.''

Lauren glanced over Beth's shoulder toward the table at which a lone man sat, just finishing his dinner. He wasn't gorgeous, but he was certainly pleasant-looking. When he looked up and caught her eye, he smiled. Curious, Beth turned also; he shared his smile with her.

"There's your chance,'' Lauren coaxed in a stage whisper filled with good-humored challenge. "I don't want him, so he's all yours. Go ahead. Take the bull by the horns.''

Turning back to their own table, Beth opened her menu and concentrated on its contents. Lauren followed suit. Neither woman noticed when the lone man took his check from the waitress and headed for the cash register.

Chapter Two

The second week of the shop's existence was as promising as the first had been. Just as Lauren was wondering how she and Beth would be able to cope with the continued pace on their own, a free-lance photographer came in, peddling his wares. He was a young man—Lauren guessed him to be no more than twenty-five—and his pictures were good. He was also looking for part-time work to pay for the increasing costs of his materials and equipment. She hired him instantly, and neither she nor Beth regretted the decision. Now they could take an hour off here or there—albeit separately—to do paperwork, go out for lunch or shop through downtown Boston.

On one such occasion, a week after Jamie had signed on, Lauren returned to the shop with a new sweater in a bag under her arm and a faint pallor on her face. Beth quickly joined her in the back room. "Are you okay?"

Setting the bag on the desk, Lauren sank into a chair. "I think so. You wouldn't believe what just happened to me, Beth. I'd bought this sweater and was walking back along Newbury Street when a car lost control and veered onto the sidewalk. I was daydreaming, feeling on top of the world, looking at my reflection as I passed store windows. I mean, I was so caught up in being happy that I wasn't paying attention to what was going on around me. If it hadn't been for some stranger who grabbed me out of the way in the nick of time, God only knows what would have happened!''

"Don't think about that. You're safe, and that's all that matters. Was the driver drunk?''

"Who knows? He regained control of the car and went on his merry way again. Didn't even bother to stop and make sure no one was hurt.''

"Bastard.''

"Mmm.''

"The stranger who saved you...was he cute?''

"He was a she,'' Lauren snapped, but her annoyance was contrived. "And what kind of question is that to ask at a time like this?''

"Have to restore a little humor here. Just think how romantic it would have been if you'd been snatched from the hands of death by a tall, dark and handsome stranger. You could have fainted away in his arms, and he'd have lifted you, holding you ever so gently against his rock-hard chest while he gazed, smitten, upon your lovely face.''

Lauren rolled her eyes. "Oh, God.''

Beth wagged a finger at her. "Someday it might happen. Miracles are like that, y'know.''

"Is this the same woman who was putting in a plug for women's lib not so long ago?'' Lauren asked the calendar on the wall, looking back at Beth only when she felt a hand on her arm.

"Are you okay now?'' The question was soft and filled with concern. "Want a cold drink or something?''

Taking a deep breath, Lauren shook her head. "I'm fine. It was after the fact, while I was walking, that the shakes set in. But I'm better now. I'd really like to get back to work. That'll keep my mind occupied.''

It did, and by the time Lauren arrived in Lincoln that evening, she'd pretty much forgotten the incident. By the next day, it was lost amid more important and immediate activities relating to the shop.

That night she went home, changed into a T-shirt and jeans and made herself dinner, dutifully following the guidelines Richard Bowen had given her. It was an effort at times, since she seemed to be eating so much, but she'd gained three of the five pounds Richard had prescribed, and she had to agree that they looked good on her.

What with the time demands that the shop had made since her return from the Bahamas, she'd had precious little opportunity to organize her thoughts with regard to renovating the farmhouse. Now, pen and paper in hand, she walked from room to room, making lists of what she wanted to have done. The realtor who'd sold her the house had given her the names of a local contractor, a carpenter, an electrician and a plumber. Though she wasn't about to hire any one of them without checking them out further, she wanted to have her thoughts together before arranging preliminary meetings.

After more than an hour of taking detailed notes, she put down the pen and paper and went out to the front porch. The night was clear, the moon a silver crescent in the star-studded sky. On an impulse, she wandered across the yard and stopped at its center, then tipped her head back and singled out a star to wish on.

But what did one wish for when life was already so good? She was totally healthy for the first time in many years. She had a new look, which she adored. She had a new business, and it was well on its way to becoming a success. She had a home of her own, with potential enough to keep her happy for a long, long time.

What did one wish for? Perhaps a man. Perhaps children. In time.

Lowering her head, she started slowly back toward the house. A sound caught her ear. She stopped and frowned. It was a sound of nature, yet odd. It had been distinctly unfriendly.

When it came again, she whirled around. A low growl. She cocked her head toward the nearby trees, then narrowed her eyes on the creature that slowly advanced on her. A dog. She breathed a sigh of relief. Probably one of the neighbors' pets.

Pressing a hand to her racing heart, she spoke aloud. "You frightened me, dog. Is that any way to greet a new neighbor?" As she took a step forward to befriend the animal, it bared its teeth and issued another growl, this one clearly in warning. Lauren held her hands out, palms up, and said softly, "I won't hurt you, boy." She lowered one hand. "Here. Sniff."

Rather than approaching her, the dog growled again, accompanying the hostile sound with a crouch that suggested an imminent attack.

"Hey, don't get upset—" She barely had time to manage the tremulous words when the dog was on her, knocking her to the ground, snarling viciously. Struggling to fend off the beast, she put her arms up to protect herself and kicked out. But as quickly as it had lunged, the dog retreated, galloping toward the trees and disappearing into the dense growth.

Trembling wildly, Lauren pushed herself up to a seated position. Then, not willing to take a chance that the dog might return, she stumbled to her feet and made a frantic beeline for the house.

Once inside, she leaned back against the firmly shut door, closed her eyes and dragged in a shaky breath. When the worst of the shock had subsided, anger set in. Had it not been so late at night, she would have called the Youngs, her neighbors on the side from which the dog had come. Then again, she realized, perhaps it was lucky it was too late to make a call. Furious as she was that anyone would let such a savage animal loose in even as rural an area as this, she was apt to say something she might later regret. She'd met Carol Young only once. She didn't want to alienate the woman, or her husband, or one of their teenaged boys. Better to let herself calm down. She'd call tomorrow.

Hence, from work the next morning, she dialed the Youngs' number and was relieved to hear Carol herself answer the phone. "Carol, this is Lauren Stevenson. We met several weeks ago when I moved in next door."

"Sure, Lauren. It's good to hear from you. How's it going?"

"Really well.... I hope I'm not dragging you away from anything."

"Don't be silly. One of the luxuries of working at a computer terminal out of my house is that I can take a break whenever I want. The boys have gone to visit their grandparents in Maryland for a week, so I've got more than enough time for a phone call or two. How's the house?"

"Pretty raw still. I've been so busy here at the shop that I haven't had much of a chance to look into hiring workers to fix things up. But that's not why I called." Lauren chose her words carefully, striving to be as diplomatic as possible. "I had an awful scare last night. I was walking out in the yard sometime around eleven when I was attacked by a dog."

"*Attacked?* Are you all right?"

"I'm fine. The dog jumped me, bared its teeth and made ugly noises, but it ran off before it did any harm."

"My God! I didn't think there were any wild dogs around here!"

"Then...it's not yours?"

"God, no. Is that what you thought?"

"It came from the trees on your side.... I'm sorry, I just assumed..."

"You should have called us last night. We might have been able to help you track it down. What did it look like?"

"It was big and dark. Short-haired. Maybe a Doberman, but it was too dark out for me to see the dog's exact coloration, and besides, I was too terrified to notice much of anything."

"You poor girl. I'd have been terrified, too." Carol paused, thinking. "To my knowledge, no one in the neighborhood has a dog like that, certainly not one that would attack a person. Sometimes strange animals do wander into the area, though. Maybe you should call the local police."

Lauren was lukewarm to that idea. As a new resident, she hated to make a stir. "I—I don't think that's necessary. As long as I know the dog wasn't from the immediate vicinity, I feel better. It's probably a watchdog that escaped and got lost. And it didn't hurt me, much as it looked like it could have."

"Listen, we'll keep an eye out for it, and I'll mention it to some of the other neighbors. But if you catch sight of it again, you really should file a complaint. There's no reason why you should be frightened to walk on your own property."

Lauren sighed. "I'll be on guard in the future. Thanks, Carol. You've been a help."

"I wish I could do more. Let me know if something comes up, okay?"

"Okay."

As Lauren hung up the phone, Beth straightened up from

where she'd been leaning unnoticed against the door. "A dog? First a car, now a dog. Lord, the new you is attracting some pretty weird elements."

"Go ahead," Lauren teased, "have a good laugh at my expense."

"I'm not laughing." Beth rubbed her hands together in anticipation of high drama. "Maybe someone's out to get you...someone who lived in that old farmhouse a century ago and whose ghost will never be laid to rest until the rightful owner of the place returns."

"Beth..."

Beth held up a hand. "No, listen. Suppose, just suppose, the ghost is determined to run you out of town, so it plots all kinds of little 'accidents' designed to scare you to death—"

"Beth!"

"And then some gorgeous hunk arrives and just happens to have a secret weapon that can zap even a ghost and reduce it to—to a shredded sheet...."

Lauren sat back in her chair, helpless to contain the beginnings of a grin. "Are you done?"

"Oh, no. The best part comes after the ghost is shredded and you and the gorgeous hunk fall madly in love and live happily ever after."

"Why aren't you working?"

"Because Jamie's working."

"I think *you* should be working." Lauren pushed herself out of her seat. "I think *I* should be working." With a fond squeeze to Beth's arm as she passed, she returned to the front of the shop.

SEVERAL DAYS LATER, Lauren knew that she had to do something about starting the renovation work on her house. The garage door had unexpectedly slammed to the ground when she'd been within mere inches of it. Ironically, if the garage had been nearly as old as the farmhouse itself, its doors would have swung open from the center to the sides, and she would never have been in danger of a skull fracture. But the garage had been added twenty-five years before. Apparently, she mused in frustration, it had been as neglected by recent owners as the house.

She made several calls, setting up appointments to discuss repairs with the men whose names she'd been given. None of them had impressed her on the phone, though she reasoned that there was no harm in meeting with them before she sought out additional contacts. She wanted her home to be perfect, and she was willing to pay to make it so.

With that settled in her mind, she sat down on the living room floor, using the low coffee table as a desk, to write up orders for the framer. But she was distracted. Repeatedly her pen grew still and her gaze wandered to the window. It was dark as pitch outside. She was alone. Anyone could see in, watch her, study her.

Cursing both Beth for her fanciful imaginings and herself for her own surprising susceptibility, she returned to her work. But that night, to her chagrin, she fell asleep wondering if one-hundred-year-old ghosts were capable of sabotaging twenty-five-year-old garage doors.

SHORTLY AFTER NOON on the following day, Lauren saw him for the first time. She was working in the front window of the shop, replacing a framed picture that had been bought that morning, when she happened to glance toward the bench just outside. He was sitting there, quietly and intently. And he was staring at her.

With a tight smile, she looked quickly away, finished

hanging the new print, then took refuge in the inner sanctum of the shop.

Fifteen minutes later, during a brief lull in business, she glanced out to find that he hadn't moved. One arm slung over the back of the bench, one knee crossed casually over the other, he appeared to be innocently people-watching—until his gaze penetrated the front window once more.

Again Lauren looked away, this time wondering why she had. There was nothing unusual about a man sitting on a bench in the Marketplace; people did it all the time. And this man, wearing a short-sleeved plaid shirt, jeans and sneakers, looked like a typical passerby. Though he wasn't munching on fried dough or licking an ice cream cone, as so many of the others did, she assumed he was enjoying the pleasant atmosphere. Or waiting for someone. Or simply resting his legs. The fact that he kept looking into the shop was understandable, since it was smack in front of him.

A telephone call came through from one of the printmakers she'd been trying to reach; then customers occupied her time for the next hour and a half. She'd nearly forgotten about the man outside until she left the shop to buy stamps, and even then she was perplexed that she should think of him at all.

He was nowhere to be seen.

AT HOME THAT NIGHT, Lauren was strangely on edge. She didn't know why, and for lack of anything better, she blamed it on the two cups of coffee she'd had that afternoon.

With a critical eye, she looked around the kitchen as she waited for the bouillabaisse she'd bought at a gourmet takeout shop to heat. She intended to do this room in white—white cabinets with white ash trim, white stove and refrigerator, white ceramic tile on the floor. The accent would be pale blue, as in enamel cookware, patterned wallpaper, prints on the wall. Perhaps she'd order a pale blue pleated miniblind—not that she'd originally planned to put anything on the windows, but it occurred to her that she might like the option of privacy for moments like these when the night seemed mysterious.

She was edgy. Too much coffee. That was all.

THE FOLLOWING MORNING, the man was back. Wearing a crisp white polo shirt with his jeans, he was sitting on the bench again, this time with his legs sprawled before him.

"Remarkable, isn't he?" Beth quipped, coming up beside Lauren.

"Who?"

"That guy you're looking at. Have you ever seen such gorgeous hair?" It was light brown with a sun-streaked sheen and was neatly brushed, but thick and on the long side.

"No."

"Or such long legs?"

"No."

"Wonder who he is."

"I don't know."

"Probably just another tourist. Why is it the good ones are here today, gone tomorrow?"

"This one was here yesterday."

"What?"

Lauren blinked once, dragging her gaze from the man to her friend. Absently she wiped damp palms on her slim-cut green linen skirt. "I saw him here yesterday."

Beth's eyes widened. "You're kidding! Do you think he's waiting for...us?"

"Come on, Beth. Why in the world would he be waiting for us?"

"Maybe he heard about these two terrific ladies who own the print-and-frame shop, and he's come to investigate."

"If he had any guts, he'd come in."

"If we had any guts, we'd go out."

"Well, we don't, and apparently he doesn't, either, so that's that." As the two watched, the man got to his feet and ambled off. "That's that," Lauren repeated, not quite sure whether to be relieved or disappointed. There had been something fascinating about the man, not only his legs and his hair but also a certain sturdiness. She wondered if he'd ever owned a black dog that snarled. Then she promptly pushed that thought from her mind, along with all other thoughts of the man—until she caught sight of him again that afternoon.

At first he walked slowly past the shop without sparing it a glance. A few minutes later he returned from the opposite direction, this time pausing near the door before heading for the bench. When Lauren saw him sink onto it, leaning forward with his knees spread and his hands clasped between them, she couldn't help but grow apprehensive. There was something definitely suspicious about the way he glanced toward the shop, then away, then back again.

"Who *is* that man?" she whispered to Beth, who promptly looked up from the VISA charge form she was filling out to follow Lauren's worried gaze.

"So he's back, is he?" Beth resumed writing but spoke under her breath. "He's a little too rugged for my tastes. You can have him."

"I don't want him," Lauren grumbled from the corner of her mouth, "but I would like to know why he's been loitering around here for two days straight."

"Why don't you go and ask him?" Beth murmured, then, smiling, handed the charge slip and a pen to her customer. "If you'll just sign this and put your address and phone number at the bottom…"

Lauren whispered back in a miffed tone of voice. "I can't just walk out there and *ask* him! He's probably got a very good reason for being there, and I'd feel like a fool."

"Then stop worrying. I'm sure he's harmless."

Lauren wasn't so sure. The man was too intent in his scrutiny of the shop, and she felt the touch of his gaze too strongly to forget him.

When a customer approached her to buy a piece of fabric and have it stretched onto a frame, Lauren welcomed the diversion. When another customer selected a print and needed advice on its framing, she was more than happy to oblige. When a third customer entered the shop in search of several prints to coordinate with swatches of fabric and wallpaper, she immersed herself in the project.

By the time the closing hour drew near, Lauren was tired. She was in the back room, dutifully updating inventory cards and looking forward to a leisurely drive home, a quiet dinner and what was left of the evening with a good book.

"Lauren?" The low urgency in Beth's voice brought Lauren's head up quickly. "He's here, asking for *you*."

"Who—"

"Him." Beth's eyes darted back over her shoulder. "The guy from the bench."

Lauren put down the cards. "He's asking for *me*?"

"By name."

"How did he…he must have…where is he?"

"Right here," Beth mouthed in a way that would have been comical had Lauren been feeling particularly confident.

But she wasn't. This man was different. Not boring-looking. Not slick and sophisticated-looking. Very... different.

Beth made an urgent gesture with her hand.

"I'm coming. I'm coming," Lauren murmured unsteadily. She stood up, smoothing the hip-length ivory cotton sweater over her skirt and squared her shoulders. Then, praying that she looked more composed than she felt, she slowly and reluctantly left her refuge.

Chapter Three

He was much taller close up than he'd appeared through the shop window. And broader in the shoulders. And more tanned. What was most surprising, though, was that he seemed just a little unsure of himself.

"Lauren Stevenson?" he asked cautiously.

She'd come to a stop several feet away and rested her hand on the butcher-block table. "Yes?"

As he studied her more closely, his puzzlement grew. "It's really strange. You're not at all as I expected you to be."

Lauren held her breath for a minute, then asked with a caution of her own, "What had you expected?"

"Someone...well, someone different."

If he had some connection to her past, she realized, not only was his puzzlement understandable but his tact was commendable. Still, she couldn't deny her wariness. The man had been staking her out for two days. "Do you know me? Should I know you?"

For the first time, he smiled. It was a self-conscious smile, endearing in its way. "My name's Matthew Kruger. Matt." He hestitated for a split second. "I was a friend of your brother's."

Lauren wasn't sure what *she* had expected, but it hadn't

been this. "Brad's friend?" She was unable to hide either her surprise or her skepticism.

"That's right. I was with him just after the accident. I'm...sorry about his death."

"I am, too," she returned honestly, her brow lightly furrowed as she studied Matthew Kruger. He didn't quite fit into the mold she'd constructed of Brad and his friends. Strange that she'd never heard of him. Then again, perhaps not so strange. She hadn't been any closer to Brad before his death than her parents had been. "But...it's been a year since he died." Silently she asked herself why this so-called friend of Brad's had waited this long to contact her.

"I know you weren't close, but Brad did mention you to me several times, and since I had to come east on business, I thought I'd look you up."

"What kind of business are you in?"

Another split second's hesitation. "I'm a builder. The development firm I work for has just contracted to do some work in western Massachusetts. I'm here to set things up— to get the ball rolling, so to speak."

She nodded. A builder. Given the pale crow's feet at the corners of his eyes, he was not a builder who directed things from his desk. He was a builder who got his hands dirty. And whose body was well-toned through hard physical labor. *That* she could associate with the image she'd formed of her brother's new life and friends, though if her parents' opinion had been valid, she would have expected someone far coarser. On the surface, at least, Matthew Kruger didn't appear to be coarse. "Clean and all-American" was a more apt description. Could the surface appearance be deceptive?

"I see," she said. Then, feeling uncomfortable, she averted her gaze. In truth, she'd known little about her brother and his way of life...and then there was the matter of this man's physical presence. He intimidated her. "Have you, uh, have you been in Boston very long?"

"A week."

She nodded.

"I'm staying at the Long Wharf Marriott."

"If your work is in the western part of the state, wouldn't it be easier to stay out there?"

"I have been, but our investors are here and there's some paperwork to do, so I decided to take a few days to sightsee." When he suddenly looked beyond her, Lauren swung her head around.

"I'm going to lock up," Beth whispered, darting a curious glance at Matt as she started to pass.

Lauren reached out and caught her arm. "Uh, Beth, this is Matthew Kruger. He is—was—a friend of Brad's." Lauren still had her doubts about that, but saying it simplified the introduction. "Matt, Beth Lavin."

Beth had known Brad Stevenson before he'd struck out on his own, and since she wasn't a member of his immediate family, she'd been more objective about his departure. Hands clasped tightly before her, she smiled shyly at Matt. "I'm pleased to meet you."

"The pleasure's mine," Matt said, returning her smile. His gaze quickly grew apologetic when it sought Lauren's again. "I don't want to hold you up if there's something you should be doing now."

Lauren opened her mouth to say that she really did have work to finish, but Beth spoke first. "Oh, you're not holding her up. We were pretty much done for the day when you came in. I finished the inventory cards, Lauren. Why don't you and Matt take off? I'll close up."

The last thing Lauren wanted to do was to take off with Matt. She wasn't convinced he was who he said he was, and even if it was so, they were on opposite sides of a rift. Besides, he hadn't asked her to "take off" with him.

As though on cue, he did. "How about it, Lauren?" He paused, then took a quick breath. "I heard there was a sunset cruise around the harbor. If we hurry, we can make it."

"Uh, I really shouldn't...."

"Go on, Lauren," Beth coaxed. Subtlety had never been her forte. "You haven't been out much. It's a beautiful night. The fresh air will do you good."

"I'd really like the company," Matt urged softly.

His last words trapped Lauren. If he'd come on strong, she might have easily refused. But he sounded sincere, and she caught a drift of the same unsureness she'd seen when she'd first faced him. Though large and rugged-looking, he had an odd gentleness to him. His eyes were brown, warm and soft. At that moment they hinted at vulnerability; above all, Lauren Stevenson was a sucker for vulnerability.

Releasing the breath she'd subconsciously been holding, Lauren acknowledged an internal truce. "I'll get my things," she whispered.

Soon after, she and Matt were walking side by side toward the waterfront. He was as quiet as she, casting intermittent glances her way, and she wondered if he felt as strange as she did.

In an attempt to break the silence, she asked the first thing that came to mind. "How did you know I was in Boston?"

"Your parents told me."

"My *parents*!"

He sent her a sidelong glance. "Shouldn't they have?"

"No—yes—I mean, I'm just surprised. That's all."

They walked a little farther before he spoke again.

"You're thinking that they wouldn't have willingly given your address to any friend of Brad's."

"I...guess that says it."

A muscle in his jaw flexed. "At least you're honest."

She shrugged. "How much do you know about Brad's reasons for leaving?"

"Only what Brad told me—that your parents couldn't accept his wanting to work with his hands rather than with his mind, that they flipped out when he left college and pretty much washed their hands of him."

Perhaps Matt had known Brad after all. "Spoken that way, it sounds cruel."

"It was, in a way. Brad was badly hurt by the split."

"So were my parents, yet none of the three tried to mend it."

"And you, Lauren? Did you do anything?"

Her gaze shot sharply to his, then softened and fell. "No," she admitted quietly. "I think I might have in time. Then time ran out."

"You regretted the distance?"

"Brad was my only brother. We had no other siblings. He was four years older than I, and his interests were always different. We weren't close as kids, but I like to think that we might have found common ground as we'd gotten older."

They had reached Atlantic Avenue. Matt put a light hand on her elbow as they trotted across to avoid an onrushing car. He dropped it when they reached the median strip, where they waited for a minute before finishing the crossing.

"Then you were seventeen when Brad left."

Lauren blew out a breath. "You really *do* know about Brad, don't you?"

"He told me he was twenty-one when he dropped out.

If you were four years his junior…'' Matt's voice trailed off and his features tensed. ''Did you think I was lying about being his friend?''

''No. Well, maybe. I have to take your word for it that you knew him, since he can't verify it, can he?''

''Are you always distrustful?''

She looked him in the eye. ''Only when I see someone lurking outside my shop for two days before coming in.''

''Oh. You saw me.''

''Yes.'' Was that a sudden rush of color to his cheeks? She wondered if it was guilt, or embarrassment. In case it was the latter, she softened her tone. ''I assume you weren't trying to hide.''

''Actually,'' he confessed, ''I was trying to get up the nerve to come in.''

That was a new one in her experience. ''Why ever would you have to get up the nerve to approach *me*?''

''Several reasons. First, I knew there were hard feelings where Brad was concerned and I wasn't sure how I'd be received. Second, I wasn't sure if it was really you.'' His gaze slid from one to another of her features. Again that puzzled look crossed his face. ''You look so different. Very…very pretty.''

Lauren clutched the shoulder strap of her bag more tightly. ''Brad had a picture.''

''An old one. You were sixteen at the time.''

For reasons she wasn't about to analyze, she didn't want to go into the matter of her reconstructive surgery. ''It was a long time ago,'' she said quietly. ''People change.''

''I'll say,'' Matt drawled. ''Still, it's amazing…'' He seemed about to go on, and for an instant Lauren wondered just how much Brad had told him about her. She was saved when he looked up and announced tentatively, ''I think this is it.''

She followed his gaze toward where the wharf and its cruise boats loomed. "Looks like it. This is really the blind leading the blind. I went to college in Boston, but that was a while ago. I haven't been back for very long."

"Are you living here in the city?"

The glance she sent him held subtle accusation, but there was a whisper of amusement underlying her words. "What did my parents tell you?"

Reading her loud and clear, he fought back a grin. "Just the name of the shop. I assume they wanted to keep things on a strictly business level."

"I'm sure they did."

"And you?"

"And me what?"

He was suddenly serious. "Would you put me down because I don't have a Ph.D. in some esoteric subject?"

"I don't have a Ph.D. in *any* subject."

"You have a master's degree in art. I never went to college."

"But you're successful in what you do. At least, if you're traveling across the country, the firm you work for must be doing well…you must be valued." Having doubted his story such a short time ago, she amazed herself by coming to his defense. Suckers for vulnerability weren't always the most prudent. She took a deep breath. "No, Matt. I'm not like my parents. Brad wasn't the only one who had differences with them. It's just taken me a little longer to act on those differences."

Their conversation was cut short when they arrived at the ticket booth. Matt paid their fare, and they boarded the boat. Wending their way through the other groups that had gathered, they climbed to the top deck and found an empty place by the rail to look back at the city skyline.

"I love Boston," Lauren mused after several minutes of silent appreciation.

"Explain."

"It's bigger than Bennington and that much more exciting, yet smaller than New York and that much more manageable. You can understand it, get to know it. It's livable."

"You have an apartment?"

"A farmhouse."

"In the *city*?"

"In Lincoln—" She caught herself and scowled at him. "That was sneaky. You took advantage of me when my defenses were down."

He grinned amiably. "Sorry about that. Do you really own a farmhouse?"

Somehow further prevarication seemed silly. "Uh-huh. It's old and needs a whole load of work before its potential can be realized, but it's on a great piece of land and has charm, real charm."

"Old places are like that. History adds character. That's one of the reasons *I* like Boston. Wandering around, seeing where the Boston Massacre took place or where the Declaration of Independence was first read—it gives you goose bumps." He paused, staring at Lauren. "Why are you grinning?"

"You and goose bumps. You're so big and solid. It seems a contradiction."

"No," he said gently. "The goose bumps I'm talking about have an emotional cause. Big and solid don't necessarily mean unfeeling."

"I didn't mean—"

"I know." His point made, he left it at that.

They lapsed into silence, watching as the gangplank was drawn up and the boat inched away from the dock. Soon the engines growled louder. The boat made a laborious turn, then picked up speed and entered the main body of the harbor, moving at a steady, if chugging, pace.

"Would you like a drink?" Matt asked.

Lauren drew herself back from her immersion in the scenery. "No—uh, make that yes. A wine spritzer, if they can handle it, or lemonade. Something cool."

With a nod, he made his way back across the deck and disappeared down the stairs leading to the lower level. Following his progress, Lauren had to admit that he was as attractive as any other man in sight. It wasn't that he was beautiful in the classic sense; his chin was too square, his nose a shade crooked, his skin too weathered. But he exuded good health and strength and competence. He'd crossed the shimmying deck without faltering.

The wind whipped through her hair as she turned to face the sea once more. She concentrated on the sights—the Aquarium, the Harbor Towers, the piers with their assortment of fishing boats and tankers, the waterfront restaurants. Only when Matt returned and she smiled did she realize how much nicer the setting seemed with him by her side.

"Two lemonades." He handed her one. "The spritzer was beyond the bartender, and the other drinks were heavier. There were some hot dogs down there, but they looked pretty sad." He took a bag of potato chips from under his arm, opened it and held it out. She munched one, then washed it down with a drink.

"Tell me about Brad," she surprised herself by saying.

Somber-eyed, he studied her expression. "I'm not sure you really want to know."

She attributed his hesitancy to her own obvious ambivalence. "You may be right. But...I guess I really am curious. I've never met anyone who knew him after he left. I'm not sure I should pass the opportunity by."

Matt tossed several chips into his mouth. "What do you want to know?" he asked between stilted bites.

"Did he work for your company?"

"No."

"Had he always been in San Francisco?" She knew that was where he'd died.

"He started out in Sacramento."

"As a carpenter."

"That's right. By the time he came to San Francisco, though, he was doing a lot of designing."

"Designing what?"

Matt hesitated for an instant. "Houses, mostly. Some office parks. As an architect, he was a natural."

"Is that how he was viewed—as an architect?"

"No. He didn't have the credentials. He was like a ghost-writer, presenting rough sketches to the company's architect, who then embellished and formalized the sketches."

"Were you familiar with his company?"

"We were competitors."

The words were simple and straightforward, yet something about the way they'd been offered gave Lauren the impression that Matt hadn't particularly cared for Brad's outfit. "But still, you were friends. How did that work?"

Matt seemed to relax somewhat. "Very comfortably. Our respective superiors held the patent on rivalry. Brad and I rather enjoyed fraternizing with the enemy."

"How did you meet?"

"In a bowling league."

Her expression grew distant. "Funny, I can't picture Brad bowling. But then, I can't picture him sweating on the roof of a house, either." She tore herself from her musings. "What else did you do together?"

"Ate out. Sometimes double-dated. We vacationed together—there were six of us, actually. We rafted down the Colorado, went on horseback through parts of Montana. It was fun."

"Very macho," she teased and was rewarded by a sheepish grin from Matt.

"I suppose."

Her smile lingered for a minute before fading. "Brad never married." She'd learned that when she'd been informed by the lawyer that she was the sole beneficiary of her brother's estate. "I wonder why."

"Maybe he never met the right girl, one who could accept him as he was."

"Have you ever married?" she asked on impulse. Matt stared at her for a minute, then shook his head. "Why not?"

"Same reason."

She pondered his answer quietly. "I can understand it in Brad's case. He grew up in an atmosphere in which intellectual excellence was the only valid goal. He struggled to keep up for a while, then simply threw in the towel. Neither my parents nor their circle of friends could accept his behavior. Long before he left, he was labeled a misfit. I'm sure he was sensitive about it."

"We all have our sensitivities."

"What are yours, Matt? Why would a woman have trouble accepting you as you are?"

He chomped several more potato chips and would have seemed perfectly nonchalant had it not been for the ominous darkening of his eyes. "I'm blue-collar all the way. I don't have a pedigree, or a series of fancy qualifying initials to put after my name. Over the years I've done well in my work, but that doesn't mean I aspire to own my own company, or that one day I won't decide to chuck it all and go back to building log cabins. If a woman thinks she's getting a future real-estate tycoon in me, she'd better think again.''

Lauren couldn't miss the bitterness in his words. ''You've been burned.''

''Several times.'' He looked out over the water and his tone gentled, growing apologetic enough to defy arrogance. ''I've always attracted women pretty easily. But physical attraction isn't enough. Not by a long shot.''

''The grass is always greener…'' she said softly. ''There are those of us who'd *love* to have looks that would attract.''

Matt eyed her as if she were crazy. ''But you *do*! I can't believe there isn't a line of men waiting to take you out!''

It took Lauren a minute to realize what she'd said and why Matt had answered as forcefully as he had. She'd forgotten. That happened a lot. A slow warmth crept up her neck. Compliments were still new to her, and from as physically superb a man as Matthew Kruger… ''I don't know about a line,'' she said simply.

''Then there's one man?''

She shook her head.

''You're a beautiful woman, Lauren. Surely you've had offers.''

Again she shook her head, this time with a self-conscious half smile.

''Why not?''

At his bluntness, she burst out laughing. ''You're almost as undiplomatic as Beth.''

''I'm sorry. I was just curious.'' He held up a large, well-formed hand. ''Not that I'm saying you should be married. You're only, what, twenty-nine, and you're obviously building a career for yourself.'' A new thought hit him, and he frowned. ''You said you haven't been in Boston for very long. Then the shop is a recent thing?''

"We've been open barely a month."

"And before that?"

"I worked in a museum back home."

He rubbed his forefinger along the rim of his paper cup. "Back home. That could explain it. Brad told me about back home."

"What did he say?"

"That it was stifling. One-dimensional. You were either an artist or an academician affiliated with the college."

"He was being unfair. Bennington's a beautiful place. Some fascinating people chose to live there. Brad just didn't."

"Nor did you, apparently. Why did you leave, Lauren?"

"Because I wanted to open the shop."

"But you could have opened a shop in Bennington."

She shook her head. "Too small a market."

"So you're going for the big time."

"I want the shop to be a success, yes," she said on a defensive note. "I may not aspire to put out one profound treatise after another the way Mom and Dad have, but that doesn't mean I can't aim to do what I do well."

There was a wistfulness to Matt's smile. "Now you *do* sound like Brad. He was so determined...." A flicker of uncertainty crossed his brow.

"So determined...?"

It was a while before Matt finished his sentence, and then it was with care. "To be successful. Recognized. I'm not sure he realized it, or realized what was driving him, but as often as he claimed that he was doing his own thing and didn't care what his family thought, I think he was kidding himself."

"Was he happy, Matt?"

Matt had to consider that. "In a way, yes."

Peering down at the bits of lemon pulp clinging to the

sides of her cup, Lauren spoke more slowly. "All we were told about the accident was that he was supervising some blasting and got caught in the mess. Was there...anything more to it?"

"That was it."

He'd answered quickly and with finality. Not knowing why, Lauren was taken aback. "You saw him right after?"

"At the hospital." His tone was clipped. As he went on, its harshness eased. "Brad was lucid for a time, but between the internal injuries and everything else—well, maybe it was for the best. If he'd lived—and the chances of that were slim from the start—he would have been a quadraplegic. I don't think he would have been able to bear that."

"No," she whispered, and when she looked up, her eyes were moist. "I feel guilty about it sometimes."

"Guilty?"

"Everything I have now—the shop, the farmhouse, this—" she gestured broadly toward herself "—has come from the money he left me. Did you know that?"

Matt put his hand on her shoulder and massaged it gently. His voice was much, much softer, his focus shifted. "That was Brad's wish. I was the one who passed it on to the lawyer. Given the circumstances, Brad gained a measure of peace from it."

Lauren nodded, then somehow couldn't stop the overflow of words. "If it hadn't been for Brad, I'd probably still be back in Bennington. Even aside from the money, his death was a turning point for me. For the first time in my life, I stopped to think of my own mortality, of what I'd have to my credit when the time came, of what I'd be leaving behind. That was when I decided to move to Boston and open the shop. I only wish Brad could know how much better I feel about myself now."

"It's enough that you know, Lauren. If Brad were here to see you, I'm sure he'd be proud."

She looked timidly at Matt, then away, and took a long, shuddering breath. "It's too bad we can't have it both ways—too bad I can't have what I do and have Brad alive to see it."

Slipping his arm across her back, Matt drew her to his side. His warmth was the comfort she needed. "Life is cruel that way, filled with choice and compromise. Even those who reach the heights make sacrifices along the way. The best we can do is to decide exactly how much we're prepared to give up and move on from there."

As she raised her gaze to his, her cheek brushed his shoulder. It seemed a perfectly natural gesture. "But that's a negative view."

"It's realistic."

"Maybe I'm more of a romantic, then. I want to focus on the goals and face the hurdles as I come to them."

He shrugged. "And I want to be prepared for the hurdles. It's just a different approach. Who's to say which one is better?"

She didn't answer. Her gaze was suddenly locked with his, lost in his, and she struggled to cope with the intensity. He was a virtual stranger, yet she'd told him things she'd never told another soul. Was it the fact that he was a link to her brother, or that he was a good listener, or that he'd shared his own thoughts with her? She'd been wary of him at first; she still was, in some respects. And yet…and yet she was drawn to him.…

The sudden blast of the boat's horn made them both jump. They looked around to find the bulk of the passengers crowded on the other side of the deck, waving to a passing tall ship. Without releasing her, Matt moved to join them.

"Impressive," he breathed, taking in the towering masts and ancient fittings of the proud vessel. "Too bad she's not under sail."

"Mmm. It's almost disillusioning. There weren't any motors in the old days."

"Or Sony Walkmans." He pointed to the sailor perched on the rigging, headset firmly in place. Lauren smiled at the sight, then shifted her gaze to the airport.

"If I had a downtown office with a view of all this, I doubt I'd ever get any work done. I could sit for hours watching the planes take off and land."

"Not me. Even watching gives me the willies. I'm a white-knuckle flier."

Lauren stared at him in disbelief. "A big guy like you?"

"Big guys crash harder."

She suppressed a smile. "I suppose you've got a point. But you do fly."

His expression was priceless, a blend of revulsion and resignation. "When necessary."

"Which is far too often for your tastes."

"You got it."

Her eyes took on an extra glow. "I don't think I could ever fly too often for my tastes. Not that I've flown that much, but I've always been so excited about getting where I'm going that I just sit back and relax. That's about all you can do, y'know. Once you're in the air, you're in fate's hands. It's not as if you have control over anything that might happen to the plane."

His grunt was eloquent. "That's what bothers me. I *like* to be in control. Just like measuring hurdles...."

Lauren narrowed her eyes playfully. "I'll bet you're the type who checks over every blessed inch of a new car before you venture to slide behind the wheel."

"I also sample the whipped cream, then the nuts, then

the hot fudge, then the ice cream before I take a complete spoonful of a sundae.''

''But where's the surprise, then?''

''The surprise is in the perfect blend of ingredients. The way I do it, y'see, I minimize the chance of disappointment. If something's not quite right, I can get it fixed, and if I can't do that, at least I'm prepared, so my expectations are on a par with reality.''

''You're a man of caution.''

''Quite.''

''Another reason why you sat outside my shop for two days.'' She tipped her head. ''Tell me, what would have happened if I'd looked exactly like that picture you'd seen?''

''I'd have come in the first day.''

Lauren had wondered if he would ever have come in. ''I don't understand. My looks made you *cautious*?''

''That's right.''

''But...I look better than I did in the picture, don't I?''

''You look gorgeous.''

''Then?'' Mired in confusion, she made no protest when he turned her into him and crossed his wrists on the small of her back.

''Gorgeous women intimidate me. I've been burned, remember?''

His smile didn't ease her this time. Her eyes widened. ''Do you think I'm after your *body*?''

He winced and shot an embarrassed glance to either side. ''Shh.''

She grasped his arms to push him away. When he held her steady, she whispered, but vehemently, ''Is that what you think? Well, let me tell you, *I* didn't ask you to walk into my shop. I didn't ask you to take me on a cruise. I don't want any part of your body! And even if I did, that wouldn't be all I'd want. Before I ever got around to your body, I'd make sure that I wanted the rest.'' She snorted in disgust and turned her face away. ''Of all the self-centered, arrogant—''

''That wasn't what I meant, Lauren. You're jumping to conclusions. Has it ever occurred to you that you can intimidate a man?''

''Me?''

''Yes, you. I'd expected to find a quiet—'' he hesitated, then cleared his throat ''—rather thin and plain-looking young woman living an equally quiet life in the country. At least, that was what Brad had implied. If he could only see you now! You own your own shop—in the city, no less. You're beautiful. You dress smartly. You're bright as all get-out. And you're sure as hell not falling at *my* feet.'' He took a begrudging breath. ''Yes, I'm intimidated.''

Lauren had felt suspended during his short speech. Now she realized how absurd her own attack must have sounded. ''Funny,'' she managed to say in a small voice, ''you don't look intimidated.''

He squeezed his eyes together. Even before they relaxed and opened, a smile had begun to form on his lips. ''I guess I'm not now, at least not as much as I was before. For someone who is beautiful and chic and super-intelligent, you're really pretty normal.''

She smiled self-consciously, averting her gaze. ''I think we're missing the sunset.''

''I think you're right.''

They returned to their own side of the boat, then switched when the vessel made a slow turn and headed back to the docks. Neither of them said very much. Lauren, for one, was lost in her own thoughts.

In spite of Matt's explanation, she still felt stunned that her looks had put him off. Initially her pride had been hurt.

The thought that she'd drastically improved her appearance only to find that it kept men away was unsettling; hence she'd lashed out.

Or had she simply been searching for a wedge to put between Matt and her?

He was too attractive, too easy to be with, too firmly aligned with Brad and a way of life that she'd been indoctrinated to frown on. No, she wasn't exactly frowning now, but neither could she turn her back on the disappointment of Brad's long-ago desertion. And then came the guilt. She'd acceded to her parents' view of Brad as a failure, yet she'd accepted his money—lots of it. Did an architect masquerading as a carpenter earn that much money? Had he banked every spare cent for some eleven years?

She realized that there were many more questions she wanted to ask Matt about Brad. In hindsight, she wondered if he'd been evasive when talking about her brother's work. His answers had been short, his expression solemn. He'd opened up more about Brad's personal life, yet she couldn't help but wonder if there were some things he hadn't said.

The boat pulled alongside the dock, its lines were secured, and the gangplank was lowered.

"You must be starving," Matt said. "Want to catch a bite at my hotel?" The Marriott was only a short distance from where they stood, but Lauren quickly shook her head.

"I'd better be getting home. It's been a long day."

"Are you sure?"

This time she steeled herself against the cocoa softness of his gaze. She needed time to acclimate herself to his appearance in her life. He was a figure from Brad's past, yet the immediacy of him unbalanced her. What she craved was the solid footing of her own home.

"I'm sure," she said with a gentle smile. "But...thank you, Matt. This has been lovely."

"At least let me walk you to your car. It's pretty dark."

"And the path to my car is well lighted all the way. Really, I'll be fine."

Matt straightened his shoulders and nodded. "Well, take care, then."

She started off, half turning as she walked. "Good luck with your work. I hope it goes well."

He nodded again and waved, then turned and headed for his hotel. Lauren didn't look back until she'd crossed Atlantic Avenue, and by then he was gone.

THE LATE-AFTERNOON SUN glanced brilliantly over the Hollywood Hills, but the shades in the study were drawn as its proprietor entered, strode across the tiled floor to the desk and picked up the telephone.

"Yes?"

"We're on our way."

"It's about time. I'd assumed I would have heard from you sooner."

"She's a clever girl. Covered her tracks like a pro—almost. I still don't know who helped her out of L.A., but you were right about the Bahamas. She went back to the same clinic she visited when the two of you were vacationing on the islands last fall. That was her only slipup."

"Then you've found her?"

"She had plastic surgery, just like you thought she would. Not much. Subtle changes. There was a phony 'before' shot stuck into the doctor's files and a bunch of misleading medical reports, but the 'after' shot had just enough similarity to the real thing to give her away. Her hair's different now, darker and shorter. And she's taken a different name."

"We knew she would. Where is she?"

"Boston. She just opened a little print-and-frame shop."

"With the money from the gifts *I* gave her. A print-and-frame shop. That's priceless."

"You'd be amazed if you saw her. She's the image of innocence. Dresses just so—stylish but understated, nothing flashy like before. Drives a Saab she must have picked up secondhand. Has this woman working with her who looks nearly as snowy-pure as she does, and a young guy who's probably eating out of—"

"What about the jewels? Have you located the fence?"

"No. No sign of the jewels at all. She may have started with the furs. They'd be easy to sell and nearly impossible to trace."

"Have you made contact with her?"

"Got a good man on it. She's already had a couple of little 'accidents'—nothing to hurt her actually, just set her to wondering."

"Is she?"

"Yeah. She's looking nervously around her front yard each time she leaves the house."

"The house?"

"An old farmhouse she picked up outside the city."

"With my money!"

"It'll all come back to you. Between the shop and the house, she's made investments that'll come back with interest."

"I want you to find the jewels."

"We're looking. She doesn't have them at home. I went through the place myself today."

"Ransacked it?"

"Nothing that obvious. Just moved little things here and there. She'll suspect someone's been snooping, but she won't be sure enough to call the cops."

"She wouldn't *dare* call the cops. She knows how long

my arm is, and she wouldn't do anything to risk blowing her cover. So where do we go from here?''

"I've got a few more mishaps up my sleeve. You want her to squirm. I want her to squirm. She's gonna squirm.''

"You're having fun, aren't you?''

"You could say that. I feel like I let you down before, and it was her fault. This is my revenge.''

"It's *my* revenge, and don't you forget it.''

"No way, boss. No way.''

Chapter Four

Beth was lying in wait for Lauren when she arrived at work the next morning. "Well? How did it go? What happened? Your parents would *die* if they knew you were dating him, but I think it's great! A sunset cruise... I've never heard of anything so romantic in my life. He may be rugged, but he's got style. Was he nice? Did you invite him back to Lincoln after the cruise? I almost called you, but I didn't dare. *Tell* me, Lauren. Tell me *everything*!"

Closely shadowed by her friend, Lauren continued through to the back room and plunked her purse in the bottom drawer of the file cabinet. "How can I tell you anything if I can't get a word in edgewise?"

"Okay. I'll shush. Give."

Lauren only wished she could. She'd spent a good part of the night thinking about Matthew Kruger, and she still didn't know what to make of him. "Yes, he was nice. Yes, the cruise was nice. Romantic? Well, I don't know about that. And no, I did not invite him back to Lincoln."

"Why not?"

"Because it wasn't called for. And we weren't on a *date*. He was my brother's friend. That's all. We talked a little about Brad and a little about other things. Period."

"Did he explain why he'd been hanging around outside for so long?"

For the first time that morning, Lauren smiled. Dryly. "If you can believe it, he was trying to get up his nerve to come in. Brad had shown him a picture of me. I wasn't quite what he'd expected."

"That's marvelous!" Beth's eyes grew rounder. "The handsome prince was so taken with your beauty that he was actually awestruck. I love it!"

Lauren screwed up her face and carefully enunciated her words. "Handsome prince? Taken with my beauty? Awestruck? What *have* you been reading, Beth?"

"Come on. I think this is great. Are you seeing him again?"

"I don't know."

"What do you mean, you don't know?"

"Just that. He didn't say anything about seeing me again, and I wasn't about to put him on the spot." Lauren reached for a can and began to spoon fresh coffee into a filter.

"'Put him on the spot.'" Beth snorted. "Straight from the mouth of the old you. The new you is sought-after. You'd be doing him a favor to *consider* seeing him again.... Well?"

"Well, what?"

"Are you?"

"What?" Lauren measured out water and poured it into the top of the coffee maker.

Beth sighed in frustration. "Considering seeing him again."

"I don't know."

As coffee began to trickle slowly into the carafe, Beth rolled her eyes and muttered, "This is absurd. We're going in circles. Do you or do you not want to see the man again?"

Lauren turned toward her friend. "I don't know! Damn it, Beth, how can I give you a better answer if I don't have one myself? Yes, I liked him, and under normal circumstances I'd be glad to see him again. But these aren't exactly normal circumstances. In the first place, the man lives on the West Coast. He's only here doing business, most of which keeps him in the western part of the state. He'll be going back to San Francisco and he hates to fly. I don't exactly have the time to zip out to see him every weekend—not to mention the money, when there are so many other things I have it earmarked for." She sucked in a breath. "And in the second place, he was Brad's friend. You're right. My parents would go bonkers."

"You're an adult. They didn't want you to go to the Bahamas, but you did it. They didn't want you to leave Bennington or open this shop, but you did both. You don't need their permission. You can do whatever you want and see whomever you want."

Lauren sighed loudly. "I know that, Beth. I'm not asking their permission for anything. I have qualms of my own about seeing Matt again. He was a friend of Brad's. He sees me and my parents through Brad's eyes. And he's a confirmed bachelor who loves taking off with the guys and shooting the rapids for a week. So what's the point?"

"The point," Beth murmured, wiggling her brows, "is that he's single and gorgeous."

"I thought he was too rugged for you."

"For me, yes. For you, no. The two of you looked great walking out of here together last night. I'm telling you, see where it leads."

"You have a one-track mind," Lauren grumbled, brushing a wisp of hair from her low-belted, apricot jersey dress.

"And you're in a lousy mood. Where's your sense of

humor? Hey, I'll bet Matthew Kruger would be the *perfect* one to ward off the ghost that's hanging out at your farm."

"Humph. I'm beginning to think I need something. That ghost was at work again."

Beth blinked once, then again. The coffee continued to trickle in the background, its rich aroma wafting from the carafe and spreading through the small room. "Excuse me?"

"That ghost. I swear it went through my things yesterday."

"Wait a minute, Lauren. There are no such things as ghosts."

"You're the one who's been touting them."

"I was teasing."

"Then I guess you've teased once too often. I'm almost becoming a believer."

"You're not serious!"

"Well, maybe not. But still...it was weird." She made a face accordingly. "I could have sworn I'd put certain things in certain places at home, and they were still there, just...shifted somehow."

Beth leaned back against the desk and crossed her arms over her chest. She might have been a psychiatrist for the indulgent tone of her voice. "I think you're going to have to be more specific. In what ways were they 'shifted'?"

"Small ways. A bottle of perfume turned around so that the sculpted bird faced the wall. A pair of shoes neatly set in the closet, with the right shoe on the left and the left one on the right. A pair of underpants perfectly folded, but inside out. I always turn them the right way before I fold them. *Underpants*." She shuddered, then whispered in dismay, "Can you believe it?"

"Maybe you should call the police."

"I thought about that, but I feel like a fool! I mean, it's

not as if anything were taken. The locks on the doors were intact, and as far as I could tell, none of the windows had been jimmied open. Ruling out a breaking and entering, I'd say someone might have just walked in, except that I'm the only one with a key.''

''How about the realtor who sold you the place?''

''I had the locks changed right after I moved in.'' Lauren gave a guttural laugh. ''That's about all I've done, but it does preclude a human visitor.'' She took a deep breath. ''So either it *was* a ghost, or I'm simply not as meticulous about things as I used to be. Maybe that's it. I mean, I suppose I have been preoccupied with the shop. It's very possible that I wasn't paying attention when I put the perfume bottle back or took the shoes off or folded the laundry.'' She looked beseechingly at Beth. ''So what are the police going to say?''

''Mmm. I see your point. Maybe you should get a dog.''

''One encounter with a dog on my property was enough.''

''Then a burglar alarm system.''

''A burglar alarm isn't going to stop a ghost. And it sure isn't going to improve my own absentmindedness, if that's what it was.'' She reached for a clean mug and poured herself some coffee. When she looked up to find a smug smile spreading over Beth's face, she scowled. ''Now what are you thinking?''

''That I was right all along. Matthew Kruger may be just the one to protect you. All you have to do is to coax him along. Before you know it, he'll be thinking of that farmhouse as his second home.''

''Matt is going back to San Francisco. How many times must I tell you that? And even if he wasn't, I can't use the man that way.''

"Seems to me he'd get something out of the arrangement."

"Humph. When—and if—I take a live-in lover, it'll be because I truly adore whoever he is, not because I need him as a bodyguard."

"You could truly adore your bodyguard."

Lauren sank into a chair and raised her mug. She spoke slowly and distinctly, as though her friend might not understand her otherwise. "I am going to drink my coffee now and gather my thoughts. Then I am going to face this new day with a bright smile and a free mind." She closed her eyes, brought the mug to her lips, sipped the coffee, then sighed.

Somewhere between the sip and sigh, Beth gave up on her and left the room.

THE SHOP GREW BUSIER as the noon hour approached, and Jamie's arrival at one was a relief. Beth ran out to pick up sandwiches, returning shortly thereafter with news far more interesting than that the rye bread had caraway seeds.

"Have you looked outside lately?" she murmured excitedly to Lauren as she passed on her way to the back room.

Lauren had been helping a customer decide which of two silk-screen prints to buy. She glanced toward the front window.

Matt. Sitting on the bench she was coming to think of as his. Reading a book.

Reading a book? That was a novel approach! Not that she doubted he was a reader; he looked more than comfortable with the paperback in his hand. But reading a book in the middle of the bustling Marketplace and on that particular bench? What was he thinking? What did he want?

She returned her attention to her customer, pleased that

in the minute she'd been distracted he'd decided on the print she'd originally recommended. Decisions on its framing proved to be more difficult, what with so many different mat boards and frames to choose from, but Lauren didn't mind. This was the part of the job she really enjoyed, and the shop made far more money on matting and framing than on the sale of the prints themselves.

It was only after she'd written up the customer's order, taken a deposit and let her gaze follow him to the door that she glanced again at the bench outside.

Matt was still reading.

Beth, who'd finished her lunch and come to relieve Lauren, was perplexed. "What's he doing out there?"

"Reading, obviously."

"But what's he *really* doing?"

"Beats me."

"Aren't you curious?"

"Sure."

"Aren't you going to satisfy your curiosity?"

"I'm going to have lunch. I'm famished."

"You're hopeless, is what you are," Beth declared. Lauren merely shrugged as she headed for the back room.

"Hopeless" wasn't exactly the word for it. She was flattered. Matt couldn't have chosen that bench by chance. But she was also puzzled. If he wanted to see her, wouldn't he simply come into the shop?

Did she want to see him? She still wasn't sure. There was something intimidating about him, and she couldn't quite pinpoint its cause.

Unwrapping her sandwich, she ate it slowly, sipping occasionally from a can of Coke. By the time she was finished, her curiosity had risen right along with her energy level. She *did* want to know what Matthew Kruger was up to. What right did he have to monopolize that bench? What right did he have to distract her? What right did he have to make her feel *guilty* for not acknowledging his presence?

Without further thought, she crossed through the shop, breezed out the door and approached the bench. Matt didn't look up. She stood there for a minute, then quietly eased herself down on the bench several feet away from him, far enough to preclude any implication of intimacy.

While he continued to read, she studied him closely. Other than his eyes, which moved rhythmically from one line to the next, his features were at rest. His lean cheeks were freshly shaved. His tawny hair was clean and vaguely windblown, haphazardly brushing his forehead and collar. He wore his usual jeans and sneakers, but today he'd put on a pink oxford cloth shirt. If she'd ever thought pink was feminine, she quickly revised that opinion. With his sleeves rolled to just beneath the elbow, and with the bronzed hue of his forearms, neck and chin contrasting handsomely with the shirt, he looked thoroughly male. Almost rawly so.

Reaching out, Lauren removed the book from his hands. She caught a brief glimpse of his startled expression before she turned the book over, carefully holding his place with her fingers, and examined the cover.

"*A Savage Place*," she read aloud. "It's a good one. But some of Parker's other books are set more in Boston. His descriptions of the city are priceless. You really should read them."

"I have," Matt answered. His liquid brown eyes caught hers when she lifted her head. "I've been a Parker fan for years."

Any indignance Lauren might have felt when she'd marched out of the shop had vanished. For that matter, she couldn't remember what doubts she'd had about Matt yesterday, last night, this morning. She couldn't seem to think of anything except the fact that his eyes were the warmest she'd ever seen and that his smile did something strange to her insides.

With a determined effort, she refocused on the book. "Like mystery and a little bit of violence, do you? Or is it Spenser's machismo that intrigues you?" The softness of her tone kept any sting from her words.

"Actually, it's Parker's writing style I enjoy. It's clean and crisp. Fast-paced. Filled with wit and dry humor."

She nodded. So it hadn't been an act, Matt's immersion in the book. He obviously knew his Parker and appreciated him.

"Why this bench?" Lauren asked suddenly. Her eyes had narrowed and were teasing in their way.

Matt stared at her, opened his mouth, then promptly shut it again. As she watched, his expression grew sheepish, filled with a boyish guilt that tugged at her heartstrings. When he finally did explain, she knew she was lost.

"I like this bench because it's close to your shop. I guess I was hoping you'd come out. What I was *really* hoping was that you'd take off with me for the afternoon and we'd rent a sailboat and join the others on the Charles. I got a view of the Basin from the thirty-second floor this morning. It looked so inviting." His voice fell, along with the expression on his face. "But you have to work. I know. It's not fair for me to come along and expect you to drop everything you're doing. You have responsibilities. I accept that, and respect it."

Lauren didn't know whether to hug him in consolation or hit him over the head with his book. "How can you *do* this to me, Matt? It's not fair!" That he should be a lovable little boy in a virile man's body. That he should be a stranger, yet so very familiar. That he should offer excitement in such a gentle and undemanding way. None of it was fair.

"Then you'll come sailing with me?"

"You were right the first time. I can't."

"But you would if you could."

"Yes."

He smiled and relaxed against the bench. "I guess I can live with that." Almost as soon as he'd sat back, he came forward again. "How about tonight? There's a Boston Pops concert on the Esplanade. We could pick up something to take out and eat while we listen."

Lauren knew that an hour later, or two or three, she'd find all kinds of reasons why she shouldn't go. At the moment, however, she couldn't think of a one. "That'd be fun. I'd like it."

"Great! What time can you get off?"

"What time does the concert start?"

Matt's eyes widened. "I hadn't thought that far." He jumped up, staying her with his hand. "Don't move. I'll be right back."

She watched him sprint toward Bostix, the ticket and information booth adjacent to Fanueil Hall, where he managed to wedge himself through the crowd at the window. Within minutes, he had trotted back to her.

"Eight o'clock. They suggested we get there early for the best spots on the grass, but the music carries pretty far, so if you can't get away from the shop until later—"

"I think I can convince Jamie to give Beth a hand until the shop closes. If we want to allow time to walk over the hill... How about your coming by at, say, seven? I'll call in an order for dinner—"

"Let me take care of that. I'm on a quasi vacation, remember? My work is done for the day, while you've still got more to do."

With a shy smile, she stood up. "Okay, then. I'll see you later?"

"Sure thing."

She nodded and had started for the shop when Matt called out to stop her. "Uh, Lauren?" Brows raised in question, she looked back. His gaze dropped from hers to the book she still held in her hand. She blushed, hurried back and gave it to him.

"Sorry. I'd forgotten I was holding it."

"I hadn't. If I can't go sailing this afternoon, I'll have to keep myself occupied somehow. Even aside from Parker's style, I suppose there is something to be said for mystery and a little bit of violence. And as for machismo—"

"Don't say it," she interrupted with a teasing glint in her eyes. "I don't think I want to hear it. A girl can take only so much, y'know." She'd pretty much reached her limit already. Another minute or two, and she'd chuck the shop and run off to the Charles with Matt. And that she would certainly regret. The shop was lasting. Matt wasn't. She'd have to remember that.

It was hard for her to remember much of anything that afternoon—other than the fact that Matt would be coming by for her at seven, of course. Beth teased her mercilessly when she rang something up wrong on the cash register, then again when she began to stretch fabric on a frame backside-to.

She thought seven o'clock would never arrive, but it did, bringing Matt, a blanket "compliments of the Marriott" and a large brown bag filled with all kinds of promising goodies. They walked over Beacon Hill, past the State House, the Common and the Public Garden, then across to Storrow Drive and the Hatch Shell.

They weren't the first to arrive, but they found a patch of grass within easy viewing of the raised stage. In truth, Lauren could have sat half a mile off under a tree by the water. The fact of the concert was secondary to that of the pleasure she felt being with Matt. She didn't analyze it, didn't stop to wonder why she was letting herself get so carried away about a man who'd be gone before she knew it. She simply wanted to enjoy, and enjoy she did.

Matt doubled up the blanket and spread it on the grass; then, after they had both sat down, he pulled out one container of food after another. He'd brought spinach turnovers, chicken salad with grapes and walnuts, Brie and crackers, fruit and a tumbler of frothy raspberry cooler. Lauren wondered where they'd ever put such a feast and told him so. He merely laughed, then laughed again when they'd eaten nearly everything. The concert was well under way by that time. He stuffed the remains of their picnic back into the bag, then sat close to Lauren with one arm propped straight on the grass behind him.

The assembled crowd was far from quiet; esplanade concerts were that way, informal evenings geared toward light-hearted company and relaxation. Families with children, young couples, middle-aged couples, elderly couples, mixed groups—all shared the pleasure of an evening along the Charles with the sweet smell of the outdoors, the gentle breeze, the exquisite blend of strings, horns and percussion.

As the evening progressed, Lauren and Matt sat closer and closer together. Lauren couldn't remember ever having felt so replete, and the dinner was only partly responsible. Matt was with *her*. Not with the pretty blonde to their right or the adorable redhead to their left. He was with *her*. She had only to drop her eyes from the stage to see his strong legs stretching endlessly before him. He'd changed into a white shirt and a pair of tan slacks that were more tailored than the jeans but no less sexy. His thighs were solid beneath the lightweight cloth, his hips proportionally lean. She felt the warmth of his shoulder as it gently supported her back; felt the goodness of its fit and its strength. His arm cut a diagonal swath to her hip, beside which his hand was flattened. His hand…long, tanned fingers, fine golden hairs, a well-formed wrist…

One song ended on a round of enthusiastic applause. When another began, the applause never quite stopped, for this song was a popular one with a heady beat, and the temptation to clap along was too great to resist. Too great, at least, for everyone but Lauren and Matt. They grinned along with the others, but neither seemed to want to disturb the physical closeness they'd captured. It seemed natural, and right, and very, very special.

Bidden by a silent call, Lauren turned her head to look up at Matt, and what she saw made her breath catch. His eyes were dark, drawing hers with a magnetic warmth, and his expression was one of gentle but insistent hunger. She might have been frightened by it, had her own body not been as insistently hungry. A glowing sun seemed to have risen inside her, radiating sparkles that speeded up the beat of her heart and her pulse and gave the faintest quiver to her limbs.

Lowering his head just the fraction that was necessary, he shadow-kissed her, openmouthed, not quite touching her lips. He drew back for an instant, dazed, then tipped his head and kissed her the same way, but from a different angle. The first kiss had been tantalizing enough for Lauren, but the second one was devastating. Acting purely on instinct, driven by the ache of desire, she opened her mouth in the invitation he'd been waiting for.

When he lowered his head this time, there was nothing shadowy about his kiss. It was full and binding, caressing her with a passion she'd never have believed mere lips to be capable of. She smelled the faint musk of his skin, tasted the fresh, fruity tang of his mouth, felt the sensual abrasion of his tongue as it swept through the moist recesses she offered.

She was about to turn into him, wrap her arms around his neck and draw him closer, when he dragged his mouth from hers and pressed it to her forehead. Though he didn't speak, the harsh rasp of his breath was eloquent and comforting, since Lauren was working equally hard to suck in the air she needed. Eyes closed, she gradually regained control.

Matt shifted and drew her back against his chest, fully this time, with her head resting on his opposite shoulder and his arms wrapped tightly around her waist. They stayed very much that way until the last encore was over. Then, with reluctance, they got up, gathered their things together and let the leisurely movement of the crowd carry them back the way they'd come.

Matt held the folded blanket under one arm. His other arm was draped over Lauren's shoulder. She held tightly to the hand that dangled by her collarbone.

They were nearly at the State House before he spoke. "I've got to be heading back to Leominster."

"When?"

"Tomorrow morning. Early. I have a nine o'clock appointment and probably should have driven out tonight, but I wanted to be with you."

She nodded, not knowing what else to say.

"I'll have to be there through Sunday. I'm sorry. It would have been nice to do something together on the weekend."

"That's okay. The shop's open seven days a week. I've forgotten what a weekend is."

"You have to have *some* time off each week."

"I will, once things get more settled. We weren't sure how soon we'd be able to hire extra help, but business has been going so well that we're trying to convince Jamie to work full-time so Beth and I can stagger days off for ourselves.''

"That'd be nice. There must be things you need to do."

"At least a million. Sundays are a help—we're only open from one till six—but I'd really like a day off in the middle of the week once in a while. If I don't start hiring people to fix up my farmhouse, it's apt to give a final groan and crumble at my feet.''

"Maybe I could help with that.''

"With the farmhouse? But you're leaving.''

"I've got some good contacts, and while I'm in Leominster I can check around for more. What do you need?''

"You name it. Plumber, electrician, roofer, carpenter. Actually, I was exaggerating before. The structure of the house is sound. I had that checked out before I bought the place. But I want to do extensive modernizing inside, and I need good people I can trust, since I won't be able to stand around and supervise.''

He gave her hand a squeeze. "Got it. I'll see what I can do.''

They walked on in silence for a time. Lauren felt simultaneously content and unsettled, if that were possible. Finally she couldn't help but ask, "When will you be flying back to San Francisco?''

"Not for another week or two. I'll be here in the city early next week, then back in Leominster.... Where are you parked?''

She pointed in the direction of the garage. "You don't need to—''

"I insist.''

"But it's out of your way.''

"What else do I have to do?'' he teased.

"Sleep. You'll have to be on the road very early to get to Leominster by nine."

"It's okay. I'll sleep tomorrow night."

All too soon, they had reached the garage, climbed to the third level and found her car. Reluctantly, she unlocked the door and opened it, only then turning to Matt. "Can I give you a lift back to the hotel?"

He shook his head. "It's out of your way."

"But this was out of yours."

"I'm on foot. It's ten times harder by car, what with one-way streets and all."

"I don't mind. Really—"

Any further words she might have said were stopped at her lips by the single finger he placed there. The dim light of the garage couldn't disguise the way his eyes slowly covered her face. They were hypnotic, those mellow brown eyes, and they conspired with the unmistakable vibrations from his body to suspend Lauren's thought processes once more.

His finger slid to her chin, where it collaborated with his thumb to tip her face up. He kissed her once, then again, then brushed his lips over her cheeks, eyes and nose. Lauren was entranced. Her own lips parted, then waited, waited until he'd completed the erotic journey and returned home.

But if she'd thought what he'd already done was erotic, she was in for an awakening. The tip of his tongue flicked out to paint her lips in the rosy hue of passion, and if she hadn't been clutching the top of the car door, she might have collapsed. She'd never experienced anything as electric, and the hardest part to believe was that the only points where their bodies touched were his tongue and her lips.

When he severed that connection, she stood still, eyes closed, mesmerized by the lingering flicker of a sweet, sweet longing. With regret, she finally opened her eyes.

"Can I come out to see you when I get back to town?" he asked. There was a trace of hoarseness in his voice.

Clearly implied was that he wanted to see her in Lincoln. Without a second thought, she nodded. "I'd like that."

He smiled, then cocked his head toward the car. "Get in. I might not let you leave if you wait much longer."

"Is that a threat or a promise?" she quipped softly, but she was already sliding behind the wheel. One part of her was tempted to wait much, much longer. The other part knew that things were happening quickly and that there were too many considerations to be made before she dared Matt to follow through.

After he had shut the door, she locked it, then started the car and backed out of the space. Matt stood to the side, watching. He gave a short wave as she began the slow, twisting descent. Soon he was lost to her view.

Lauren smiled all the way down Cambridge Street. She was still smiling when she curved into Storrow Drive and was ebullient enough to ignore the harsh beam of headlights from a car following too close on her tail. When she crossed the Eliot Bridge onto Route 2 and the same car remained behind her, she indulgently assured herself that if she was patient, the car would turn off soon.

It didn't.

She passed through Fresh Pond, circled the far rotary and moved into the right lane of what was now a comfortable superhighway. The car stayed with her. She tossed frequent glances in the rearview mirror and frowned. The traffic wasn't heavy. Surely whoever it was could move to the left and pass her, rather than tail her at forty-five miles per hour.

The highway was well lighted. She could see that the car was a late-model compact and that the driver was alone. Some kid having fun? There was no weaving to suggest he was drunk. Neither was there any hint that he was trying to tell her something, such as that her car had a flat tire or was on fire. He was simply following her and succeeding in making her extremely nervous.

Lauren pressed her foot on the gas pedal, pulled into the middle lane and held steady. The other car accelerated, pulled into the middle lane and held steady. She moved back into the right lane. The compact followed suit. She pumped her brakes lightly in an attempt to signal the driver to pass her, but he only slowed accordingly, then resumed speed when she did. In a last-ditch attempt to free herself of the tail, she flicked on the signal lights, moved into the breakdown lane and came to a cautious stop, prepared to floor the gas pedal if the other car stopped.

It swung to the left and passed her.

Breathing a shaky sigh of relief, Lauren sat for several minutes to recompose herself. Since she'd realized she was actively being followed, her imagination had taken her to frightening places. Too many little things had happened to her lately—the near accident on Newbury Street, the vicious dog in her yard, the garage door's fall, the subtle suggestion that someone had been in her home—for her to dismiss summarily this instance as a prank.

Yet as she entered the driving lane once more, that was exactly what she forced herself to do. A prank. A dangerous prank.

Then she crested a hill and saw taillights in the breakdown lane. She passed them by, instinctively speeding up, but within minutes the same car was behind her once more.

She swore softly, but that did no good. The car remained in pursuit. Five minutes went by. She searched the road for a sign of a police cruiser she might hail, but there was none. Another five minutes elapsed, and her knuckles were white on the steering wheel.

She approached her exit and held her breath, praying that

when she turned off, the driver of the compact car would consider the game not worth any further effort.

He exited directly behind her and proceeded to follow her along the suddenly darker, narrower road.

Praying now that her car wouldn't break down and leave her at the mercy of the nameless, faceless lunatic, she drove along the road as fast as she dared, heading directly for the center of town.

For the first time she blessed every chase movie she'd suffered through in which the dumb innocent was pursued up and down hills, around corners and through dark alleys without grasping at the simplest solution. Lauren Stevenson was no dummy. She had no intention of heading off into a side street, much less leading someone to her farmhouse, where she would be totally unprotected.

She headed for the police station.

What she hadn't expected when she pulled up in front was that the car that had been on her tail all the way home would swing smoothly—with no qualms or hesitation—into a space in the parking lot. Between two police cruisers.

Lauren quickly shifted into drive and headed home.

She was mortified. Apparently she'd imagined the worst for nothing. Yes, she was angry. For an officer of the law, plainclothes or otherwise, to have behaved in such an irresponsible fashion was inexcusable!

But what could she do? If she marched into the police station and complained, she'd be making a certain enemy. Policemen protected their own, and if what she'd read so often in the newspapers was correct, they weren't beyond administering their own subtle forms of punishment. Someday she might need them, really need them. Could she risk turning them off to her now?

Moreover, what could she say? That she'd been terrified because so many strange things had happened to her of late? They'd think she was nuts. A wild dog. A garage door that went bump. A ghost in her underwear. Maybe she *was* nuts.

No one was following her now, but then, she hadn't expected that anyone would be. Some cop had been playing his own perverse game, perhaps simply practicing up on the technique of the chase. It must be boring being a cop in as peaceful a town as Lincoln. No doubt he'd enjoyed the excitement of his little escapade. At that moment he was probably sitting in the back room with his police buddies, having a good laugh.

Lauren put the car in the garage, then all but ran for the side door of the farmhouse. No doubt about it, she was spooked. She'd left her pursuer at the police station. She'd reasoned away all of her other little near-mishaps. Still, she was spooked.

Coincidence and imagination were a combustible combination.

Turning on every available light, she walked from room to room before satisfying herself that everything was the same as when she'd left that morning. That morning seemed so very far away. And that evening had been so very special, but somehow tarnished by the terrifying experience she'd just been through.

After leaving a single bright light on downstairs, she went up to bed, thinking about the outside floodlights she would have put in when she finally found an electrician. Perhaps she *should* consider a burglar alarm. God, she hated that thought. One of the reasons she'd bought a home in the country was to avoid the stereotypical city fears.

She was making something out of nothing, she reminded herself for the umpteenth time as she lay in the dark of her bedroom, afraid to move. She was letting Beth's wild imagination get to her. She was letting her own wild imagination get to her. Maybe Beth was right. Maybe she did need a bodyguard. The thought of Matt Kruger—strong, capable of protecting her, capable of thrilling her with a kiss—brought some measure of relaxation, so that at last she was able to fall asleep.

THAT WEEKEND, working around the hours when the shop was open, Lauren met with three different general contractors to discuss what she wanted to do with the farmhouse. None of the three impressed her.

The first was too traditional in his orientation. What she wanted wasn't exactly restoration, she tried to explain. Yes, she wanted the outside of the farmhouse to look much the way it always had. But she wanted the inside to be a modern surprise of sorts.

Unfortunately, number one didn't have much imagination when it came to modern surprises.

Number two was both patronizing and condescending. "I know exactly what you want," he informed her, then proceeded to tell her what he'd do to the farmhouse. It was exactly what she didn't want.

Number three was not only late for the appointment, but both he and his truck were filthy. That said a lot in her book. She could just picture hiring the man and having him show up for work when the mood suited him. He'd probably leave a mess behind every day for her to trip over, and then she'd have to hire a team of workers to clean up after him.

She'd gone to the contractors first in the hope of finding someone who would then issue subcontracts for things like plumbing and electricity. Now, having struck out, she debated calling the plumbers and electricians herself. Lord only knew she desperately needed to get the job done.

She decided to wait for Matt to return. He'd help her.

And she trusted him. She'd never seen his work, but she somehow knew that any recommendations he made would be solid.

By Sunday night, she was thinking of Matt more and more, wondering when he'd be returning and what would happen then. She liked him—very, very much. She wanted to believe that his finest qualities—his gentleness, honesty and spontaneity—were indicative of the way Brad had been, too. She still wondered about Brad, still had questions for Matt to answer. But when she was with Matt she wasn't thinking brotherly thoughts. Matt intrigued her. He excited her. He seemed to take the best of both worlds—brain and brawn—and emerge superior. He wasn't quite like anyone she'd ever known before.

Nor did he kiss like anyone she'd ever known before. Not that she was anywhere near to being an expert on kissing. But she'd dreamed of feeling things in a kiss, and Matt had taken her far, far beyond those dreams—so much so that the restlessness she felt was no mystery.

Knowledge of the cause of a problem was not, however, a solution in itself. And since the solution was for the present out of reach, Lauren did the next best thing. Leaving a light burning in the living room, which had become a habit, she headed upstairs to treat herself to a long, soothing shower.

"Treat" was the operative word. As with most everything else pertaining to the farmhouse, the hot-water heater was small and outmoded. Even with its thermostat set on high, the "hot" was negligible. She'd quickly learned that she couldn't take a shower and then expect there to be enough hot water for the laundry. But she wasn't doing laundry that night, and she fully intended to indulge herself until the water ran cold.

Tossing her clothes into the hamper, she took a fresh

nightgown from her drawer and went into the bathroom. The shower was little more than a head rigged high in the bathtub, but it served the purpose. She turned on the water, drew the curtain, waited until steam rose above it, then stepped inside.

Heaven. Just what the doctor ordered. Eyes closed, she tipped back her head and let the warmth flow over her hair, shoulders, back and legs. Soap in hand, she lathered her body, then turned, inch by inch, to rinse off. Relaxation seeped through her. She rocked slowly to the pulse of the water.

Then she heard a noise. Her head shot up and her eyes flew open. The slam of a door? Or was it her imagination? She lingered beneath the spray, listening closely. She thought she felt vibrations.

Without pausing to decide whether the vibrations were footsteps or her own thudding heart, she reached back and quickly turned off the water. Then she grabbed her towel and, with jerky movements, began to dry off. Under the circumstances, she did a commendable job, though her nightgown didn't realize that. It stuck so perversely to the damp spots she'd left that she was all but screaming in frustration by the time she finally managed to get it on properly.

Holding her breath, she peered around the bathroom door into the bedroom. When she didn't see anyone there, she dashed out to her closet and grabbed the first weapon she could find. The heavy, workhorse of a Nikon camera, which she hadn't used in years, would certainly serve as a make-shift club, particularly when heaved from its strap.

She tiptoed to the wall by the open bedroom door, flattened herself against it and listened. And listened. Nothing.

She took a deep breath, then yelled as forcefully as she

could, "I've already connected with the police department and they're on their way! Better get out while you can!"

Silence.

Of course, she hadn't connected with the police department. They'd think she was a fool. Old houses made noises all the time, and she wasn't sure she'd lived long enough in this one to be able to identify all its characteristic moans and groans. No, she wasn't convinced there was an intruder.

On the other hand, she wasn't convinced there wasn't one, either.

Figuring that she'd need every precious moment if someone should storm in, she reached for the light switch and threw the room into a darkness that was broken only by a faint glow from the bathroom. Then, moving as silently as she could, given that she was more than a little unsteady on her feet, she wedged herself behind the bedroom door and peered through the crack, waiting for someone to creep up the stairs or emerge from one of the other two bedrooms.

No one did.

Noiselessly, Lauren sank to the floor, her gaze never once leaving the narrow slit of a peephole. She waited and watched and listened, growing stiff with tension but not daring to move. Five minutes passed, and there was nothing. Ten minutes passed, and she continued to wait, her temple now pressed wearily to the wall. By the time fifteen minutes had elapsed, she had to admit that she'd very possibly jumped to conclusions.

She wasn't convinced enough to leave herself unprotected, though. To that measure, she carefully closed the bedroom door, carried over a chair and propped it beneath the knob. Then, with the strap of the camera still wound around her hand, she climbed into bed and lay stiffly, listening, waiting. The only thing she was sure about as the hours crept by was that she very definitely would have a burglar alarm system installed when the house was sufficiently readied for it. Nights like this she didn't need.

Unless, of course, she had that bodyguard.

Chapter Five

When the phone rang early the next morning, Lauren jumped. She was in the kitchen, trying to force down a breakfast she didn't really want, and the unexpected sound jarred her already taut nerves. Snatching up the receiver after the first ring, she gasped a breathless "Hello?"

"Lauren? It's Matt."

Hand over her heart, she let out a sigh of relief. It wasn't that she'd actually expected someone menacing to be on the other end of the line but, rather, that the sound of Matt's voice was an instant and incredible comfort. "Matt," she murmured. "I'm so glad...."

There was a slight pause. "Is something wrong?"

"No, no. Just me and my imagination." She put her hand on the top of her head and found herself spilling it all. "I had the worst time last night. I was in the shower and thought I heard a noise. It turned out to be nothing, but the weirdest things have been happening lately, Matt. You wouldn't believe it. After I left you the night of the concert, some car tailed me all the way home. Well, not all the way, but almost. And before that the garage door had missed me by inches, and the dog had attacked me, and the car had swerved into the sidewalk—"

"Whoa, sweetheart. Slow up a bit. It doesn't sound like it's all been your imagination."

"No, but my imagination has been connecting all these little things that have nothing to do with one another and could really have happened to anyone—"

"But they happened to you." His voice was low and distinctly grim. "When did this all start?"

"I don't know…maybe a week and a half ago. It's like every few days something happens. I never thought I was accident-prone, but I'm beginning to wonder. Beth thought it was a ghost—"

"A ghost? Come on!"

"I know, I know, but if someone's trying to scare me out of this farmhouse, he's doing one hell of a job."

Matt was silent for several long seconds. "Listen, I'm still in Leominster, but I'll be driving back later this afternoon. Why don't I meet you at home? If I get there before you do, I can take a look around."

Lauren was without pride at that moment, and self-sufficiency was a luxury she couldn't afford. "Would you? I'd be so grateful, Matt! I've never been one to be spooked, but I'm as spooked as they come right about now. I don't think I slept more than two or three hours last night, and that was with a chair propped against the bedroom door and a camera nearby."

"You were going to take pictures?" he asked in meek disbelief.

"I was going to hit whoever it was over the head! My camera was the closest thing to a weapon I had. And then this morning I crept around the house looking for signs of an intruder. Crept around my own house in broad daylight—I must be getting paranoid!"

"Shh. Don't say things like that, Lauren. I'm sure there

are perfectly logical explanations for everything that's happened.''

"That's what I've been telling myself, but it's getting harder to believe. I mean, I can't deny that a car nearly ran me down, or that a dog attacked me, or that the garage door fell...but someone going through my lingerie?"

Matt cleared his throat. "Someone going through your lingerie?"

"See? You think I'm crazy, too!"

"I do not think you're crazy. Never that. You strike me as one of the most together women I've ever known."

"But you don't know me. Not really."

"Well, we'll have to do something about that, then. Tonight?"

"Promise you'll come?"

"I promise."

Lauren gave him directions; then, for the first time that morning, she smiled. "Thanks, Matt. I feel better already."

"So do I, sweetheart. See ya later."

LAUREN ARRIVED HOME from work that night to find a car in the drive. It was a brown Topaz and had local license plates. She assumed it was Matt's rental, but, seeing no sign of him, she felt a momentary tension. The car that had tailed her the Thursday before had been of a similar size, and though she'd had only glimpses of it when it passed beneath lights, she'd guessed it was either maroon or brown.

Staying where she was, safely locked inside her car with the motor running just in case, she leaned heavily on the horn. Then she waited. She seemed to be doing a lot of that lately.

This time she didn't have long to wait. Within a minute, Matt opened the front door of the house and loped out to greet her. The relief and sheer pleasure she felt upon seeing him eclipsed the fact that he'd somehow entered her house without a key.

Killing the motor, she scrambled from the car and threw herself into his arms. It seemed the most natural thing to do and, given the way Matt's arms wound tightly around her, he appeared to have no objections.

When at last he set her down, they exchanged silly grins.

"You look wonderful," he said. "A little tired, maybe, but a sight for sore eyes."

"I could say the same." Her hands were looped around his neck, her lower body flush with his. He looked positively gorgeous, sun-baked skin, slightly crooked nose, too-square chin and all. "Thanks for coming, Matt. I really needed you here. Did you have any trouble finding the place?"

"Nope. Your directions were perfect. I got here a couple of hours ago. It's a nice place, Lauren. I can see why you bought it. It does have charm."

"But does it have ghosts? That's what I *really* need to know."

Taking her hand, he started with her toward the house. "No ghosts. Just lots of things that need repairing." He cleared his throat. "For starters, the lock on one of the back windows is broken. I had no trouble climbing inside."

So that was how he'd done it. Simple enough. "But I tested all the locks. I was sure they worked!"

"Oh, this one works, all right. Until you raise the window. The wood around the screws has rotted. The entire lock simply slides up with the window. Close the window and the lock is in place again." He paused. "Which means that there's good news and bad news."

"Mmm." She dropped her purse on the chair just inside the front door. "The good news is that there's no ghost.

The bad news is that the moving around of things inside the house was caused by a human intruder.''

"Right. Hey, don't look so down. Every other lock in the house is solid, so it's just a matter of fixing this one. I've already been to the hardware store and picked up larger screws and packing. That'll hold the lock until the wood can be replaced.''

"Oh, Matt, you didn't have to.''

"I did it for my own peace of mind, if nothing else. Besides, fixing things is my speciality." He eyed her apologetically as they entered the kitchen. "I'm not sure I did as well with dinner. I picked up some things in town, but I'm afraid I'm not all that good a cook.''

"I could have taken care of that.''

"You'll still have to. I made a salad and husked some sweet corn, but I didn't know what in the hell to do with the chicken. At home I douse it in barbecue sauce and throw it on the grill, but you don't have a grill, and for the life of me I couldn't figure out how the broiler in that stove of yours works." His eyes shot daggers at the appliance in question.

She laughed. "It doesn't. The stove has to be replaced along with the refrigerator, the hot-water heater, the furnace—I could go on and on.''

"So what do we do with the chicken?" Opening the refrigerator, he removed the plastic-wrapped package.

"We bake it. And I've got a super sauce. You'll think you're eating the best of barbecue." She looked toward the single cabinet on the wall beside the sink, then down at her sleeveless beige jump suit. "I'd better change first. By the way, was that a bottle of wine I saw in the refrigerator?''

He nodded. "California's finest, already chilled. I'll pour while you change. Then we can talk.''

Talk. For a minute she'd forgotten what they needed to

discuss. She felt so good, so safe, with Matt that the last thing on her mind had been her series of recent misadventures. But she wanted to tell him. Matt was levelheaded and straightforward. She trusted that he'd be honest with her and let her know if she was making a mountain out of a molehill.

She trotted upstairs to her bedroom, changed into a pair of jeans and an oversize gray shirt that she knotted at the waist, then returned to the kitchen in record time.

Matt stood at the kitchen window, looking out at the field beyond. He spun around in surprise when she breezed into the room, then stared at her and swallowed hard.

"I...is something wrong?" She glanced down at herself.

"No. Not at all. It's just that I've never seen you in play clothes."

Lauren could have kicked herself for not having taken the time to touch up her makeup and brush out her hair. In the past those things had never mattered. She'd looked as good—or as bad—with or without the primping. She'd forgotten that she had something to work with now. But it was too late.

Self-consciously, she reached up to finger-comb her hair toward her cheek, but Matt crossed the room in two long strides and stayed her hand. "Don't. Don't do that." Releasing her hand, he used his own fingers as a comb to smooth the hair back. "You look so pretty. I want to see your face."

You look so pretty. I want to see your face. So hard to believe. So...strange. "I look tired. I should have done something."

"You look beautiful—and with only two or three hours' sleep." Dipping his head, he brushed a kiss on her cheek, another closer to her mouth, then another closer still. His hand was curved around her jaw by the time he reached her lips, though Lauren wouldn't have pulled away even if he hadn't held her. His nearness was drugging, his kiss intoxicating. His breath mingled with hers, seeming to bring her to life as she'd never lived it before. She forgot all else but the sweet sensation of closeness, of awareness, of longing that the caress of his mouth inspired.

"Ahh," he breathed against her lips at last, "your kiss takes me…"

"You have it…the wrong way around."

"Then it's reciprocal, which is why it happens to begin with."

"This is getting confusing."

"Mmm." He smacked his mouth to hers, then set her back and put his wineglass in her hand. She sipped the wine, perfectly content to drink from his glass while he laid claim to the second he'd poured. "Now, let me watch you make this super sauce of yours. I want to see what you put in it."

She grinned. "Cautious, Matthew. Hungry but cautious."

"Quite" was all he said, but the grin he gave her stole her breath almost as completely as his kiss had. Fearing for the state of her health, she quickly set to work mixing the ingredients of her super sauce, then indulged Matt by offering him the spoon for a taste.

"Mmm." He licked his lips. "Not bad. Not bad at all."

"Don't give me 'not bad.' It's *super*. At least," she added in a demure undertone, "that's what it was called in the cookbook I took it from."

"Ah, a cookbook reader." He glanced around. "But I don't see any cookbooks."

She flipped open the cabinet and pointed.

"Two cookbooks? That's all? A cookbook reader is supposed to have a huge collection."

"I'm, uh, I'm a little new at it." She unwrapped the chicken and rinsed it under the faucet.

"You didn't used to cook?"

"I didn't used to eat."

Matt chuckled and scratched his forehead. "That picture. I'd forgotten. You were pretty skinny back then—no offense intended."

"None taken. You're right, I was pretty skinny. It's just recently that I've been forcing myself to eat. I don't dare tell that to many people, mind you," she added, patting the chicken dry with a paper towel. "Most of them get annoyed."

"Jealousy, plain and simple."

She sent him a mischievous grin, then knelt down to remove a baking dish from the lone lower cabinet. That took some doing on her part. Pots were piled on top of pots, which were piled on top of pans, which were piled on top of the baking dish. "Top priority in this kitchen," she announced, rising at last, "is new cabinets, and plenty of them."

"Cabinets—easily done. What else?"

As Lauren dipped the pieces of chicken, one by one, into the sauce and placed them in the baking dish, she outlined her concept of the perfect kitchen, only to find that Matt's suggestions and additions made her plans more perfect than before.

"Why didn't *I* think of a center island?" she asked as she shoved the baking dish into the oven.

"Because you're not a builder."

"And you do this kind of thing?"

His shrug was one of modesty. "The development we're planning in Leominster is a cluster-home type of complex, a planned-community thing. Modern and elegant but also practical. Island counters in the kitchens are an option.

They can be used for storage underneath and eating above, or for a sink and a stovetop. Lord only knows, this kitchen's big enough to handle an island.''

"And you know people who can do this for me?''

He patted the breast pocket of his shirt. ''Names and numbers, already checked out.''

With exaggerated greed, she put out her hand. ''Gimme. I'll make the calls tomorrow.'' She proceeded to tell him of the contractors she'd interviewed herself; well before she had finished, he'd closed her fingers around his list. She promptly secured the piece of paper with a decorative magnet on the refrigerator door, then reached for the foil-wrapped loaf of French bread Matt had brought.

He clasped her wrist. ''Set the timer for twenty-five minutes. That'll be plenty early to put the bread in the oven.'' While she did so and then put a pot of water on to heat for the corn, he refilled their wineglasses. ''Come on. Let's go out back. I want to hear more about your... escapades.''

With vague reluctance, since she'd enjoyed talking with Matt about lighter subjects, Lauren led the way through the back door to the yard. A weathered bench under the canopy of an apple tree provided them with seats. Sunset approached; shards of orange and gold sliced through the trees and threw elongated shadows on the grass.

"Okay," he said. "Start from the top. I want to hear about each thing as it happened.''

Encouraged that at least he was taking her seriously, she turned her thoughts to the days that had passed. ''The first incident took place more than a week and a half ago, I guess.'' She related the Newbury Street story. ''I don't know if the driver was drunk. I don't even know if it was a man or a woman.''

"How about the car? Size? Color?''

She shook her head. "It came from behind. I don't think it was red or yellow. Nothing bright—that would have stuck with me. It must have been some nondescript color. As for the size, God only knows."

"Did you go to the police?"

"What could the police do? The car was gone."

"Maybe there was a witness who caught the license number."

"If there was one, he or she certainly didn't come forward. I just assumed I'd had a close call with a freak accident and left it at that."

He nodded. "Okay. What next?"

"Next was the dog. My run-in with him was...I don't know, maybe two days after the incident with the car." She described what had happened. "As soon as I was down on the ground and thoroughly frightened, he took off. Like he'd simply lost interest."

"You said it was a Doberman?"

"I said it *might* have been a Doberman. It's the same with the car. You're so stunned when it happens that the details slip by you. And anyway, it was dark."

"Was the dog wearing a collar?"

"That's the last detail I'd have noticed."

"Not if your hand had hit something when you tried to push him away."

"My hands were busy protecting my face. I kicked out with my legs—pretty ineffectively, I'd guess. If that dog hadn't wanted to leave, he wouldn't have."

Matt seemed about to say something, then stopped and took a breath. "Did you call the police?"

Lauren shook her head. "The dog was gone. It hasn't been back since."

Even in the fading light, the tension on Matt's face was marked. "Then what?"

She took a drink of wine for fortification. On the one hand, Matt's grim concern was reassuring. On the other, it seemed to make the situation all the more real and, therefore, ominous. "Then the garage door crashed down. It's an old garage, an old door. I'd simply assumed it would hold."

"I checked it out. There's no apparent reason why it didn't. The chains are strong. So are the coils."

"Then what could explain it?"

He looked off toward the shadowed trees and didn't speak for several minutes. "There are ways to rig a door like that."

"But it worked perfectly the next day, and every day since!"

"There's rigging—and unrigging."

Apprehension made her gray eyes larger. "You're suggesting that whoever might have tampered with it before it crashed down went back and fixed it again? But why would anyone *do* that?"

"What happened next?"

Lauren stared at him. He hadn't attempted to answer her question. Not that he ought to have an answer when she didn't, but at least he could have tried to soothe her. Brows lowered, she looked away. What had happened next? "I'm not sure about the next thing. It wasn't as obvious as the others...I mean, it could have been me."

"What was it, Lauren?"

She took a short breath. "After we'd gone on the cruise that night, I came home and noticed that some things were out of place in my bedroom. At least, they seemed out of place to me, but it might have been my own carelessness." When his silence demanded further explanation, she told him about the perfume, the shoes and the underwear.

"Nothing was taken? Money? Jewelry?"

"I don't have much of either lying around, but no, nothing was taken."

"And it was only the bedroom that was touched?"

"As far as I could tell."

"Did you go through the other rooms?"

"Of course I did! And nothing was touched—*as far as I could tell*. Honestly, Matt! I mean, it's possible that the spoons in the kitchen drawer were rearranged, but I don't set them up in any special pattern, so how would I know?"

He held up a hand. "Okay, okay. Take it easy."

Even the softening of his tone did little to calm her. "How can I take it easy? I feel like I'm at an inquisition, and the implication is that you think I've been irresponsible. Well, I haven't! Taken separately, not one of these incidents is particularly unusual. People on the streets have close calls with cars all the time. Wild dogs get loose; they attack innocent victims. Garage doors malfunction. And as for my personal effects, that could just as well have been my own fault. I'm not perfect! I might have been distracted! And *don't* ask me if I called the police, because I didn't!"

"I didn't ask," he said. His words were gently spoken; his gaze was solicitous. "And I'm sorry if I sounded critical. It's just that I'm concerned…and I'm a stickler for details. I like to know exactly what I'm facing." He slanted her a lopsided smile. "You were supposed to know that already."

Immediately ashamed of her outburst, Lauren sent him a look of apology. "I forgot."

"Well, don't," Matt went on in the same soft voice. "I'm looking for any possible detail that would give us some clue to whether the things that have happened are unrelated or not."

She shivered at the latter thought. "I know. And I appreciate your listening to all this. But I don't know in which direction to turn at this point.''

''Which is why you should tell me everything.'' He paused. ''All set?'' When she nodded, he released a breath. ''Okay. Some things were amiss in your bedroom. Possibly your own fault. What was the next thing that happened?''

''The car followed me home.''

''Did you see where it picked you up?''

She shook her head. ''It could have been anywhere. I was on Storrow Drive when I first noticed the headlights in my rearview mirror.''

''Make of the car?''

She shrugged and shook her head.

''Color?''

''Dark. At the time I thought it was maroon or brown, but it was hard to tell.'' Her eyes widened. ''Do you think it could have been the same car that nearly hit me on Newbury Street?''

''I don't know. There are a hell of a lot of maroon and brown cars on the road. Without a make and model, we're clutching at straws.''

''I'm sorry,'' she murmured. ''Cars aren't my thing. I'm no good at identifying them.''

''That's okay, Lauren. Do you remember when it finally dropped away?''

''It didn't, in a sense.'' She explained how she'd headed straight for the police station, where the car had nonchalantly pulled into a parking space. When Matt remained silent, she feared that he would chide her for not entering the station and complaining; she still wondered if she should have done that. ''Well?''

''It's odd,'' he said at last. ''Could have been a policeman having a little fun on his way to work, but all the way from Boston? And he stopped, then picked you up again.''

"But he had to be harmless if he was a policeman."

"If, and that's a big if."

"Matt, he pulled into that space as if he knew just where he was going!"

"He may have pulled out just as smoothly once you drove on."

"And if I'd gone in to file a complaint?"

"He could have driven off anyway. You would have led the officer on duty to the parking lot, only to find that there wasn't any car there."

"Mmm. And the officer would have thought I'd dreamed the whole thing up."

"Possibly. Okay, the only thing left, then, is the matter of strange noises last night. Tell me exactly what you heard."

She did. "By the time I came out of the shower, there was nothing. Maybe I imagined it all."

"Maybe."

Then again, maybe not. "If someone had gotten *in* the house, wouldn't he have had to get *out*? I was so spooked that even the tiniest creak in the floorboards would have sounded like thunder to me. But there was nothing. I'm sure of it."

"And when you got up in the morning, there was no sign of an intruder?"

"Nothing."

"No window partway open? No dirt tracked onto the floor?"

"Nothing."

"And is that it? No other suspicious incidents in the past few weeks? Anything that, with a twist of the imagination, might seem odd?"

She thought about it, going back over the days with a

fine-tooth comb. Eventually she shook her head. "Nothing."

Matt sat back on the bench, deep in thought. Sandy brows shaded his eyes. His mouth was drawn into a tight line. Lauren studied him, waiting to hear what he had to say. When he stood up abruptly and began to walk back toward the house, she was mystified.

"Matt?" She bolted to her feet, jogging to catch up. He looked at her almost in surprise, and she wondered where his thoughts had been.

"Oh. Sorry. I thought I'd put the bread in the oven now."

"But the timer—"

"We wouldn't have heard it." Sure enough, as they mounted the back steps they caught the insistent buzz.

Biding her time with some effort, she watched him open the oven door, flip over each piece of chicken, then slip the prebuttered loaf onto the lower shelf. Without missing a beat, he carefully dropped the husked ears of corn into the now-boiling water.

Finally she couldn't wait any longer. "Well? What do you think?"

"Mmm. Chicken smells good."

"Not the chicken. My *predicament. Is* someone after me?"

Straightening, he leaned back against the chipped counter and studied her. "Is there a *reason* that someone should be after you?"

She couldn't believe the question. "Of course not! I haven't done anything. I haven't hurt anyone. To my knowledge, I don't have any enemies. I'm amazed you'd even ask that!"

"Just ruling it out. It's as good a place as any to start."

"Well, we've started. A more probable possibility is that

these incidents have something to do with the farmhouse. Everything began after I moved in.''

"When, exactly, did you move in?"

"The first week in June."

"And the car incident took place, what, at the end of the month?" He thrust out his jaw. "The delay doesn't make sense. If someone legitimately didn't want you living here, the incidents would have started while you were first looking over the place, or certainly as soon as you'd moved in. Besides, not all of the things have happened here. Nah, I don't think they have anything to do with the farmhouse.''

"That'd be the most plausible explanation," she pointed out. "And it'd be the easiest one to follow up. I've considered the possibility that one of the neighbors doesn't want me here, but the few I've met have been pleasant enough, and I can't think of any reason that my presence would be objectionable. I know nothing about the former owners, though. I could speak with the realtor and go through the records of who has lived here in the past. If necessary, I could call in a private investigator, or even the police—"

"Don't do that," Matt interrupted, then quickly gentled his voice. "Not yet, at least."

Though Lauren herself hadn't been anxious to call the police, she was surprised by his vehemence. It occurred to her that he might be indulging her in her fancy while not quite taking it to heart. "What do you suggest?" she asked more cautiously.

"Let's consider the possibilities." He squinted with one eye. "Are you sure you can't think of someone who might get his jollies by scaring you?"

"Like who?"

He shrugged. "An old boyfriend?"

"An old boyfriend who'd come all the way from Bennington in search of a little mischief?"

"Then maybe someone you might have met since you've been here. Someone who asked you out. Or followed you around. Or just…looked at you for hours on end."

"You're the only one who's done that," she replied with a smirk. "Maybe you've got a Jekyll and Hyde thing going."

The twitch of his nose told her what he thought of that idea.

"Well," she went on, thinking aloud, "it could always be a random lunatic."

He shook his head. "Too persistent. Your average random lunatic may hit once, even twice, but not six times. Your average random lunatic wouldn't have access to a trained attack dog—"

Horrified, Lauren interrupted him. "Trained? Do you think that dog was trained?"

Matt gnawed on his lower lip, as though regretting what he'd said, but the damage had been done. "It's possible. If it was trained to respond to a high-pitched whistle that our ears can't detect, that would explain why it retreated so abruptly."

"Just enough to frighten me…not enough to harm me. What kind of insanity are we dealing with?" Her voice had reached its own high pitch.

He gave her shoulder a reassuring squeeze. "We don't know anything for sure, except that so far you haven't been hurt."

"But I *could* have been. If I'd been a little slower in leaving my garage that night…if there'd been no Good Samaritan near me on Newbury Street that day…"

Responding to the sudden pallor of her skin, Matt drew her against him and slowly rubbed her back. "Don't think about what might have been," he murmured. "Nothing's happened, and if I have any say in the matter, nothing will."

With her head pressed to his heart, Lauren believed every word he said. She didn't stop to ask him how he intended to protect her. She didn't stop to ask herself why she, who valued her independence highly, welcomed the protection. She only knew that Matthew Kruger filled a spot that, at this particular point in her life, was open and waiting for him.

He drew back from her to ask, "Think that chicken's almost ready?"

"The chicken!" Pushing herself away from him, Lauren flung open the oven door, reached for a pair of mitts and pulled out first the chicken, then the bread. "Thank goodness it's not burned! I'd forgotten all about it!" She teased him with a punishing glance. "And it's *your* fault."

"My fault?" He was the image of innocence. "You said *you* were the cook around here."

"But you've kept me preoccupied. I haven't even set the table!" The item in question was of the card-table variety, albeit inlaid with cane, and there were folding chairs to match. She'd picked them up to use until she bought regular furniture.

"Then you do that while I toss the salad," Matt suggested. He was already draining the sweet corn. "I picked up a creamy cucumber dressing—unless you've got a super dressing of your own."

The twinkle in his eye brought fresh color to her cheeks and a momentary curl of warmth to the pit of her stomach. "Creamy cucumber's fine. Super sauce I can handle; super dressing is still a way down the road." As she reached for the dishes, she said, "It's amazing..."

"What is?" Matt asked, removing the salad from the refrigerator.

"That you can take my mind off things. Not only dinner, but everything else. One minute I can be worried sick about what's been happening; the next, I forget all about it."

"Maybe you've been worrying for nothing," he ventured quietly. "Maybe all that's happened really *is* a coincidence."

"Maybe...but it's crazy. Everything's been so wonderful. I left Bennington. I have a new job, new home, new look—" The last had slipped out. She rushed on. "Maybe it's all too good to be true."

Matt poured dressing on the salad and began to toss it. "I'm sure that whatever's been going on can be taken care of."

"But how can it be taken care of if I don't know what it is?"

"In time, Lauren. In time. Let's get back to the random-lunatic theory. Lunatic, perhaps. Random, unlikely." He held the salad tongs in the air for a minute before resuming his tossing. "Are you absolutely sure you can't think of anyone who might be behind it?"

Lauren set the silverware on the table with far greater force than necessary. "Yes, I'm sure. I've told you that, Matt. I don't know anyone who'd be capable of doing what has been done. Why do you keep harping on it?"

He hesitated. "Because the only other possibility is that we're facing someone who is neither lunatic nor random, but who has a very specific ax to grind. Maybe someone who has a grudge against your family."

Her jaw fell open, then snapped back into place. "If you knew my parents, you'd never even suggest that. They are utterly harmless. They live in an insulated little world. There may be competition within the academic community, but my parents have been so well accepted for so long that I can't begin to imagine anyone's acting out of jealousy, much less trying to seek revenge. And if someone did, he or she sure as hell wouldn't do it through me. I've declared my independence in ways that have my parents climbing those ivy-covered walls of theirs—'' Her voice broke abruptly, and for a minute she wished she could retract what she'd said. Then she realized that there was no point in being coy. Matt, more than anyone, would understand.

He brooded for a minute as he placed the salad on the table, then reached for the wine. ''What do you mean?''

Lauren opened the foil-wrapped bread with care. It was hot. ''What I'm doing with my life isn't exactly what my parents had wanted me to do.''

''In what sense?''

''Oh,'' she began, juggling the steaming loaf into a bread basket, ''they would have preferred that I stay in Bennington and work at the museum. I'd be surrounded by culture, attend plays and lectures, take part in a weekly reading-and-discussion group. Then I'd marry some nice, pale-faced fellow whose interests lay in Babylonian astronomy or medieval art or comparative linguistics. I'd go on to have sweet little children who would take up the cello at age four, read Dostoyevsky at age eight, write a novel at age twelve and beg for college admittance at age fourteen.''

''And you? What would you prefer?''

''Me?'' She set the bread basket on the table and looked up at him pleadingly. ''I want to be happy. I want to do well at whatever I choose to do. I want to feel good about myself.''

''And a husband and children?''

Shrugging, she brought the plates to the stove. ''I haven't thought that far yet.''

''Sure you have. Every woman dreams.''

"Every man does, too," she countered.

"But I asked you first. What do you want in a husband? What do you want for your children?"

She put two pieces of chicken on Matt's plate, a single piece on her own. "The same thing I want for myself, I suppose. If a person is happy, and feels good about himself, everything else falls into place." She added an ear of corn to each plate before bringing both to the table.

"How can your parents argue with that?"

"They believe that certain things make a person happy. We just disagree on what those things are."

Matt was standing with one hand on his hip as he watched her. Straightening suddenly, he tilted a chair out and gestured for her to sit. "Brad's philosophy was similar. It's amazing how alike you are in so many ways. Then again, there are differences."

"Tell me more about him, Matt. Did he really feel the same way I do?"

Matt slowly seated himself and didn't speak until he'd pulled his chair in and spread a napkin on his lap. His expression was pensive. "He felt that what your parents wanted was different from what he wanted. But you already know that. I think he would have been surprised that you agree with him. He saw himself as the black sheep of the family."

"So much so that, regardless of what he did, it didn't seem to measure up?" she asked.

Matt frowned, then shifted in his seat. He drew the salad bowl toward him and prodded the lettuce with the tongs. In a sudden spurt of movement, he began to pile salad on Lauren's plate. "Is that the way *you* feel? That nothing you do can measure up?"

"Hey." She put her hand on his and pushed the tongs toward his own plate. "That's enough."

He served himself. ''Do you feel that way, Lauren?''

''No. I'm pleased with what I'm doing. Brad tried to meet my parents' expectations, failed, then took off. I went along with their wishes and was fairly successful at it before realizing that it wasn't what I wanted. I left because I chose to. Brad left because he had to. I could have gone on forever up there, I suppose. Brad couldn't have survived.'' She took a breath. Her fork dangled over the chicken. ''It wasn't that he didn't have the brains for it, but his temperament was totally different. He was more impulsive, more restless. Hyperactive, my parents always said, but I think they were wrong. He just wanted to use his brains for things other than scholarly pursuits.''

''He did that,'' Matt drawled under his breath, but there was no humor in his expression. When he saw Lauren staring at him, puzzled, he spoke quickly. ''Designing houses, interesting houses, takes brains, although it's not considered a scholarly occupation. It's too bad your parents couldn't have seen some of the work Brad did.''

''They never even knew about it'' was her sad reply. ''They didn't know who he worked for or what he did. They were shocked at the amount of money that came to me when he died.'' She rolled her eyes. ''For that matter, so was I.''

Matt's hesitation was a weighty one. ''They didn't begrudge it to you, did they?''

''No.'' She snorted. ''The only thing they begrudged was what I *did* with it.'' Spearing a tomato wedge, she waved it for an instant. ''Family interrelationships are weird things. Expectations are often so unrealistic. It's as if we have blinkers on. I suppose I'm not that much more understanding of my parents than they are of me, but it's a shame. I'm an adult now. They're adults. Wouldn't it be nice if we *liked* one another?''

"It's not that simple. You're right. Unrealistic expectations can stand in the way. Or ego needs. It must be difficult in a situation like yours, where it would be impossible for you to rise above what your parents have done. They've been so successful in their fields. Maybe that's why both you and Brad felt the need to strike out on your own."

"Maybe. I hadn't thought about it that way." Lauren mulled over the prospect for several minutes, but what lingered with her was how insightful Matt was. "What about you? Are you close to your family?"

"Very."

"Are they in San Francisco, too?"

He shook his head. "L.A. I guess I needed a little distance, just as you do. The pressure coming from my parents was a more traditional one. They're retired now, but for years they both worked in a factory. They wanted my sister and me to rise higher, to advance socially. Unfortunately, there wasn't much money for college. I suppose I could have tried for a scholarship, but I wanted to work. Once I got going, I discovered that I could get the education I needed on the job. I've taken business courses here and there, and I've advanced, so I can't complain."

"How about your sister?"

Matt warmed Lauren with a grin. "Maggie's a speech therapist. She *did* go for a scholarship, won it and wowed 'em all at UCLA. I'm really proud of her. We all are."

"I can see that," Lauren said. His grin was contagious, or was it the way his cheeks bunched up and his eyes crinkled? Whatever, she was grinning back at him, wondering how a man could be so gentle and giving, yet so wickedly attractive. "Tell me more," she urged. "About when you were a kid, what you were like, what you did."

He made a face and tilted his head to the side. "It's really not all that exciting."

"Tell me anyway." She perched her chin in her palm and waited expectantly.

"Only if you eat while I talk. You haven't had more than a bite, and the chicken is fantastic."

Listening to Matt and watching him drove all thought of food from her mind. But if eating was his precondition, well...

He talked and she ate. She made observations and asked questions while he ate, then resumed her own meal when he talked more. By the time they'd had seconds of just about everything, including wine, she'd learned that, though a mischievous Matt had received his share of spankings as a boy, he'd grown up in a house filled with love. She'd also learned, but between the lines, that what Matt craved most was his own house filled with love.

When he offered to help her clean up, she accepted. It wasn't that she needed the help or that she was liberated enough to demand it. She'd thoroughly enjoyed the way they'd worked together getting the dinner ready, and she wanted to draw out the evening as long as possible.

Apparently Matt had the same idea. When the kitchen was as spotless as one that age could be, he suggested they relax for a few minutes before he left. They settled in the living room, which, aside from Lauren's bedroom, was the only room with furnishings. There was one sofa and two side chairs. They shared the sofa.

Lauren felt peaceful and happy and tremendously drawn to the man beside her. His arm was slung across the back of the sofa, his fingers tangling in her hair. The clean, manly scent that clung to his skin heightened her senses, while his warmth bridged the small space between them with its invisible touch.

"This has been nice," she told him, slanting a shy glance his way. "I'm glad you came."

His voice was like a velvet mist. "So am I." Sliding his arm around her shoulders, he drew her closer even as he met her halfway. His lips touched one corner of her mouth, then the other, then her cupid's bow, then her lower lip. He'd opened his mouth to kiss her fully when, unable to help herself, she laughed.

He drew back and stared at her for a minute, then cried in mock dismay, "Lauren! What kind of behavior is that? Didn't anyone ever tell you not to laugh in a man's face when he's about to kiss you?"

"I'm sorry... It's just that...you were tasting me one little bit at a time.... You really *are* cautious!"

His eyes danced mischievously. "Caution's gone" was all he said before he covered her mouth with his and proceeded to deliver the most thorough kiss she'd ever received. No part of her mouth was left untouched by any part of his, and by the time he buried his face in her hair, she felt totally devoured. She might have told him so had she been able to speak, but her breath was caught somewhere between her lungs and her throat, for his hand was sliding over her waist, over and up, ever higher, and anticipation had become as tangible as those long, bronzed fingers. When at last they reached her breast, she let out a soft moan and succumbed to the exquisite sensations shooting through her.

Lauren had never been touched this way, yet there was nothing demure in her response. Both mind and body said that what she was experiencing was right and natural; instinct, goaded by desire, set her fingers to combing through his thick hair, running over his broad shoulders, splaying eagerly across his sinewed back.

"Lauren." His voice was hoarse. "Lauren...I have to...we have to stop...."

"No," she whispered. She held his head with one hand,

pressing it to her neck. Her other hand covered his at her breast. "Don't stop."

A groan came from deep in his chest. "Do you know what you're saying, sweetheart? What it does to me?" His voice was thicker now, foreign to her ears yet exciting. She held her breath when he transferred her hand to his own chest and slowly slid it lower.

Lauren could feel the strength beneath her palm, the tautness of his stomach, then the stunning rigidity beneath the fly of his jeans. She wanted to hold him, explore him, let him satisfy the ache that had taken hold deep in her belly, but the newness of it all brought a measure of sanity. With a shuddering breath, she sagged against him.

"Yes. Do stop," she whispered. She was shocked by her own abandon, not quite sure what to make of it. "Everything...everything's happened so fast...and there's still the other matter." Of her own accord, she retreated from him, taking refuge in her corner of the sofa and clasping her hands tightly in her lap. The aura of arousal, a telltale quiver, lingered in her body, but thought of that "other matter" gradually put it to rest.

Matt, too, retreated to his corner of the sofa. He shifted in an attempt to get comfortable, finally hunching forward with his elbows on his knees. His fingers were interlaced, not quite at ease. He cleared his throat. "Yes...that other matter."

"We didn't reach any conclusions."

A pause. "No."

"What do you think?"

Another pause. "I don't know."

"Should I call the police?"

"No." Emphatically.

"Why not?"

He didn't answer, but studied his hands and frowned. "I

have to ask you this, Lauren. I know it may sound terrible…but you did mention that your parents were against your coming here—''

"My parents? You think my *parents* could have been behind what's happened?" Vehemently she shook her head. "No. Absolutely not. They may disagree with me, but they'd never try to harm me."

"Maybe just scare you into going back—"

"No." She was still shaking her head. "Not possible! They wouldn't be capable of conceiving of violence."

"Maybe not violence, but if they've already lost one of their children—"

"Forget it, Matt. It's simply not possible…. I think I should call the police."

"No."

"You've been very firm about that. Why, Matt?"

He offered the longest pause yet. "Maybe it's… premature."

"Premature? Then you don't think there's a connection between the things that have happened?"

"I didn't say that. I just think we ought to give it a little time. Let me see what I can do."

"What can you possibly do? Neither of us knows where to begin!"

He didn't argue with her; neither did he agree. Instead, he scowled at his hands.

"Matt, I'm frightened." As much by the strangeness of his response as by everything else, she told herself. "I haven't been hurt so far, but maybe I've just been lucky. What if the next time—"

"You won't be hurt," he gritted out, raising his dark brown eyes to hers. She tried to read his feelings, but they were shuttered. "I'll stay here. If something happens, I can take care of it."

Lauren stared at him. "You can't stay here! My bed's the only one—and—and anyway, you can't be with me every single minute of the day. You have to work. So do I. How can you anticipate when something will happen?"

"*If* something happens."

She bolted from the sofa and began to prowl the room. She was confused and upset. "You think I'm paranoid. I know you do. You think I'm making something out of nothing." Whirling to face him, she stuck her fists on her hips and glared. "The little lady with the rampant imagination. The fanciful little woman to be indulged—that's the macho attitude isn't it? That's where *you're* coming from!"

Matt's face paled. He sat up straight, then rose and began to walk stiffly toward the front door. His voice was flat. "I think I'd better leave. If that's the way you feel…"

Lauren watched him open the door, then close it behind him. What had she said? Had *she* put that look of hurt in his eyes? Had she been responsible for draining the emotion from his voice, that very same voice that had always been so wonderfully expressive?

Her gaze flew to the window. It was dark outside. Once Matt left, she'd be alone. Unable to take back the ugly words she'd said. Open prey to her own impulsiveness and…

The growl of his engine hit her ears as she wrenched open the front door. "Wait!" she cried, arms waving as she tore down the walk. "Matt, wait!" The car was halfway down the drive. Thinking only that she needed him with her, she flew in pursuit. "Don't go, Matt! I'm sorry! Please…don't…go!"

The taillights went on at the end of the drive, and the car slowed, about to turn onto the street. Lauren's steps faltered. She came to a tapering halt. She'd lost him. He was gone.

The car began to turn, then stopped.

She held her breath, then started running again. "Matt! Please! Wait!"

His tall figure emerged from the car but didn't move farther. Again she faltered and stopped. But the hesitation was only momentary. She knew what she wanted, knew what she needed. With a tiny cry of thanks that she'd been given a second chance, she raced forward.

Chapter Six

Flinging her arms around him, Lauren hung on for dear life. "I'm sorry—so sorry, Matt!" She pressed her cheek to the warm column of his neck. "I didn't mean what I said. I was nervous and frustrated. I took it out on you." Slowly she eased her grip on him and met his gaze. Her voice grew softer. "Don't go. Please?"

"I don't disbelieve you, Lauren," he stated quietly.

"I know that. I accused you unfairly. I expected you to have answers where I didn't. It was wrong of me."

"Nothing's changed. I still don't have answers."

"I know that."

"And you still have only one bed." His hands came to rest lightly on her hips, fingers splayed. "If I were a saint, I'd offer to sleep on the couch, but I'm not a saint."

His words and the look in his eyes sent ripples of excitement through her. "I know that," she whispered.

"Then you know what I want?" he asked as softly.

Unable to speak, she nodded.

His gaze held hers captive for a minute longer; then he grabbed her hand. "Get into the car."

"What—?"

He was urging her into the driver's seat, his hands on her shoulders. "Slide in. Over a little. That's it." He was mere inches behind her, then flush to her side. "I'm not taking the chance that you'll change your mind." Tucking her arm through his, he put the car in reverse and sped backward up the drive. Then he all but swung her from the car, fitted one strong arm over her shoulder and half ran to the house.

"Matt?" She was laughing, breathless.

"Shhh."

Once inside, he continued up the stairs, straight to her bedroom. The light was off. He made no attempt to alter the darkness, and Lauren was relieved. She knew that she wanted what was about to happen. She also knew that the darkness added to its dreamlike quality. That a man like Matt wanted *her* was mind-boggling. Surely if he turned on the light, he'd have second thoughts; she'd have second thoughts....

He took her in his arms and kissed her until the only thoughts she had were how wonderful he was, how unbelievably desirable he made her feel, how lucky she was to have found him. She gave herself up to his kiss, to his hands as they unbuttoned her shirt and unclasped her bra, to his fingers as they charted her flesh, branding her woman with fire and grace.

A soft moan came from deep in her throat, and she arched her back to offer herself more fully. Acceding to her wordless plea, he stroked her with gentle expertise. His fingers made firm swells of her breasts; his thumbs, tight buds of her nipples. And all the while his tongue correspondingly familiarized itself with every nook and cranny of her mouth.

His hands left her only to free himself of his shirt, and then he was back, crushing her close. His chest was warm and lightly furred. Its texture exhilarated her, though she wondered if it was simply the closeness, male to female, that pleased her so. There was something very, very right about what she felt. There was something very, very right about Matt. At that moment she didn't know how she'd ever doubted him.

While he held her lips captive, he reached for the snap of her jeans, released it, lowered the zipper. She gasped for breath when he knelt and eased the denim from her legs, then did the same with her panties. She clutched his shoulders for support and shivered, though her blood was hot, her body aching for completion. Modesty was nonexistent; she wanted him too badly.

"Please," she whispered shakily, "I need you, Matt."

For an instant, he buried his face in her stomach while he caressed the backs of her legs and her bottom. His breath was ragged, his hair damp against her hot flesh. She drove her fingers into the thick, sun-streaked pelt and held him closer, then urged him upward.

He didn't need much urging. Standing, he shed the rest of his clothes, then came to her naked, pressing her to him, graphically showing her that the need wasn't hers alone. She thrilled to the knowledge, unable to be afraid when Matt was all she'd ever wanted, all she'd ever dreamed about. The fact that she could arouse him to the state he was in was as heady as the state of arousal he'd himself brought her to.

He moved from her only to tug back the spread before lowering her gently to the sheets. "Lauren...God, Lauren..." he murmured, then kissed her again. He caressed and teased with his hands, his lips, his tongue, but the play took its toll. His body seemed on fire, trembling under the strain of the heat, finally unable to withstand it. Threading his fingers through hers, he anchored them by her shoulders and positioned himself between her thighs. With one powerful thrust, he surged forward.

Lauren arched her back against the sudden invasion, and a tiny cry escaped her lips. When he stiffened, she wrapped her arms around him to draw him close to her. He resisted.

"Lauren?" His voice was little more than a throaty whisper.

"It's okay...don't stop...don't stop."

His breathing grew all the more labored and he pressed his forehead to her shoulder. "I couldn't if...I wanted to," he finally managed, "but I can be more...gentle."

"Don't be!" she cried, for the instant of pain was gone, leaving only that swelling knot of need low in her belly.

But he was gentle and caring, moving slowly at first, letting her body adjust to his presence before he adopted the rhythm designed to drive her insane. What he didn't realize was that even his initial, cautious movements were delicious. His fullness inside her gave Lauren an incredible sense of satisfaction; the idea of receiving a man, of receiving Matt in this way, was the sweetest delight.

By the time he moved faster, Lauren was right with him. She adored the way his thighs brushed hers, the way their stomachs rubbed. When he bent his head, she strained higher. His mouth closed over her breast and began a sucking that pulled at her womb from one direction while the smooth stroking of his manhood pulled at it from another. Her hands roamed over and around his firm body, but even had she not touched him, she would have been intimately aware of every hard plane and sinewed swell he possessed. Their bodies were that close, working in tandem.

He murmured soft words of encouragement and praise. "That's it, sweetheart...ahhh...your legs...yes, there...so good..."

They moved as one then, each complementing and completing the other. Lauren experienced a beauty she'd never imagined. She was drawn beyond herself into Matt, sharing, collaborating, merging with him into a greater being for those precious moments of emotional and physical bliss.

After the climax had passed, it was a long time before either of them could speak. They gasped for air, alternately panting and moaning, laughing from time to time at their inability to do anything more. At last Matt slid slowly to her side, leaving one leg and an arm over her in a statement of possession she had no wish to deny. His head was beside hers on the pillow, his cheek cushioned in her hair.

"How do you feel?" he asked in a thick whisper.

"Stunned," she whispered back. "I never imagined…"

"*You* never imagined…"

She forced her lids open and looked at him. "Then…it was okay?"

"It was more than okay," he teased in throaty chiding, "but you had to know that."

"No. I didn't."

His grin faded, replaced by a look of tender concern. He brought a shaky hand up to smooth damp strands of hair from her brow. "I'm sorry if I hurt you, Lauren. If I'd known, I might have been able to make it easier."

"It couldn't have been easier. I've never felt so wonderful in my life."

"Even at the start?" His arched brow dared her to deny the moment of pain she'd felt.

"Even then. If I hadn't felt a thing, something would have been lost. I wanted the pain. Does that make any sense?"

He didn't answer. Instead, he traced her eyebrow with his finger. "Why didn't you tell me, sweetheart?"

"I didn't think it mattered." She paused, experiencing a frisson of apprehension. "Did it? I mean, we're both adults. I knew what I was doing."

"Did you?"

"Yes!" She didn't understand what he was getting at.

"Lauren, I didn't do anything to protect you. It's possible I've just made you pregnant."

Her jaw slackened only slightly. Then, unable to control herself, she burst into a smile. "What an exciting thought!"

Matt closed his eyes for a minute. "You're supposed to be worried, sweetheart." He propped himself up on an elbow and looked down at her. "You're supposed to be thinking about this new life you have, the shop, your independence."

"But a baby!" Her eyes were wide. "I could adjust to that. It would be marvelous!"

"I didn't know you wanted a baby so badly."

"Neither did I." She scrunched up her nose. "But it probably won't happen. Just once, Matt. And it's the wrong time of the month." She brushed the strands of hair from his forehead and left her fingers to tangle in the wet thatch. "Are *you* worried?"

"Of course I'm worried. Babies should be planned, the logistics worked out. Everything should be clear from the start."

"There you go again. So cautious." She tugged playfully at his hair. "If I were to become pregnant, I'd manage. One way or another I would, because I'd want the baby enough to make everything fall into place."

"Such a romantic," Matt murmured, but there was a sadness in his eyes.

Her smile faded. "You're thinking that you'll be leaving soon."

"Sooner or later I will."

"It's okay, Matt. There are no strings attached to what happened tonight. I won't ask any more of you than you want to give."

He snorted and flopped back on the pillow. "That's cavalier of you."

"Would you rather I demand marriage?" she asked, confused. "Times have changed. Just because we made love doesn't mean you have to make an 'honest woman' of me. I don't feel dishonest. I feel...lucky."

He turned his head on the pillow so that he faced her again. "Explain."

"I never expected what happened tonight. What I felt, what I experienced, were so much more than I've ever dared to dream."

"Why not? That's what I don't understand. I don't understand why you were a virgin. You're beautiful, charming and intelligent. And you're right. Times have changed. Women your age are rarely inexperienced."

"Would you have had me throw myself at just any old man for the sake of experience?"

At the sound of hurt in her voice, he rolled over to cover her body. With his large hands cupping her face, he spoke gently. "No, sweetheart. Of course not. I'm the one who's been lucky tonight. To know that you've given me what you've given no other man...that was one of the reasons I couldn't stop when I realized what was happening."

"One of the reasons?"

Even in the dark she caught his sheepish grin. "The others are right here." He dropped a hand to her knee and lifted his body only enough to permit that hand a slow rise. He touched each and every erogenous zone before tapping his finger against her temple. "All of you—mind, body, soul. You turn me on, Lauren."

"Oh, God" was all she could whisper, because his tactile answer had set her body to aching again, and she hadn't believed it could be possible. She didn't know whether to be pleased or embarrassed, but that was her mind talking.

Of its own accord, her body shifted beneath his with a story of its own.

As she'd already learned, Matthew Kruger was a good reader.

When the last page of this second chapter had been turned, she fell asleep. Her body was exhausted yet replete, her mind at peace. She was totally unaware that Matt lay awake beside her for long hours before curving his body protectively around hers and at last allowing himself the luxury of escape.

LAUREN AWOKE the next morning to a strange sensation of heat running the entire length of the back of her body. Her lids flew open and she held her breath. Only her eyeballs moved, questioning, seeking, finally alighting on the large, tanned hand flattened on the sheet by her stomach.

Matt.

Shifting her head, she followed a line from that hand, up a lean but powerful arm to an even stronger shoulder.

Matt.

Quietly, almost stealthily, she turned until she faced him, and her heart melted. He was sound asleep, tawny lashes resting above his cheekbones, his mouth slightly parted, lips relaxed. Unable to help herself, she let her gaze fall along his body. Last night she'd savored him with her hands; this morning it was her eyes' turn to feast.

He was magnificent. Soft hair swirled over his chest, tapering toward his navel, below which the sheet was casually bunched. His hips were lean, as she'd known they'd be; the sheet was nearly as erotic a covering as the air alone might have been.

A self-satisfied smile spread over her face. She felt good. Complete. All woman. Giving in to temptation, she leaned forward and kissed his chest. He smelled of man, earthy but wonderful. Eyes closed, she drank in that essence as she continued to press the lightest of kisses into the warmest of skin.

When a hand suddenly tightened around her waist, her head flew up. Matt's eyes were still closed, but he wore the roguish shadow of a beard on his cheeks and a faint smile on his lips. "Am I dreaming?" he whispered.

In answer, Lauren shimmied higher, slid her arms around his neck and kissed his smile wider. She was further rewarded when he rolled onto his back and hauled her over him. Only then did he open his eyes.

For long minutes, they simply looked at each other. She wasn't sure what her own eyes were saying, but Matt's quite clearly spoke of pleasure. And affection. They made her feel special.

"Hi," he whispered at last.

She swallowed the lump of emotion in her throat. "Hi."

"How'd you sleep?"

"Fine."

"No ghosts?"

She shook her head.

"No strange noises?"

She shook her head. "Beth was right. She said I needed a bodyguard."

He closed his hands around her bottom and gave her a punishing squeeze. "So that's why you did it? Because you wanted a bodyguard?"

"You know better than that." She sucked in a breath when his hands pressed her intimately closer. "Matt?"

He was grinning. "It's your fault. You started it. In case you didn't know, a man's at his peak in the morning."

"I thought a man was at his peak in his twenties, and you're a mite beyond. You're shocking me."

"You're the one with the bag of surprises. A virgin is supposed to be shy and demure."

She grinned. "I'm not a virgin anymore, so my behavior is excusable."

Rolling over, he set her on her back, then held himself up so that he could look at her. Just as hers had done moments earlier, his eyes touched her body as only his hands had done the night before. "You are beautiful, Lauren. God, I can't believe it." He met her gaze. "No regrets?"

Still basking in his approval, which both stunned and thrilled her, she shook her head. "How about you?"

One long forefinger drew a bisecting line from the hollow of her throat to the apex of her thighs. "No," he answered, but gruffly. "Not about this. About not having the answer to your problem, yes, I have regrets."

"Don't think about that," she whispered, feeling a strange urgency not to let anything intrude on this precious time with Matt. "Not now."

His grin was lopsided, slightly forced, and his eyes lingered on the soft curves of her body. "I think I'd better. It's either that or ravish you again, and I imagine you're going to be a little sore."

"Me? Sore?"

"Yes. You, sore."

"Oh."

With a deep growl, he gathered her into his arms and held her tightly. When his grip loosened, it was with reluctance. "I could use a shower and some breakfast. It's a workday, or had you forgotten?"

"Oh, my god!" She twisted toward the clock on the dresser, then pushed herself from his arms and bolted out of bed. "I'll take the shower first," she called over her shoulder. Remembering her sadly deficient water heater, she added, "Real quick."

Lauren was true to her word, but by the time she had returned to the bedroom, Matt was nowhere in sight. For a split second she panicked. Then she caught sight of his clothes on the floor. "Matt?" Wrapped in her towel, she headed for the stairs. "Matt?"

The aroma of fresh coffee filled the air, but he didn't answer. She was halfway down the staircase when the front door opened and Matt strode through, carrying a large leather suitcase. He was stark naked.

"Matthew Kruger! Where is your sense of decency? If one of my neighbors saw you—"

He'd taken the stairs by twos, and the smack of his lips on hers cut off her teasing tirade. He continued upward. "The trees were my cover. It's a gorgeous day outside."

Lauren couldn't think to argue. He was spectacular. Tall and straight. Broad back, narrow hips, tight buttocks. If it hadn't been for the time, she'd have followed him into the shower just to touch him again. The mere sight of him took her breath away.

But time was of the essence. She blow-dried her hair and put on makeup while Matt showered and shaved; then she dressed quickly and hurried to the kitchen. They were seated side by side, finishing off the last of the scrambled eggs and toast, when Matt laid out his plans for the day.

"I've got meetings set for ten and two. We can take my car into Boston, meet for lunch, then grab something on the way home tonight. Sound okay?"

His words were offered gently, not at all imperiously, yet they brought back to Lauren the crux of Matt's present mission. He intended to protect her as he'd promised, which meant that he was going to stick as close to her side as possible. On one level, she was thrilled with that prospect. On another...

"About my problem, Matt. Are we just going to... wait?"

"Pretty much. It'll be interesting to see if my presence here makes any difference."

"But if nothing happens, we won't know if you've scared someone off for good or simply put him off for a while. And you can't stay here forever."

"I know." He looked away. "I'm going to make some calls today."

"What kind of calls? To whom?"

"People who may have more insight than we do." There was an edge to his voice, but his gaze was soft when he glanced back at her. "Let me do the worrying for now, Lauren. You've done your share."

"But it's my problem! I can't just dump it on your shoulders and wipe my hands of it. That's not fair to you. You don't owe me anything."

For a minute he looked as if he would argue. He gnawed on the inside of his cheek, then lifted his mug and drained the last of his coffee. "Let's just say I owe it to Brad, then. He was my friend and you're his sister. The least I can do is to help you out when you need it."

That wasn't quite the answer she wanted, but she knew she'd have to settle for it.

"Anyway," he added with an endearing grin, "I've got broad shoulders. I can handle it. Maybe it's the Spenser in me coming out, after all."

"Better you than Robert Urich. But are you sure?"

"Very sure. Hey, as far as work on the house goes, are you going to call those names I gave you or would you like me to do it?"

She winced. "Got a cold shower, did you?"

"Well..."

"I'll do it. You're doing enough. I'd love it if you were

here when I meet with them, though. I have a feeling some of those guys show more respect when a man's around." The last had been offered on a dry note. She paused, then asked cautiously, "How long will you be here?" She envisioned two or three days, and the thought left her feeling empty.

He rubbed the back of his neck. "I was thinking about that last night. I have to be in Leominster on Thursday and Friday, but I could almost commute from here." He took a fast breath. "Unless you'd rather have the house to yourself again. I'll understand, Lauren. It's okay, really it is— Hey, crumpled napkins in the face I can do without first thing in the morning!"

"Then don't give me that little-boy pout," she chided as she carried their plates to the sink. But when she returned to the table, she gave him a hug from behind. "Of course I want you here," she murmured with her cheek pressed to his. "For as long as you can stay. Besides, you *do* owe it to me."

His hands clasped hers at the open collar of his shirt. "I do?"

"Uh-huh. You've awakened me to some of the finer points in life. Seems to me there's got to be an awful lot I still don't know."

"Then you *are* after my body! I knew it all along!"

"Could be," she answered with a grin. "Could be."

DURING THE NEXT FEW DAYS, Lauren and Matt spent every possible minute with each other. They drove to and from Boston together. They met for lunch each day. When Matt wasn't working but Lauren was, he was parked so frequently on the bench outside the shop that Beth suggested they charge him rent.

"Either that, or hire him part-time."

Lauren wrinkled her nose. "After all we went through to convince Jamie to start full-time next week? No way. Besides, what does Matt know about art?"

"What does he know about *other* things?" Beth drawled suggestively. "That's what *I* want to know."

"Oh, quite a bit" was all Lauren would admit. She knew Beth was fishing. She hadn't made a secret of the fact that Matt was staying with her in Lincoln. But some things were sacred, not to be discussed with even the closest of friends, and for more than the obvious reasons. Lauren felt she was living a fairy tale. By her own admission, Beth was envious. The last thing Lauren wanted to do was to rub it in.

"Well," Beth said with a sigh, "at least he's managed to keep you safe."

"That he has."

Since Matt had been with her, there'd been no accidents, no close calls, no questionable occurrences. Indeed, Lauren felt safe enough almost to forget there was a problem.

Almost, but not quite.

Tuesday evening she asked Matt if he'd made any calls to those "people who may have more insight than we do." He said he had and that the ball was rolling. His tone was light. She hadn't dared ask more.

Wednesday evening, though, she couldn't help herself. As gently as she could, she inquired about it again.

"Have you heard anything yet?"

"No. It takes time."

"Time to do what? I don't understand."

"Questions can be asked, people consulted. Trust me, Lauren. Please?" Put that way, with an eruption of tension dissolving abruptly into beseechfulness, she'd surrendered.

But much as she tried, she couldn't shake the conviction that the things she'd experienced were linked and that, despite Matt's protective shield, they were bound to resume at some point. And she was frightened.

THURSDAY MORNING Matt crawled out of bed at dawn, showered, shaved and dressed, then woke Lauren to say goodbye. She was groggy. It had been another late night of sweet, prolonged loving. Only the realization that Matt was leaving brought her from her self-satisfied stupor.

"You should have wakened me sooner," she whispered, reaching up to touch his freshly shaved cheek. "I'd have made you breakfast."

"No time. They'll have coffee and doughnuts there."

"I wish you didn't have to go."

"I'll be back tonight."

"I know, but I've been spoiled. Leominster seems so far away."

He sighed. "I agree." He pressed his lips together, then forced a smile. "You take care of yourself, sweetheart, you hear? Drive carefully, and be sure to lock the doors."

"I will."

Lifting her in his arms, he hugged her before setting her back with a kiss on the tip of her nose. She knew not to ask for more. Where temptation was concerned, they were both decidedly weak.

"Good luck, Matt. I hope everything goes well."

He waved as he left the room. Climbing from the bed, she crossed to the window and watched him slide into his car, start the engine and drive off. In an attempt to parry the unease that settled over her, she took a shower and dressed, then forced herself to make breakfast for one and eat every last bit.

Only when she'd finished did she permit herself to sit back and think. She missed Matt. Already. After only two full days together, she'd gotten used to his presence. More than used to it. Addicted to it. Breakfast wasn't the same without him. Neither would lunch be. For that matter, she'd miss being able to look up at odd times and find him on the bench outside the shop.

She wished he could stay forever, but that was an unrealistically romantic thought if ever there was one. Today he was off to Leominster. Next week, or soon after, he'd be back in California. What then? Would they talk on the phone? Visit each other from time to time?

She knew it wouldn't be enough for her. She wanted him in Lincoln with her. Whatever initial reservations she'd had about his background, his occupation or his character were nonexistent now. His background was blue-collar and strong, his occupation solid, his character sterling. She'd never once glimpsed anything coarse in him. Rather, he'd proved to be unfailingly gentle and giving. Even his reticence about discussing Brad had ceased to matter. He was simply protective, skirting around what he knew to be a sensitive subject.

And he'd brought out a new side of her. Since she'd met him, she'd matured as a woman. He made her believe in both her looks and her sexuality. Whereas her confidence had come from looking in the mirror when she'd first returned from the Bahamas, now it came from the reflection of admiration in Matt's eyes. She didn't care what anyone else thought of her. Only Matt mattered.

So where was she to go from here? Sighing, she rose from the table. She'd clean up the kitchen, go to work and come home. Soon after that, Matt would return. She wasn't even going to think about tomorrow.

One day at a time. All she could do was take one day at a time.

Cleaning up the kitchen was no problem at all. Going to work was another matter. When she tried to start her car, the engine refused to turn over. Not one to beat a dead horse, she returned to the house, called AAA, then sat waiting for half an hour until the tow truck arrived.

"Battery's dead" was the mechanic's laconic diagnosis.

"But that's impossible. This battery's barely four months old!"

"It's dead."

"How can a four-month-old battery die?"

Taking jumper cables from his truck, the man set to work recharging the battery. "Maybe you left the headlights on."

"I never do that."

"Anyone else drive this car? A kid? Maybe he forgot and left 'em on."

"There's no kid, and I'm the only one who drives the car. It's been sitting in the garage since Tuesday morning—" that was when Matt, in fact, had put it away, but he wouldn't have left the lights on "—but it's sat for longer than that without any trouble."

"No sweat, lady. The battery looks okay otherwise. I'll have it working in no time."

He did, and Lauren was only fifteen minutes late for work, but she was bothered by the incident. It occurred to her that the same person who'd sabotaged her garage door might have entered the garage during those days when the car was idle, switched the lights on for a good, long time, then switched them off without her being any the wiser. She decided to discuss it with Matt that night, but the sense of solace in that resolution wasn't enough to prevent a certain nervousness when she returned to the car after work. She found herself glancing around the large parking garage and into the back seat of the car before she dared climb into the front.

She held her breath. The car started. She drove to Lincoln without any trouble.

Matt wasn't due back until nine at the earliest, so she took the time to stop for groceries before arriving at the farmhouse. It was still light out, and she was grateful. She imagined herself being watched and knew that, had it been dark, she would have been terrified.

Relief came in small measure after she was locked safely inside the house. Focusing determinedly on Matt's return, she stowed the groceries, prepared all the fixings for dinner, then poured herself a glass of wine and took refuge in the living room. While lights were burning in the rest of the house, she chose to sit in the dark. Hiding. Brooding. Wondering. Worrying. She knew that her imagination was getting the best of her, but that didn't stop it from happening.

Minutes seemed to stretch into an eternity, though it was barely after nine when finally she heard a car whip up the drive. Hurrying to the window, she peered cautiously out. Her relief was immediate and considerable when Matt climbed from the car. Even before he'd stepped over the threshold, her arms were around his neck.

"Matt, it's wonderful to have you back!"

He had one hand at the back of her head, the other arm around her waist. "Mmm. You're good for my ego. Such a welcome, and I haven't even been gone fourteen hours."

"Close. Thirteen and a half." She lifted her face for a kiss that was instantly comforting and thoroughly satisfying. "How did it go?"

"Very well. I think we've finally worked out the last of the bugs with the locals, so we can get the permit we need, which is great, since we've got everyone else lined up and ready to go."

"Good deal!"

"And I spoke with Thomas." Thomas Gehling was the general contractor whom Lauren had called on Tuesday.

"He's looking forward to meeting with us Sunday morning."

"But if he's going to be involved with your project, will he have time to do mine?"

Matt threw an arm around her shoulder and drew her into the house with him. "You have to understand construction lingo. When I say that everyone is lined up and ready to go, it means that if we're lucky, we'll have broken ground within six weeks. And then there's the heavy work that has to be done first—blasting, digging, pouring foundations. The plumbers and electricians and carpenters you'll need won't be required at our site for three months minimum. Thomas will have more than enough time to oversee work here—that is, if you find that you like him and what he has to say. You're under no obligation to use him. There are other names on that list."

"Of the ones I spoke with, I liked him the best. Call it instinct, or whatever, but something meshed even on the phone." She was well aware of the fact that Matt's using Thomas Gehling for his own work might have slanted her view. She trusted Matt's judgment. But she had liked Thomas. He spoke intelligently and seemed perfectly comfortable dealing with a woman.

"I think you'll be impressed when you meet him." Having reached the kitchen, Matt went directly to the sink, turned on the water and squirted a liberal amount of liquid soap on his hands. "So how was your day, sweetheart?"

"Fine—I mean, okay. God, I can't believe it happened again."

"What?"

"I've been a nervous wreck all day, counting the minutes until you got back so I could tell you what happened. Then you walk in here, bringing a sense of security, and I forget all about it."

He stared at her over his shoulder. "What happened?"

"My car wouldn't start this morning. The battery was dead. I had to get a truck here to jump-start it."

"The battery was dead? Didn't you say you'd gotten a new one just before you left Bennington?"

"I did. That's what's so weird. The man from the garage suggested that I'd left my lights on by mistake. I'm sure I'd never do that."

A thick cloud of suds coated Matt's hands, but he paid it little heed. His brows knitted low over his eyes. "I was the last one to drive your car. I put it in the garage Tuesday morning before we left for Boston in mine. I'm sure the lights were off. There'd have been no reason for me to turn them on to begin with, and the car started perfectly, so they couldn't have been left on the night before."

"That's what I figured." She was standing close by the sink. "The only logical explanation is that someone's been tampering in the garage again."

He shot her a sharp glance. "Was anything else wrong with the car?"

"No, and it started perfectly when I left work tonight."

Bending over the sink, Matt splashed soapy water on his face. Lauren reached into a drawer and had a clean towel waiting by the time he'd rinsed and straightened up. No amount of wiping, though, could remove the concern from his features.

"It may have been a fluke," he suggested quietly.

"Do you believe that?"

He hesitated. "No."

"Matt, don't you think it's time we called the police? I mean, when it was only a couple of incidents, they might have thought I was crazy, but at this stage the situation has to be considered suspicious. At least if the police were aware of the possibilities, they could patrol the area more closely.''

Matt's expression grew more troubled than ever. "The police might scare him off, and then he'd only wait for things to die down before starting again. What we need to do is to catch him.''

"Come on, Matt," she chided, "I was only kidding about playing Spenser.''

"It wouldn't be too hard to rig up some booby traps.'' His eyes were growing animated; he was obviously warming up to the idea. "I think I could manage it, with a little help from a friend.''

"From what friend?''

"One of the guys I met in Leominster. He works at a nearby lumberyard.'' Matt gave a mock grimace and scratched the back of his head. "Seems to me that he mentioned something about having done time.''

"A convict? You're going to enlist a *convict* to save me?''

"An ex-convict. And he's been straight for ten years.''

"Matt, what *is* this?''

"His specialty was breaking and entering, and he was a genius at it.''

Lauren narrowed her eyes. "How long did you spend with this guy?''

"Not long. Can I help it if he's proud of what he's done?''

"Not only after, but before.'' She grunted, then muttered under her breath, "I can't believe I'm standing here listening when I should be on the phone talking to the police.''

Matt put his hands on her arms and stroked her coaxingly. "Come on, Lauren. It's worth a try. You know how the police are—''

"I don't know how the police are. I've never had dealings with them before, contrary to *some* of your friends."

He kissed her forehead. "The police ask millions of questions and then get their minds set on an answer that isn't the one you've given or the one you want to hear. These local departments just aren't geared to taking the offensive, and they sure as hell wouldn't call in the state police or the FBI in a situation like this." His voice softened, taking on a hint of teasing that was reflected in his eyes. "If you were worried about contractors being chauvinists, just wait until you've met the police. They'll treat you like a sweet little thing who's slightly soft in the head." He cupped said item in his hand and gently massaged her scalp. "And even if they decided that you just might be on to something, there's the matter of red tape. They could step up their patrols, but that'd be all. They'd have trouble getting authorization for much else. More than anything, they'd be reluctant to do something that might backfire in court."

Lauren was having trouble fighting him when he was so close and touching her so gently. "You're not reluctant," she stated, but the accusation she'd intended came out sounding more like admiration.

"Not one bit." His thumbs traced the delicate curves of her ears. "I want whoever's been harassing you to be caught. I have to believe that once we find out who it is, we'll find a motive as well."

"You're seducing me," she breathed.

"Me?"

"Don't look so innocent. You're seducing me."

"I am not. I'm simply trying to convince you to let me have a go at it."

"At what? That's the issue." Her voice was whisper-soft, not seductive in itself, simply…taken. "Do you want a go at playing cops and robbers, or at making love with me?''

''I'll make you forget, Lauren,'' he murmured, lowering his head until his lips feathered hers. ''I'll make you forget everything else.''

She caught her breath when he nipped at her lower lip. He was already making her forget, damn him—bless him. At this moment, she wanted to forget.

''I'll make you forget everything else,'' he repeated hotly against her neck. ''And that's a promise. Word of honor.''

MATT MADE GOOD on his promise. Right there, propping Lauren against the kitchen counter, he made love to her with such daring that she forgot everything else but what she felt for him, with him.

He also made good on the promise to call his friend, the breaking-and-entering expert, who showed up at the farmhouse bright and early the very next morning with a carload full of booby-trap makings the likes of which Lauren had never imagined. She had to leave for work before the last of the snares were set, and remarked only half in jest that she'd never make it back into the house alive.

Matt called her from Leominster in the middle of the afternoon to say that he was going to have to attend a dinner meeting and that he wouldn't be back until late. Disappointed but fully appreciative of the demands of his work, she decided to stay in the city after the shop closed to have dinner with Beth and then see a movie.

''Nervous about going home?'' Beth teased.

Lauren chuckled—yes, nervously. ''It'll be dark, and they've hooked up so many gadgets that it's very possible I'll be the first one caught. You wouldn't believe it, Beth. There's a gizmo on the garage door that has to be deactivated, or else a huge black net descends on an intruder.

And once the net falls, *it* sets off a god-awful clanging. The doors to the house have hidden latches that are attached to electrical devices that deliver a shock powerful enough to stun, and the shock in turn sets off an alarm.''

"You're right in the middle of a spy novel. I love it!''

"You wouldn't if you had to negotiate everything yourself. There are even hidden snares along the edge of the woods. You'd think we were trapping mink.''

"I'm telling you, you've got all the makings of a bestseller. Just think, when this is over, you can write it up. Before you know it, you'll be signing autographs and doing the talk-show circuit.''

"Thank you, Beth. I'll settle for catching one man and turning him over to the police.''

"But what if it isn't *one* man?'' Beth tossed out with imaginative anticipation. "What if there's a whole syndicate that's got some kind of grudge against you? What if you catch one man and another takes over where the first leaves off, so you catch the second? Meanwhile, the first dies mysteriously in jail, so the second decides to sing, and before you know it, there's enough evidence to convict the *entire* syndicate. You'll be a hero!''

"Heroine,'' Lauren correct dryly. "And I don't believe we're dealing with any syndicate. What would a syndicate have against me?''

"Maybe it was using your vacant farmhouse as its headquarters, and then you came along and, boom, moved in lickety-split, and there's still some very valuable and potentially condemning material stored in the cellar—''

Lauren scowled at her. "What happened to your theory about the ghost of inhabitants past?''

"Too passé. I think I like the syndicate idea better.''

"I don't like *either* of them, and if we're going to have

dinner together, you'll have to swear you won't go on like this. You're making me nervous.''

"I thought you were already nervous."

"You're making me *more* nervous."

Beth patted her arm, then squeezed it. "I'm just teasing, Lauren. You know that. Just teasing.''

THAT WAS WHAT LAUREN told herself when, later that night, after the movie had let out and she and Beth had gone their separate ways on the streets of Boston, she had the uncanny sensation of being followed.

Chapter Seven

The sensation was vague at first, and Lauren wondered if her imagination was simply working overtime. She glanced over her shoulder, then faced forward again. There were people around—she wished there were even more—but none appeared to be suspicious. At least, no one had ducked into a doorway when she'd looked back.

She had walked a bit farther and turned a corner when the sensation intensified. A prickling arose at the back of her neck, accompanied by a frisson of fear. Instinctively she quickened her step, mentally charting the course she'd have to take to reach the garage. It consisted of main streets for the most part, with a single alleyway at the end.

She darted another glance behind her and saw the same outwardly innocuous people—several couples, a handful of singles, all staggered at intervals. If someone grabbed her, she'd yell. There were plenty of bodies to help.

She walked on. Fewer people were ahead of her now; some had turned off toward the subway stop. She assumed the same was true for those behind her, and the thought added to her unease.

She turned another corner. There was no one ahead of her now, and she didn't dare look back. Unbidden, she recalled her childhood. There'd been a dog in the neighborhood, a large German shepherd of which she'd been terrified. Her mother had always instructed her to walk calmly past it on the theory that dogs could smell fear. Could people smell fear? Lauren wondered now. She was sure she reeked of it.

Imagination. That was all it was. Imagination getting a little out of hand. The sounds she heard not far behind weren't footsteps. They were the knocking of the air-conditioning unit in the building she passed…or the creaking of heat as it escaped from the engine of a newly parked car alongside the curb…or…

Eyes wide, she shot a frightened glance over her shoulder and gasped. There was a man. He was very tall, large-set, dressed in black, and he was not twenty feet behind and gaining steadily on her.

Uncaring if she was jumping to conclusions, she began to run. She turned another corner and ran even faster. Her heels beat a rapid tattoo on the pavement, merging with the thundering of her heart to drown out all other night sounds of the city.

She passed another long—agonizingly long—building, then reached the alley, in actuality a single-lane driveway. At its end stood her salvation, a guard booth.

She was breathless and shaking, terrified of looking back and losing time, tripping or slamming into the wall. She cursed her side, which ached; cursed the shoes she wore and the heat that seemed to buffet her and slow her progress. By the time she reached the booth, she felt as though she'd run a marathon.

"Thank God," she whispered, panting as she sagged against the thick plastic enclosure. Then, with a burst of energy, she scrambled to the booth's opening. The guard, a young man with a punk hairstyle at odds with his uniform, sat balanced on the back legs of his chair. A dog-eared magazine lay open on his lap. The heavy beat of rock music thrummed from the stereo box by his side. He was chewing gum; the vigorous action of his jaw only enhanced the indolence of his stare.

"Someone was following me," Lauren gasped and darted a frantic glance toward the alley through which she'd run.

Looking thoroughly bored, the guard followed her gaze. There was no one in sight.

"He must have turned away when he saw me heading toward you," she explained, trying to calm herself enough to think clearly. "Listen, I need a big favor."

The young man blew a bubble, popped it and licked the gum back into his mouth. "Depends what it is."

"Could you walk me to my car?"

He gave a one-shouldered shrug. "I'm on duty."

"I know, but there aren't many cars leaving the garage now. With the gate down, they'll wait. It won't take you long—two, maybe three minutes. Just until I lock myself in."

He fingered his earlobe, which sported a crescent of multiple studs. "I'm not supposed to leave this booth."

"But I'm in danger!"

Slowly, his head nodding in time with the music, he looked back toward the street. "Don't see anyone."

"He may have taken the stairs. Please! I need your help!"

After what seemed forever, the front legs of the chair hit the floor. "So. Chivalry calls." The guard stood up, yawned, then pushed his shoulders back.

The show was wasted on Lauren, who saw right through it to the scrawniness of his physique. Not much to protect her with. But he wore a uniform. There was safety in a uniform.

"I'm the new guy on the block," he drawled. "I was given specific instructions—"

She felt sweat trickling down her back. "Look, I'll argue on your behalf if you get into trouble. It seems to me your boss would reward you for helping a regular tenant."

"You're a regular tenant?" His gaze drifted down her body.

"Yes." She sighed in exasperation, feeling suddenly tired. Instinctively she knew she was safe standing at the booth with even as unlikely a guard as this, but there was still the threat of the inner garage to overcome. She wanted nothing more than to be locked in her car and on the road, headed for home. "Please. Just walk me upstairs. You could have been up and back in the time you've spent talking with me."

He grinned. "Yeah, but talking with you beats sitting here by myself." He cocked his head to one side. "Sure. I'll walk you upstairs."

Lauren jerked her eyes toward the thick pipes overhead. "Thank you," she breathed. By the time she looked down, the guard had let himself out of his cage and was swaggering toward her.

She glanced worriedly back toward the exit, but it remained empty.

"Come on, love. Up we go." He took her elbow and she jumped, wondering for an instant if she'd leaped from the frying pan into the fire. Unfortunately, she was the proverbial beggar who couldn't be choosy. So she clamped her mouth shut and let her cocky gallant lead the way to the stairs.

He dropped her elbow to open the door. Her apprehensive gaze examined every nook of the stairwell as they started up.

"Floor?"

"Third." Had the stairwell always been this narrow? He chewed away at his gum. "Work around here?"

"Yes." Had the stairwell always been this confining?

"Kind of late leaving, aren't you?"

"Yes." He wouldn't try anything. He wouldn't dare. She knew where and for whom he worked.

"Hot date?"

"Yes…he'll be waiting for me on the corner as soon as I leave here."

They climbed the last set of stairs in silence. Though Lauren didn't look, she could feel the smirk on her companion's face. He hadn't believed her. She'd hesitated too long, then spoken too quickly. Damn, but she wasn't good at this.

He swung open the door, then stood aside to let her through. "Always park on the third floor?"

She was looking nervously from side to side, trying to see into corners where a tall, large, dark form might be lurking. "It depends," she offered distractedly. With no assailant in sight, she blindly fumbled in her bag for the keys.

"Where's your car?"

She pointed. They reached it half a minute later.

"There," he announced as she unlocked the door, checked the back seat, then all but threw herself behind the wheel. "Safe and sound."

She locked the door and rolled her window down, just enough to murmur a heartfelt "Thank you. I do appreciate what you've done."

"How about a ride down?"

"Uh…" Dumbly, she looked at the passenger seat, then leaned over and tugged up the button on the opposite door. Already striding around the front of the car, the guard let himself in.

She had her window up tight and the car started before he'd closed the door, and she took the ramps at breakneck speed. Her passenger didn't seem to mind. She suspected he enjoyed the daring ride.

She brought the car to an abrupt halt by the booth, let the guard out and quickly relocked the door. By the time she'd straightened up, he was at her window and making a rolling gesture with his hand. Again she lowered the window several inches.

"Your card?" he asked with an impudent grin.

"Oh." She rummaged in her purse, drew out the card and handed it over. While he studied it, her gaze alternated between the rearview mirror and the windows on either side.

"Looks okay...Lauren." Chomping briskly on his gum, he returned the card, then winked. "Drive carefully now." The last word was muted through her reclosed window. He twisted backward in a move she was sure he practiced regularly on the dance floor, pressed a button and released the gate.

Without another word, Lauren stepped on the gas. She held her breath and didn't expel it until she'd reached the relative safety of Government Center.

With great effort, she forced her rigid fingers to relax on the steering wheel. She took long, deep breaths, feeling safer with each block she put between herself and the parking garage. No one appeared to be following her. To double-check, she swung from one lane to the other, then, a block later to the first lane. She annoyed several drivers, but she didn't care. All that mattered was that the headlights in her rearview mirror were ever varied.

During the drive home, her emotions ran the gamut from fear to confusion to anger. It was the latter that was dominant by the time she pulled up in front of her own garage.

She left the engine running and the headlights on; she had a death grip on the wheel again, and her teeth were clenched. She barely had time to debate whether she should sit this way until Matt returned—she didn't expect him for a while yet—when a pair of headlights pierced the darkness behind her.

She sucked in a breath. It was *him*! He'd followed her after all! Frantic, she struggled to decide on the best course of action. The other car neared. She had to think quickly. She could make a mad dash for the safety of the house, but it would take time for her to work around the booby traps.

Too late.

She could run from the car and head for the woods in an attempt to make it to a neighbor's before being over-taken, but the woods, too, were booby-trapped, and that man had been large and ominously physical-looking.

Too risky.

She could lean on the horn in the hope that the noise would either scare him off or arouse someone's attention.

That seemed her only option.

Her hand was on the horn, about to exert force, when the car behind her sounded its own horn in short, repetitive blasts. Her fear-filled gaze snapped to the rearview mirror.

Matt! It was *Matt*!

Lauren had never felt so relieved, or so foolish, or so furious in her entire life. Storming from her car, she met him halfway between the two. "I cannot *take* any more of this!" she screamed, hands clenched by her sides.

"Lauren, what—"

"It's gone on too long! Why *me*? What have *I* ever done to deserve this—this torture?"

"Take it easy, sweetheart—"

"I've *had* it, Matt!" She took a step back, eluding the

hands he would have put on her shoulders. "This isn't fair! I'm a nervous wreck. I'm getting a permanent crick in my neck from looking over my shoulder. Someone's following me. Someone isn't. Someone's been in the house. Someone hasn't. Someone's sicced a dog on me. Someone hasn't. I don't know who to trust and who not to. For all I know, *you* were the one who stalked me in Boston!"

"*Me?* I just this minute got back from Leominster!"

"But how do I know that?" she fired at him. She was visibly shaking; the emotional strain was taking its toll. "How do I know *anything?* It's always in the dark. *I'm* always in the dark. I'm afraid to pull into my garage for fear I'll become a sitting duck in a big black net. I'm afraid to go into my house for fear I'll be electrocuted at the front door." Her voice grew as wobbly as her knees. "I can't live this way." She ducked her head and withered into herself, whispering, "Damn it, I can't live this way."

She didn't have the strength to elude Matt this time. He put his arms around her and held her while she cried softly.

"It's okay, sweetheart," he murmured. "Let it out. You'll feel better, and then we'll talk."

"I won't feel...better...."

His arms tightened, hands gently kneading her back. "Sure you will. You're upset now. Sounds like you had a bad day."

"Bad night...."

"Come on. Let's go inside."

A short time later, Lauren was huddled in a corner of the living room sofa, holding the glass of brandy Matt had pressed into her hand. He drew one of the side chairs close and propped his elbows on his knees. "Okay. From the top. What happened tonight?"

"It's not just what happened tonight. It's *everything.*"

"But tell me about tonight. I need to know, Lauren."

She studied the rim of the brandy snifter and shrugged. ''I panicked.'' Painstakingly, she explained how she'd walked back to the garage. ''Then there was that awful last stretch when only one man was behind me.''

''Did you see what he looked like?''

She tipped the snifter until the brandy came perilously close to its rim. ''Not really. I glanced back once and got the impression of someone big and tall and dark. Then I started running and didn't look back again.''

''He didn't follow you once you ran?''

''I don't know. I didn't look. By the time I reached the garage, I couldn't see him. I conned the guard into walking me up to my car.''

''Smart girl.''

She snorted. ''Fine for you to say. You didn't see the guard.''

''It was still smart. A paid guard wouldn't try anything. He'd never get away with it.''

''That was what I figured, not that I had much choice at the time.''

''But you made it to your car safely. Did you see anyone when you were driving away from the garage?''

''I wasn't looking.'' She paused to take a healthy swallow of brandy, made a face, recovered, then went on. ''I just locked the doors and drove. No one followed me home, at least no one I could see. I was checking for that.'' Her voice rose. ''But when I got here, I didn't know what to do. Everything was dark, and I was sure that if I tried to get into the house, I'd get caught in one of your snares. Then you drove up, and I thought it was *him*—but I really don't know if there *was* a him. The man I saw could have been after me. Then again, he could have been minding his own business.''

Matt closed his hand over hers and urged the snifter to

her lips again. The brandy was doing its thing; at least she'd stopped shaking.

"I'm sorry I frightened you," he said.

"I thought you'd be later."

"I left Leominster as soon as I could. I was worried."

The eyes Lauren raised brimmed with discouragement. "What am I going to do, Matt?" she whispered. "I can't go on this way."

"I know, sweetheart. I know." His expression was grim. "Do you think someone's keeping tabs on you during the day?"

"While I'm at work, you mean?"

He nodded. "Have you ever gotten the feeling that you're being followed in broad daylight?"

She thought for a minute. "No."

"Ever remember seeing anyone who might fit the description of the man you saw tonight?"

Again she pondered his question, then shrugged in frustration. "There have to be dozens of tall, large-set men who wander through the Marketplace each day. I've never noticed anyone special...other than you." When he glowered at her, she added a sad "That was a compliment," and his glower promptly faded.

"Oh. Thank you."

"What *am* I going to do?"

"I'm thinking. I'm thinking." It was a while before he spoke again, and then it was almost to himself. "You haven't gotten any strange phone calls, heavy-breathing type of thing? And there hasn't been any direct contact, like a note or anything?"

She shook her head, but Matt's attention was on the floor. His brows were knitted together, his lips clamped into a thin line.

"I think," he said at last, "that you should finish your brandy and get to bed. You've had a frightening—"

"Finish my brandy and get to bed? That won't solve anything!"

"There's nothing to be solved tonight. You're safely locked in, and I'm here."

"But tomorrow! I have to go to work tomorrow! You can't be with me every minute, and I don't even want that. I've never been helpless or clinging before, but it seems that lately I'm throwing myself at you the instant you get here."

"I don't mind," he volunteered with a half grin, only to be cut off.

"Well, I do! I don't like what I've become, Matt. I can't continue living this way. I won't!"

What had existed of a grin was wiped clean from his face. "I agree, Lauren. Something has to be done. It's simply a matter of deciding what. Just...just let me sleep on it, okay?"

"I know what should be done. The police should be called in."

He took her hand. "Do you trust me?"

"Of course I trust you. I just think that—"

"Do you *trust* me?"

She knew he was testing her. There was nothing of the little boy about him now. He was all man. Eyes locked with his, she nodded.

"Then let me sleep on it. Give me until morning to figure out what the next step should be."

At that moment, Lauren came out of herself enough to see the lines of fatigue that shadowed Matt's face. He was tired. And worried. "But it's not your responsibility—"

"Till morning?"

She clamped her lower lip between her teeth, then let it

slide out. Her nod was slower in coming this time, but when it did, it conveyed the trust he sought.

MORNING ARRIVED, and Lauren awoke to find that Matt was no longer in bed. Tossing her robe on, she hurried off in search of him. He was just replacing the telephone receiver when she entered the kitchen.

"Matt?" She halted abruptly and stood suspended on the threshold. There was something about the tired slump of his shoulders that filled her with dread.

He covered the distance between them and took her in his arms. His words came out in a rush. "I have to go back to California for a couple of days, Lauren. I've just spoken with the airline and made a reservation."

For a minute she couldn't say anything. She'd known that sooner or later he'd be leaving, but... "Now?" she whispered through a tight throat. "Why *now*?"

"It's important. You know I wouldn't leave if it weren't."

"But...what should I do?" The instant she said the words, she hated them, hated herself, hated the situation.

"I think you should consider visiting your parents."

"No."

"What about Beth? You could sleep over at her place."

"No."

"Then take a room at a hotel. Maybe the Bostonian, or the Marriott. Something close to work."

"No!" She freed herself from his grasp and wrapped her arms around her waist. "I'm not running away. I won't be forced out of my own home!"

Matt ran a hand through his hair, which looked as if he'd done that more than once. For that matter, between the creases on his brow and the weary look in his eyes, she wondered if he'd slept at all. He seemed to be exerting a taut control over himself, but then, so was she. She refused to fall apart, to be reduced to a simpering weakling. No strings, she'd told Matt, and no strings there would be.

"It's very important that I go, Lauren."

Her chin was firm. "It's all right. You can go."

"I don't want to."

"But it's all right. I'll be fine." Hadn't she always been before?

"It's just for two or three days."

"I understand."

"No, you don't. You think I'm running out on you."

"I think just what you told me, that it's important for you to fly back." She was feeling distinctly numb. "When does your plane leave?"

He glanced at his watch. "In two hours."

"I can drop you at the airport on my way—"

"You'll be late. I'll drive myself and leave the car at the airport."

She nodded. Without another word, she turned and retraced her steps to the bedroom. She thought of nothing but getting ready for a regular day's work.

Matt showered while she dressed. They said little to each other during breakfast. Only when she had swung her pocketbook to her shoulder did she look at him. Even her self-imposed anesthetization couldn't fully immunize her against the swell of emotion that hit her.

"Have a safe flight," she whispered.

He walked her to the door. "You know how to work the latch for this thing?"

"Yes." He'd reviewed the process in detail when they'd entered the house last night.

"Be sure to reset it once you've let yourself in or out."

"I will."

They passed through and headed for the garage. "And this one?"

"Yes. I've got it now."

"Lauren, I really wish—"

"Shh. Please, Matt. You have to do your thing, and I have to do mine." She pressed the hidden switch that allowed her access to the garage without mishap, but before she could enter the car, Matt stopped her. He put both hands on her shoulders and looked her straight in the eye.

"I know you're angry, Lauren, and hurt. Believe me, I'd never be leaving if I didn't think it was absolutely necessary."

She stared up at him, saying nothing because there was nothing she would permit herself to say. Only when he tugged her close and wrapped his arms tightly around her did she allow herself a moment's softening. Closing her eyes, she leaned into his strength. By the time he'd released her, though, she was on her own again.

"Be cautious, Lauren," he said. His voice was thick, his gaze clouded. "When in doubt, go with your instincts. They're good. Trust them."

For a split second, she wavered. Her instincts told her that Matt shouldn't go, that she needed him here, that whatever it was that drew him back to California wasn't as important as what was happening between them in Massachusetts. Her instincts told her that his trip would bring no good where they were concerned.

But reason ruled. Matt's home and job were in San Francisco. She had no claim on either. She was right in what she'd told him; he had to do his thing and she had to do hers. And hers was to carry on with her life, just as it had been before Matthew Kruger had entered it.

"Take care," she whispered, then slipped into her car. She didn't look back to see Matt by the garage door after she'd backed out and around, or to see him still standing there when she drove down the drive and turned into the street. If she was aware that she'd left part of herself with him, she put that particular ache down to the general upheaval her life had gone through in the past few weeks. Doggedly she kept her sights ahead.

As THE DAY PASSED, Lauren had less control over her emotional state than she might have liked. Much as she tried not to, she thought of Matt. *He's arriving at the airport now. His plane is taking off now. He's over Pennsylvania, Illinois, Kansas, Utah.* Out of the blue, she'd feel tears in her eyes, and though she cursed her preoccupation, she knew that it was diverting her mind from other thoughts.

Beth, who'd been quick to sense something amiss, tried to get her to talk, but all Lauren would say was that Matt had been called back to his home office for a few days.

"But I thought he was here for another week at least."

"Things come up."

"And he didn't elaborate?" There was an undercurrent of accusation in Beth's words.

Lauren, who was carelessly flipping through the morning's mail, ignored it. "Other than to say it was important that he go." She frowned. "I don't believe it. Another letter for Susan Miles."

"Who's Susan Miles?"

"Beats me. But it's addressed to her, care of this shop. There was one yesterday, too."

"Mark it 'return to sender, addressee unknown' and stick it back in the mail."

"I would if I could, but I can't. There's no return address."

"Postmark?"

"Boston. If whoever sent it doesn't get an answer, he'll just have to show up here to see what's wrong."

"He? How do you know it's a he?"

Lauren held out the letter. "Look at the handwriting. It's heavy. And messy. Has to be a he."

Beth donned her imagination-at-work look. "A he. Hmm, I smell possibilities in this one. You've already got a guy, so forget you. Let's concentrate on me. Suppose, just suppose, some fellow was given the name of a girl he was told worked here. A blind-date kind of thing. Only either he got the girl's name screwed up or the friend who set him up was playing a joke."

"Why would a guy *write* to set up a blind date?"

"Maybe he's too shy to call. Or he's simply taking a new approach. A new approach—that's it." She eyed Lauren through a playful squint. "Not all that different from sitting on a bench for two days, or sitting on it for hours a third day just reading."

"Point taken," Lauren admitted dryly. "I suppose this guy's gorgeous and witty and bright."

"Naturally."

"Then why does his handwriting look like a thug's?"

"It's not like a thug's. It's…creative."

"Ahh. Then whatever is inside this envelope," Lauren said, waving it, "must be equally as creative."

"I'm sure it is." Beth's voice dropped conspiratorially. "Let's open it."

"We can't do that, Beth. It's not addressed to us."

"It's addressed to our shop."

"And what if your gorgeous guy comes in to collect the letters he's incorrectly addressed? He'll be mortified."

"He'll be so taken with me that he won't have time to be mortified. Besides, we can say we threw the letters out.

So what harm is there in opening them first? Do you have the other one?''

"Yes, but, Beth, I don't think this is a great idea."

"Don't think." Snatching the gray envelope from Lauren's hand, Beth quickly opened it. She removed a sheet of matching stationery, unfolded it, then turned it over, puzzled. "Blank. There's nothing on it."

Lauren, too, stared at the blank sheet. "Maybe he lost his nerve the second time around."

"Where's the first?"

Lauren fished the envelope from a drawer in the desk and, her own curiosity piqued, opened it. "The same. The paper is blank. What's going on here, Beth?"

"Who knows?" Beth continued the game, but her enthusiasm was waning. "Maybe his tactic is to be mysterious for a while."

"So we have to wait for the next installment to find out who the mad letter writer is?"

Beth shrugged. "Looks that way." She headed for the front of the store, leaving Lauren to dispose of the blank love letters as she saw fit. For some reason Lauren herself didn't understand, she folded both sheets back into their envelopes and tucked the envelopes into the drawer.

This activity had provided only a temporary respite for Lauren, as did most of work that day. Unfortunately, by the time she knew that Matt had landed and been swallowed up in his own life again, she could no longer free herself of those other, more ominous thoughts.

"How'd you like a roommate for a night or two?" she asked Beth when they were getting ready to close the shop. She'd tried to sound nonchalant, but the gesture was lost on Beth, who knew better.

"I'd love it, Lauren. You know that. You're welcome to stay at my place whenever you want."

"I know you have a date—"

"No, I don't."

"Listen, it's okay. I just don't feel like driving back to Lincoln. You can go out. I'll make myself at home."

"I don't have a date, Lauren."

"But that fellow Joe—"

"Asked me out and I refused. He wanted to go camping. Overnight. I didn't have equipment, and I'm not keen on camping, and I'm even less keen on Joe."

"How do you know? You've just met the guy."

"Exactly. Have you ever heard of camping overnight for a first date?"

Lauren shrugged. "Might have been interesting."

"Maybe for you and Matt. No, chalk that." Beth grunted. "Matt might have left you stranded in the woods while he raced off to scale some nearby peak. How could he simply abandon you this way, Lauren? I still can't believe it."

Lauren kept her voice calm. "He has his own life."

"But he's barged his way into yours—"

"He didn't barge his way in anywhere."

"Okay, then he wormed his way in. He's made himself nearly indispensable—"

"He has *not*. I can do just fine without him."

"Mmm. That's why you can't bear the thought of going home."

Lauren's gaze lowered to the scrap of fabric she was fraying. "It's not that. But after last night I feel... uncomfortable." She'd told Beth earlier about the episode near the garage. "It's still too fresh in my mind."

"Matt wasn't around then, either. Why do men do this, Lauren? Why aren't they around when you need them?"

"It's not a question of need," Lauren rationalized. "I'm independent. I can take care of myself."

"You should go to the police. I think what you're facing is more than even Matt can handle. Why is he so vehement against it?"

"He has good reasons. He may be right."

"Maybe his reasons aren't so noble."

Lauren tensed. "What do you mean?"

"It's occurred to me that much of what's happened to you has been since Matt showed up."

"That's not true! Three of those incidents happened before he ever got here!"

"No," Beth returned, determined to make her point. "If my memory's correct, three of those incidents happened within mere days of his first introducing himself to you. He said he was here in Boston on business. For all you know, he was here in the city that very first time, when the car just missed you on Newbury Street."

"I'm not sure I like what you're implying."

"I'm not sure I do, either, but it may be worth considering."

"Absolutely not! What could Matt possibly have to do with those incidents? What reason could he have to wish me harm?"

"Maybe something to do with Brad?"

"That's impossible. Don't even think it, Beth. It's out of the question."

No more was said about it, but Beth had accomplished her objective. Lauren fought it. She told herself that Beth was either playing the game she played so well or simply jealous. Lauren closed her mind to it while she and Beth walked over Beacon Hill to Beth's apartment, where they shared a congenial dinner and evening. Later that night, though, while Lauren lay quietly on the sofa bed trying to fall asleep, unwanted thoughts flitted in fragments through her mind.

Ironically, Matt's phone call didn't help. It came at two in the morning, shortly after Lauren had fallen into a restless sleep. The phone was on the table by her head. She nearly jumped out of her skin when it rang.

"Hello?"

"Lauren! I've been worried sick! When there was no answer at the farmhouse, I started calling hotels. You said you *weren't* going to Beth's!" He sounded angry. That was all Lauren needed.

"Why, Matt, how good of you to call in the middle of the night. I'm fine, thank you. How are you?"

"Lauren, you said you weren't going anywhere!"

"I changed my mind."

"Damn it, you could have let me know. I was sure something had happened!"

"How could I have let you know? I don't know where you are, much less at what phone number."

"I'm at home, and I'm the only Matthew Kruger in the San Francisco book!"

"How did I know you'd be trying me? You didn't say anything about calling."

She heard a deep sigh at the other end of the line. "Right. I'm sorry. It was my fault. Are you okay?"

"I'm tired, Matt." *And confused. Very confused.* The sound of Matt's voice, imperious, then gentle, only added to her confusion.

"I'm sorry to be calling so late. I started trying the house an hour and a half ago. When there was no answer, I figured maybe you'd gone to another movie or something, but when you didn't return, I started imagining things and it all began to spiral. You are okay?"

"Yes, I'm okay."

"Nothing happened today?"

"No, nothing happened."

"Thank goodness."

His voice clearly held relief. For that matter, Lauren mused, everything about his voice was clear. He could just as well be calling her from around the corner....

"Well," he went on, less sure of himself now, "I just wanted to hear your voice. And to tell you that I'm going to try to catch an afternoon flight out of here tomorrow. By the time I get into Logan and on the road, it's apt to be pretty late. It may be easier if I go to a hotel—"

"No!" she interrupted. She could hear the fatigue in his voice, and it pulled a string somewhere deep inside her. This was Matt, the man she missed, the man she wanted to see, to be with. "No. Meet me in Lincoln. I'll be there."

"But you may be sleeping. I'll frighten you."

"Just give a honk like you did the other night and I'll know it's you."

"Are you sure?"

"I'm sure."

"Okay, sweetheart." His voice lowered. "I miss you."

"Me, too, Matt."

"See you tomorrow night, then?"

"Uh-huh."

"Take care, sweetheart."

"You, too. Bye-bye, Matt."

She replaced the receiver and sank back to the bed, only then realizing that she hadn't even asked how he was doing. Maybe she hadn't wanted to. Maybe she'd been afraid he'd give her an evasive answer. He hadn't spelled out the reason for his abrupt return to San Francisco—if indeed he was there. Was his business on the West Coast shrouded in mystery, or was her imagination at work again?

After tossing and turning for better than an hour, she finally fell back to sleep. When she awoke on Sunday morning, she felt weary and tense. Even Beth's lighthearted chatter didn't lighten her mood; irrationally, perhaps, she blamed Beth for having planted the seeds of doubt in her mind.

Driving to Lincoln in broad daylight was accomplished comfortably. Lauren arrived there moments before Thomas Gehling pulled up. She liked him instantly, finding him easygoing, intelligent and polite. As they walked through the house, they discussed a wide range of possibilities. She hired him on the spot.

That was the high point of her day. The tension, the confusion, the worry, were back in full swing by the time she'd returned to Boston. Work at the shop was a blessing, but a short-lived one. All too soon she was headed back to Lincoln. This time around, she was a bundle of raw nerves.

A confrontation was imminent. She felt it in every fiber of her being. By nature she was a peaceful, accommodating sort, but the events of the past few weeks had upset her equilibrium. It was one thing to suspect that an unknown lunatic was after her, yet quite another to suspect that it was Matt. He was either with her or against her. She had to know one way or the other.

Arriving home at dusk, she was assailed by every one of the fears she'd been free of that morning. Glancing anxiously from side to side, she inched her way up the drive. Her first thought was to leave the car outside, but she knew that its protection, and hence her own, came from the trap that was set inside. Dashing quickly from the car to the garage, she fumbled to disengage the alarm and raise the door. That done, she quickly brought the car inside, lowered the door and reengaged the snare, then tackled the front door of the house. Beads of sweat were dotting her upper lip by the time she'd finally closed the door behind her and reset the alarm.

Then she made dinner, ate practically none of it and

waited. She picked up a book, turned page after page without absorbing a word and waited. She dozed on the living room sofa, awakening with a jolt at the slightest sound—though most were in her dreams—and waited.

Midnight came and went. Then one o'clock. It was nearly one-thirty when she finally heard a car approach. This time she didn't rush to the window. She didn't so much as shift on the sofa. She sat quietly in the dark, waiting.

Chapter Eight

Lauren held her breath when she identified the click and scrape at the front door as the disengagement of the make-shift electrical alarm. Her eyes pierced the darkness, never once leaving the broad oak expanse as, with an aged creak, the door slowly opened. The man who came quietly through was tall, very tall, and large-set. Though he could have doubled for the man she'd seen behind her in Boston on the previous Friday night, there was no doubt in her mind that this time it was Matt.

"You didn't honk," she accused in a voice that shook.

His head twisted. "Lauren!" Setting his suitcase on the floor, he groped for the light switch. The weak glow that subsequently filtered into the living room from the hall was enough to reveal her position on the sofa. "What are you doing up, sweetheart? I thought for sure you'd be in bed."

"You didn't honk."

He paused, turning his head slightly. "The thought of it seemed jarring at this hour. I really didn't want to wake you up." He stood backlighted in the archway of the living room, his face in shadows. "But you weren't sleeping, were you?" Crossing the room, he hunkered down and curled his fingers lightly around her arms. Her skin was cold. "Why aren't you in bed?" he asked softly.

"We have to talk."

"You sound strange. What's wrong?"

She didn't move. "I'm not sure. That's one of the things we have to discuss."

He frowned at his hands, dropped them to the sofa on either side of her hips, then met her gaze. "What is it, Lauren?"

"I've been sitting here thinking. I've spent most of the day thinking. And last night, too."

He sank back on his heels, hands falling to his sides. "About what?"

"You. I want the truth, Matt." It was a struggle to keep her voice steady when so much was at stake, but she managed commendably. "I want all of it. No evasion. No seduction. I want to ask questions and have them answered."

"I don't understand. I've always given you answers—"

"They were never enough, but that may be my fault. Maybe I haven't *asked* enough."

"I don't know what you're getting at."

She tucked her legs more tightly beneath her. "Three weeks ago I was happy. My life was shaping up so beautifully that I had to pinch myself to make sure it was real. Then certain things started happening, and I'm suddenly stuck in the middle of a nightmare. Someone is after me. I don't know who or why."

"What's this got to do with *me*?"

"You showed up right after it all began, Matt. By some coincidence, you appeared out of nowhere. You claim to be a friend of my brother's, but my brother has been dead for a year, so I can't ask him about it. You have biographical facts about Brad, any of which you could have picked up by reading a standard job résumé. You have insight into his character, most of which you could have gained in one night of heavy drinking with him, even if he'd been a total stranger up until then.''

"I don't believe this," Matt muttered, but Lauren was just beginning.

"That first night when you introduced yourself to me, you said you'd been in Boston for a week. It was during that very week that I was nearly run down by a car on Newbury Street. Nothing about the car registered with me. It could very easily have been a nondescript rental, just like the one you've been driving."

"Lauren—"

"Then a dog attacked me. You were the one who suggested it might have been trained to pull away when a special whistle was blown. That thought wouldn't even have occurred to me, yet it did to you. Why?"

"It's common knowledge—"

"And then my garage door crashed down." Despite the warmth of the night, her hands were freezing. She tucked them more deeply in the folds of her shirt. "You're a builder. You seemed familiar enough with the workings of that door to be able to rig, and unrig, a malfunction."

"This is absurd, Lauren! Do you know what you're saying?"

"I'm not done," she declared. "Let me finish."

He was on his feet, prowling the room. "I can't wait to hear the rest."

She ignored his sarcasm, knowing only that the time for silence had passed. "There was the matter of an intruder in my house. You found the problem immediately. A lock on one of the windows was broken. In fact, you used that very window to get into the house, supposedly to scout around. How can I be sure it was the first time you'd entered the house that way?" When Matt took a sharp breath to defend himself, she rushed on. "The car that followed me all the way home from Boston was compatible in both size and shade to your rental. And the timing was perfect. You could have left me at my garage, picked up your own car—even on another floor of the same garage—and tailed me out. Then there was the night when I heard strange noises. You said you were in Leominster. It was a convenient alibi, but I have no proof, do I?''

"I'll give you names and numbers—"

"My car battery went dead; you were the last one to drive the car. Someone followed me late at night in Boston; you conveniently arrived here within minutes after I did.''

"I was in *Leominster*—but I told you that once before, didn't I? I thought we agreed on it.''

"That was what you wanted, for me to agree on it.''

"I wanted you to trust me.''

"So you told me. Many times. And I've been completely taken in, because I thought you were one of the most sincere, straightforward men I've ever met. Maybe I was wrong, Matt. Maybe I've been playing into your hands all along.''

He stood before her then, hands on his hips, his face a mask of steel. The oblique light from the hall did nothing to blunt his obvious irritation. "What brought all this on? That's what I'd like to know. You did trust me. At least, I thought you did. Where did I go wrong?''

Lauren's composure was beginning to slip. If Matt was innocent—and his reaction was far from conclusive on that score—she was going to hate herself for the accusations she'd made. On the other hand, if he was guilty as charged, she was in a lot of trouble.

"You went wrong," she began with a shaky breath, "when you took off for California on Saturday morning.''

"You *were* angry.''

"No. But I was puzzled and maybe a little hurt, because

the trip was so sudden and you were so tight-lipped about it. And that got me to thinking, and suddenly there were more questions than ever. I'm an intelligent person, Matt. 'Together,' to quote you. You could have told me anything and I'd have understood. Okay, what happens with your work is your business. But you've shared other things with me, which I realize in hindsight you've been very selective about. Why discuss some things and not others? Unless you're hiding something. Unless there's something you don't want me to know.''

He threw a hand in the air. ''It's Beth. You've been listening to Beth. This sounds like one of her harebrained plots.''

Lauren stared him out. ''Days ago I wanted to go to the police. Any person in his right mind would do that in a situation like mine. But I didn't go to the police, because you told me not to. You've been adamant about it! *Why?*''

''You want to know why?'' Matt raged suddenly. His eyes were narrowed, his head thrust forward. ''I'll tell you why! Because your brother, Brad, was up to no good during the last few years of his life, and if I'd gone to the police when I suspected that Brad's boss was behind what was happening to you, it would have all come out. *You'd* have been hurt. I was trying to protect *you*!''

Lauren sat in stunned silence as the warm summer night crowded in on her. One minute she felt smothered, the next chilled. In the third, she was stifling again and began to sweat. Dropping her gaze to the floor, she pressed a finger to her moist upper lip, frowned, then looked back at Matt. ''What did you say about Brad?' she asked in a timid whisper.

Matt stood with his feet braced apart, one hand massaging the taut muscles at the back of his neck. At her question, he lowered his head, put two fingers to his forehead and rubbed. "Brad was in trouble." His voice held a blend of sadness and defeat. Lauren knew he'd have to be a consummate actor to produce such a heart-wrenching tone on cue.

"What kind of trouble?" Her stomach had begun to jump. She pressed a hand to it.

"Please. Lauren, you don't want—"

"What kind of trouble?" When he didn't answer, she repeated the question a third time. *"What kind of trouble?"*

Matt sighed in resignation. "He'd been padding invoices and expense vouchers, then pocketing the difference."

"I don't believe you."

"Maybe that's just as well. Brad's dead. Nothing will ever be proved one way or another. Just rumors. Lousy rumors."

"You believe them."

"I knew Brad." He took a quick breath. "Please, don't misunderstand me. Brad and I were close. He was a loyal friend. I respected him in many, many ways."

"But?"

"But all along I knew there was one part of him that was unsettled. It was as if he was looking for an opening, and his boss unwittingly gave him one. Chester Hawkins was a crook. We both knew it. We discussed it many times. Bribes, kickbacks—you name it, Hawkins did it."

"But padding expense vouchers—that's small-time stuff. What could Brad have hoped to gain?"

"It's not small-time when it's done over and over again."

"For how long?"

"Two years, maybe three. It adds up."

"But *why*? Why would he have done it?"

Matt dropped into a side chair. "Maybe he felt it was poetic justice, stealing from a thief. More likely he felt that an accumulation of wealth was the only way he could prove his worth.''

Lauren moaned softly. Her head fell back against the sofa and she closed her eyes. When she spoke, her voice was wobbly. ''I knew there was too much money. It didn't make sense. Right from the start I wondered, but I took it. I took it and I used it.''

''Which was exactly what you *should* have done!'' Matt sat forward and spoke with renewed force. ''Brad earned every cent of that money. He was overworked and underpaid for years. What he did might have been punishable in a court of law, but there was still a certain justice to it. He gave Hawkins his life, for God's sake, and there was only a piddling insurance policy on it! Hawkins wasn't big on employee benefits. He gave the bare minimum. Brad earned that money, Lauren. And he wanted you to have it.''

Lauren swallowed hard, trying to ingest all that Matt had told her. ''Did he really? Or did you tell me that just to make me feel better?''

''He said it. Believe me—ah, hell.'' Matt flopped back in the chair. ''Believe what you want. The fact is that you've put the money to good use. No one can ever take it away from you.''

They were back to square one. ''Someone's trying. Is it this fellow, Hawkins?'' she asked nervously.

''He claims not.''

''You *spoke* to him?''

Matt was out of his seat, pacing again. ''What did you think I went to San Francisco for?''

''I didn't know! I assumed it had something to do with your own work. You didn't volunteer any details!''

''I went to confront Hawkins.''

''And?''

''He says he's innocent.''

"Do you believe him?"

"I'm not sure." Matt stopped his pacing and stared at her. "On the one hand, he wouldn't dare try anything. I wasn't the only friend Brad had. If Hawkins tries to pin something on Brad, even posthumously, any number of us will cry foul. Hawkins can't risk that. There's too much that can be pinned right back on him."

"On the other hand…"

He took a deep breath. "On the other hand, I wouldn't put it past him to try something on the sly. He and Brad had reached a stalemate. Each knew what the other was doing, so it was a form of mutual blackmail. Hawkins didn't dare fire Brad for fear he'd squeal. But Brad's gone now. It's possible that Hawkins thought he'd go after some of that money—"

"By terrorizing *me*?"

"Sick minds work in sick ways. Besides, Hawkins wouldn't do it himself. He'd hire someone. If he's discovered that you've invested the money between the shop and this place, he may be out for his own private form of revenge."

"So we're back where we started."

"Not…quite," Matt stated with such quiet thunder that Lauren's pulse skipped a beat before racing on. "There are still certain allegations you've made that have to be resolved. Y'know, you're right." He cocked his head and eyed her insolently. "I may well be the man Hawkins hired, playing you now just as I've played you all along—orchestrating events, then showing up and explaining them away."

"But why *would* you?" she cried.

"You're the one with the answers." He flung himself back into the chair. "You tell me."

"I don't *have* the answers. That's what this—this is all

about! I don't have *any* answers. My mind is running in circles!''

"Could be I'm getting paid a pretty penny for this."

"You don't want the money," she protested. "You're not ambitious that way! You told me so the first time we met!''

"Could be I was lying. Could be it was all an act." He jacked forward in the chair. "And since you're hurling accusations, I've got a few of my own. You were a virgin for twenty-nine years. Then you met me, and within a week we became lovers. Strange things were happening to you. You were frightened. You needed protection." He snorted. "Pretty high price to pay for it, I'd say."

She felt as though she'd been slapped. "No! I didn't—"

"Then again, maybe you were truly infatuated. I was different from the men you'd known. More physical. Brawny. But now that you've gotten what you wanted, you're scrabbling for reasons to put me off."

"No, Matt! How can you—"

"I don't meet your high standards. Is that it, Lauren?" His eyes bore into hers. "You're prepared to believe the worst because you just don't think I'm good enough for you?"

Unable to bear another word, Lauren sprang up from the sofa and rounded on him. "That's not true!" she screamed, grabbing his shoulders and shaking him. It was a pitiful gesture, since he was so much larger than she, but her fury was beyond reason. "It's not true! And I wasn't *prepared* to believe the worst!" His face blurred before her eyes. "But I had to know—had to know. I'd never been with another man, because no man had meant anything to me until you came along!" Tears trickled unheeded down her cheeks, and her hands stilled, impotent fingers clutching fistfuls of his shirt. "I've been dying, slowly dying for the past two days, grasping at straws, wondering if it was possible that—that I'd made a big mistake and given you everything and that you were really on the other side.''

Her knees gave out then, and she sank to the floor between his legs. Her head was bowed. She wept softly. ''It hurt so to…to think that, and I knew I had to get…get it out in the open, but that hurt, too…and…and…'' Her fingers curved around his knee, gently kneading in a silent bid for forgiveness.

Matt put a tentative hand on her hair. ''And what, Lauren?'' he asked softly.

Her head remained down, her muffled voice punctuated by sniffles. ''I love you…and I've hurt you…and somehow this new life that was supposed…supposed to be so wonderful is all messed up!''

With a low groan, he slid to the floor. His thighs flanked hers as he took her into the circle of his arms. ''Oh, baby. Sweetheart, shhh.'' He rocked her tenderly. ''You've just said the magic words. Nothing's messed up. Everything's suddenly clear.''

She shook her head against his chest, too upset to comprehend.

He spread a large hand over the back of her head, buried his face in her hair and pressed her closer. ''It's all right,'' he whispered between soft kisses. ''Everything's going to be all right.''

Lauren let her tears flow. They were a purging of sorts. It wasn't that she agreed with Matt or understood things as he seemed to, but being held in his arms this way, absorbing his strength and incredible tenderness, she felt herself slowly emerging from the hell she'd been living for the past few days.

He rubbed her back, caressing her gently. He whispered soft words of endearment and encouragement; with each one the darkness receded and she moved closer to the light. The warmth of his body thawed her inner chill. She fed on his strength like a creature starved for it.

Then he tipped her chin up and kissed her, and the last of her anguish broke and dissipated like a fever at the end of a long illness. She felt suddenly free, lightheaded and very much in love. Shaping her hands to his cheeks, she gave herself up to his kiss; but because she offered as much as she received, Matt was as aroused as she by the time they finally parted, panting.

While she strung slow kisses along the line of his jaw and his chin, she worked at the buttons of first her shirt, then his. His hands were already in full possession of her breasts before she'd finished the latter, and when she came to her knees to press closer, the squeeze of her thighs against the mounting ache between them was a necessity.

From numbness such a short time before to this rich blossoming of the senses, Lauren reeled. Everything about Matt turned her on, from the vitality of the thick, sun-burnished hair through which her fingers wound to the musky scent of the rough, sweat-dampened skin beneath her lips to the virile cords of muscle straining against the rest of her body.

"I love you," she whispered against his mouth. "I love you, Matt." Her hands slid from his head down his chest, savoring the journey. But urgency was quickly mounting. She released the snap of his jeans, then the zipper, and worked her way beneath the waistband of his shorts until her fingers found what they sought. He was thick and hard, needing her in the same way that she needed him.

He gave an openmouthed moan and whispered her name, then set her back and shoved his jeans lower. "Hurry," he rasped as Lauren rocked back on her bottom and tore her own jeans off in jerky movements. He reached for her with urgent fingers, bringing her close until she straddled his thighs.

"Love me, Matt. Please, love me…"

"God, yes…"

His hands covered her buttocks, urging her downward even as she guided him inside her, and there was nothing then but paradise. His hands on her body, stroking…inflaming…lifting. His tongue wet and greedy on her throat, her collarbone, her breasts. Her own hands clutching his bronzed flesh, molding…straining…her mouth rapacious, her hips meeting his every thrust with matching ferocity.

They brought each other to near-peak after near-peak of exquisite sensation, and when the final climax hit, their cries were simultaneous, prolonged and distinctly triumphant.

For long moments, Lauren was aware of nothing but the state of heavenly bliss in which she floated. Then came Matt's ragged breathing. It took her a minute longer to realize that her own throat was contributing to the rasping sound.

Very gradually the gasping eased, then ended, yet neither of them made a move to leave the other's arms. Their bodies remained joined, and Matt defied the limpness of his limbs to hold her even closer.

"I love you, Lauren," he murmured hoarsely. "Please, please don't doubt me again. I think it would—" His voice broke. "It would destroy me."

Her face buried in the warm crook of his neck, she whispered his name over and over again. Her arms, too, had taken on a strength that denied passion's drain, and she held him with no intention of ever letting go. "I'm sorry" came her muffled cry. "I shouldn't have suggested those awful things."

"No, it's good you did. You were right. They had to come out in the open." He tipped her head back and looked into her eyes. "We need the truth, sweetheart. Both of us. There are so many things we can't figure out, but the situation becomes only more complicated if we can't be honest about ourselves and our feelings." With one arm supporting her back, he gently smoothed damp tendrils of hair from her cheeks. "I have insecurities. Lots of them. They hit me like a ton of bricks when I first met you, and they've kept me a little off balance ever since."

"You didn't need to worry about *anything*!"

"But I did. At the start I worried that you'd associate me only with Brad and that you'd transfer the rift between you and him to me. I worried that you'd turn down your nose at my occupation, that you'd categorize me and put me in a slot and wouldn't like the things I suggested we do. Then, when I began to realize how I felt about you, I was afraid you wouldn't feel the same." He slid his cheek against her temple. "And all the time I was worried about what was happening to you. I imagined Hawkins might be behind it, and I was reluctant to tell you the truth. Maybe I wouldn't be able to protect you or catch the bastard before he really hurt you."

"You'll be dead long before I will if you keep up that worrying," Lauren quipped softly, "and *then* where will I be?"

"Do you love me?"

"I do love you."

"And you're not bothered by who I am and where I come from?"

"Only that you come from the opposite coast, and that's much too far away."

A tremor shot through his body and he gave her a bone-crushing squeeze. "God, you're wonderful. You're beautiful and bright and warm and giving. What did I ever do to deserve you?''

Lauren was thinking the very same thing, but with the pronouns reversed. ''I love you,'' she whispered. She'd never tire of telling him so, and with that knowledge and the intimate closeness of his body, her insides began to quiver. She tightened her lower muscles and was rewarded by the faint catch in Matt's breath; then, as he grew inside her, she began to move.

It was much, much later, after they'd finally sought out her bed, that she turned in his arms. ''Matt?''

His eyes were closed. She was wondering if he was asleep when she heard his low ''Hmm?''

''Do you realize what we did?''

He shifted his hips and smiled smugly. ''Mmm-hmm.''

''But without anything.'' After that first night, Matt had taken the responsibility of protecting her. ''Aren't you worried?''

''You told me to stop worrying.''

''But if we make a baby…''

His eyes opened slowly, but the smugness remained on his face. ''If we make a baby, we'll have it. It'll be beautiful and bright and healthy.''

''But the planning, the logistics…''

The light in his eyes grew brighter. ''I love you, Lauren. If a baby comes out of that love, I think I'd be the happiest man alive.''

With a soft sigh of elation, she nestled more snugly against him. ''Oh, Matt, I love you so.'' Basking in a special glow, lulled by the strong and steady beat of his heart, she fell into a deep and untroubled sleep.

COME MORNING, Lauren and Matt awoke together, showered together, dressed together, cooked and ate breakfast together. Neither seemed to tire of touching the other, or smiling, or whispering those three precious words.

It was only when they were getting ready to drive into Boston that Lauren permitted herself to think beyond the fact of their newly shared love. Matt sat sideways on the sofa, sorting through papers in his briefcase. Curling an arm around his neck, she slid onto his lap.

"We can't go to the police," she began quietly. "You're right. If they start looking into things and somehow come upon Brad's dealings, his memory will be sullied. I'm not sure my parents would care, but I would. So that leaves us back where we began. What should we do?"

Matt finished straightening a pile of letters, set them in the briefcase and snapped it shut. "I think maybe it's time to call in some help. Not the police—someone private." He slipped an arm around her waist. "That way we can control what comes out. Hawkins may be behind this, or it may be someone totally unrelated to him."

"In which case the motive is still a mystery."

"We need a fresh ear, someone who might ask questions we haven't thought of or see things from a new angle." He paused. "Should I get a name and make a call?"

"Yes. We have to do something. I don't want to live with a shadow hanging over me, especially not now."

Matt was in total agreement. Through one of the corporate powers he'd been dealing with in Boston, he contacted a reputable private investigator by the name of Phillip Huber and set up a meeting for the following morning. In the meantime, he stayed as close to Lauren as he could, returning to the shop between business meetings of his own, taking her to lunch, then dinner. When they finally arrived back in Lincoln, it was late. Given the minimum of sleep each had had—not to mention the strain of jet travel on Matt, about which Lauren teased him unmercifully—they were both tired.

Absently she picked up the mail and flipped through it. Gas bill. MasterCard bill. Advertisements. She lifted the next piece of mail, a disconcertingly familiar gray envelope, and stared at it.

Susan Miles. Addressed directly to the farmhouse.

Fingers trembling, she tore open the flap, pulled out the stationery and unfolded it. A separate piece of paper floated to the floor, but once again, the stationery itself was blank. Stooping, she lifted the paper that had been enclosed. Roughly cut at the edges, it was a picture of a gleaming fox fur coat, apparently taken from a magazine. The model had been unceremoniously decapitated.

"Matt?" she called faintly, then louder: "Matt!"

He appeared at the top of the stairs, his shirt unbuttoned, its tails loose. Lauren's anxious expression brought him trotting down immediately.

She spoke quickly. "Last Friday and again on Saturday we received a letter at the shop addressed to a Susan Miles. Neither Beth nor I know anyone by that name. We assumed it was simply a mistake. Now there's a letter addressed to Susan Miles *here*." She held out the piece of stationery and watched him turn it from front to back.

"It's blank."

"So were the other two. The only difference is that this one came with a magazine clipping." She offered it as well. "Just a picture of a fur coat. Nothing else."

Matt studied the clipping, frowned back at the blank sheet of stationery, then took the envelope from her hand and examined the raggedly scrawled address. "There's got to be a message here," he said at last. "We may not be understanding it, but there's got to be one. You say the other two letters were exactly like this one, but without the clipping?"

"That's right. Same gray stationery."

"Same handwriting on the envelope?"

"Yes. And the same Boston postmark. I didn't think much of the first two. They were addressed to the shop. It could have been a simple mistake. Taken with this last one, though, there has to be something more personal in it. Whoever sent them knows my home address. He's got the name wrong, but he knows where I work *and* where I live."

Much as Lauren's stomach was doing, Matt's jaw clenched. "Right." He rubbed his forehead with his finger. "Is it possible that you've been mistaken for someone else? For this Susan Miles, perhaps?"

Lauren didn't say anything. Her heart was hammering, and the knots in her stomach had tightened painfully.

Matt's focus remained on the pieces of paper he held. "Mistaken identity...that would make sense. All along you've had no idea who would have a reason to threaten you. We know there's a chance it could be Hawkins, but if it's not, this might be something to go on. If we could identify and locate this Susan Miles..." He looked up and caught Lauren's stricken expression. "Sweetheart?" When she swayed, he held her arms to steady her. "What is it?"

"I don't believe this is happening," she whispered. Her eyes were wide, dry but filled with the horror of conviction. "I don't believe it. I knew it was too good to be true."

Matt ducked his head, bringing his face level with hers. Every one of his features broadcast love and tenderness, and his voice was filled with hope. "It's okay, sweetheart. It's good, in fact. At least it's another lead to follow, and now that we've contacted an investigator—"

She covered her face with her hands. "My parents were

right. I shouldn't have done it. I played with what fate had decreed, and now I'm paying for it.''

"Lauren, what—"

"My face, Matt!" she cried. "It didn't always look this way. When I was a very little girl, my bones developed improperly. I was ugly. You saw a picture! You know!"

"My God," he whispered, finally putting the last piece of the puzzle into place. "I thought it was just a bad picture. I never dreamed…" Seizing her wrists, he drew her hands from her face and clutched them to his chest. His eyes slowly toured her features. "You had surgery," he said in amazement.

She nodded. "My chin was practically nonexistent, and my jaw was so badly misaligned that I had trouble eating. That's why I was so skinny."

"And you're so beautiful now. It's incredible!" He took her chin and turned her face first to one side, then the other. "No scars," he announced excitedly. "It must have been done from the inside. When, sweetheart?"

"This past spring, right before I came to Boston. I went to a clinic in the Bahamas. The recuperative period was ten weeks. Part of that time I stayed in a rented apartment and returned to the clinic on an outpatient basis."

"Unbelievable." Done with its journey, his gaze coupled with hers. "Just this past spring. So if I'd come six months before, I'd have found you in Bennington looking exactly as I'd expected. It all makes sense now—your inexperience with men, your talk of a new life, a new look…" His eyes lit with pleasure at a new thought. "Part of Brad's money went toward this, didn't it?"

"Some. Insurance paid for most of the surgery, since it had become a legitimate medical problem."

"And you feel better?"

"Physically *and* emotionally." She hesitated. "What about you, Matt? How do you feel?"

"How do I feel?" he echoed, puzzled.

"About what I did. Having plastic surgery and all."

"I think it's marvelous! If you'd looked this gorgeous much earlier, you'd have been snapped up before I could have found you."

"But what do you think about the surgery itself? Does it...bother you?"

"Of course not! Why would it bother me?"

"It bothers my parents. They were against my doing it."

"Hell, it's no different from a kid wearing braces on his teeth to correct a bite problem that would become troublesome in time. Or someone having his nose fixed to correct a deviated septum."

Lauren blushed. "I had that done, too."

"You did!" He grinned. "What did it look like before? The picture I saw was a head-on shot."

"It was crooked," she admitted sheepishly. "And lousy for breathing. I used to snore something awful."

"You sure don't now. I love your nose." He ran a finger down its smooth slope. "It looks so—so natural. The whole thing looks so natural! I'd honestly decided that the picture was just a bad one. Either that, or you'd simply come into your own as you'd grown older."

"Then Brad didn't say anything specific?"

Matt's voice mellowed. "No. It wasn't often that Brad spoke of home, but when he mentioned you, there was always a certain tenderness in his voice. In spite of the rift, you had a special place in his heart. He worried about you. Wow, if he could only see you now!"

"Yeah," Lauren drawled wryly. "I've got a new face that apparently looks so much like someone else's that an enemy of that someone else is out for blood."

"Hey, we don't know that!"

"Well, maybe not blood, but something, that's for sure."
She sent a pleading look to the ceiling. "I don't believe
this. I just don't believe it. It's like something only Beth
could have dreamed up, but she didn't." She arched a brow
at Matt. "You do agree that the mistaken-identity theory is
the strongest one we've had?"

"Mmm. Not that I'm ruling out Hawkins. But, given the
letters for Susan Miles, this theory is more plausible."

"What could the newspaper clipping mean?"

"I don't know. If the letters were real letters with writing
and all, it wouldn't be so bad. But three blank sheets of
stationery—that's odd."

Lauren sighed. "So, we look for Susan Miles."

"It's the way to go. Seems to me that'd be right down
our investigator's alley."

IT SHOULD HAVE BEEN. Lauren and Matt met with the detective at a small coffee shop in Boston early the next
morning. They told him everything, from a detailed account
of each of Lauren's mysterious incidents to their theories
involving, alternately, Brad's boss and Lauren's new face.

Phillip Huber went off in search of Susan Miles. Unfortunately, after a full day of poring through State House and
registry records, he could find no evidence of anyone by
that name living in the area.

The next day he went through the records of the local
and state police, and the day after that he made use of his
considerable network of contacts to broaden the search to
include the rest of New England and New York.

By Thursday night, Lauren and Matt were no closer to
finding Susan Miles than they'd been at the start, and by
Friday afternoon, the search was temporarily abandoned.

LAUREN LEFT THE SHOP shortly before four, intent on getting to the bank and back before Matt came for her. He'd been her shadow for most of the week, and she'd loved it. But that day he'd had business to attend to, so she set out on the errand alone.

With the luxury of Jamie's working full-time, Lauren was taking off early. It was a beautiful day. She and Matt planned to return to Lincoln to change, then drive one town over, rent a canoe and explore the Concord River.

She walked at a confident pace, buoyed by the anticipation of the outing, lulled into security by the peaceful week it had been. Since Monday, when the letter for Susan Miles had arrived at the farmhouse, there had been no incidents. Of course, Matt had been close at hand, a visible deterrent to mischief, and Phillip Huber had taken his turn when Matt had been busy.

Lauren had barely turned down the side street on which the bank was located when a car slid smoothly to the curb. Its door opened, and she was jostled inside by a burly hulk that had come from nowhere on her opposite side. Before she knew what had happened, she was seated in the back seat of a car that would have been roomy except for the two giants who crowded her between them.

She tried to squirm, but she was solidly pinned. "What— what is this?" she cried between attempts to free herself.

"Sit still, pretty lady," the man on her left said. "You know what it is."

"I—do—not." She was trying to elbow herself out of the human vise, only to find that the vise had tightened. "Let me out of this car!" she gritted. She began to pound at the thighs flanking hers but succeeded only in having her wrists immobilized by a single beefy paw on either side. "You can't do this!"

"We've just done it," the same man pointed out. His voice was calm, matter-of-fact, infuriating.

"Well—" she kicked out "—I'm not—" she writhed lower in the seat "—having it!" She managed to hike herself forward but was pitched back by the arm of steel that crossed her collarbone and tightened. She bit at the arm and heard a low grunt. Before she could struggle free, she was slapped viciously across the side of her head. Sharp pain radiated through her entire skull, rendering her utterly dazed. She sagged limply against the seat and fought to catch her breath.

"That's better," the man on her left said. "Now sit there and *don't move*."

She couldn't have moved if she'd tried, and she couldn't even try. The blow had robbed her of what little strength had remained after her futile attempt to escape. Her head lolled against the upholstered seat, and for long moments she could do nothing but hope to regain her equilibrium. Her jaw hurt something fierce, and she felt a momentary flash of hysteria. If they'd broken her jaw after all she'd gone through to set it right, after all she was going through because she *had* set it right...

"You've got the wrong girl," she managed to mumble through stiff lips.

"Mmm" came a hum from her left. "Somehow we knew you'd say that."

"You do." Gingerly she worked her jaw. It was sore, but at least it functioned. "I don't really look like this...I had repair work done to correct a problem..."

"We know the problem."

The one on the left was apparently the designated speaker. She dared a glance at him. He was dark-haired, dark-eyed, dark-looking in every respect. His eyes were focused straight ahead, following the course the driver was taking.

"If you know the problem," Lauren ventured, "then you know this is all a mistake."

"The problem is that you didn't want to be found." He looked at her then, and she cringed under his scrutiny. "It's subtle, I have to say that much. You're clever. Didn't do anything drastic, thought we'd be off looking for someone *completely* different. Or maybe you just thought what you had was too beautiful to tamper much with. You always were a haughty bitch."

"You've got the wrong woman," Lauren pleaded in a shaky voice. "As God is my witness, I'm telling the truth. The surgery I had was to correct a problem I've had from childhood. You can contact the clinic. My doctor will tell you."

The man was looking forward again, a smug look on his face. "We've already been to the clinic. That was a fancy job you did with the records, and if we were stupid we might have been put off. But we're not stupid, Susan. I think it's about time you realize that."

"I'm not Susan! I know you think I'm Susan Miles, because that's the name on those envelopes, but *my* name is Lauren Stevenson! Lauren Stevenson, from Bennington, Vermont. I have family and friends still there—you can check."

"Lauren Stevenson." He rolled the name around on his tongue in a way that made her want to vomit. "It's as good an alias as any."

"It's *not* an alias!"

Dark eyes glittered dangerously back at her. "Keep your voice down. I have a headache."

"I'll talk as loud as I want—" she fairly shouted, only to have her words cut off by the human mitt that clamped over her mouth. It had come from the right, but the voice, as always, came from the left.

"I'll gag you. Is that what you want?"

"No," Lauren answered the instant the mitt had left her mouth. She had to be able to communicate if she was to get anywhere.

"Then keep your voice down. And talk with respect." The last had been tacked on almost as an afterthought, but the man appeared to find immense satisfaction in it.

She wasn't about to argue. Physically, she was outsized and outnumbered. All three men—one on either side of her, plus the driver—were huge. Their sedate business suits did nothing to disguise the bulk of their physiques. Intellectually, though, she had to believe she was at least on a par with them, if not above. Yes, she was terrified, and terror had a way of fudging the workings of the mind. But if she could stay cool and somehow control her fear, she had a chance.

In keeping with that, she considered her captor's command. If it was a respectful tone he wanted, a respectful tone he'd get. Far more could be accomplished with sugar than with vinegar.

"Who are you?" she asked quietly, directing her efforts solely to the man on the left.

"Now, that is an insult if I ever heard one. You know who I am."

"I don't."

"I sure know you." He tilted his head to the side and studied her lazily. "You're looking good, Susan. Hair's a little shorter. Face looks good. Makeup's different. Easing up on it, are you?"

"Where are you taking me?"

He gave a careless shrug. "I'm not sure."

"What are you going to do with me?"

"I'm not sure."

"You must have a plan."

"Oh, yes."

She waited, but he said nothing more, so she dropped her gaze to her lap. "The plan is to make me nervous. Just as you've been doing for the past two weeks."

He puckered his lips, then relaxed them in acknowledgement of her perception. "Very good."

"But you do have the wrong person," she argued, albeit in a respectful tone. "The first few things you did didn't even make me nervous, because I had no reason to suspect there was anything to them."

"You wised up."

"Not really. It was the mail for Susan Miles that pulled it all together. Up until then I couldn't imagine what anyone would have against me." The issue of Chester Hawkins was irrelevant. "That's when I realized it had to be a case of mistaken identity."

"Sure," he drawled.

Lauren felt a movement in the arm that was pressed against her right side, and she looked sharply toward the hulk connected to it. The man was laughing. Silently, but laughing nonetheless. On the one hand, she was livid; on the other, she was more frightened than ever. They were obviously prepared for her denials, which practically defeated her efforts before they'd begun, but she wouldn't give up. There had to be *some* way out of this mess—if only she could find it!

Chapter Nine

For the first time since her abduction, Lauren looked beyond the confines of the car to the outside world. If she'd expected to see narrow, unfamiliar streets, she was mistaken. The car was on Storrow Drive, taking the very same route out of the city that she traveled every day.

She wished she knew what her wardens were up to, but she hadn't gotten that far yet, so she thought of Matt. Surely he'd have arrived at the shop. Surely he and Beth would be getting nervous when she didn't return from the bank. The bank!

"I have money," she exclaimed in a burst of hope. "If it's money you want, I'll give you all I've got." She fumbled in her purse for the envelope containing the cash and checks she'd been on her way to deposit, but her offer was immediately denied.

"We don't want money. The boss pays us plenty."

"Who's the boss?"

"Come on, Susan. We're not really as dumb as you'd like to think."

"I don't think you're dumb at all," Lauren declared quietly. "You've just made an innocent mistake. I'm not Susan, and I don't know who 'the boss' is. And *because* you're not stupid, you'll realize that I'm telling you the truth before you do anything drastic. If you go ahead with whatever you're planning, sooner or later someone *will* call you stupid—because you'll have done whatever you're planning to do to the wrong person.''

He shot her a sidelong glance. ''You've gotten quick with words. You never used to talk this much.''

''Maybe Susan Miles didn't, but I always have. Look, there are any number of people—people who've known me for years—who can vouch for my identity.''

''Like the medical records in that clinic did?'' His question dripped of sarcasm.

''If you don't believe the records, that's not my problem.''

''But it is. Seems to me it's very much your problem.''

He was right. She had to take a different tack. ''Okay. So you don't believe the records and you won't believe my friends. You tell me. Who am I supposed to be? Just who *is* this Susan Miles?''

''You want to play games? I'll play games. Susan Miles was the boss's best girl. He gave her everything any woman could want—'' his eyes pierced Lauren's and his voice grew emphatic ''—like a safe full of jewels and a closet full of furs. Where are they, Susan? We haven't been able to find them yet. Did you sell everything to bankroll that little shop you've got, or the house?''

''Jewels?''

''And furs.''

''That clipping,'' she murmured, horrified. ''Matt was right. There was a message in the clipping, but we just didn't get it.''

The man on her left said nothing.

''I don't have jewels *or* furs. I bought the shop and the house with a legacy from my brother, who died a year ago.'' In other circumstances she'd never have volunteered that information, but these were unusual circumstances, to say the least.

"A legacy from your brother. Touching, but not terribly original, although I suppose it is different from the dead-uncle or maiden-aunt story, or that of the parents who were tragically killed in an automobile accident."

"My parents are alive and well and living in Bennington, Vermont. Check it out in a phone book. Colin and Nadine Stevenson."

The man on her left was silent.

"How *else* would I get money to open that shop? I've never had anything of my own like that before."

"Oh, please."

"I did?"

"How quickly you forget."

"What was it? What did I own?"

"A charming little boutique in Westwood Village. Actually, you were running it into the ground. After you died, the boss put one of his own men in charge, and it's begun to turn a pretty profit."

"I *died*?" Lauren felt as if she were in the middle of a slapstick comedy, only nothing was funny. She was totally bewildered. "But if I died, what am I doing here and why are you after me?"

The man on her left seemed to weary of her questions. "You didn't die," he growled. "You just made it look like you'd died. You took off with the jewels and furs, changed your face, bought your shop and your house and thought you could get away scot-free." His expression grew even darker. "Well, let me tell you, no one does that to the boss and gets away with it. And no one does it to *me*!"

"What did I do to you?" she whispered fearfully.

"You made a fool of me. I was the one who reported that you burned to death in that car."

"Oh."

"Yes, 'oh.' It's been a sweet pleasure putting you through hell these past couple of weeks. What was it like, Susan, knowing someone was on to you?"

"I *didn't*. I told you—"

"I'll bet you didn't believe it at first. You always were arrogant, with your pretty little nose stuck up in the air."

"It's not my nose—"

"When you finally admitted to yourself that you'd been found out, did you think of running? It wouldn't have done you any good. We'd have been right on your heels." He sniffed loudly. Lauren decided he had a deviated septum of his own. "I've enjoyed it. And the best is yet to come. What I've got planned for today will singe your hair. I mean *really*, this time. Think about *that* while we take our little drive."

Their "little drive" had already taken them to the outskirts of Lincoln. Lauren stared out the window and swallowed hard. *Singe?* She began to shake. What was he planning? Did he intend to kill her? She had to escape. And soon. But how?

They turned off Route 2 and began the drive down the street she took each night. She would have stiffened in her seat, or sat straighter, but she had precious little room to move in and barely more strength. Her arms and legs were beginning to ache from a combination of tension and the steady pressure applied from both sides. Her face hurt. Her stomach was knotting.

"Where are we going?" she asked in a small voice.

"Don't you recognize the streets?"

At that moment they turned down the very road that would lead to her house.

"Thought you might want to take a last look."

"A...last look?"

The man on her left said nothing.

"This is a mistake. It's all a mistake. I really am Lauren Stevenson. *Really*."

"Sure."

She took a quick breath. "Look, you can come inside the house and I'll show you everything. I have identification—a birth certificate, college diplomas, even pictures of my family." Her captor's snort told her what he thought of the validity of that identification. She barely had time to wonder how one could possibly forge family pictures when another thought hit her. "I have a passport! Picture and all!" It didn't take a snort from her left for her to realize she'd struck out again. The passport would do her no good. If there'd been various point-of-entry stamps recorded over a period of time, she might have proved that Lauren Stevenson had existed long before Susan Miles had supposedly died. But Lauren's passport had been issued shortly before her trip to the Bahamas. Ironically, she hadn't needed it; it had never even been stamped. And yes, the picture was of her "before" face, but the files in the clinic had contained a similar picture, which these men had written off.

"So much for identification," she muttered under her breath. Then her head shot up. "My car! The registration!" Her face dropped again. "I reregistered it when I came to Massachusetts."

The man on her left seemed to be enjoying himself. "Keep thinking, pretty lady. See if you can come up with something we haven't already looked over. Don't forget, we've been through most of your belongings."

Lauren's nostrils flared, and for a minute she forgot herself. "You know, it wasn't so bad that you sampled my perfume and fiddled with my shoes. If that's what turns you on, okay. But my *underwear*? I mean, there's kinky and then there's—ahh!" Her arm had been wrenched up sharply against her back. She twisted to ease the pain. "Please," she gasped out in a whisper. "Please—that hurts!"

"I don't have to take your smart mouth. You're not calling the shots around here—*I* am!"

"Please," she begged, then gasped again when her arm was released. She hugged it close and alternately rubbed her elbow and her shoulder.

By this time the car was approaching the farmhouse. Lauren held her breath as she peered out the window, praying that Matt might be there, though she knew he wouldn't be. He was in Boston, waiting for her, maybe out looking for her by now.

The driver slowed in front of the garage, shifted into reverse, backed the car around and headed for the street again.

"Weird place," the man on her left said. "Pretty rundown. I really thought you had more class."

Lauren bit her lip and said nothing. She gazed longingly out of the window, hoping to see a neighbor walking along the side of the road, in which case she'd force some sort of ruckus inside the car that would attract attention. But she saw no one. The road was as quiet and peaceful as it had always been.

To her amazement, they drove on into the center of town. She marveled at the gall of her keepers, until she realized that she couldn't have made a stir if she'd tried. Large hands suddenly manacled both of her arms, just as burly legs had gripped her calves. She might have bucked in the middle, but no one outside the car would have noticed. And if she yelled—

"Don't even think it," the man on her left advised. "Mouse here has a mean right hook. It'll be even meaner the second time around."

"But if you're going to kill me anyway, why would it matter?"

He grinned. "The pain, Susan. The suffering. It'll be bad enough for you as it is. If you want it worse, well, then, go ahead and scream."

Lauren didn't scream. But she did decide that this man's grin had to be the ugliest thing she'd ever seen. And she vowed that if she ever escaped, she'd take great pleasure in personally wiping if from his smug face!

They passed the police station, and she stifled a cry. They passed the market, and she bit her lip. "You won't get away with this. There are two good men who are probably on our trail right now."

"Two good men? Well, I know about the dick you hired. I suppose he's a good man, but he won't find a thing. As for Kruger, haven't you figured that out yet?"

"Figured what out?"

"He's one of ours."

She didn't even blink. "You're lying."

The man on her left shrugged. "Suit yourself. Cling to romantic illusion if you want."

"You can say anything else and it might make me nervous. But Matt—one of *yours*? Not by a long shot."

"What do you think his quickie trip to the coast last weekend was for, if not to check in with the boss?"

"I know what his trip was for, and it wasn't your boss he was checking in with."

"You're awfully sure of yourself."

"Where Matt's concerned, yes."

"Why? What proof do you have that he's not with us?"

She knew she'd be wasting her breath to mention things like love and trust. "He has the proof. Or, if you want to be crude, it was on my sheets the morning after we first made love. I was a virgin. If Matt had been with you, he'd have known something was strange. Unless, of course, your boss is some kind of eunuch.''

"A virgin," the man on her left mused. "Kruger didn't mention that to us.''

"Of course not. He doesn't know you from Adam."

When he shrugged again and simply repeated, "Suit yourself," Lauren knew she'd scored a point.

That was the last bit of satisfaction she was to have in a while. They left Lincoln behind and drove along back-country roads with no obvious destination, at least none obvious to Lauren. Her mind jumped ahead, touching on possible stopping places and possible forms of punishment in store for her, then recoiled in fear, seeking refuge in more purposeful thoughts.

"Did she have any birthmarks?" Lauren asked suddenly.

The man on her left frowned at her.

"Susan Miles. Did she have any distinctive birthmarks? There had to be *some* way I can prove I'm not her.''

"Birthmarks. That's an interesting thought. I could ask the boss about it. Do *you* have any distinctive birthmarks?''

"No.''

"Are you sure?''

"Yes.''

"Maybe we should pull over to the side of the road. If you strip, I can check you out.''

He was goading her. She looked away. "I don't have any birthmarks," she muttered half to herself as she shriveled into the seat. Her arms and legs had been released once they'd left Lincoln proper, but she might as well have been shackled for the little freedom she'd gained. Shoulders hunched, she tried to minimize contact with the bodies on either side by making herself more narrow. It was a token gesture; the more she narrowed, the more the two men spread.

They drove on and on. She lost track of their direction, and much of the scenery was unfamiliar. With each mile, though, she grew more edgy. They couldn't drive forever. Sooner or later they'd have to stop. And what then?

"Y'know," the man on her left offered, "you really blew it. You had it all. The boss adored you—"

"Who is he?"

"Oh, Lord."

"What's his name? If he's the one who's behind all this, don't I have a right to know his name?"

"You don't have *any* rights, pretty lady. You gave them up when you double-crossed him."

"I didn't double-cross anyone!"

His nonchalance faded. "I'd watch my tone if I were you. It's getting uppity, and if there's one thing Mouse can't stand, it's uppity women. Right, Mouse?"

Mouse grunted.

"I'm sorry," Lauren said as conciliatorily as she could. "I didn't mean to sound uppity. It's just that you assume I know everything, but I don't, and I feel as if this whole thing has to be an awful joke, except no one's laughing, and I'm sitting here trying to figure out a way to prove to you who I am, but my mind is getting all foggy and... and..." She'd begun to shake. Tucking in her chin, she closed her eyes. "I don't feel very well."

"Throw up in this car, lady, and I'll make you lick it up."

She swallowed hard against the rising bile and took several deep breaths through her nose. The strain was getting to her. Her insides continued to shake; she wrapped her arms around her middle as though to hold them still, but it didn't work. She was hot and tired and positively terrified.

"It's amazing," the man on her left said. "You're quite

an actress, after all. Funny, you should be such a flop in Hollywood.''

''I thought you said Susan had a boutique,'' Lauren murmured weakly.

''Yeah. But she was like everyone else in that town. Between running the boutique and pleasing the boss, she read for every bit part she could. Had a couple of walk-ons.'' He sent her a look of ridicule. ''She wasn't much of an actress, at least not on the silver screen. What she's doing now is remarkable.''

''I have never been, nor had the slightest desire to be, an actress.''

''Sure.''

Lauren didn't have the strength to argue further, and they didn't stop driving. Dusk fell over the landscape. She thought she'd explode if something didn't happen soon. Once she cast a glance over her shoulder. The man on her left picked up on it instantly.

''Sorry. No one's following.''

She grew defensive. ''Aren't we stopping for dinner or something?''

He simply laughed.

''Or the bathroom? Don't any of you need one?''

''We're like camels. You'd better be, too. No, we're not stopping. Sorry, but you'll have to think of some other way to escape.''

She tried. Oh, Lord, she tried. But, imprisoned in the car between two dark-suited sides of beef, she was hamstrung. There was no hope for escape unless they stopped, and it terrified her to think of where that would be and what they had planned for her then.

Just as she was beginning to bemoan the darkness, she noticed that the car was heading back toward the city. Of course. It made sense. Psychological torture. The purpose of the long ride had been to set her further on edge.

"Look, you've accomplished what you've wanted," she confessed without pride. "I'm thoroughly frightened. You can drop me off anywhere. I'll even take my chances and thumb a ride home."

"Is that what you thought, that we'd just let you go? Susan, Susan, how naive you are."

"What are you planning?"

The man on her left made a ceremony of debating whether or not to tell her. He moistened his lips, scratched the back of his head, then shrugged. "I guess it's time you knew. We're gonna do what we thought had been done months ago."

Lauren's heart was slamming against her breast. "What was that?"

"Your car plunged off the road and burst into flames. There was nothing left but ashes. The ashes were supposed to be you, so the boss gave you a fine burial." He sighed. "In this case, the burial came before the death, so we're kinda doing things ass-backward. But you will burn, Susan. Take that as a promise. You will burn."

Where Lauren got the breath to speak was a mystery. Perhaps the source was her desperation. "It's a threat, and you won't get away with it."

"Oh, we'll get away with it, all right. We're not novices at this type of thing."

"You're killers, then. Hit men. Is your boss connected with the mob? Well, let me tell you, if the mob kills its own, that's one thing. But I've got nothing to do with the mob or your boss or Susan Miles or you, and that makes me an innocent victim. I swear, you won't get away with it!"

The man on her left laughed. "Ah, pretty lady, that's

priceless. Tell me, what do you intend to do once you're dead? Haunt us?" He laughed again.

Lauren gritted her teeth, no mean feat since they were chattering. "You'll get yours. So help me, you'll get yours."

When his laugh only came louder, she lapsed into silence. She'd save her strength, she decided. At some place, at some time, she'd glimpse a chance to escape. She'd need every resource she had when that time came.

Unfortunately, she couldn't seem to glimpse that chance to escape. After they had arrived back in Boston, the car drove down Atlantic Avenue, parallel to the harbor. It turned into a darkened path, continued to the end and stopped.

"Let's go," the man on her left said.

Before he'd even left the car, the man on her right had seized her. His arms were like cords of steel around her legs and shoulders. She was literally crunched into a ball with her face smothered against his chest. As she was carried from the car, she called on those resources she'd saved to try to free herself, but her bonds only tightened. Her scream was a pathetic sound muffled against the man's shirt, and she grew dizzy from the lack of air.

Terror was a driving force, though. Frantically she fought against the arms that held her. Futilely she tried to turn her head and gasp for air. While the doomed battle waged, she was carted up a flight of stairs, then another and another. Her captors' footsteps hammered against the wood planks, each forceful beat driving another nail into her coffin.

Then she was released, dumped unceremoniously onto the floor of a cavernous room. Gasping and trembling, she pushed herself up and looked around. It was dark, but she knew she was in a warehouse—rank and decaying, abandoned warehouse.

The two men loomed over her. Their bodies were straight, their legs planted firmly apart. Their stance was aggressive, but it couldn't have intimidated her any more than she already was.

The man who'd been on her left abruptly hunkered down. She inched back on the floor, but she couldn't escape his hand when he took a strand of her hair between his fingers. He spoke with lethal quiet. "Your final resting place, pretty lady. Take a look around. Try to find a way out. It'll keep your mind busy."

"Where are you going?" she whispered.

"I've got a call to make."

"To whom?"

He let the strand of hair sift through his fingers. "Who do you think?"

"Your boss?" A sudden flare of fury gave her voice greater force. "You tell him for me that he's an idiot! You tell him that he's murdering the wrong woman and that he'll pay—"

When the man raised his hand, palm up, she ducked her head and shrank back. But he didn't hit her. Instead, he slowly lowered his hand until it gently brushed her cheek. "Such a pretty face," he murmured. "Such a shame—"

Her lips moved in a mere whisper. "You know I'm telling the truth. You do."

"I know you'd like to think that. It's okay. Hold on to the hope if you want. It won't be much longer. We'll be back soon."

"And then?" The devil made her ask that. Her eyes were wide with pleading.

"Then," he answered quietly, ever calmly, "we will sprinkle you with gasoline and set you on fire." She gasped and began to shake her head, but he went on. Too late, she realized she'd played into his hands by asking what he planned to do. Clearly, he took pleasure in her horror. "We'll watch you burn, Susan. This time there will be no doubt that you've died."

"Someone...will find me."

"I think not. Y'see, there's a contract out on this building. The man who owns it wants to build condominiums here, like those others along the waterfront, only he's a little strapped for money." The man glanced at his watch. "Roughly two hours from now, one of Boston's best torches will set fire to this place. It'll go up so quick that by the time the fire department gets here, the floor you're on will have long since fallen through. Your ashes will be hopelessly scattered. There's no way anyone will know you've been here, much less be able to prove you died here."

"Please," she cried, feebly grasping the lapels of his jacket, "please don't do this."

"Are you sorry, Susan? Do you finally regret what you've done?"

Lauren was weeping softly. "I haven't done anything...you *have* to believe me...*I'm not Susan Miles!*"

The man threw back his head, took a deep breath and stood up. Together with his sidekick, he made the long walk across the rotting floor. At the door, he looked back.

"You can scream as much as you want. No one will hear you. And Mouse will be right outside this door in case you decide you want to take a walk." He glanced at his buddy. "I think he'd like to get his hands on you again. Right, Mouse?"

Lauren never heard Mouse's answer. She found herself alone, trembling wildly and feeling more frightened than ever. For long moments of mental paralysis, she remained where she was. Then the bottom line came to her. It was do or die. Life or death. Scrambling to her feet, she began to explore her prison, seeking any possible hole or loose plank or trapdoor that might offer escape.

THE BOSS WAS LOUNGING by the pool when his houseboy brought out the cordless phone. He took it, nodded at the boy in dismissal, then put the instrument to his ear. "Yes?"

"We have her. She's safely tucked away. And she's dying just thinking about dying."

"Good. When will you do it?"

"Soon. Uh—did you get the pictures I sent?"

"This morning."

"What do you think?"

"With her hair that way and the clothes, she looks a little younger, more innocent, but it's Susan, all right."

"Are you sure?"

There was a pause. "Aren't you?"

"I thought I was until we picked her up today. Somehow, close up, she seems different."

"That was her intent."

"No. Not just in looks, but in character. The woman we've got does seem more innocent. Susan would have tried a come-on. She'd have promised us all kinds of little favors if we let her go. This one hasn't done that—like it's never occurred to her that she's got a marketable commodity. She's terrified, but half of it seems to be that we won't believe her story. Either Susan has suddenly become one hell of an actress, or we've been tricked."

The boss lit a cigarette and took a long drag. "You think it's someone else?"

A pause. "I'm not sure."

"Is it possible that Susan could have set up someone else to smoke us out?"

"Possible, but not probable. This one claims she had her face fixed to repair a medical problem, just like the clinic records said. If she's telling the truth, it'd be just too convenient that Susan would have happened to find her, looking so similar and all. And if she knew about Susan, she'd have squealed by now. She's scared, really scared."

"So it wasn't a setup. It has to be Susan."

"Or someone who looks like her."

Silence dominated the next half minute. Then, "It's not like you to get cold feet."

"That's what I've been telling myself, but something just doesn't feel right. If we do have the wrong woman, we'll be in trouble."

"I thought you had it arranged so that no one would know."

"I do. It's foolproof."

"So what's the problem? If it's really Susan, she'll be getting her due. If it's not Susan, but someone she set up to take the fall for her, let her take the fall. That'll get Susan to shaking all the more."

"And if it's simply a case of mistaken identity?"

"I can't believe that. The resemblance is too strong."

"But we'll never know. That's the problem. Once this one's dead, we'll never know for sure whether we've taken care of Susan or not."

"Damn it, what do you suggest?"

"I suggest…that we let this one escape and then continue to follow her for a while. If she suddenly runs from Boston and tries to change her looks again and sets herself up somewhere else, we'll know for sure that she's Susan. She won't have a head start on us this time. We'll be watching her constantly."

"I don't like this. I want Susan dead."

"So do I. But I want to make sure it *is* Susan who's dead."

"I thought this was all clear-cut. You'd found her. You'd

been tormenting her. You've got her set to fry. It's all very neat. I don't like waffling.''

''It's your decision, Boss.''

The silence this time was the lengthiest yet. It ended with a low growl of frustration. ''Ah, hell. Let the girl go. Then follow her. Do you understand? *Follow her.* If you lose her, so help me, you'll die right along with her!''

''Right.''

''*And let me know what's happening.*''

''Right.''

LAUREN WAS AMAZED by the simplicity of her escape, although she assumed anything would have seemed simple in comparison to what she'd been through and the fate she'd so vividly been made to envision. After a lengthy search of the room, she'd found old planks sealing up a shaft. She'd pried them off—most had crumbled in her hands—and discovered a door leading to what was a cross between a dumbwaiter and a freight elevator. After climbing onto the platform, she'd pulled and tugged on a fraying cord of rope until she'd lowered the platform to its base. Then she'd shouldered her way through the rotting wood of the door and burst into a run along the street floor of the warehouse. Moments later, she was in the summer night's air.

Smelling vaguely of dead fish and other refuse, the air was the sweetest she'd ever breathed. But she didn't pause to savor it. She continued running out to Atlantic Avenue, veered left around the corner and didn't stop until she'd reached the first of the waterfront restaurants. She barged inside and made her way to the maître d's desk.

''I need a phone,'' she gasped, hunching her shoulders against the pain in her chest.

The maître d' smiled politely and gestured. "Right over there, in front of the rest rooms."

"No! I don't dare!" She shot a glance at the phone by his hand. "You've got one here. I'm being followed, and if I go back there, they're apt to catch…me again and I can't risk it…because they want to kill me and I…have to make this call. Please?" Her breath was coming in agonizing gulps, but she was beyond caring.

"This phone is reserved for—"

"Please!" she whispered. "It's critical!"

"I could call the police for you."

"Let me…please?"

Whether he acquiesced because, in her disheveled state, she didn't look like a troublemaker, or because he had a hidden streak of protectiveness in him, Lauren would never know. As soon as he reached to turn the phone her way, she snatched up the receiver and began to punch out the number of the shop. It was the closest place Matt might be, unless he was out searching. She had to try three times before her shaking fingers hit the right buttons.

"Lauren! My God, where *are* you?" Beth exclaimed. "We've been looking all over for you! Matt's half out of his mind, and the police won't do anything about a missing person for at least twenty-four—"

"Where is he? I need him, Beth. Where is he?"

"You sound awful!"

"Where's Matt?"

"He's out looking for you. He calls in here every few minutes. We've got Jamie stationed at your house."

Lauren's fingers had a death grip on the ridge of wood running around the top of the maître d's desk. "I'm at Fathoms. The restaurant. On Atlantic Avenue. Tell him to come *right away*."

"Where have you been? Are you all right?"

"Just tell Matt. I have to go." Lauren set the receiver back in its cradle, looked up at the maître d' and said, "You can call the police now." Then her knees buckled and she sank to the floor in a dead faint.

By the time she came to, she was lying on a couch in the manager's office. It took her a minute to get her bearings; then she bolted up, only to be restrained by two firm but gentle pairs of hands.

"It's all right, miss. You're safe. The police are on their way."

She recognized the maître d' but looked warily at his companion.

"I'm the manager, and you're going to be just fine."

"Matt...Matthew Kruger...he'll be looking for me."

"It's all right," the manager assured her. "The police will be here any minute. We won't let him get to you—"

"No! He's my—my—he's okay. He's not one of them. I need him."

The two men exchanged a glance before the manager spoke again. "Then we should let him in?"

"Yes!"

He nodded toward the maître d' who turned and left. When the door opened several minutes later, two uniformed officers entered. By this time, Lauren was sitting upright, sipping shakily from a glass of water. One of the officers sat down beside her on the couch; the other knelt before her and began to ask questions. Lauren barely heard the questions, much less her answers. At the slightest movement or sound, her eyes flew toward the door.

After what seemed forever, but was probably no longer than fifteen minutes, Matt burst in. His eyes were wild, his tanned skin was pale and his entire body was trembling, but that didn't stop him from catching Lauren when she rocketed into his arms or from crushing her tightly to him

Brokenly, he whispered her name. He took her weight when her legs seemed to dissolve from under her and melded her body to his. She was crying softly, clinging to his neck, unable to say anything for a very long time. At last he lifted her and carried her back to the couch, which the seated officer had vacated for that purpose. Taking her onto his lap, Matt began to stroke her hair, her back, her arms.

"It's all right, sweetheart. Everything's going to be all right. I'm here. Shh." His breath was warm on her forehead, her ear, her cheek.

"Oh, Matt...you have...no idea..."

Framing her head with his hands, Matt examined her closely. "Are you all right?" His gaze focused on the faintly discolored side of her face, and his voice came out in a croak. "What happened to your cheek?"

"He hit me. It was Mouse, but he wasn't the one in charge."

Matt looked up quickly at the manager. "Can we get some ice for this?"

The man nodded and hurried out, but Matt's attention was already back on Lauren. "Can you talk about it, sweetheart? From the beginning?" His thumbs stroked the tears from beneath her eyes. "The officers will listen. You'll have to go through it only once."

Nodding, Lauren slowly launched into her tale. It was interrupted from time to time—when the ice arrived; when she began to cry again; when Phillip, who'd been out searching for her, too, joined them—but she managed to get through it all before she collapsed, emotionally drained, against Matt.

It was Phillip, soft-spoken and dependable, who turned to the officers. "You'll look for the car?"

"You bet," the older of the two answered. "And if the

warehouse hasn't already been torched, we'll search it.'' He grimaced and rubbed his neck. ''I'm afraid we don't have much to go on. Dark blue Plymouths are pretty common. But we'll check out the local rental agencies and the hotels. Three oversize men might be remembered, particularly if they've been here for a while. Of course, they could be staying somewhere other than at a hotel.''

Matt was cradling Lauren against his chest. ''We'd be grateful for anything you can do. And we'd like to be kept informed.''

''Can we reach you at—'' The officer flipped back several pages in his notebook and read off Lauren's Lincoln address.

Matt caught Phillip's headshake. ''No. They know the house. I can't take the chance they won't return. We'll be at the Long Wharf Marriott. You can either call us there or leave a message at the print shop.''

With a nod, the policemen left, followed several minutes later by Phillip. Matt studied Lauren with tender concern. ''Feel up to moving, sweetheart?''

When she nodded, he helped her to her feet, then wrapped an arm around her waist and guided her out. Less than half an hour later, they were in a spacious hotel room overlooking the harbor. Despite her exhaustion, Lauren insisted on taking a shower. She felt dirty all over. With her eyes closed or open, she could smell the men who'd abducted her.

She scrubbed herself until her skin was pink, while Matt stood immediately outside the shower. He helped her dry off, tucked her in bed, then sat down beside her. If she'd ever doubted his love, she doubted no more; it was indelibly etched on every one of his features.

''Want some aspirin?''

She shook her head and managed a wan smile. "We don't have any, anyway."

"I could call down for some."

"I'm okay." She reached for him and whispered, "Just hold me, Matt. Just hold me."

He did. After a time, he moved back to shed his own clothes, then climbed under the sheets with her and held her for the rest of the night.

Come morning, Lauren had recovered to the point where she could think more clearly. Matt had been at that stage from the moment she'd fallen asleep in his arms.

They were sitting cross-legged on the bed, dressed only in white terry velour robes. She'd begun to gnaw on a strip of bacon when she set it back down. "I've been thinking, Matt. Theoretically, those guys are still after me. But something's odd. I escaped too easily."

Matt wasn't eating, either. "I know."

"It took me a while to find that shaft, but the one who went to make a phone call hadn't returned. No one heard me tearing off the strips of wood. No one heard the elevator. No one chased me down the street. Considering the way they manhandled me earlier and spelled out exactly what they planned to do to me, it just doesn't make sense."

"Maybe the terror they put you through was the end point of the exercise."

She thought about that for a while as she leaned against the headboard and sipped her coffee. "I suggested that to him, and he denied it. Maybe I managed to convince him that I wasn't Susan Miles, or at least plant some doubts—"

"In which case he *let* you escape. If only we knew for sure whether your escape was deliberate or accidental. I have no intention of assuming that you're off the hook until I have proof of it, which means either finding those thugs or—"

"Finding Susan Miles."

"Right. If we could find her and convince her to go to the police, they could question this boss of hers. At least then he'd know he had the wrong woman in you, and we could breathe freely."

Lauren sat forward and reached for the bacon. Matt's presence, his commitment to her cause, the fact of the two of them working together to resolve the problem—all gave her a sense of optimism that, in turn, awakened her appetite. "So," she said between bites, "we have to find Susan Miles, which may be easier said than done. No doubt she's using a different name, and she's probably had plastic surgery to alter her looks, so that's where we'll begin."

He nodded. "The clinic in the Bahamas."

"Right. That's where the boss found out about me, though how he knew to check out that particular clinic is a mystery. I wonder if Susan had been there before, or if she'd mentioned it to him at some point."

"If that was the case," Matt reasoned, "I doubt she'd be stupid enough to go back there when she was trying to flee him. On the other hand, the boss may have had some information we don't. Airline tickets, hotel reservations, something. I think we should fly down and talk with your doctor. Can they spare you at the shop?"

"They'll have to. The shop means a lot to me, but my own health and safety mean more. Between Beth and Jamie, things will run smoothly."

Matt popped a cube of cantaloupe into his mouth. "That Beth is a character. You wouldn't believe some of the stories she came up with to explain your disappearance. She even dared to hint that Brad had come back from the dead and taken you off to some hideaway to heal old wounds!"

"Did she really say *that*?" Lauren grimaced, then

sighed. "She's got an unbelievable imagination. I think she's incurable."

"I think she's also incredibly devoted and loyal. She refused to budge from that shop yesterday because she wanted to be there if you called, and when you finally did, she all but sent out the cavalry to find me. She called Jamie to pass on your message in case I contacted the farmhouse first. She got in touch with Phillip—he has a phone in his car—and sent him looking for me. She was ready to tell the police I'd stolen her car so they would go out in pursuit. You're lucky to have her for a friend, Lauren."

Lauren reached out and touched his cheek. There was warmth in her fingers and love in her eyes. "I'm lucky about a lot of things. Very, very lucky."

THE POLICE weren't so lucky. They had nothing to report to Matt except the fact that shortly before they'd arrived to search it the night before, the warehouse had gone up in flames. The fire marshal's office was investigating arson, but that case had little to do with Lauren's, and there was no sign whatsoever of either the dark blue Plymouth or the three oversize thugs.

Accompanied by a pair of officers from the Lincoln police department, Lauren and Matt returned to the farmhouse at noontime on Saturday, packed their bags and headed for the airport. Matt took a few minutes to phone Phillip to keep him abreast of their plans. Then he and Lauren were airborne, en route to the Bahamas.

To the best of their knowledge, they hadn't been followed.

Chapter Ten

Upon landing, Matt took Lauren directly to one of the plush hotels on the island. It had become clear to him in the course of the flight that she was suffering a delayed reaction to what had happened the day before. She'd been shaky and restless, unable to do more than pick at the meal that was served. She'd dozed off, then awakened with a start to a fit of uncontrollable trembling. He'd teased her, saying that *he* was the one who was supposed to be nervous, but his fear of flying took a back seat to her upset. He'd known that what she needed most was a peaceful restorative night.

First thing the next day, though, they went to the clinic. Purposely, they didn't call in advance. They knew that the boss's men had been there, and they weren't sure how they'd be received. Lauren was convinced that the doctor would not have willingly colluded with thugs, but Matt reserved his own judgment until their meeting.

Richard Bowen was in surgery. They insisted on waiting in the room just outside his office and caught him the minute he returned. Richard was surprised and pleased to see Lauren, doubly pleased to find her with Matt. After the brief introductions, he ushered them into his sanctuary. Neither Lauren nor Matt missed the subtle blanching of his face as she explained what had happened.

"They made it very clear that they'd seen your files," Matt concluded for her when he sensed that Lauren wasn't sure exactly how to confront the doctor. She obviously liked and trusted him, and she was loath to toss accusations his way. Matt had no such qualm. "Did you show anyone those files, or know that they'd been seen?"

To Lauren's relief, Richard was not offended and deeply shared their concern. "My files are confidential. The only way I'd have shown them to anyone would have been if Lauren had specifically requested it."

"Then how—" Lauren began, only to be interrupted.

"About a month ago there was a break-in here. My file cabinets were forced open and the files rifled. Records of hundreds of patients were left scattered all over the office. Nothing was taken that I could tell. Until now I've had no idea what the burglars were after."

"And Susan Miles?" Matt prompted. "Have you treated a patient by that name?"

Richard widened his eyes for an exaggerated second. "Treated, no. Spoken with, yes. Oh, yes. She came by to see me last fall, maybe early winter. She wanted to discuss having some minor work done. It never got past the discussion stage, so I don't have a file on her, but I'll never forget her face. She was stunning. A real beauty." He cast an apologetic glance at Lauren. "Yes, Lauren, you do look a lot like her now."

"Did you do it intentionally?" Matt growled. It was obvious that Richard Bowen had been taken with Susan Miles's looks. For him to try to form another woman in her image might have been conceivable, if infuriating and possibly unethical.

Richard chuckled. "I'm a plastic surgeon, not a miracle worker. It's only in the movies that one face can be completely altered to look like another. No, in Lauren's case, it was pure coincidence. The hair's the same in texture and color, and the figure is complementary, now that Lauren's put on weight. The eyes were alike all along. But, if I remember correctly, and I'm sure I do, Susan Miles wore much more makeup. As for the rest—the nose, the cheekbones, the jaw—they all just came together. You have to understand that in cases like Lauren's, the end results are sometimes a mystery even to the doctor until everything's done. Reconstructive work can go this way or that in the healing process." He smiled ruefully at Lauren. "Yours went the way of Susan Miles."

"From what you say, I should be happy about that," Lauren mused, "but given all that's happened…"

"There are differences," Richard pointed out, "but mostly I think they come from within. The woman I spoke with had a harder edge to her. She was very much like so many of the others I treat, women whose inner tension does things to their faces that no amount of plastic surgery can correct."

"Then she didn't really need plastic surgery?" Lauren asked. She looked at Matt. "Maybe she was planning on disappearing even back then."

Richard spoke before Matt could comment on that supposition. "There were a few things that could have been touched up, but basically they could have gone another five or ten years without attention. People would have thought her beautiful if she'd done nothing."

"Did you tell her that?" Matt inquired. Richard gave him a wry, what-do-*you*-think look. "But she didn't come back."

"No. I never saw her again."

Lauren sat forward. "We have to find her. We know she came from the L.A. area and had a boutique there. Did she say anything to you—drop any names—that might give us a clue?''

Richard sat back in his chair and frowned, trying to absorb all that Lauren had told him. "I don't think so."

"She was probably with a man," Matt offered. "A very wealthy and powerful man."

"Wealthy and powerful men are a dime a dozen on the islands. She did say that she was here on a pleasure trip and had heard about the clinic from a friend."

"No name?" Matt asked.

Richard shook his head. "Fully one-third of my patients have been from the West Coast. They like coming here for the ambience, and for the distance. They can go on an extended vacation far from home, then return looking positively marvelous with no one the wiser." His frown deepened, and he chafed one eyebrow with the knuckle of his forefinger. "I can picture her sitting here talking with me. I'm sure I asked her where she way staying—it's standard small talk in a place like this—and I don't think it was one of the large hotels, because I would have formed a mental image of her there. Maybe a smaller—no—" He hesitated, concentrating. "A boat. I think she mentioned something about the marina."

Matt grunted. "There have to be dozens of marinas. She didn't say which one?"

"If she did, I don't remember."

"Then it'll be like finding a needle in a haystack, and we don't even know which haystack to search."

"How about other clinics on the islands?" Lauren asked.

"There are none I'd recommend, and I doubt a woman like that would go to a second-rate place." Richard held up a hand. "No conceit intended."

"None presumed," Matt offered in his first show of

faith. "Can you tell us anything else about her—how she wore her hair, any distinctive jewelry or style of dress?"

Richard closed his eyes as he called back the full image from his memory bank. "Her hair was pulled away from her face in a chic kind of knot. She was wearing gold jewelry—large hoops at the ears, a chain around her neck. She had several rings, maybe one with a stone, and she was wearing white silk slacks and a blouse. Oh, and high-heeled sandals. I noticed that because her toenails were polished to match her fingernails, and the pink was the same color as the sash around her waist."

"You were very observant." was Matt's wry comment.

Richard laughed good-naturedly. "It's my business to be observant when it comes to women's looks, and this woman was well worth the look. I remember thinking how elegantly she'd coordinated everything. She was stunning. Truly stunning."

Matt pushed himself from his chair. "The description may prove to be helpful somewhere along the line. I hope." It went without saying that they were still at the very start of that line. He held out a hand for Lauren. "Come on, sweetheart. We'll have to rethink our strategy."

Richard walked them to the door. "I'm really sorry I have no more information. If only—" His brow rippled. "Wait a minute. There is something. I mean, it'd still be a long shot, but—"

Matt and Lauren had turned hopeful faces his way. "What is it?" Lauren asked, holding her breath.

"She smoked. I remembered thinking that in time her face would show it. It does, you know."

"But where does that get us?" Matt prodded.

"She was using a little green box of matches. Not a matchbook, but a little green box. I remembered thinking, 'Ah, she's been to Terrance Cove.' It's one of the more showy restaurants around here. Just the place for the wealthy and powerful.''

Matt and Lauren exchanged a look of excitement. ''Let's try it, Matt,'' she said. ''We've got nothing to lose.''

It was Matt who turned to shake Richard's hand and thank him. Belatedly, and purely on impulse, Lauren gave the doctor a hug. ''You've been great, Richard. How can we ever thank you?''

His grin was crooked. ''You can find Susan Miles and get both of you out of danger. Her friends don't sound very charitable.''

Lauren agreed, then slid her hand into Matt's.

A taxi took them to Terrance Cove, which, fortunately, had just opened for lunch.

''What are you going to say?'' Lauren asked. ''If Susan Miles was with the boss, who presumably made the reservations, the people at the restaurant would have no way of knowing, much less remembering, her name.''

''But the face,'' Matt cooed. ''Ah, the face. Susan Miles had a memorable face. And, sweetheart, you've got that face. *I* always knew it was memorable, but then, I'm slightly biased.''

Lauren pinched him in the ribs, but she was buoyed. She held her head high when they entered the restaurant, and tried to look every bit the boss's woman while Matt did the talking. His story sounded conceivable enough.

''My fiancée is looking for her identical twin. They've been separated for two years, and we just got word that she was here last winter. Her name is Susan Miles.'' He looked at Lauren affectionately. ''And this is her face. Does it look at all familiar? Ring any bells? Susan might have had her hair pulled back, and she was probably wearing more makeup and jewelry. But the similarities are marked.'' He paused. "She might have been with a rather impressive man, and if we can find him, we can get a lead on her."

The maître d' stared at Lauren long and hard. "I'm sorry," he said in crisply accented English. "I don't recognize her. But I only work afternoons. The man who was working evenings last winter was recently retired. He is living in Miami with his daughter and grandchildren."

"It's very important that we reach him," Lauren urged. "We have no other leads. Do you have an address or a phone number?"

The man seemed to waver. His indecision came to an end when Matt pressed a folded bill into his hand. "Wait here, please. I'll see what I can do."

As soon as he had disappeared, Lauren leaned close and whispered to Matt, "Why does that always work?"

He whispered back, "It doesn't, at least not always. I was prepared to give him another. He sold himself cheap."

"That was quite a story. *Identical twin?*"

"Beats the other explanation."

Neither of them commented on the fiancée part of the tale.

Within minutes the man returned with a small index card on which he'd printed the name of the former employee and his Miami address. Matt pocketed the card, and he and Lauren headed back to the hotel.

"To Miami?" Lauren asked.

"To Miami."

"When?"

Matt glanced at his watch. "As soon as we can get a flight."

They both knew that the personal visit was a must. They could easily get the man's phone number and call him, but Lauren's face was the key. So they put back the few things they'd taken out of their suitcases, returned to the airport they'd landed at less than twenty-four hours before, and caught the first plane to Miami.

The flight was short and uneventful. As always, they were watchful, alert to any face that would be familiar, or threatening, or in any way suggestive of a tail. As always, they saw none.

After the plane had landed, they took a taxi straight to the address printed on the index card—a modest house on the outskirts of the city. Various bicycles and toys littered its driveway. Instructing the driver to wait, they approached the door.

It was opened by a gentleman in his early seventies. The children crowding behind him called him "Papa," but his actual name was Henry Frolinette.

Matt repeated the story they'd given the maître d' at Terrance Cove, stressing simultaneously their regret at disturbing him and the urgency of their mission. The man nodded, looked closely at Lauren and nodded again.

"I don't know the name," he admitted, "but I do remember the face. They came to the restaurant more than once."

"They," Matt echoed. "Then she was with the man."

"Oh, yes. A dapper sort, and a generous spender. There were usually eight or ten in his party, though the individuals differed—except for the woman. Miss...Miles, you say?" When Lauren nodded quickly, he went on. "Miss Miles was always with him. And Mr. Prinz always picked up the check for the entire group. He paid in cash, too, I might add."

Lauren's gaze met Matt's. "Prinz," she breathed.

Matt was already looking back at Henry. "Do you know his first name?"

"Oh, yes. He's been quite a presence in the islands over the years. Theodore Prinz, from Los Angeles. Not that everyone speaks highly of him, mind you. There have been rumors about the nature of his work. I never believed them, personally. He is a good-looking man, very well behaved and dignified, and he was always more than gracious to me.''

Unfortunately, Henry Frolinette was unable to give them any specific information on Susan Miles. Lauren and Matt discussed it that night over dinner at the beachfront hotel they'd checked into.

''At least we have the boss's name,'' Lauren mused, ''but that's about all. I suppose we could show up on his doorstep and tell him he's made a mistake, but—''

''He wouldn't believe us, and we'd only be putting ourselves right back in his hands. No, if anything's going to stick, we have to find Susan Miles. If Henry had been able to pinpoint a marina, maybe we could have gone back and found someone who might give us a clue to where she went when she left Prinz. But to use Theodore Prinz's name alone would only be asking for trouble. Word is bound to get back to him, and if he's half as powerful as I suspect, we'd be playing with fire.''

''So?''

''We call Phillip, who can use his contacts to get the lowdown on Prinz. If Prinz is involved enough with that boutique to have his own man running it, the name of the place will be sandwiched in there with the rest of the information. At least, it will be if Phillip is worth his salt, and from what I've seen, he is.''

Lauren didn't understand. ''But what good will it do to know the name of the boutique? We can't show up there, any more than we can show up at Prinz's home. If we start asking questions of nearby shopkeepers, they're apt to call Prinz. Besides, I'm sure he had his men question everyone in sight when he started looking for Susan himself.''

"True. But what if we go further back? What if Phillip can get hold of the original papers for that shop?"

"What if Prinz bought it for her in the first place?"

"Maybe he did and maybe he didn't. If he didn't, there might just be some information—even data on loan applications—that could lead us to where she came from—or even to a friend or a family member whom she might have contacted when she relocated."

"But wouldn't Prinz have done that?"

Matt's eyes were filled with excitement, and his voice held a kind of restrained glee. "Prinz went forward. He obviously felt he knew Susan well enough to anticipate what she'd do. He must have known of her visit to the clinic when they were in the Bahamas. That's why his men went there right away. They found what they were looking for, so why look further?"

"But you'd go backward," Lauren stated with sudden comprehension. And admiration. "Cautious Matt. Wants to know the ingredients before he takes a taste."

"It makes sense, doesn't it?"

"Sure does. And in spite of the danger, you're enjoying yourself."

"Sure am. I read somewhere—maybe not in a Spenser novel, but somewhere—that private investigators often locate people who've been missing for years by staking out the graves of their parents. Unless this Susan Miles is truly made of ice, she's been in touch with someone from her past, and more likely than not, that someone is a family member." He straightened in his seat and sighed. It was as though he'd suddenly set down the mystery novel he'd been reading and returned to reality with a jolt. "All *we* have to do is find that family member."

"WHAT'S HAPPENING?"

"They flew back to Boston. Looks like she's not trying

to disappear. Kruger's with her constantly. They're staying in a hotel in town, but that may be because workmen have started tearing up her farmhouse.''

"Tearing it up?"

"Remodeling. At least, that's what it says on the side of the truck parked out front. I don't think she's planning to abandon the place, Boss.''

"Then she's not Susan.''

"Looks that way. She's still pretty nervous, y'know. Looks all around her whenever she goes out, and, like I said, she doesn't go anywhere alone. More than that, the police are in and out of her shop.''

"Susan wouldn't have dared call the police.''

"Right.''

"So. She's not Susan. Do you think she's given up the search for Susan?''

"I don't know. Word has it that the detective's been doing some research.''

"About what?''

"The boutique.''

"You have to be kidding! How did they find out about that?''

"I told her.''

"Not smart. Not smart at all.''

"It was when I had her in the car. I thought she was Susan then.''

"They'll get my name.''

"They've already got it.''

There was a pause, then an arrogant "No problem. The boutique's on the up-and-up. You'll just have to be doubly careful with Susan's demise.''

"What about Lauren Stevenson? And Kruger? And the dick, for that matter? If they do manage to find Susan for us and then something happens to her, they'll know who to blame.''

"But Susan's death won't be traceable to us. It could be an accident; it could be part of a larger scheme. If it looks like someone else kills her, that's not my worry. And if a whole bunch of people shoot each other to bits, so much the better. I don't care how you do it, but keep us clean. I pay you good money to handle things like this. Do what you have to. Don't bore me with the details. I want Susan dead!''

"WE'VE HIT PAY DIRT!" Matt exclaimed with a broad grin as he set down the telephone. He was seated at the desk in the back room of the shop, and Lauren was propped expectantly at its edge.

"What did he say?" The call had been from Phillip. She'd known that much, but had been unable to follow the conversation, which had been distinctly one-sided in favor of the detective.

"He said," Matt began slowly, savoring the suspense, "that Susan bought the boutique herself and she financed it with a loan from a local bank. The loan application listed two people as references, neither of whom are named Miles, but both of whom are from Kansas City.''

"Kansas City. Where she grew up?"

"Either that, or where she was living before she hit L.A. It doesn't really matter. At least we have contacts." He patted the scrap of paper on which he'd jotted the two names.

"But what if these contacts are somehow related to Prinz? What if one or the other of them was the instrument of Susan's introduction to him?"

Matt was shaking his head. "According to Phillip, neither of the names has shown up in any of the information he's gathered on Prinz. There's still that possibility, but I think it's remote. And even if it's not, neither one has any direct association with Prinz now, which means that we'll be safe.'' He lifted the receiver again and called the airport. Within hours, he and Lauren were headed for Kansas City.

"Poor Matt," Lauren mused when they were airborne again. "For someone who hates flying, you've done your share in the past few days."

He leaned close to her, denying the steel arm between them. "It's worth it. Every hateful minute."

Lauren smiled and whispered. "You are a wonderful man."

"Nah. I'm just along for the ride."

"That's one of the reasons I love you." She kissed his too-square chin. "You didn't ask for any of this."

"But I asked for you," he murmured deeply. "All my life I've been asking for you, and now that I've found you, I'll take any ride, as long as you're along." He sought and captured her lips, kissing her thoroughly. "And when this is all over," he whispered against her mouth, "we are going to take a vacation to beat all vacations. We'll fly somewhere and stay put for two weeks, just the two of us. Sun and sand and moonlit nights…"

"Sounds wonderful, but you'll have used up all your vacation time by then."

"So I'll take more."

"And if your boss objects?"

"I'll quit."

She grinned. "Mmm. I'd like that. San Francisco's too far away."

"My thoughts exactly." He kissed her again, softly, deeply. His mouth was just leaving hers when the flight attendant came by with lunch.

Beneath the lighthearted teasing, Lauren had been very

serious. San Francisco *was* too far away. But she couldn't think about the future. Not yet. There was still too much to be done to ensure that she had a future at all.

BRIGHT AND EARLY the next morning, Lauren and Matt showed up in the office of one Timothy Trennis. The office was done in obvious taste and at obvious cost; the man was in his early forties, neatly dressed and pleasant-looking. When he saw them, his mouth dropped open. His eyes were riveted to Lauren's face.

"Susan?" he asked uncertainly.

"Almost," Lauren said gently, "but not quite. I am looking for her, though. We thought maybe you could help us."

Timothy continued to stare at her, then slowly shook his head. "The resemblance is remarkable. It's been a long time since I've seen Susan. I could have sworn—" He seemed to catch himself, and his cheeks reddened. "But you'd know, wouldn't you?"

Lauren nodded. "It's very important that we reach her. Do you have any idea where she might be?"

"Is she in trouble?" he asked with genuine concern.

Lauren looked hesitantly at Matt, who took over. "She may be if we don't find her. Someone else is looking for her. It's critical that we find her first."

"It's that Prinz guy, isn't it?"

"Do you know about him?" Lauren asked.

Belatedly, Timothy gestured for them to sit. When they'd done so, he lowered himself into a chair near his desk. "Susan and I dated for a time. I always knew she had greater ambitions—ambitions that went beyond Kansas City, I mean. When she decided to move to Los Angeles, I wasn't surprised. We kept in touch for a while, so I knew she was seeing Prinz. I made it my business to find out about him, and when I tried to caution her subtly, she pretty much severed all contact between us.''

''When was the last time you heard from her?'' Matt asked.

Timothy thought about that for a minute, making rough calculations in his mind. ''It had to have been more than three years ago.''

''And there's been nothing since then?''

Timothy shook his head.

''Is there someone she *might* have contacted? Someone she's kept in touch with—family, maybe?''

''If there is, I don't know about it. Susan rarely talked about family. There was an older sister, and her mother. The father died when she was a child, and the mother remarried. Susan detested her stepfather. She left as soon as she could.''

''Do you know where the mother lives?'' Lauren asked.

''Susan grew up in a small town in Indiana. Whether the mother's still there is anyone's guess. I don't even know her married name.''

''How about the sister?'' Matt queried.

''The sister was older by five or six years, took off after high school and got married. Susan never mentioned her. I simply assumed they'd lost contact, too.''

Matt looked at Lauren. ''Another strikeout.'' He fished the scrap of paper from his pocket. ''What about, uh, Alexander Fraun? Do you know him?''

Timothy nodded. ''Susan worked for him. He owns a pair of dress shops in the area. Nice-enough fellow. You could try him. He may have information I don't.'' As Lauren and Matt stood up to leave, he added, ''I hope you find her. I always wished her happiness.''

Lauren smiled warmly. She liked this man and felt he'd given them the first positive picture of Susan Miles to date.

"We'll tell her that when we find her," she said. *When*, not *if*. Pessimism had no place here; there was too much at stake for all of them.

"THEY'RE IN KANSAS CITY."

"Kansas City? Clever. Susan was from Kansas City. They *are* looking for her."

"Will they find her?"

"In Kansas City? No. She wouldn't go back there. It's too obvious." There was a pause. "It is possible, though, that she's contacted one of her old friends there." A smug smile. "And if that's the case, Kruger and the girl will find out. They're doing our legwork for us."

"Seems to me I'm doing it anyway, following them around like this."

"You're not stupid enough to let them see you, are you? After that little kidnapping stunt, the girl would recognize you instantly."

"Don't worry. We've got Jimbo tailing them close, and she never saw him, so we're safe."

"But you're not far."

"No, sir."

"Good. I don't trust Jimbo to do the heavy work."

"Neither do I, and I have a personal investment here, too. Susan's kept us running in circles. That kind of thing inspires revenge."

"Mmm. I like that. Very good."

ALEXANDER FRAUN was harder to reach. When Lauren and Matt arrived at the address Phillip had given them, they were told that Fraun was at the other store. When they arrived at that one, they were told that he'd gone to a luncheon meeting and would be back at the first store that afternoon.

They went to lunch themselves, then returned to the first store to await the elusive Mr. Fraun. Shortly before two o'clock, he entered the small outer office in which they sat. He had started to pass through into his own office, after glancing briefly their way, when he did a double take on Lauren and came to an abrupt halt.

"Susan?" he asked uncertainly.

"Almost," she said gently, "but not quite." She felt she was living a broken record and quickly moved to free the needle from its cracked groove. "My name is Lauren Stevenson. And this is Matt Kruger. We're looking for Susan and thought you might have some idea as to her whereabouts."

"Come into my office," the man said with a broad wave of his hand. He was as different from Timothy Trennis as night from day. Not only was his office a disaster area, but the man himself looked as though he'd seen better days. Lauren estimated that he was in his late fifties. His bald pate was scantily covered with strands of gray that had been called to the rescue from somewhere just above his ear. He had chipmunk cheeks and a multitiered chin, both of which coordinated perfectly with his girth. There was something about him, something strangely genuine, that made Lauren like him on the spot.

"Now," he said, scooping a pile of ancient magazines from the torn vinyl sofa so that Lauren and Matt could sit down, "what's this about Susan?" He propped himself on the edge of the desk. The wood groaned.

"We're trying to find her," Matt explained. "We were told she worked for you once."

"What do you want with her?" Fraun shot back with such suspicion that Lauren, for one, wondered if Prinz's men had reached him first.

Matt did the talking, apparently taking the man's suspicion for protectiveness. He explained just why he and Lauren were anxious to find Susan.

Fraun shifted his gaze back to Lauren. "You look just like her. For a minute when I walked in, I thought she'd come back."

"We know that she went to Los Angeles when she left here," Lauren offered, "but we were hoping that you might have heard from her."

"She's not still there?"

Lauren shook her head.

The wrinkles on Fraun's brow echoed higher on his bald head. "I thought she was. Last thing I heard from her, she had her own boutique." He smiled. "Susan was good. She had a way with color and style." He gave his head a little toss. "She was wasted here. I told her so. I mean, my goods are nice enough, but she needed high fashion to make the most of her talents."

"When was the last time you heard from her?" Matt asked.

Fraun suddenly scowled at him. "How do I know you're on the up-and-up? How do I know you two haven't come to do her harm?"

Lauren, too, saw protectiveness this time. As briefly but meaningfully as she could, she told him where she'd come from and where she worked, then did the same for Matt. "We don't wish Susan any harm. We have no reason to do her harm. If Matt and I can locate her, Susan and I stand to benefit—Susan, because she'll be aware of the danger and be able to do something about it; me, because if Susan does something about it, I'll be out of danger, too."

Fraun tugged a slightly warped pad of paper from beneath a haphazard pile of letters. "I'm going to write down your names and addresses. That way, if anything happens to Susan, I'll know who to call."

"Then you know where she is?" Lauren asked in excitement.

"Driver's licenses, please."

Lauren and Matt exchanged a glance and dug into their respective pockets for identification. Only when the man had taken notes to his satisfaction did he put down the pad and face them.

"No, I don't know where Susan is," he admitted. "The last time I heard from her was nearly two years ago. She sounded fine then. Why did she leave L.A.?"

"We're not sure," Matt answered. "But we do know she left. We'd hoped she'd contacted you, or someone else she knew before."

"You could try Tim—"

"We already have. He suggested we try you."

Fraun sighed and gave a shrug that made his belly shake. "I don't know what to tell you. I can't believe Susan's in trouble. She was always honest, and a hard worker."

"She probably still is," Lauren speculated. "It's just that she had the ill fortune to get mixed up with a man who's probably neither of those things. Can you think of anyone she may have contacted? Timothy said she wasn't close to her family, but there's always a chance she could be in touch with one of them."

Fraun shook his head. This time his jowls shimmied. "Tim was right. She wasn't big on her family. She did mention the sister from time to time."

"Do you know her married name," Matt asked, "or where she's living?"

"Nah— Wait just a minute." He bounced off the desk and tugged at the drawer of a file cabinet. It resisted his efforts, yielding at last, but with reluctance. Lauren understood why. The drawer was nearly as overstuffed as was the man rummaging through it.

"How can you find anything in there?" she asked on impulse.

"I find. I find. It just takes a little time."

It took a good fifteen minutes, during which Lauren and Matt sat by helplessly, glancing from each other's faces to the man at work to the calamity of his office.

"Here we go!" Fraun exclaimed at last. He held up a sheet of paper that had a permanent press running diagonally through it. "Susan's original employment application. You see," he cried victoriously, "it sometimes pays not to clean out drawers." Holding the paper at arm's length, he ran his eyes down the form. "Aha! Person to call in case of emergency: Mrs. Peter—Ann—Broszczynski. Relationship: sister." Proudly, he offered the form to Lauren. "St. Louis. Think you can get there?"

Lauren looked from the form to Matt and grinned. "You bet we can." When she returned her gaze to Alexander Fraun, she realized that, with a beard and a little more hair, he would have reminded her of Santa Claus.

ANN BROSZCZYNSKI was not living at the address listed on the employment application, which was understandable, Lauren and Matt told each other, since the application had been filled out seven years before. The people presently living at that address didn't know what had become of the Broszcynskis, but the telephone company did.

A phone booth with its book miraculously attached and intact gave them the information they needed, and a taxi delivered them to the right address. It was another apartment, but a nicer one, more a garden complex. Lauren felt a certain pleasure that Susan's sister had moved up in the world.

The door was answered by a teenage girl who reminded Lauren of the guard at the garage where she parked. Definitely a music fan. If the net of lace banding her curly hair, the penciled mole just above her lip, or the abbreviated top and minuscule straight skirt hadn't given her away, the fingerless lace glove on her hand would have.

"Mmm?" the girl mumbled.

"We're looking for Ann Broszczynski," Lauren explained. "Is she in?"

The girl tilted her head back and hollered to the ceiling, "Mom!" A minute later she stepped aside to make room for the woman who approached.

Ann Broszczynski was a clean and attractive representative of middle America. She wore jeans, a sleeveless blouse and an apron, the latter serving at the moment as a towel for her wet hands. Her hair, a little lighter than Lauren's, was shoulder-length and swept behind her ears. Even devoid of makeup, her face was lovely.

It was also momentarily stricken. Her eyes were huge. She opened her mouth, then closed it and stared at Lauren in puzzlement.

Lauren smiled. "I look a lot like Susan, I know, but my name's Lauren Stevenson. This is Matt Kruger. We wonder if we could talk with you for a few minutes."

"Are you friends of Susan's?" the woman asked, more wary than curious, a fact that Lauren attributed to the distance between the sisters.

"Indirectly, yes," Lauren answered. "May we come in?"

Ann didn't budge. "Susan and I don't see each other," she returned a little too quickly. "We go our own ways."

"I know that. But we need to talk with you. No one else has been able to help us."

"Why do you need help?" Ann shot back.

Matt, who'd been silent up to that point, suddenly understood the problem. "We don't wish Susan any harm,

Mrs. Broszczynski. If anything, the contrary is true, which is why we're here. Susan is in danger. Apparently you know that, or at least you know she's living somewhere new under an assumed name and that there's a potential for danger if she is discovered. What you don't know is that Lauren was mistaken for Susan by Theodore Prinz's men. For weeks they've put her through hell, using one scare tactic after another. Last week they abducted her and came very close to killing her. It was during the time she was being held that she learned about Susan.'' He spoke with soft urgency. ''We need to find your sister. She must be told that she's being hunted. We have to convince her to go to the police. Between her testimony and Lauren's, we know that something can be done about Prinz.''

Ann was pale. She gnawed at her lower lip and clutched the folds of the apron in her fists.

''May we come in?'' Lauren asked again, this time pleadingly.

After another moment's hesitation, the woman nodded. Shooing her daughter away, she led them into a small, modestly furnished living room. None of them sat; the air was too tense for that.

''I'm not sure if I know what you're talking about,'' Ann burst out. ''I'm not involved in Susan's life.''

''We realize that,'' Matt said quietly, intent on convincing her of the legitimacy of their mission. ''We've just come from Kansas City, where we spoke with both Timothy Trennis and Alexander Fraun. Do those names ring a bell?''

After a pause, Ann nodded.

''Do you trust them?'' he asked. When, after another pause, Ann nodded again, he went on. ''Alexander Fraun was the one who found your name on Susan's old employment application. He was obviously fond of Susan and

wouldn't have given us your name unless he trusted us."
Though he raised a hand to emphasize his point, his voice
remained soft. "We wouldn't be bothering you if we had
anywhere else to turn, but no one seems to know where
Susan is or what she's doing. Prinz doesn't seem to be
aware that Susan had any family, which may explain why
no one has reached you sooner. But it's simply a matter of
time before he gets to you, and then to Susan, because it
may well be that you're the only one who knows Susan's
new name and address." He paused, gentling his voice all
the more. "Will you tell us, Ann? We only want to help."

"I wish my husband were here," Ann wailed softly,
hands tightly clenched before her. "I'm no good at things
like this."

"You're Susan's sister. It's your decision, more so than
your husband's."

"But things are so tenuous between Susan and me," she
argued. "For years we had very little contact. She was in
one world, I was in another. There was no middle ground
between us. I don't want to do something that will anger
her, or worse, put her in danger."

"Then you have to tell us where she is," Lauren urged.
"*None* of us will be safe until we find her and convince
her to go to the police with us. For all we know, Matt and
I are just one step ahead of Prinz's men right now."

Ann pondered Lauren's words nervously, her gaze shifting from one spot in the room to another. Then she brightened. "Why don't you let *me* call Susan? I can tell her
everything you've told me—"

"Do you think she'll believe you—or that we're legitimate?" Matt cut in. "She'll run, Ann. She's done it before,
and she'll do it again if this isn't handled right. She needs
to *see* Lauren and the physical similarity between them in
order to believe what's happened."

Ann looked from one face to the other. "You're asking an awful lot."

Lauren nodded. "We know."

"If you turn out to be the bad guys—"

"We're not! You can call the police back home, either in Boston or Lincoln. They'll verify everything that's happened to me."

"And Fraun took precautions of his own," Matt added soberly. "He has our names and addresses. He knows where to send the police if anything happens to Susan."

"I'll never forgive myself if she's hurt because of me!"

Matt put every ounce of feeling into a single, last-ditch plea. "*No* one will be hurt if we reach her in time. But time is of the essence, and we can't reach her if we don't know where she is."

Ann worried the issue for several minutes longer, her eyes filled with concern, her lips clamped tightly together. Her gaze slid from Lauren to Matt and back to Lauren, asking questions for which there were, as yet, no answers.

Just as Lauren was about to scream in frustration, Ann straightened her shoulders, took a deep breath, let it out in a sigh and surrendered.

Chapter Eleven

A single long shadow stretched across the grass behind him as Ted Prinz stood in his garden staring out over the hills. Absently he lit a cigarette and dragged deeply on it. Pensive, he narrowed his eyes through the tunnel of smoke.

So Susan was in Washington, D.C. That made sense. He could picture her trying to hook up with a politician who had enough clout to protect her.

He grinned. She'd never make it. His men would make sure of that. At this very moment Kruger and the girl were being staked out at the Hay-Adams House. When they moved, his men would, too.

And Susan would regret the day she'd been born.

"WHADDYA THINK?" Matt asked, looking at his watch. "Should we make a stab at it tonight?"

Lauren pressed a hand to her chest. "My heart is pounding. I can't believe we've found her."

"Don't believe it until you see it. There could be a catch yet."

But Lauren was shaking her head. "Ann said she'd spoken to her just last week. Oh, she's here all right. I can *feel* it."

Slinging an arm around her shoulder, Matt tugged her

close. "My eternal optimist." He popped a kiss on her nose. "So. What will it be? Tonight, or tomorrow morning?"

Lauren pondered the choice. "If we go tonight, it'll have to be to her apartment. Ann said it's a nice place, which means there will be security guards—"

"Who call up to announce your arrival and get permission to let you in. Susan doesn't know us. She'll never allow it. No, I think we'll have to take her by surprise. Any advance announcement of our presence will put her on guard and, in turn, put us at an immediate disadvantage."

"On the one hand," Lauren mused, "I hate to wait. The sooner we get to her, the sooner we'll all breathe freely. But another twelve hours, after all this time…it can't hurt."

Matt nodded his agreement. "We know where she works. If we surprise her there tomorrow, she won't have a chance to turn us away sight unseen. And if she gets scared and tries to run, we can stop her."

"But we need time with her, time to explain what we're about." Lauren ran her tongue back and forth over her lower lip, then expressed her thoughts aloud. "She's a beauty consultant, Ann said. That figures. From what we've learned, she has a way with makeup and color and style. What if I call first thing in the morning and make an appointment? If we just drop in, she's apt to be with a client. On the other hand, if I can guarantee us a piece of her time…"

A slow grin spread over Matt's face. "Smart girl. I *knew* there was a reason why I brought you along."

Lauren grabbed his ears, tugged him down and kissed his yelp away. She lingered to savor his returning kiss, her fingers tangling in his sun-kissed hair. At last she dropped her arms to his waist and pressed her cheek to his chest. They were silent for a time, enjoying the closeness. But

Lauren's thoughts of the day to come refused to stay in abeyance for long. "Poor Susan. If she only knew tonight what was in store for her tomorrow."

"Save your sympathy, sweetheart," Matt murmured. "Susan Miles may still put us through an ordeal. Confronting her is one thing, convincing her that we're on the level is another, but selling her on the idea of going to the police may be a different can of worms entirely."

MICHELE SLOANE, as Susan now called herself, had set up her business in fashionable Georgetown. Lauren got the phone number from directory assistance and started calling at eight-thirty in the morning on the chance that the shop opened early for the prework set. It wasn't until nine that she got through.

Luck was with her. Michele had a cancellation and could see her at eleven-thirty.

The minutes ticked by with agonizing slowness as Lauren and Matt pushed their breakfasts around their plates in the hotel dining room. Then, to expend nervous energy, they went out for a walk. But while the White House, the Mall and the Lincoln Memorial should have inspired awe, they were too preoccupied in anticipation of the coming meeting to award these sights their due.

Ten o'clock came and went, then ten-thirty. Back in their hotel room, Lauren began to pace the floor. By eleven she was ready to jump out of her skin, but it wasn't until eleven-ten that she and Matt left the room, rode the elevator in silence, walked calmly through the hotel lobby and climbed into the cab that the doorman had whistled up. They'd calculated well for the traffic. It was eleven-thirty on the dot when the cabbie pulled up at the address they'd given him.

For a minute Matt and Lauren stood before the stately

brownstone on the ground floor of which was Susan's shop. The sign on the front window, a contemporary logo in burgundy, read "Elegance, Inc." Smaller letters, far below, advertised fashion advice and salon services.

Taking a collective breath for courage, they crossed the sidewalk, descended three steps to the door and entered the shop. An aura of quiet dignity surrounded them instantly. The reception area was done in shades of a soothing pale gray and peach. Soft pop music hummed in the background, low enough to create a modern mood yet be unobtrusive.

A woman sat in a chair reading a magazine, apparently awaiting her appointment. Lauren and Matt made their way directly to the receptionist.

"May I help you?" she asked politely.

"Yes. My name is Lauren Stevenson. I have an eleven-thirty appointment with Michele Sloane."

The receptionist consulted the large book open before her, put a tiny dot next to Lauren's name, then smiled up at her. "Why don't you have a seat? Michele is just finishing up with another client. She'll be with you in a minute."

Lauren thanked her and settled into one of a pair of chairs farthest from the receptionist. She crossed her legs, folded her hands in her lap and leaned closer to Matt, who'd taken the chair immediately on her left.

"When was the last time you were in a place like this?" she whispered in an attempt at levity.

His soft grunt was the only answer she got, the only thing that betrayed his mood. He looked self-confident and composed. Taking her cue from him, she breathed deeply and straightened her shoulders. They were so close, so close....

Moments later another woman entered the shop, checked in with the receptionist and was sent directly through to one of the back rooms. Lauren stared after her, noting a long hallway sporting two doors on the side she could see. She assumed another two doors were on the opposite side.

Just then, from that blind side came the soft murmur of conversation. It was immediately followed by the appearance of two women, but Lauren's eyes homed in on only one of them.

Susan Miles was everything she'd been built up to be. She was indeed stunning. Very much Lauren's own height and build, she wore a pale yellow dress whose shoulder pads gave a breadth that narrowed, past a hip belt, into a pencil-slim skirt. Chunky beads hung around her neck. A coordinated bracelet ringed her wrist. Whether she wore earrings was not immediately apparent, for her chin-length hair was a mass of thick waves that framed her face in haphazard tumble.

The entire look was chic without being ostentatious. Lauren, who mere moments before had felt sufficiently confident in her own stylish tunic and slacks, was envious.

She was also puzzled. Susan Miles looked very much like her, yet very different. Apparently the receptionist had missed the resemblance. Now, studying Susan, Lauren could understand why.

Susan's hair was far lighter than Lauren's, for one thing. It had obviously been colored, though there was nothing obviously doctored about the blond, sun-streaked tangle. It blended perfectly with Susan's skin tone and makeup and looked completely natural.

Makeup. Yes, another difference. While Lauren wore it lightly and for simple enhancement, Susan's makeup sculpted her face, shading and contouring with a skill that was remarkable. Plastic surgery? Lauren doubted it. Yet there was something about the nose…a small bump…

The woman who'd been with Susan left. Susan bent over the desk to examine the appointment book, then followed the receptionist's finger to Lauren and Matt. She smiled as she straightened and approached them, but her smile wavered as she neared. Lauren thought she saw a faint drain of color from Susan's face. The smile remained but was more forced.

Lauren stood up, finding solace in the warmth of Matt's body by her side. If Susan was playing a part, she herself was doing no less. She held out her hand, willing it not to shake. "Michele?"

Susan met her clasp. "Yes. You're Lauren. And…" Her gaze slid to Matt.

"Matt Kruger," he said with a smile.

Susan nodded, but she was already looking back at Lauren. She folded her hands at her waist, hesitated a minute too long, then cleared her throat. "Well. You're here for a consultation. Why don't you come back to my office?"

They followed her down the hall to the last door on the right. The office they entered was simply decorated and furnished, exuding the same quiet dignity as the front room had. Large semiabstract watercolors—one of a woman's face—hung on the walls. Had it been another time, Lauren would have paused to admire the pictures themselves, if not their matting and framing, but she was too busy trying to organize her words and thoughts to handle anything else.

They were all three seated—Susan behind her desk, Matt and Lauren in comfortable chairs before it—when Susan spoke. "What can I do for you?" she asked. Her tone was thoroughly cordial, even warm. The wariness in her eyes was subtle enough to go unnoticed by any but the most watchful of observers. Lauren and Matt were that.

Lauren went straight for the heart. "You've noticed the resemblance, haven't you?"

Susan frowned. "Resemblance?" Her expression was

one of confusion, but it was studied. A second, almost imperceptible drain of color from her face betrayed her.

"I have a problem," Lauren explained softly, her eyes never once leaving Susan's. "I was hoping you could help me. Several months back I had plastic surgery, reconstructive work, actually, to correct a long-standing medical problem. The work was extensive, and when it was done, I looked like a new person. But after I returned to the States—the clinic where I had the surgery was in the Bahamas—I ran into trouble. Things started happening. Odd things. Dangerous things." She gave several examples, then paused, looking for a reaction in Susan. But the latter, aside from her underlying pallor, remained composed, so Lauren went on.

"Matt and I put two and two together when I began to get letters addressed to Susan Miles. We realized that I was being mistaken for someone else, but we couldn't find a Susan Miles in the area and we didn't know what to do next. Then, just about a week ago, I was abducted, forced off the street into a car by two men who firmly believed I was Susan Miles."

Susan blinked. That was all.

"They drove me around for hours, finally brought me to an abandoned warehouse and told me their plan. They meant to set me on fire and watch me burn. They had every intention of seeing me dead, as their boss wanted me to be." Lauren paused again, this time out of necessity. Her voice began to shake, whether from remembered terror or the utterly bland look on Susan Miles's face, she didn't know.

Matt came to her aid. "Lauren managed to escape. But we don't know if they're still out looking for her or if they actually let her go because she managed to convince them she wasn't Susan. The police have nothing to go on, at least nothing that's leading them anywhere, and Lauren can't live under guard indefinitely. We realized then that our only hope was in finding Susan.''

For the first time, Susan stirred. She propped her elbow on the arm of her chair and rested her chin on her knuckles. Her fingernails were beautifully shaped and painted a sheer pink noncolor. ''I'm not sure I understand. I'm a beauty consultant, not a detective. Why have you come to me?''

Lauren resumed speaking, more calmly, now, and briefly sketched the course of their search. She concluded with a soft ''Ann Broszczynski sent us here.''

Susan's eyes were blank and she was shaking her head, but her knuckles had curved into a fist. ''None of those names mean anything to me. Ann—whoever she is—must have been wrong. I have no idea why she sent you here.''

''I think you do,'' Matt challenged. ''You saw the resemblance to your old self the minute you looked at Lauren, and we saw the resemblance the minute we looked at you.''

A hoarse laugh tripped from Susan's throat. ''This is ludicrous! I don't know why I'm even sitting here listening to you.'' But she didn't move. ''Do you really expect me to swallow the story you've told? I'm sorry. Even if I believed it, which I don't, I don't know why someone would have sent you to *me*. And as far as the resemblance is concerned, you're mistaken—''

''No.'' Matt spoke softly, trying his best to understand her fear as he tamped down his own impatience. ''We're not here to hurt you. You have a problem, and because of that, Lauren has a problem. I, for one, don't think it's fair that she's been saddled with it. She did nothing but try to correct a medical deficiency, and now she's being punished. We know that Theodore Prinz is at the root of the problem. We also know that unless you agree to go to the police and testify along with Lauren, he'll snake his way free.'' Susan's telephone chirped melodically. Matt ignored it. "It's only a matter of time before he finds you—Ann realized that—and he may well kill Lauren along the way."

When the phone on the desk chimed a second time, Susan picked it up. Her every movement was carefully controlled. "Yes?... She's back?... No, no, don't let her go. I'll be there in a second." Replacing the receiver, she rose from her seat and headed for the door. Matt was instantly on his feet, but she held him off with a hand. "There's a problem at the front desk. I have to see to it, but I'll be back. Please don't go anywhere. I'd like to hear more about this Theodore Prinz."

With that, she left the office. The door had no sooner closed behind her than the phone rang again, that same soft tinkle. Matt stared at it and frowned. When he made a move toward it, Lauren was one step ahead. Their lines of sight merged on the keyboard. A red dot flashed beside the bottommost number, one that was separate from the others, one totally apart from that marked "X" that would connect the interoffice line.

"Damn it," Matt barked, heading for the door, "she's gone! That wasn't the receptionist. It was someone on her personal line, someone who's calling back now to find out what in the hell she was talking about." He was in the hall, looking first one way, then the other, with Lauren by his side. "I'll take the back, sweetheart. It probably leads to an alley. No, you take the back. I'll circle around and head her off." He burst into a run toward the front of the shop.

Brushing past the white curtain at the end of the hall, Lauren raced through the back room, threw open the door and dashed up the steps. Yes, there was an alley, a long, long alley strewn with trash cans and miscellaneous other debris. Susan Miles was about halfway down its length and running.

"Michele!" Lauren screamed as she, too, broke into a run. "Wait!"

Susan wasn't waiting. She was running as if the devil himself were at her heels, and would have long since made it to the end of the alley had it not been for the dodging the obstacle course demanded.

"Michele! Wait! It's dangerous!"

But Susan had no intention of stopping. Had it not been for Matt's timely appearance at the end of the alley, she'd have escaped. As it was, when she saw him, she whirled around, saw Lauren, whirled again and made for the nearest doorway. Matt reached her before she made it.

Capturing her bodily, he swung her up and wrestled her back until he'd pinned her to the nearest brick wall. "I am *not* going to hurt you, Susan," he gritted out between breaths, "but neither...neither am I going to let you get away. Not...after all we've been through to find you, not after all Lauren's been through *because* of you."

Lauren came to a breathless halt just as Susan sagged lower against the wall. Matt simply shifted his grip, veeing his hands under her arms and propping her right back up. She'd tricked him once. Lauren agreed with his caution.

"It wasn't my fault," Susan gasped. Her composure had vanished. There was near panic in the eyes that skipped from Matt's face to Lauren's and back. "I'd been with Ted for two years before I discovered who he really was. I wanted to leave him then, but he wouldn't hear of it. For a year, a whole year, I tried, but he threatened awful things and I kept giving in until I hated myself nearly as much as I hated him. I was desperate...so desperate that I tried to kill myself."

"A suicide attempt?" Matt drawled. "We knew about the accident, but that's a new twist to the story."

"Why else would I drive over a cliff? You thought I

wasn't in the car when it went over the edge? I was. *I was.* But I was thrown free when the car began to roll." Trembling, she shoved the hair from her forehead. Just below her hairline was a three-inch scar. "I broke an arm and several ribs, but I could breathe and think and feel, and it was then that I realized I'd been given a second chance. So I let them think that I'd died, and I ran. Don't ask me what hospital I went to—it was in some godforsaken town in northern Arizona."

"How did you get there?"

"I hitchhiked."

"Talk of ludicrous stories!"

"It's the truth. At the time, nothing was more dangerous than staying where I was."

"Why didn't you go to the police? If Prinz threatened you—"

"Ted *owns* the police, or half of them, and what he doesn't own he has connections to. I know what I'm talking about. I've seen him buy his way out of serious investigations. That was what tipped me off in the first place!"

Lauren entered the conversation at that point. She was beginning to feel sorry for Susan. While she understood Matt's anger, she wanted to put the other woman at ease. They still needed her cooperation. "Okay," she said gently. "You felt you couldn't go to the police. Where did you go? What did you use for money? The two men who kidnapped me mentioned furs and jewels."

"I had both. Ted had given them to me. As far as I was concerned, I'd earned them."

"But how did you get them? You'd have to have gone back to Los Angeles."

"A friend did it." Susan's voice softened. "He was a little old man who used to sell flowers on a street corner not far from the boutique. I liked him. He reminded me of my father—or what my father would have been like if he'd lived beyond forty," she added in a whisper. "Sam was kind and gentle. I knew he'd do anything for me." She averted her gaze. "Maybe it was wrong of me, or arrogant. I knew Sam was dying. He'd told me that he'd been given six months to live. I figured that he wouldn't mind the risk, that he'd take pleasure in helping me out." Her eyes met Lauren's. "And he did. He told me so in a note he stuck inside the pocket of one of the coats."

"An old man, breaking into your apartment and stealing your things?" Matt was clearly skeptical.

"He didn't steal them," Susan shot back. "He simply returned to me what was mine. As for breaking into my apartment—he had friends who would have done anything for him, just as I would have."

"But you never got the chance," Matt concluded sarcastically, only to be instantly corrected.

"I did. After I sold the very first ring, I sent him a large chunk of the money. I know he received it, because I called him to make sure." Susan took a ragged breath. "Whether he lived long enough to enjoy it, I'll never know. I've tried to call him again, but there's been no answer. He may be using the money to travel, or he may be...well, I'll never know."

Matt stared at her. "Prinz's men may have had him killed."

"Do you think I don't know that?" Susan cried. "I've *seen* Ted in action—"

"Isn't it about time you did something about it?"

The air between the two sizzled. Lauren set about diffusing it. "We're getting ahead of ourselves. Did you come directly to Washington from Arizona?"

Susan was leaning against the brick on her own now, Matt having released her and stepped back. She took several calming breaths. "I made a few stops. I wasn't sure where I wanted to settle. But each time I stopped, I felt I was still too close to Ted, so I kept going. When I reached Washington, it was either stay or swim. So I stayed."

"What about your nose?" Lauren frowned as she leaned to the side for a profile view. "We assumed you'd have plastic surgery to change your looks. Prinz's men assumed the same, which was how they got onto me."

"I figured they'd think that, so I avoided it." Susan gave a self-conscious half shrug. "My nose had been broken in the accident, and I didn't trust the doctors in that hospital to do more than tape it up. When the bandages came off, I saw the bump. It was subtle enough to change my profile just that little bit. I told myself it'd give my face character." She snorted. "Obviously it didn't fool you."

"We started with an advantage." It was Matt speaking, more gently now. "We had your name and knew where to find you. Even before you walked into that reception area, we were primed to see Susan Miles."

With an air of helplessness, Susan raised her eyes to the sliver of sky above. "Well, you saw her. And you have her cornered. I suppose I knew that someday someone would find me. In some ways, it's a relief that it's you."

"Then you do trust us?" he asked.

Her gaze met his. "Trust? Maybe that's going a little too far."

Lauren grasped her arm. "But you do believe that what we've told you is the truth."

Susan studied her for a long time. "The resemblance…it's amazing. What did you look like before?"

Dropping Susan's arm, Lauren glanced awkwardly at Matt, who nodded. "I was awful." Lauren proceeded to paint a brief, if blunt, picture of her former self. "Richard took care of it all, bless him.'' She winced. ''Then again…''

Matt curved his hand around her neck. ''No, no, sweetheart. From a purely medical standpoint, it is a blessing, what he did. And as for this other, we'll work it all out. Susan will go to the police with us—''

''Whoa. I never said that.''

''But you have to!'' Lauren cried. ''It's your only chance. Sooner or later those guys will find you—''

A deep voice cut her off with an ominously sarcastic ''Hel-lo, hel-lo.''

All three heads jerked around. Lauren and Susan gasped in tandem. Matt grew rigid.

''What have we here?'' drawled the man whose face and voice Lauren would never in a million years forget. He stood several yards away, a human wall with a gleaming gun in his hand. ''Matthew Kruger, Lauren Stevenson…and if it isn't the elusive Miss Susan Miles.''

''What do you want, Leo?'' Susan demanded. Her eyes were hard, glittering more with disgust than with fear.

Leo grinned, that ugly grin Lauren remembered so well, and looked first at Mouse on his left, then at another thug on his right. The eyes he refocused on Susan were nearly black. ''You know what I want. I want you.''

''I'm not available.''

''Seems to me you are.'' He cocked his head toward Lauren and Matt. ''These two don't want you, that's for sure. You've been a thorn in their sides.''

''I'd pick her any day—'' Lauren began, only to be silenced by the restraining hand Matt put on her arm, and by his own retort.

''You've got the three of us, and you know damn well that if you so much as touch Susan, we'll go straight to the police. Do you plan a triple murder?''

"Wouldn't bother the boss any. I have his okay."

"Think, Leo, think," Susan urged. "There are too many people involved now. If you do something to Matt and Lauren, someone *else* will go to the police. This isn't another one of your little in-house jobs. If you kill one of your own, you're doing us all a favor. But to kill me—and these two, who are totally innocent... The police will get you one day, Leo. And if you think Ted will come forward on your behalf, you're crazy."

Leo laughed. "The police won't get me. I'm good at what I do. We'll have it arranged so it looks like you shot the others, then killed yourself. Very clean."

"Very simpleminded," Susan retorted. When Leo made a move toward her, she slipped into a half crouch, arms raised. "I think it's only fair to warn you that I've learned karate."

Lauren and Matt glanced at each other, then at Susan. Leo threw back his head and laughed louder. "Talk of simpleminded. That threat's the oldest in the book, and in your case it's empty. You haven't had the time to learn enough karate to protect yourself."

"I'm a quick study."

"Against a gun?"

Susan had no answer for that, and Matt and Lauren said nothing. They were concentrating on the gun, measuring the distance between Leo and his accomplices, peripherally evaluating the potential weaponry within reach.

"Gotcha there, don't I?" Leo said. He took a step back. "Okay, I want the three of you to start moving. Straight to the car at the head of the alley." He gestured at Susan with the gun. "You first."

Lauren swallowed hard. She had no desire to be in a car with Leo and company. She knew the helplessness of that. No, if a move was to be made, it had to be now.

Matt's hand remained on her arm, but it was steadily tightening. He agreed with her. She waited for his signal.

Slowly Susan moved forward. She hadn't taken two steps, though, when her ankle turned and she buckled over.

"Ah, hell," Leo moaned. "That's the corniest move I've ever seen. It won't get you anywhere, Susan, and if you think I'm going to carry you, you're nuts."

"These heels," Susan gasped. "They're too high."

Matt's hand tightened all the more on Lauren's arm. They both knew from personal experience how well Susan could maneuver, high heels or no. Internally coiled and ready, they watched her unstrap the thin buckles and remove the shoes.

"Come on, come on. We haven't all day—" Leo's words were abruptly cut off by a totally unexpected, lightning-quick move. As Susan straightened, she hiked her slim skirt high on her thighs, spun around and delivered a kick that would have made her instructor proud.

The gun went flying, as did Matt, who barreled into Leo's midsection, knocking the burly man to the ground. Susan, meanwhile, turned her attention to the other men, throwing strategically placed kicks with such speed that they barely knew what hit them. When Mouse doubled over in pain, she whirled around and into his pal, and by the time she was done with him, she was aiming lethal chops at Mouse again.

Lauren came to her aid. Grabbing a heavy shovel from its resting place beside a nearby trash bin, she slammed it repeatedly against the back of whichever man Susan wasn't battering. Each slam vented a little more of her anger, and she might have actually enjoyed herself if she hadn't shot a glance at Matt.

He and Leo were fighting hand to hand, tumbling on the filthy pavement, each landing his share of punches.

Dropping the shovel, Lauren scrambled along the alley, returning seconds later to put an end to the fray. *"That's it!"* she screamed. *"Enough!"* She stood a safe distance back with her feet planted firmly, both hands curved around Leo's gun. The fact that she didn't know how to use it was secondary to the proprietary air with which she held it. Her chest was heaving, the only part of her that betrayed any weakness.

Later she realized that if she'd had to shoot, she'd never have been able to separate Matt from Leo, so fast were they shifting. But her strident yell brought all heads up in surprise. Matt took advantage of the precious seconds to free himself and stumble to her side. He grabbed the gun and turned it on the trio.

"Susan! That's enough!" he ordered. She'd been poised to deliver another side-handed slice to Mouse's head, and only with reluctance did she lower her arm and move back.

Matt motioned with the gun toward the three. "Okay, up! And if you think I don't know how to use this, think again. I'm an avid hunter." His knees were bent; both hands were on the gun, holding it aimed and steady. Not once did his eyes leave the men. "Lauren, go back inside the shop and call the police—"

The sound of shoes clattering on the pavement interrupted him, and seconds later the police themselves rounded the corner and entered the alley with their guns drawn. Slowly Matt straightened. He didn't lower his arm until each of Prinz's men had been handcuffed.

"Mr. Kruger?" one of the officers asked. He was the only one not in uniform and was obviously the man in command. "I'm Detective Walker. Phil Huber gave me a call and told me to keep an eye out. He sensed there might be some trouble."

"How did you know where to come?" Matt wondered.

His voice shook. He shot a glance behind him to make sure Lauren was safe.

Walker smiled and cocked his head toward Susan, who stood warily at the side. "Miss Miles's receptionist gave us a call when she found out that something had gone awry with your, uh, beauty consultation. Sorry we didn't get here sooner." He studied Matt's face. "We might have spared you a little of that."

Gingerly Matt fingered his cheek, then his mouth. In the next instant, he reached out for Lauren and hauled her close. She was eager to support him; he'd fought valiantly and had to be uncomfortable.

"Those three thugs intended to kill us," he said.

Lauren pointed. "Those *two* were the ones who kidnapped me back in Boston."

"No doubt," Matt added, his eyes filled with venom, "the third is another of Prinz's men."

"His name is Hank Ober, but he's called Rat," Susan stated stiffly. "The one with the ugly nose is Leo Charney, and the other, Mouse, is Malcolm Donnia." She watched as the three men were hustled off. "What will you do with them?"

The detective faced her. "Book them for attempted murder."

"Then what?"

"They'll be arraigned, and if they can post bond, they'll be released until their trial."

"*Released!* Do you know what they'll do once they hit the streets? They'll disappear. But before they do that, they'll finish off one or another of us, if not all three!"

"Susan..." Matt took her shoulder with his free hand. "That won't happen. The police won't *let* it—"

"The police! If they're not already in Ted's pocket, they will be soon!"

"Just a minute now," Walker growled. He took a menacing step closer. "I have never been, and will never be, in anyone's pocket, and I can safely vouch for three-quarters of my men."

"And the other quarter?"

"They won't be allowed anywhere *near* this case. The Ted Prinzes of the world would like to believe they can buy their way out of trouble, but it won't work here."

"You know of Ted?" Susan asked, wavering.

"Every major law-enforcement officer in the country knows of him. It will be one of the greatest thrills of my career to nail him, but I can do that only if you're willing to testify."

"You have to, Susan," Lauren begged. "Once and for all, it has to be put to rest."

Matt echoed her sentiment. "Lauren's right. If the three of us work together, we can do it. Lauren and I alone... well, it'll be tougher."

"He'll still come after me. It won't matter if he's in prison."

Walker spoke up. "He won't *dare* come after you. Nor will he send anyone else. He knows we'll be watching his every step. I've seen how these men work, Susan. Revenge may eat them alive, but in the end they opt for survival. Prinz will be signing his own death warrant if he comes near you again. He'll know that. Believe me, he'll know it."

Susan swallowed and looked from the detective to Matt and Lauren. "I want to believe. Really I do."

"Trust him," Matt urged. "Trust *us*. But then, you already do, don't you?"

"What makes you think that?" she returned, but there was a softness in her tone.

Matt smiled, then winced when his bruised lip protested.

He soothed the spot with his finger. "You really do know karate, but you don't try it on me. One kick, and you'd have escaped. The fact that you didn't try it had to mean something." He ventured a second smile, this one more carefully. "How *did* you learn it so quickly?"

Susan shrugged and gave a tentative grin of her own. "Like I told Leo, I'm a quick study."

Matt chuckled softly. Reaching out, he drew Susan to his side at the same time that his arm tightened around Lauren. "You'll work with us, Susan, won't you?"

Susan moistened her lips, but it was Lauren she was looking at. "After all you've gone through for me, I guess I'll have to." She jerked her head toward Matt. "Where did you even find this big lummox, Lauren? Do you think maybe he has an identical twin stashed away somewhere?"

Lauren grinned up at Matt. "I don't think there's another man like him on the face of the earth. He's pretty special, isn't he?"

Purpled cheek, bruised lip, battered ribs and all, Matt sucked in a deep breath and threw back his head. "Ahhhh. Paradise. One pretty lady on the left, one pretty lady on the right…if only my buddies at the beer hall could see me now!"

"THE BEER HALL? You never talked about a beer hall. For that matter," Lauren said, scowling, "you never said you were an avid hunter." They were back in the hotel room after spending the afternoon at the police station. Lauren had insisted that Matt take a long, hot bath to soothe his aching body, but now she had him in bed, exactly where she wanted him.

Matt looked up at her through one half-lidded eye. "Where did you think construction workers went for fun?" He steeled himself against an attack that never came.

"Did you get drunk?" Lauren asked.

"On occasion."

"What were you like...drunk?"

He shrugged the shoulder she wasn't leaning against. "I don't know. I was too far out of it to tell."

She grinned. "And the hunting?"

"Wooden ducks at an amusement park. We should go sometime. I'll win you a huge stuffed teddy bear."

Lauren settled onto him, gently and with a sigh. "Thanks, but I've already got one." She rubbed her ear against the tawny hair on his chest and stilled only when he began to stroke her back.

"You're pretty special yourself," he murmured. "The way you thought to go for that gun, and then the way you held it...I thought for a minute that *you* were the one with experience."

"All a bluff. I've never held a gun in my life."

"Not even a water gun?"

"Nope. My parents were pacifists. Dead set against weapons of any kind. That's one of the things that drove them crazy about Brad. He used to make guns out of whatever toys he had handy. Some of them were pretty creative."

"Lauren?"

She took a deep breath, inhaling the clean, male scent of his skin. "Mmm?"

"What will your parents say about me?"

"That depends," she said softly and raised her head. "It depends on what I tell them first."

"How about you tell them that I love you and want to marry you?"

"How about I tell them that you're fearless and strong, or that you've got brains as well as brawn, or that you saved my life?"

"I didn't save your life. You escaped from the warehouse on your own. Then, today, you were the one who saved all of our lives."

"You saved my life."

"How did I save your life?"

"You gave it deep, deep, lasting meaning. A good job is fine. So's a good house, even a pretty face. But the thing that really pulled it all together was you. I love you, Matt. Love is what counts. Always has been, always will be."

Matt cleared his throat, but his voice still came out hoarse. "How about you tell them that I love you and want to marry you?"

"They'll hit the roof, but you know something?" Lauren asked, pushing her chin out. "I don't care! If they love me—and I'm sure they do—they'll come around in time. So. Any other questions?"

"Just one. Aren't you worried about where we'll live?"

She turned the tables on him. "Are you?"

"No."

"Why not?"

"Because I've already decided that if my boss won't open a permanent Boston office, I'm quitting. I've made enough contacts here to get another job. And I love the farmhouse in Lincoln." He paused, narrowing his eyes. "But you knew that. You've known all along. You're too smart, that's what you are. You've got me wrapped around your little finger. Y'know, maybe I ought to rethink this. If I'm going to be led around by the nose for another fifty or sixty years—"

Lauren's lips silenced him, and within seconds he was fully involved in the nonverbal give-and-take of love. Belying the punishment he had taken that day, he rolled over to cover her with his body. Hands buried deep in her hair, hips poised above hers, he whispered thickly, ''...for another fifty or sixty years, I'll love it...every... sweet...minute.''

HARLEQUIN®
INTRIGUE®

HER SECRET PAST

Amanda Stevens

Amanda Stevens has written over twenty novels of romantic suspense. Her books have appeared on several bestseller lists, and she has won Reviewer's Choice and Career Achievement in Romantic/Mystery awards from *Romantic Times Magazine*. She resides in Cypress, Texas, with her husband, her son and daughter, and their two cats.

From the Editors...

Amanda Stevens has a special gift for creating intensely romantic characters and situations. Her deft plotting and emotional characterizations draw readers in and keep them turning pages as quickly as they can. Her strong heroines never fail to meet their matches in some of the most charismatic heroes around. You'll fall in love with Amanda's stories!

"Amanda Stevens always delivers what I want most in a book—excitement, romance, adventure.... Her stories are filled with a tenderness that keeps the reader emotionally involved to the very end." —Susan Wiggs

Her Secret Past
Amanda Stevens

PROLOGUE

Magnolia Bend, Mississippi

FRANKIE BODINE CUT the outboard motor on his flat-bottomed fishing boat and drifted toward the iron girders of the old Choppowah River bridge. Tying off, he threw a fishing line overboard and then situated himself in the bottom of the boat, head propped on one of the plank seats as he gazed at the stars.

It was so quiet out here, he sometimes imagined he could hear the phantom cries of the Confederate soldiers who had been ambushed in the piney woods just upstream. He knew the sounds were made by the whippoorwills and the hoot owls that nested in the trees, but it was easy to get spooked on the river.

One night, peering over his boat at the blackened surface of the water, Frankie could have sworn he'd seen a reflection that wasn't his staring back at him. The image had been that of a woman with long blond hair.

Frankie had convinced himself that the face hadn't been a reflection at all, but the ghost of Miranda Tremain, who had thrown herself off the bridge a few years back. The body— what was left of it—hadn't been found until two weeks later, thirty miles downstream, and by then, the catfish and the gar had been at her.

Frankie shuddered, remembering the stories he'd heard all his life about the man-size alligator gar that lay on the muddy river bottom near the bridge, waiting for someone to fall into the water. Or to jump, like Miranda Tremain had done.

But in spite of his fears, Frankie loved the river. It was the only place where he could feel at ease. His sister, Winny, called him special—others in town called him slow. He didn't learn things the way regular people did, didn't understand some of their ways, so when he'd turned fifteen, Judge Tremain had sent him away to a special school, one with bars on the windows and locks on the doors. One far away from the river.

There had been times when Frankie thought he might die in that place, had even wished for it. His hatred for the judge had festered deep inside him back then, but by the time Frankie was let out at eighteen, his rage had turned into a strange kind of acceptance.

He'd been free now for over two years, and except for the occasional visit from Winny, he lived alone in the old two-room house where he'd grown up. He kept to himself mostly, and generally, everyone left him alone.

A car engine sounded in the distance, but Frankie tried to ignore the intrusion by counting the lightning bugs that darted through the cypress knees near the bank. As the sound drew nearer, he sat up in the boat and listened.

The car came to a stop almost directly over Frankie. He waited for the whoops and rebel yells of the teenagers who came out here to drink beer, but when all remained silent, he decided it must be a couple who'd come to park. The thought made him a little uneasy, and he wondered if he should start up his motor and take off.

But he remained where he was, and after another few moments of silence, a car door opened. Footsteps rumbled on the wood flooring overhead, and then another door opened. As Frankie looked up, he saw the shimmer of illumination between the cracks in the planks where the interior light was on in the car. The light went out when the door was closed, and then he heard scraping sounds against the wood, as if something were being dragged.

He thought at first someone was dumping trash. The river bottom was littered with old stoves and refrigerators, even a car or two that had been pushed into the water to collect insurance. Frankie wondered if he should holler up at them, let them know he was there so maybe they'd just up and go away. But before he could decide what to do, something fell from the bridge, and a loud splash set his boat to rocking.

Someone had jumped off the bridge!

Frankie's heart slammed into his chest, and for a split second, he couldn't breathe. Someone had jumped off the bridge—just like Miranda Tremain had done.

But even as that thought came to him, footsteps hurried along the plank flooring above him. A car door opened and closed, and the engine, which had been idling the whole time Frankie realized now, gunned as the car was put into gear. The vehicle shot forward at a dangerous speed, and Frankie thought for a moment the car might come hurtling over the railing, too.

But at the end of the bridge, the car slowed and pulled off the road to make a sweeping turn, and then roared across the wooden planks again, back in the direction it had come from. When it reached the end of the bridge, the headlights came on.

Frankie watched as the car rounded the sharp curve in the road that made it visible for an instant from where he sat beneath the bridge. He couldn't tell in the dark the make or model of the car, but he knew it was headed back toward town.

Or was it?

In the distance, the white chimneys of Amberly gleamed in the moonlight. The place was gloomy in the dark, full of legends and ghosts. It was a house that had driven Miranda Tremain to her death one night.

The roar of fear in his ears brought Frankie's attention back to the water, to the rippling circles that marked the spot where the body had gone under seconds before.

What in the world should he do?

CHAPTER ONE

Houston, Texas, nine years later

THE WOMAN WITH the platinum hair was staring at her again. Caught in the act, the blonde dropped her gaze to the menu in front of her, but Amy Calloway knew the woman had been watching her ever since she'd followed Amy into Miguel's, a Mexican restaurant popular with the downtown lunch crowd.

Turning the tables on the woman, Amy studied her for a long moment, but didn't recognize her. The layered hair, dark suit and lacquered nails could have belonged to any number of the young professional women—including Amy, who worked for a small but innovative advertising firm—populating downtown Houston during work hours.

But whoever the blonde was, she didn't appear threatening, so after another moment, Amy gave up the game and idly sketched on a paper napkin while she waited for her fiancé to join her for lunch.

She scowled as her pen flew over the paper. It was still hard to believe she was getting married in two weeks. Harder still to believe that a man like Reece Kantner, a handsome, ambitious, brilliant attorney, was willing to accept her just the way she was. No questions asked.

And maybe, just maybe, that was why those nagging doubts had been plaguing her for the past few weeks, Amy mused. Maybe she'd feel a little better about the impending marriage if Reece *would* ask those questions, if he weren't quite so willing— eager even—to accept the fact that she couldn't remember anything beyond nine years ago.

"You must at least be curious about my past," she'd said to him recently.

"How many times do I have to tell you? I know everything about you I need to know. I'm only interested in the woman you are now." And then, to prove just how insignificant her memory loss was to him, he'd persuaded her to move up their wedding date. The sooner they married, the sooner she could get rid of her fears, he'd reasoned.

His arguments had made sense at the time, but now Amy regretted having given in to his wishes. She felt rushed and off balance, and found herself wondering, all too often, if she was doing the right thing.

It was probably just a case of nerves, she told herself firmly. Prewedding jitters. She'd been alone for so long the prospect of sharing her life with someone was bound to be daunting.

Sighing, she glanced down at the drawing on her napkin. The masculine features she'd sketched were not those of her fiancé, but in some ways, they were more familiar to her than Reece's.

Amy had no idea who the man was. Over the

years, she'd simply come to refer to him as the Face, the unknown man with the dark eyes and the angry expression.

For all she knew, he didn't even exist outside her imagination, but he'd come to her nine years ago, after she'd awakened in a strange hospital with no recollection of who she was or what had happened to her.

Her aunt Nona, after a while, had gently explained to Amy that she'd been in a tragic accident. A fire had taken her parents' lives and destroyed their family home in Iowa. Amy had been seriously injured after a fall from her upstairs bedroom window while trying to escape the burning house.

Nona, Amy had soon learned, wasn't a blood relative but her dead mother's best friend since childhood and Amy's godmother. Since Amy had no other family and no one to take care of her, Nona had traveled to Des Moines and brought Amy back to the Houston hospital where Nona worked as head nurse.

Upon Amy's release from the hospital, Nona had insisted she move in with her, and Amy had been very grateful. With her parents gone and her personal belongings all destroyed in the fire, there was nothing left of her former life, not even memories. The past, with all its tragedy and heartache, appeared to be lost to her forever, and maybe, Nona had often said, it was better that way. Maybe it was better if Amy never remembered what had happened.

But shortly after she'd gone to live with Nona,

the Face had begun to appear to Amy, sometimes in her dreams, sometimes when she was fully awake. She would draw him, over and over, and when she showed the sketches to Nona, her aunt explained that he was probably someone Amy had known back in Iowa. A neighbor or a boy from school. Someone from her past but no one important. No one for Amy to worry about.

Why, then, couldn't she forget him? Why did his face haunt her at the oddest times—during a crucial meeting, in the middle of the night, in the arms of her fiancé? Why were the visions almost always accompanied by the coldest of chills, the blackest feelings of dread and fear?

Amy stared down at the Face and shuddered. She literally had hundreds of drawings of this man. His face—the shadowy eyes, the sensuous mouth that contrasted sharply with the rigid set of his jaw and chin, the angry scowl—was the only image she had from her past.

But Nona had been so meticulous in supplying Amy with the details of her life before the fire that she sometimes thought she *could* remember her home in Iowa, her parents and even the little Scottish terrier named Mickey she'd had as a child. The vivid images Nona created were like the homey figures in a Norman Rockwell painting.

But the Face didn't belong with those memories. To that contentment.

The Face sparked a turmoil inside Amy she didn't dare explore.

Sensing the woman's gaze on her again, Amy

looked up. This time, the blonde didn't glance away, but held Amy's gaze for a long, enigmatic moment. Then she rose from her table and walked toward the booth where Amy sat facing the entrance.

When she stopped at the booth, Amy stared up at her. The woman hesitated, biting her lower lip as if not quite certain what to say. A cloud of musky perfume enveloped her as she bent forward slightly, staring into Amy's upturned face. "I can't believe it," she finally murmured.

"Excuse me?"

The woman shook her head. "I know it's impossible, but…" She trailed off, her gaze raking Amy's features.

Amy frowned. "Do I know you?"

The woman remained silent for a moment, her gaze one of astonishment. Then, as if collecting herself, she explained in a rush, "I'm…sorry. I know you must think I'm crazy, but I'm not a stalker or anything like that. It's just…when I spotted you out on the street, I thought I'd seen a ghost, so I followed you in here, just to get a better look. But even up close like this…my God—" She broke off, shaking her head in disbelief. "The resemblance is uncanny. The hair…those eyes…"

Amy shifted uncomfortably against the red vinyl upholstery. She wished the woman would go away and leave her alone. The intense scrutiny was unnerving.

As if sensing Amy's discomfort, the blonde apologized again. "I'm sorry. I don't mean to stare, but you look exactly like someone I went to high school with back in Mississippi.''

"I'm afraid I couldn't be her, then," Amy tried to say lightly. "I'm originally from Iowa. I've never even been to Mississippi." But even as she voiced the denial, a powerful emotion swept over her, a longing so intense it was almost a physical ache. The scent of magnolia blossoms swirled through her senses, and the sound of a whisper came to her. A man's voice murmuring to her how much he loved her. How much he wanted her.

What he would do if he couldn't have her.

Startled by the memory, Amy glanced down at her drawing. Without knowing why, she picked up the napkin and turned it over, so the blonde couldn't see the Face.

"Oh, I know you're not her," the woman was saying. "You couldn't possibly be her. Amber Tremain is dead."

Her words sent a chill coursing through Amy's veins. "Dead?" she repeated vaguely.

The woman nodded, her eyes glittering. "She drowned in the river, just like her poor mother. It must have been a family curse or something." She paused, then said, "Of course, there were some who thought she'd just run off. That would have been like Amber."

Amy had no idea why the woman's story distressed her so much, why that name had jolted her. She'd never seen the blonde before. Had never been to Mississippi. Had never heard of anyone named Amber Tremain.

And yet…

A memory tugged at her. Maybe she *had* heard that name before.

And then it came to her all of a sudden. Her aunt had mentioned an Amber Tremain several months ago, after Nona had first been diagnosed with breast cancer and she'd learned her prognosis wasn't good. She'd broken the news to Amy over dinner, and then the two of them had stayed up all night talking.

For the first time since Amy had moved in with her aunt, Nona had told her about growing up dirt-poor in a rural Mississippi town, the same place where Amy's mother had been raised.

Nona had also talked about a younger brother, who still lived there, even though he'd been ostracized by the community because of his learning disabilities. When he was fifteen, a girl had accused him of trying to assault her.

"My brother wouldn't hurt a fly," Nona had said angrily. But the judge who heard the case had been good friends with the girl's mother. He'd sent the boy to a state mental hospital until he turned eighteen. The incarceration had all but killed him. When he'd finally gotten out, Nona, by then a widow, tried time and again to get him to move to Houston and live with her so that she could protect him, but he refused because of his almost fierce sense of independence.

"The judge's name was Tremain. Emmett Tremain," Nona said, studying Amy with an intensity she didn't understand.

"He doesn't sound like someone I'd want to know," Amy replied loyally.

Nona shrugged. "The Tremains had their good points. Though I never could forgive the judge for what he did to my brother, I always admired his first wife. Her name was Miranda. She was a lovely woman, the best I remember. Very kind and gentle. She committed suicide one night by jumping off a bridge into the river. Her body was found two weeks later."

A profound sadness came over Amy. She hugged her arms around her middle, as if in protection. "Why did she kill herself?"

Nona shook her head as her gaze grew even more intense. "No one ever knew. But it must have been something terrible for her to leave behind her two daughters. The youngest, Jasmine, I think her name was, was hardly more than a baby. The other one was a teenager. Her name was Amber. Amber Tremain."

As the memory faded, Amy realized she was gripping the edge of the table so hard her knuckles whitened. She stood abruptly, feeling as if those dark waters that had taken Miranda Tremain's life were closing over her own head. Amy didn't understand her panic. Her sudden fear. All she knew was that she had to get out of the restaurant and fast. She thought, somewhat dramatically, that her very life might depend on it.

"Excuse me," she blurted, glancing at the blonde. "I have to go now. I just remembered an appointment."

The woman looked alarmed. "I hope I haven't upset you."

"No, of course not." Amy gathered up her purse and briefcase. But when she tried to brush by her, the woman caught Amy's arm, and for a moment, they stood staring into one another's eyes.

"It's amazing. You really are a dead ringer for Amber Tremain. Same height, same body type, same hair. Even your eyes. I've never seen anyone else with those same strange-colored eyes. If I didn't know better..." She broke off, shuddering. "Amber's body was never found," she murmured, almost to herself.

Her gaze lifted to meet Amy's, and Amy suppressed her own shudder, pulling her arm from the woman's grasp. "I assure you, I'm not her. I've never seen you before in my life, and I don't know anyone named Amber Tremain. Now, if you'll excuse me—"

Amy turned and hurried through the crowded restaurant, refusing to look back even though she could feel the woman's gaze on her. But once she reached the door, she couldn't resist. She glanced over her shoulder and saw that the blonde was still standing at the booth, scowling down at the table. As Amy watched, the woman reached down and picked up the napkin Amy had left behind.

The napkin on which she'd drawn the Face.

The woman looked up, and her gaze met Amy's once more. Slowly the woman smiled.

"IT WAS THE strangest encounter," Amy told Reece that evening as she sat across from him at a beautifully set dinner table in his uptown apartment. The crystal and china gleamed in the flickering light from a dozen votive candles, but the effect was lost on Amy. Her fingers trembled as she smoothed the linen napkin over the skirt of her green silk sheath.

"I haven't been able to get it out of my mind. I keep asking myself what I would do if I found out I'm not really Amy Calloway." She hesitated. "What would *you* do?"

Reece, pouring his favorite Chilean wine into two crystal goblets, glanced at her with amused indulgence over the dancing flames. "You mean if I suddenly found out I'm not Reece Kantner? That's an interesting question. I don't know what I'd do, but I'm sure my mother would be greatly relieved."

Amy frowned, in no mood for levity. "I'm serious about this."

His smile disappeared, and his expression grew sober. He sat back in his chair and sighed. "I know you are. And I'm sorry if I tried to make light of what happened. I know this has been bothering you all day, but I still think you're making too much of it. Just because a woman in a restaurant thought you looked like someone she used to know doesn't mean you have some deep, dark, mysterious past." He cut a piece of tomato in his salad and speared it with his fork. "Besides, you know what they say—everyone has a double. I'm always being told I look like someone's cousin or neighbor or college roommate. It happens all the time."

"Yes, but that's not the same thing," Amy said

impatiently. "You don't have a past you can't remember."

Restless, she picked up her wineglass and turned to stare out into the darkness while Reece ate his salad. The view from his high-rise usually enthralled her, but tonight the string of lights along Post Oak Boulevard and the 610 Loop seemed as chaotic and aimless as her thoughts.

The soft click as the central-air-conditioning unit came on caused her to jump, giving away her edginess, and she turned back to gaze at Reece across the candle glow. More than anything, she wanted to take comfort in his presence tonight, in the familiarity of their relationship, but for some reason, his good looks were even more intimidating than usual to her. Was it because their wedding day was only two weeks away?

It was only natural to have reservations, Amy reminded herself. After all, she'd only met Reece a few months ago, under very trying circumstances. How well did she really know him? How well *could* she know him when she'd suddenly discovered she might not even know herself?

"You haven't touched your salad," he commented.

Amy shrugged. "I'm not hungry tonight."

Reece placed his knife and fork on his salad plate and shoved it aside. "Talk to me, Amy," he urged softly. "Don't shut me out."

"I'm not trying to shut you out. It's just…" She waited a heartbeat, then said, "I can't explain what's happening to me. It's like I've been blindsided. Everything has changed suddenly. The moment that woman mentioned Amber Tremain..." She trailed off again as a quiver of emotion shot through her.

"But you said you'd heard your aunt mention the name before," Reece pointed out. "Don't you think that's why you reacted to it?"

"I think that only adds to my confusion. Just before she died, Aunt Nona mentioned someone named Amber Tremain, and then I'm told, months later, that I look exactly like her."

"I admit, it is a strange coincidence."

"But you told me once you didn't believe in coincidences."

They'd first met five months ago at the M. D. Anderson Cancer Center, where Amy's aunt and Reece's father were undergoing chemotherapy at the same time. Reece had told Amy from the first that their meeting in the face of tragedy wasn't due to coincidence but fate.

Amy had desperately wanted to believe him. With her aunt gone, Amy had had no one to turn to, no one to count on. Reece had been there for her in the days following Nona's death when Amy had needed him the most, and she knew he would be again. So why wasn't that enough?

As if reading her thoughts, he leaned toward her. "Let's assume, for the sake of argument, that none of this is a coincidence. Why didn't you have the same reaction when your aunt first mentioned Amber Tremain several months ago?"

"I've thought about that," Amy admitted. She bit her lip for a moment, contemplating. "I think I did have some of those same feelings I had today, but I was still in shock from learning about my aunt's cancer. When she told me about Amber's mother committing suicide, I felt an almost overwhelming sadness, but I thought it was because Aunt Nona had just told me *she* was dying.

"But now that I look back, now that I remember her expression, the way she studied me that night...even her timing...it was as if she was leading up to something. Trying to tell me something, but just couldn't quite bring herself to do it."

"Are you saying you think you *are* this woman?" Something that might have been excitement flashed in Reece's eyes, but in the next instant, his brows drew together in a deep frown. "How could that be possible? The woman in the restaurant told you Amber Tremain is dead."

"She also said Amber's body was never found."

A pall fell over the room. Somewhere in the background, Amy was aware of the steady hum of the air conditioner, the faint ticking of the grandfather clock in the foyer, a myriad of tiny sounds but none so loud as her own heartbeat, drumming an unsteady rhythm in her ears. Did she really believe she was Amber Tremain?

The scent of magnolia blossoms filled the air suddenly. It was as if the ghost of Amy's past, wearing a sweet and haunting perfume, had drifted into the room. Amy knew the scent wasn't real, and yet the fragrance was so overpowering, so provocative, she found it difficult to breathe.

"I don't know what I believe," she said with a

sigh. "I don't know who I am anymore. If I am Amber Tremain, why did Aunt Nona feel compelled to lie to me? Why did she tell me I was from Iowa, that my family died there, when all along she knew it wasn't true?"

Reece took another sip of his wine. His attitude was almost casual. "Even if Nona did lie to you about certain aspects of your past, it was probably because she was trying to protect you. From everything you've told me about her, and from what little I saw of her before she died, she loved you very much. You were like a daughter to her. If there was something in your past she thought might cause you pain, she would have wanted to shield you from it."

"Like what?"

He shrugged. "I don't know. Didn't the woman say that some people thought Amber had run away? Maybe there was some kind of turmoil in her life."

Amy put her hands to her face for a moment. Her fingers trembled against her skin. "None of this makes any sense. Aunt Nona told me so much about my past, how wonderful my parents were. She even told me the reason I had a Southern drawl was because my mother had grown up in the Deep South, and I'd picked up her accent. She had an answer for everything, and it all made sense. My past sounded so idyllic—" She broke off, her gaze darting to Reece's. "So...perfect. A past too good to be true."

Reece reached across the table and took her hand. "Let's not jump to conclusions. We'll figure this thing out together."

But Amy barely heard him. She stared off into

space, her thoughts chaotic and troubled. "I keep asking myself all the questions I should have asked before. Why did I never meet Aunt Nona's brother? I never knew about him until she was dying, and even then she wouldn't tell me his name. I didn't know how to get in touch with him when she died."

"You said Nona's lawyer took care of all the details, including disbursing her estate. Maybe her attorney notified the brother, and for whatever reason, he couldn't be here for the funeral."

"Maybe. But it all seems so secretive now." Amy let out a shaky breath. "There are a lot of other things that bother me, too. I don't understand why I didn't go back to Iowa when I got out of the hospital. I was desperately trying to get my memory back. Why didn't Aunt Nona encourage me to go back? Surely that would have been the logical treatment for an amnesiac, and yet I can't remember that I ever seriously considered the possibility. It was as if I knew, on some level, that the memories Aunt Nona gave me, the home and family she created for me, weren't real. But to question them, to not have accepted them, would have meant facing something I didn't want to face." Rather than confronting a fear greater than anything she could imagine, an unknown terror she couldn't begin to explain, Amy had believed in those memories Nona had given to her. She'd accepted the past her aunt had created for her. And she'd tried, for nine long years, to be a woman who may never have existed.

Pushing herself from the table, Amy got up and walked to the windows, staring out. A mist had de scended over the city, obscuring the tops of the downtown skyscrapers, making the buildings seem shimmery and nebulous in the distance, as if they were floating in clouds.

Like my past, Amy thought, staring at her reflection in the glass, studying her features and seeing, as if for the first time, the thick blond hair pulled back from an oval face with cheekbones a little too prominent, a mouth a little too generous and a nose a little too straight. But her most dominant feature had always been her eyes. Light golden brown, almost tawny, they tilted slightly at the corners, giving an exotic touch to what otherwise would have been a mildly attractive face.

So who are you? she wondered uneasily. Amy Calloway? Or the ghost of Amber Tremain?

The image in the window wavered, then reformed as if someone else's features had been superimposed over hers. The dark eyes, the seductive mouth, the angry expression seemed to taunt her. Only he knew the secrets of her past.

So come and find me, his image whispered to her. *Come and find me…if you dare.*

Amy shivered as those same intense emotions rolled over her again—dread, fear and an almost excruciating excitement that tingled like an electrical shock through every nerve ending in her body.

Was it possible? Did she have a family out there somewhere? People who loved her, missed her, wondered what had happened to her?

The loneliness of the past nine years filled her with an unbearable sadness, a yearning deep inside her that Amy could no more explain than she could wish away. It had been a part of her, of who she was, for far too long.

When Reece came up behind her and wrapped his arms around her, she tensed, unable to relax in his embrace. Taking a deep breath, she turned to face him. "I have to pursue this. I have to learn the truth about my past. If Aunt Nona did lie to me, then I have to find out why."

"I know you do."

Surprised that he'd given her no argument, Amy turned back to the window. She could see his reflection in the glass, could see that he was smiling, and a tiny shiver of unease raced up her spine.

He bent and nuzzled the back of her neck. "I'm here for you, Amy, just like I was when Nona died. I'll do whatever I can to help you." His voice was soft and warm, gently coercive, but Amy found herself recoiling this time from his seductive persuasion.

"I'm...not sure how I want to go about this."

"Then let me handle it for you." He massaged the tense muscles in her shoulders. "I'll get one of the investigators we use at the firm to do some checking for you. By the time we get back from our honeymoon—"

"No!" The word almost exploded from Amy, shocking them both. She shook her head. "I don't want some stranger poking around in my past." Why? Because she was afraid of what he might find?

After a moment, Reece said, "Okay. We'll do it

ourselves, then. They say you can find out almost anything on the Internet these days.'' His tone was ironic as he smiled at her reflection.

Amy said slowly, ''I'm not sure that's what I want, either.''

His hands stilled on her shoulders. ''What *do* you want?''

She hesitated. ''This is something I have to do alone, Reece.''

''Alone?'' He sounded incredulous. ''But why? Why won't you let me help you?''

Amy couldn't explain it, but exploring her past and discovering her true identity was a journey she had to make by herself. She couldn't allow anyone, not even Reece, to uncover her memories and secrets until she had a chance to sort through them on her own.

Because there was a chance, she thought with a shudder of fear, that she might need to rebury them.

Avoiding his question, she said, ''In some strange way, I think I've always known that I'm not Amy Calloway. I'm not the nice, sweet, uncomplicated girl from Iowa Aunt Nona tried to create. Which means I'm not the woman you want to marry.''

''You're wrong about that.'' Reece turned her again in his arms. His eyes glinted with a sudden emotion Amy was hard-pressed to name. ''I know everything I need to know about you, and I still want to marry you. More than ever. You have to believe that.''

Amy wished she could believe it, but unfortunately, along with all of Reece's good qualities came

an ambition to succeed that almost bordered on obsession. She supposed it resulted from never measuring up to his parents' expectations. Reece's older
brother had been the golden child, and had, upon
their father's death, inherited the bulk of the family
fortune.

Reece had been devastated, and his ambition had
only grown keener since then. He had his eye on a
full partnership in his law firm, an almost unheard-
of accomplishment for someone his age. What
would happen if something from Amy's past—some
forgotten scandal—surfaced to threaten his position,
his future?

An image of the Face suddenly burned in her
mind, and Amy shuddered. Who was he, and why
was his angry expression the only thing from her
past she could remember?

Had he been someone special to her?

Or someone dangerous to her?

Amy closed her eyes briefly, willing her strength.
"I can't marry you, Reece—"

Putting a fingertip to her lips, he cut her off before
she could finish. "Don't say that. Don't even think
it. You're just upset. Confused. You didn't mean
it."

"But I did mean it. I can't plan a future with you
when all of this is hanging over my head. It
wouldn't be right. It wouldn't be fair to you."

He gripped her shoulders, his eyes flaring with
sudden anger. "Why don't you let me be the judge
of what's right or wrong for me? For God's sake,
you're overreacting. Think about it. The wedding is

only a couple of weeks away. It's only natural you'd have jitters. Second thoughts, even. You're just using all this other stuff as an excuse.''

"Reece—"

"You *need* me. You need me now more than ever. Haven't I always been there for you?"

His grasp tightened on her, and Amy winced at the pain. She tried to pull away, but he wouldn't let her go. A tiny bubble of panic rose inside her.

"Please don't make this harder than it already is," she whispered. "I don't want to hurt you. That's the last thing I want. But I've been having doubts for weeks, and if you'd be honest, I think you'd have to admit that you have, too. You know as well as I do this wedding would be a mistake.''

He stared down at her, his gaze dark and turbulent. "Damn you, I've come too far to let you pull the rug out from under me now. I won't let you stop this wedding.''

Amy stared at him in shock. He'd always been so gentle with her, so accommodating, but the man she saw before her now was almost a stranger. "What do you mean, you've come too far?"

He paused, drawing in a long breath as if to quell his growing temper. Turning away from her, he rubbed the back of his neck. "I'm sorry. Forgive me. I shouldn't have spoken to you like that. I only meant that I've let my feelings for you go too far. I care about you too much to let you walk away from everything we could have together.''

"I'm sorry, too," Amy said, staring at his profile.

"But this is something I have to do. And after you've had time to think about it—"

"I'll what? Come to agree with you?" He gave her a quelling glance. "Don't count on it. And don't expect me to make this easy for you. I'll fight for you, if that's what you want. I'll do whatever I have to, but this isn't over. I won't let it be."

He turned his back on her then, and Amy watched him for a moment longer, wondering how she could have let things get this far. Loneliness was a powerful motivator, but even that was no excuse for making bad decisions. Reece was not the man for her. A part of her had known that all along, even as another part, the lonely part, had wanted to believe that marriage and a family could fill the dark void inside her heart.

But now Amy knew the truth. There was only one way to fill that emptiness. She couldn't go forward with her life until she'd gone back to search for her past.

The scent of magnolia blossoms rose around her as she slipped the engagement ring from her finger and placed it on the table.

CHAPTER TWO

Magnolia Bend, two weeks later

AMY STARED DOWN at the river, the calm surface discordant with the turmoil raging inside her. She wiped her clammy palms on the sides of her white sundress, unmindful of the rusty streaks she left behind as she forced herself to study her surroundings, trying to conjure a memory.

What was she doing here anyway? What force had compelled her to leave the main road, which would have led her, according to her map, to a new bridge a few miles farther downstream? Once across the river, she could have either turned left off the highway onto a two-lane blacktop road that would take her into town, or she could turn right and go directly to Amberly, the plantation home where Amber Tremain had been born and raised.

But some strange impulse had caused her to turn off the highway and follow a narrow, dusty road that snaked along the river's edge. Then, rounding a corner, she'd spotted the rusted iron girders of the bridge rising over the water, and at that very moment, Amy had been overcome with fear. Heart-pounding, mind-numbing terror had washed over her like sheets of cold, hard rain.

She'd given in to the panic for only a split second before she'd stopped the car, gotten out and walked to the bridge, determined to face this first hurdle head-on. Gingerly, she'd stepped across the wood flooring to stand at the railing, gazing at the water some thirty feet below her.

But the fear wouldn't abate. If anything, it grew more overpowering the longer she stood there. And yet for some unexplainable reason, Amy couldn't move. She remained on the bridge, letting the terror crawl through her, almost welcoming it, because the emotion told her exactly what she needed to know.

She'd been here before. She knew this bridge. There was a very good chance, as she'd come to believe in the past two weeks, that she was Amber Tremain.

Once Amy had seen the picture of Amber Tremain in an old Jackson, Mississippi, newspaper, her doubts had all but vanished. The resemblance was too great to pass off as a coincidence. And the fact that Amber had disappeared nine years ago, almost to the day that Amy had awakened in a Houston hospital without her memory, was even further proof.

None of it was a coincidence; of that, she was certain, but why the lies? Why had Nona painstakingly created such an idyllic past for her? Why had she never told Amy the truth? What had the woman who claimed to be her aunt been protecting her from?

The answers, Amy was almost certain, lay hidden here on this bridge, in those murky depths thirty feet below her, in the shadowy countryside that wrapped all around her.

"So it is you," a masculine voice said behind her.

Amy hadn't heard him approach. She whirled, and as her gaze met his, her heart vaulted to her throat. For one dizzying moment, she couldn't breathe.

The Face swam before her, no longer a figment of her imagination, but terrifyingly real. The dark eyes, the sensuous mouth, the angry expression were all the same, but there was no mistaking the fact that this man was flesh and blood.

In the space of a heartbeat, Amy's gaze flickered over him. She'd sketched his face hundreds of times, but she'd never wondered about his overall appearance, perhaps because she'd managed to convince herself he wasn't real. But now, in an instant, she noticed breathlessly how tall he was, how menacing he seemed.

He wasn't handsome, not even very attractive with a day's growth of beard shadowing his face and a body lean to the point of gauntness. The faded jeans and white, sleeveless undershirt he wore hung loosely on his thin frame, but there was still something about him, an innate magnetism, that made Amy's heart flail painfully against her chest. Who was he and why was she so afraid of him?

"I heard you were coming back, but I didn't much believe it." His voice was low and husky, edged with something that might have been anger.

When Amy remained silent, he cocked his head and stared down at her. "It is you, isn't it? Or am I seeing a ghost?"

"I'm not a ghost," she finally managed to say.

He lifted a dark brow. "No? Maybe I should check that out for myself." He reached out a hand to touch her, but Amy flinched away. His dark brown gaze narrowed on her as his expression hardened. "What's the matter, Amber? Don't you remember me?"

"No. I'm afraid I don't." She put a hand to her throat, trying to stifle the rush of fear. "I don't remember anything, or anyone, before nine years ago."

"I heard that, too," he said. "But I didn't much believe that, either."

Amy stared at him helplessly. "Why not? It's the truth."

"The truth?" He gave her a quizzical smile. "I doubt you'd know the truth if it smacked you right in the face. But amnesia, that's good. And the P.I. you hired to come snooping around down here was a brilliant touch—I'll give you that."

"P.I.?" she said weakly. Had Reece sent an investigator against her wishes? "I don't know what you're talking about."

The man's smile turned into a smirk. "You always were one hell of a liar."

At his biting words, Amy experienced a sinking feeling in the pit of her stomach. She'd had such hopes, when she'd first begun her quest, of finding a family and friends who had been missing her all these years, who had been desperately trying to find her, who would welcome her back into their hearts. Then she would finally *belong*.

But this man's animosity dashed those dreams. What had she done to him? What had Amber Tremain done to him?

"Who are you?" she blurted.

"Why don't you think on it for a while? I'm sure it'll come back to you." His gaze swept over her in a manner so familiar, Amy's insides trembled in warning. But she returned his stare, refusing to give in to the panic that told her to head back to Houston as fast as she could.

From some hidden place inside her, an unfamiliar emotion rose to the surface, momentarily overshadowing the panic. Amy barely recognized the defiance, the foolhardy recklessness that made her lift her chin and glare at him with chilly disdain. "I'm sorry, but I *don't* remember you," she said. "I do have amnesia, whether you believe it or not. I only came back here to—"

"I know why you came back," he cut in. "Everyone in town knows. Little sister's eighteen now." He waved a hand toward the river, encompassing the hardwood forest beyond and the white chimney tops peeping through the trees. "Amberly would have been all hers…if you hadn't come back."

Amy frowned. "Look, I didn't hire any private investigator to come snooping around down here, as you put it—and my interest in Amberly is solely because it's Amber Tremain's ancestral home." She stopped and drew in a deep breath. "The only reason I'm here is to try and find out who I really am. I don't even know if I am Amber.''

''Oh, you're Amber, all right.'' The dark gaze, insolent and thorough, moved over her again.

''How can you be so sure? I've been Amy Calloway for a very long time. I doubt I'm anything like the person you knew.''

''Some things, and some people, never change. But there's one way to find out for certain.'' He moved toward her slowly, in a manner so deliberate Amy was reminded of a wild animal stalking its prey. Instinctively, she took a step back from him, and felt the iron balustrade on the bridge give way against her weight.

The railing tore loose from the rusted support with a shrill metallic squeal. Amy felt herself plunging backward, and in the split second before he caught her, an image flashed through her. A disembodied hand reaching out of darkness. Someone falling from the bridge…

Shaken by the vision, Amy gasped and glanced over her shoulder at the water far below. His grip tightening on her wrists, he let her waver on the edge, his gaze smoldering. ''Careful,'' he warned. ''This bridge is dangerous. You could get hurt if you don't watch out.''

Amy had never seen eyes as deep and ominous as his. Mesmerized, she couldn't seem to look away as he held her there, at the very brink of disaster. But even through her panic, she realized instinctively that she was not in immediate danger. She wasn't going to fall—not if he didn't want her to.

In spite of his lean appearance, he was very strong. A tiny snake tattooed on his left arm drew her attention to the bulging, well-defined muscles, and Amy's fear gave way to something darker and far more dangerous.

She lifted her gaze to meet his, trembling in spite of herself, and a look of almost perverse satisfaction flickered in his eyes before he pulled her away from the edge of the bridge. He didn't release her, though, and for some reason Amy couldn't fathom, she didn't struggle to get away from him.

"Who are you?" she whispered.

He hesitated, as if deciding whether or not to answer. Then he shrugged and said, "My name's Conner Sullivan. People around here call me Con."

"Why do you hate me…Con?"

At the sound of his name on her lips, his expression froze. He released her so abruptly she almost stumbled. "Who said anything about hate?"

"You didn't have to say it," she told him. "I can see it in your eyes. Hear it in your voice. What did I do to you?"

He didn't say anything, but turned away from her instead to scan the wooded countryside behind her. His eyes grew distant and bleak and for a moment, Amy thought she glimpsed something beyond the darkness. A glimmer of pain that made her, for some insane reason, want to reach up and caress the beard-roughened cheek. To smooth back the short dark hair that had fallen across his forehead. To lift her lips to a kiss she instinctively knew would be soul shattering.

"You wanted me to believe you were dead."

The emptiness in his voice seemed to mirror the void deep inside Amy. She felt tears spring to her eyes, though she had no idea why. "Why would I do that? What happened the night I…Amber disappeared?"

He turned back to her then, his expression so cold Amy thought she must have imagined the hurt. "The night you left, you mean."

He'd released her, but he hadn't moved away. He stood so close, Amy could see the deeply etched lines around his mouth and eyes, the hardened resolve in a face that shouldn't have been alluring, yet somehow was. She said uncertainly, "Do you really believe that's what happened? That…Amber just left? Some people thought she drowned."

"They were fools," he said, his eyes blazing with sudden anger. "They didn't know you like I did."

"But…how can you be so certain I am Amber?"

"Because I *know*."

"How?" She'd meant to challenge him, but somehow that one word seemed to provoke him. He grasped her shoulders, pulling her toward him again, bringing his face so close to hers that for one breathless moment, Amy was sure he would kiss her. Her heart beat wildly inside her as she wondered fleetingly what she should do. Push him away, risk angering him even more or…succumb and hope for the best.

"*How?*" He flung the word back at her. "Jesus Christ, did you think I wouldn't recognize you? That hair, those eyes, those…lips?" He said the last word almost brutally, closing his eyes briefly as if trying to beat back some untamable beast inside him. "I don't care what name you call yourself now—I'd know you anywhere. You can't fool me. I'm the guy who stood right here on this bridge with you that night, Amber."

The image of the disembodied hand, reaching out of the darkness, shot through Amy again, and she put a hand to her mouth, trying to suppress the scream that rose inside her. She knew without a doubt this man was dangerous to her, but she couldn't move away from him. He held her prisoner, more with his dark gaze than with his hands.

Amy opened her mouth—to say what—she wasn't quite certain—but he never gave her the chance to speak. Instead, he pulled her even nearer, until their lips were only inches apart, until her knees grew weak and her heart beat a painful staccato against her chest.

"Look me in the eye and tell me you don't remember," he demanded. His voice was rough with anger, deep with an emotion that might have been anguish. Or passion. "Tell me you don't remember the man you promised to love, honor and cherish that night."

Amy gasped at his words. Terror, like nothing that had ever preceded it, surged through her, but still she couldn't tear herself away from him. She stood helpless while he threaded his fingers through her hair, holding her face still beneath his scrutiny.

"That's right, Amber. Take a good, long look at the poor, dumb son of a bitch you married before you decided to up and skip town."

CHAPTER THREE

SHE STARED UP AT him, pale as the ghost he'd earlier thought her to be. "M-married..."

The word was barely out of her mouth before her legs buckled and she pitched forward into Con's arms. Catching her limp body, he eased her down onto the wooden floor of the bridge.

"Amber?" When she didn't respond, he swore under his breath and gently slapped her cheeks. "Amber, come on. Snap out of it."

Her features were so still, a ripple of panic coursed through him. He felt her pulse, somewhat reassured by the weak, erratic beat.

She was out cold, and it occurred to Con that her reaction to his announcement could hardly be termed flattering. Neither could the look of pure terror he'd glimpsed in her eyes before she'd fainted. She was scared to death of him, and after that night nine years ago, she damn well ought to be.

Still, he couldn't deny her response to him had taken him by surprise. The Amber Tremain he'd known hadn't been afraid of anything or anybody. The girl from his past would never have allowed him to talk to her the way he had minutes ago. She would have thrown his scorn right back in his face and told him to go straight to hell with it. But this woman was different.

And maybe that was precisely why, Con thought suddenly. She was no longer a girl, but a woman. No longer wild and rebellious, but mature and restrained.

Something that might have been regret rolled through him as he touched two fingers to the pulse in her throat and found that the beat was getting stronger and steadier. She'd probably come around in a few minutes, but until then, he didn't think it was a good idea to leave her lying on the bridge in direct sunlight. The day was sweltering, with humidity rising off the river in thick, steamy waves. Sweat trickled down his backbone as he struggled to his feet, then lifted Amber's pliant body and heaved her over his shoulder.

He carried her off the bridge, down the embankment, and settled her beneath the shade of a water oak. She didn't weigh much, but Con wasn't in the kind of shape he'd once been in. Breathing heavily, his knee throbbing, he stripped off his undershirt and dipped the cotton into the river, then came back to stand over Amber's supine body, dripping water onto her face.

She stirred, turning her head from side to side. Then her eyes opened and she stared up at Con. For a split second, he could have sworn he glimpsed recognition in those tawny depths before her lids came down to shutter her unguarded emotions. When she opened her eyes again, the fear and confusion had returned.

She tried to sit up, but fell back against the bank, groaning and clapping a hand to her mouth as if to quell a rising tide of nausea.

Con tossed her his wet shirt. "Here. Use this."

Lying on her back, she took the shirt gratefully and wiped away the beads of sweat from her forehead, then held the damp cloth to her face for a moment. "I don't feel well," she muttered.

"You'll be all right in a minute."

She glanced up at him doubtfully. "What happened?"

"You blacked out on the bridge. You're lucky you didn't fall off the damn thing."

She rolled her head, gazing up at the bridge. Con wondered what she was thinking. She had a dazed look on her face he couldn't quite decipher. Then she turned away from the bridge and sat up, handing him his shirt. "Thanks."

"Don't mention it." He tossed the wet garment over one shoulder as he stared down at her. She still looked pale, and when the slender hand she lifted to her forehead trembled, he couldn't help thinking again how different she seemed.

He'd never known Amber to faint. She'd always been able to hold her own under extreme circumstances, but this woman seemed frail and vulnerable, two words he would never have thought he would use to describe any of the Tremains.

Could he have been wrong about her? Con wondered uneasily. Could she really be suffering from memory loss? Was that why she seemed so different?

But even total amnesia couldn't bring on this kind of personality metamorphosis. Assuming the changes in her were genuine, something else must have happened to her. But what? Or...who?

He turned his gaze to the water, away from her upturned face and eyes—those damn cat eyes—that had always made him think and act irrationally. He was doing that now, he realized, falling right back under Amber Tremain's devious little spell. Hell, she probably didn't have amnesia any more than he did. She was probably lying about everything.

Now that, Con thought grimly, would be totally in character for Amber.

"Did you carry me down here?" she asked.

He shrugged, still refusing to look at her. He wouldn't let those golden eyes cast their spell on him again. Nine years was a long time. He'd been through a lot. Seen a lot. Done even more. Amber Tremain, with or without her memory, meant nothing to him anymore.

But when he heard her stirring, he couldn't help glancing over his shoulder. She'd risen unsteadily to her feet and was brushing dirt from her dress. As if testing his resolve, she walked to the river's edge and stood beside him.

Something light and airy drifted between them, a sweet, heady fragrance that took Con straight back to the tortured summers of his youth, to the secret longing that had led him to the darkest days of his life. No matter how far he'd traveled from home, the scent of magnolia blossoms always brought him back to that night.

She lifted a hand to tuck a tangled strand of hair behind one ear. "You said something earlier…right before I fainted…." Her voice trembled as it trailed away, but when Con turned to stare down at her, her chin lifted in a defiant manner that made him think she hadn't changed after all.

"I said a lot of things on that bridge." He watched her expression, fascinated in spite of himself by the struggle of emotions he saw in her eyes.

She bit her lip uncertainly. "You know what I mean. You said we…were…"

"Married." He gave a low, bitter laugh when he saw her flinch.

"Were you just saying that?" Her tone was almost desperate. "Were you trying to provoke me?"

"Now, why would I do that, Amber?"

She put her hand to her temple and rubbed, as if trying to eradicate a headache. "I don't feel comfortable with you calling me that name. I'd rather you call me Amy. At least until—"

"Until what? You slip up?"

Her brows knitted together in confusion. "You still don't believe I have amnesia, do you? I don't know what I can say to convince you. Or why I should even try, for that matter."

"I think you do know why." He let his gaze linger on her features—those damnable eyes, that perfect nose, the wide, generous lips that had once been as familiar to him as his own. He'd wanted her for so long back then, had loved her so much, and she'd put him through an unspeakable hell. And now she claimed she didn't even remember him. The irony of that was enough to send Con straight to the near-est liquor store.

Instead, he tried to shrug it all away. "All right, so maybe I'll give you the benefit of a doubt—for now. Let's say you do have amnesia. It doesn't change anything."

"What do you mean?"

"What do you think I mean?"

Nervously, she wiped her hands down the sides of her dress. The cotton fabric, probably once as cool and crisp as a snow cone, was now rumpled and stained with rust from the bridge railing. Her hair was tangled and windblown, her makeup long since melted away. She looked like hell, but it didn't seem to matter to Con. She was still Amber Tre-main.

As if reading his thoughts, she turned away from him slightly, so that her gaze could trace the con-tours of the bridge towering over them. Con thought he saw her shudder before she turned back to face him. "I couldn't have been more than eighteen."

"And I was nineteen," he said dryly. "But it was all legal and binding. I have a marriage license to prove it."

Her face looked pale as she stared up at him. "That was nine years ago. Are we still—?"

She couldn't even bring herself to say the word. Con gave her a long, hard look. "I never divorced you, if that's what you mean, though I'm damned if I know why."

For a moment, she looked as if she might pass out again, but then she rallied, straightening her shoulders and pushing the damp strands of hair from her forehead. "Tell me about that night," she said urgently. "Tell me what happened."

When he didn't answer right away, she reached out to touch his arm, but then hesitated. She let her hand drop to her side as she gazed up at him. "Look, I know you still don't believe I have amnesia, but please, just humor me. What can it hurt?"

Con wasn't sure what to believe anymore. Was she lying to him? God help him, he couldn't tell. But when she looked up at him like that…when he saw with his own eyes how much she appeared to have changed…it was hard *not* to believe that something very significant had happened to her. "There's not much to tell," he said finally. "We eloped."

"Eloped?" An emotion he couldn't define flashed in her eyes. "Why?"

"That's the way you wanted it. You didn't want anyone to know until afterward. So we drove up to Memphis where we could get a license without a waiting period, and then we saw a justice of the peace. A couple of his fishing buddies were our witnesses."

"What happened then?" Her voice sounded breathless and shaky.

It was all Con could do to keep his own tone even. "We came back here, and you went home to tell your old man what we'd done. You wanted to talk to him alone, so we agreed to meet later right here on the bridge. But you never came back." After that, Con's life had become a living nightmare, but he wasn't sure he wanted to tell her the rest. Not yet. Not until he was certain she couldn't remember on her own.

"What was the date?" she asked suddenly.

He answered without having to think. "July 8. We'd saved some fireworks from the Fourth of July...." He trailed off, shrugging. It sounded like kid stuff now, but the roman candle he'd lit that night on the bridge had seemed symbolic of their passion—fiery, explosive and potentially very dangerous.

Her frown deepened as she gazed at the river. He wondered if she was thinking, as he was, that the Fourth of July was only a few days away—and so was their anniversary.

"My first memory is waking up in a Houston hospital," she said, her tone pensive. "It was the day after that, I think. July 9."

"What the hell were you doing in Houston?"

"I have no idea. But when I came to, I couldn't remember anything. Later, I was told that my name was Amy Calloway, and that my parents had both died in a fire that destroyed our home in Iowa. I was told...I had no one else."

Con stared at her in disbelief. "Who told you that?"

"A woman I believed was my aunt."

"You mean Corliss?"

"Corliss?" Amy shook her head. "I don't know anyone named Corliss. This woman's name was Nona. Nona Jessop. Have you ever heard of her?"

He shook his head. "Can't say as I have. Was she from around here?"

"She told me that she and my mother grew up together in a small town in Mississippi. That's actually how I was able to trace...Amber Tremain to Magnolia Bend. But the newspaper accounts I read about the disappearance never mentioned anyone named Nona Jessop. She told me she had a brother who still lives here, but I haven't been able to find out anything about him, either."

"As far as I know, there aren't any Jessops around here." Con still wasn't sure whether or not he believed a word she was telling him. It was the strangest story he'd ever heard, but he wasn't certain even Amber could make up anything this bizarre.

She made a helpless gesture with her hand. "Anyway, when I awakened in the hospital, Nona was at my side. She didn't tell me much at first, not for several weeks, only that she would take care of me. She kept asking if I remembered what had happened to me, and then she took me to see a therapist. But when my memory didn't come back, she eventually started telling me things about my past, about my parents and the fire. She said she was my mother's best friend, my godmother, and that she would take care of me since I had no one else." Amy paused. "I believed her. I had no reason not to."

Con dragged a hand through his short hair. "Do you really expect me to believe all that? You've told some whoppers in your time, but this has got to take the cake. What I can't figure out is why. What are you up to, Amber? Is it Amberly you're after? Have you come back here to claim your half of the inheritance?"

Amy's eyes flashed with sudden fire, reminding Con of the way she'd looked once before, when he'd accused her then of lying to him. "I'm telling you the truth! I don't know what happened here nine years ago, or how I ended up in Houston with Nona. That's what I've come back to find out. That's the only reason I'm here. She died a few months ago without ever telling my why she lied to me about my past. She left no records, no papers, nothing. I don't even know what her brother's name is, or if he even exists. I don't have any idea what—or who—she was trying to protect me from, un-less—" Her voice broke suddenly as her eyes wid-ened in revelation. Con could almost see the fear churning inside her.

"Unless what?" he demanded. When she didn't say anything, he took her arm. She tried to flinch away, but his grasp tightened. "Unless what, damn it?"

She stared at his hand on her arm for a moment, then slowly lifted her gaze to meet his. And he knew instantly what she was thinking. He could read it in her eyes—Nona Jessop, whoever she'd been, had taken Amber miles away from Mississippi to protect her from him.

Whatever satisfaction her fear might have given him earlier vanished. Staring down into her face, Con realized, with an insight that was almost dev-astating, everything she'd told him was true. She didn't remember him. She didn't feel anything for him except terror.

Something sharp and bitter stabbed through him,

and as abruptly as he'd grabbed her, he released her. He took a step back from her, distancing himself from the temptation—and the threat—she posed to him. "Maybe you'd better get on home, Amber. I'm sure everyone there is waiting with bated breath for your return."

She cringed at the sarcasm in his voice, but she didn't say anything. Instead, she turned and walked away, exactly as she'd done nine years ago. And watching her go, Con had an odd sinking feeling in his stomach that the girl who'd disappeared that night was never coming back.

AMY SAT IN HER CAR, hardly aware of the stifling heat as she watched Conner Sullivan walk along the riverbank to a path that led through a thicket of brambles and cypress trees. Emotions tumbled through her. It couldn't be true. She couldn't be married to him, and yet...

Was that why she'd never been able to forget him? Was that why his dark, angry features had always haunted her?

Was that why she hadn't been able to marry Reece?

God, she thought, scrubbing her face with her hands. Until two weeks ago, she'd been engaged, and now to learn that she'd been secretly married to another man for nine years. *Nine years!*

Her gaze traveled along the river's edge, to where Con had left the bank to follow the path back into the copse. The rugged terrain made his gait appear unstable, but his pace didn't slow. It was as if he couldn't wait to put as much distance between them as possible.

He was still shirtless, and his back and shoulders looked deceptively thin. But up close, the definition of muscle beneath his bronze skin had told Amy that at one time—and probably not all that long ago—Conner Sullivan had been in peak physical condition.

What had happened to him? she wondered, as she watched him disappear into the trees. What had his life been like for the past nine years?

And why, if she was so terrified of him, did she wish suddenly that he would turn and come back? That he would tell her more about that night—their wedding night—and somehow make her remember?

But he didn't turn, not even once to glance back at her, and Amy knew she should probably be relieved even as a faint measure of disappointment trickled through her.

CON LIMPED UP THE PATH toward his trailer, fighting the urge to turn and look back at her, to reassure himself that he'd really seen her, had really talked to her. Christ, he'd even held her in his arms. It hadn't been a dream this time, or a nightmare from which he would awaken in a cold sweat, reliving the details of a night that would haunt him for the rest of his life.

Amber Tremain had really come back.

She'd even worn white, damn her, but that shouldn't have surprised him. Amber had always worn white on significant occasions. Like on her birthday. On Christmas and Easter and the Fourth of July. And on the night she died, he remembered.

So why wouldn't she wear white on the day of her resurrection?

Bending, he picked up a rock, rubbing the smooth surface as the unwanted memories crowded through him. His whole past had been such a damn cliché. A drunken, abusive father, a browbeaten mother and a girl from the other side of the tracks. Or in this case, river.

No matter how far he'd traveled or how many years had gone by, Amber's ghost had always been there, lurking somewhere in the deepest, darkest hideaways of his mind. He'd tried to convince himself a long time ago that she really was dead, because to believe otherwise…

Shoving away the thought, he threw the rock toward a rusted beer can, missing his target by more than an inch. He'd lost his touch, Con reckoned, along with a few other things over the past nine years. Innocence? He gave a biting, inward laugh. You couldn't lose what you'd never had.

No, he'd lost things a lot more valuable than innocence. His mother, last year. His career, just before that. His right kneecap, in a covert war in South America no one back home in Mississippi had ever even heard of. On good days, he could walk without a noticeable limp. On bad days, like today, it was all he could do to drag himself out of bed.

That's what you get for running out on PT, a little voice taunted him. The knee might have gotten better in time. But after a half-dozen surgeries in less than a year, he hadn't had the patience, or the pain threshold, to endure endless months of physical therapy. He'd opted out of the service—where was there to go anyway, except a desk job maybe, or a training assignment?—to come home and lick his wounds. And after some of the places he'd been in the past several years, even Mississippi had seemed a little like paradise. At least at first.

But then he'd learned that his mother was dying. Her heart, the doctors had told Con, had simply been overworked for far too long. There was nothing they could do for her.

Naomi Sullivan had worked like a dog all her life, waiting tables, taking in laundry, accepting whatever menial job she could find so that her son, her boy, could have a better life. So he wouldn't turn out like the mean, drunken son of a bitch who had fathered him.

And the irony of it was, the goddamn, stinking irony of it all was that if she'd lived a little longer, she would never have had to worry about money again.

But she was gone now, and so was the judge. Emmett Tremain would never look across the river and view the vacation homes and golf course that would one day populate what used to be the worthless old Sullivan place. He would never know the bitterness of defeat or the irony of fate.

But maybe that was just as well. If Con had learned anything in the past nine years, it was that old wounds—anger, hurt, betrayal—meant very little in the face of survival. He'd come to terms with the past a long time ago.

He would never have come back here if he'd thought otherwise. He sure as hell wouldn't have stayed on after his mother died. He would have sold the property, made his killing and gotten the hell out if he'd thought there was even a remote chance that his marriage to Amber would ever come to light.

He glanced back at the river, but the trees hid Amber from his view. Which was probably a good thing. He didn't trust himself with her right now. There was too much unfinished business between them. Too many things left unsaid.

Too many emotions Con had never dealt with.

In some ways, it would have been easier if she'd just stayed dead.

CHAPTER FOUR

TEN MINUTES LATER, Amy backtracked along the dusty river road and found her way onto the main highway. Another twenty minutes or so had her crossing a different bridge, this one a modern affair with gleaming steel girders and four lanes of traffic.

Once across the river, a truck bearing down on her rear bumper gave her only a split second to decide which course to follow: Left and head into town, or right and go to Amberly.

Taking a deep breath, Amy cut the wheel to the right and whipped her rental car onto a smooth blacktop road that angled away from the river and cut like a straightedge through acres and acres of flat bottom land.

The crops rippled in a stray breeze, like yards and yards of undulating green satin. Almost mesmerized by the rolling movement, Amy lost all sense of time and direction until a sharp bend in the road headed her back toward the river, away from the sun.

The farmland gradually gave way to meadows and pastures lined with white wooden fences, and around another curve in the road, she saw the turnoff to Amberly, just as it had been described to her. The wrought-iron arch over the gravel lane was partially hidden by a dense stand of oak and pecan trees that, like towering sentinels, had guarded the narrow entrance for over 150 years.

Driving through the gateway, Amy eased her car along fence rows overgrown with blackberry, honeysuckle and morning-glory vines. She rolled down her window, and the cloying scent drifted through the car like a soft summer dream.

A mile down the gravel lane, the woods thinned and the hedgerows gave way to a wide, sloping lawn. A peacock, tail feathers spread wide, strutted onto the road a few yards in front of her car, and Amy slowed, giving him time to cross while she caught glimpses of a white plantation house through an alley of tall, shadowy magnolias.

The river was nowhere in sight, but Amy could smell it. The damp, musty scent was unmistakable as it seeped through the open car windows and mingled with the honeysuckle.

The only visible water was a man-made lily pond ringed with deep purple irises and black-eyed Susans. Swans and ducks glided effortlessly on the smooth surface, their grace and cool beauty almost dreamlike in the stifling heat.

But more surreal than anything was the house itself. Amberly.

Amy pulled through the rows of magnolias, stopped her car on the gravel drive and got out, her heart pounding in excitement. Or was it fear?

No one waited on the porch for her with bated breath, as Con had suggested, but she knew she was expected. She'd written the family days ago, when she'd first learned of Amber Tremain's origins, explaining her uncanny resemblance to Amber and the fact that she had no memory of her life prior to nine years ago. She'd also sent a recent photograph of herself and detailed briefly the life she now led.

She'd gotten a prompt, though somewhat wary, reply from the family's attorney, Darnell Henry, requesting more details and a face-to-face interview. After a series of phone calls, he'd flown to Houston, the two of them had met for several hours and the very next day, she'd received a call from Lottie Tremain, Emmett Tremain's widow, who had issued a cordial invitation to Amy to come for an extended visit with the family at Amberly.

Evidently, Mr. Henry had been convinced that she was Amber Tremain, because Lottie had assured Amy that everyone in the family was very excited to see her. The sooner she could come the better. As they'd talked, the woman's tone had warmed, but Amy had still sensed an undercurrent in Lottie's voice that was more than a little troubling.

Even so, Amy had made her travel plans immediately. She'd already had vacation time scheduled for her canceled honeymoon, two whole weeks that she could use to discover who she really was. Who Amber Tremain had been.

Shivering, she stared up at the house, letting her gaze slide over the gleaming white facade, the steep angles of the gabled roof and the eight columns that dignified a wide porch with granite steps.

As she stood there, the history of the place

seemed to wrap around her, like the arms of some forgotten ancestor summoning her home.

But her initial awe paled as she slowly climbed the steps. The granite was chipped in places, and the porch roof, supported by the stately columns, sagged precariously at one end. The faded splendor of the house depressed Amy, though she couldn't say why. She had no memory of Amberly. In fact, she still couldn't quite believe she had once lived here, been born and raised here, and that something must have happened to drive her away.

Suddenly chilled in the afternoon heat, she lifted her hand to knock, but the door was drawn back so abruptly, she was left standing with her fist in mid-air. Lowering her hand, she cleared her throat and shifted uncomfortably as the woman on the other side of the threshold stared at her in mute shock.

"Amber? Oh, my heavens—" The soft Southern drawl broke off as the woman took a step toward her. She lifted her hand, perhaps to touch Amy's face, but almost unconsciously, Amy moved away from her.

Something that might have been hurt flashed in the woman's eyes. As if needing to do something with her hands, she wiped them on a tattered white apron that tied around her neck and again around an ample waistline. She wasn't fat nor did she appear out of shape, but was plump in a pleasing, down-home sort of way that spoke of fried chicken, potato salad and luscious pecan pies.

Her red hair, tinged with gray, was pulled back into a knot, but wiry tendrils frizzed along her forehead and at her nape. She looked to be comfortably in her fifties, unassumingly attractive with a pale, lovely complexion and eyes the color of a summer sky.

Amy said tentatively, "I'm Amy Calloway. I spoke with Mrs. Tremain on the phone yesterday. I believe she's expecting me."

The blue eyes danced with sudden amusement. "Indeed, I am! We've all been dying to see you since we received your letter."

Amy's face flamed in embarrassment. So this was Lottie Tremain. The woman looked nothing like Amy had pictured her, and she realized guiltily she'd been expecting the proverbial wicked stepmother—tall, elegant and coldly remote. "I'm sorry. I didn't recognize you—"

The woman waved aside her apology. "I'm the one who should be sorry. I should have introduced myself right off, but it's hard to remember that you *don't* remember. Amnesia, for heaven's sakes!" She held out her arm. "Look! It gives me chicken skin, just thinking about it. Mama, God rest her, was senile for years and almost as blind as a bat when she died, but that's not the same thing, is it?"

She continued the patter as she took Amy's arm and ushered her into the house. Amy stopped in the cool foyer, her breath suspended somewhere in her throat. Whereas the outside of the house looked worse for a century and a half of wear and tear, the inside had been beautifully preserved.

Fanlights over the double oak doors illuminated the high gloss on the hardwood floors and showcased a spectacular freestanding staircase that curved regally toward a wide, open gallery above. Carved moldings and whimsical frescoes adorned the high ceiling, and a crystal chandelier tinkled in the breeze of a lazy tropical fan.

But what stopped Amy's breath, what made her heart slam against her chest in slow, painful strokes, was the echo of a thousand voices, whispering to her, calling out to her, telling her that at long last, she had finally come home. The feeling was so strong, the house almost seemed like a living entity to her.

Lottie Tremain touched Amy's arm. "Are you all right?"

Amy started a bit. "Yes, I'm fine. It's just this place…it's so beautiful."

"It is magnificent, isn't it?" Lottie's eyes glowed with pride. "Many of the furnishings are original to the house, as is most of the woodwork. Sometimes, even after all these years, I still have to pinch myself to make sure I'm not dreaming. Who would ever have thought that someone like me—" She broke off, biting her lip as her blue gaze searched Amy's features. "But you, of all people, would know how I feel. You used to love this place as much as I do."

A frisson of tension went through Amy, as if something unspoken had passed between them. But the feeling was gone in an instant, and Lottie smiled warmly, taking Amy's arm again. "Welcome home, Amber, honey. If only Emmett could be here to see you—" She paused, looking distressed. "You do know about your daddy, don't you? He died last year."

"Yes, I know." Darnell Henry had told her about her father's death, but Amy had already read his obituary in a Jackson newspaper. Until now, however, the impact hadn't fully hit her. She'd believed her parents dead for the past nine years, but her father had been alive for most of that time. The realization of what her memory loss had cost her made Amy suddenly want to cry.

As if sensing her emotion, Lottie squeezed her hand. The faint scent of lemon sachet seemed to emanate from her clothing, from the essence of the woman herself. "You can't begin to imagine how he suffered when you disappeared like that. It very nearly killed him."

"I'm sorry," Amy murmured, helpless to know what to say or do in such a situation.

"Now, why should you be sorry? It wasn't your fault. You explained in your letter about the amnesia, and how that strange woman kept you down there in Houston and somehow managed to convince you you were somebody else. Who in the world was she, and whatever possessed her to do such a thing?"

Obviously not expecting answers, Lottie drew Amy into a square room off the foyer. An antique sofa and Hepplewhite chairs were grouped around a huge marble fireplace that had been swept clean of winter ashes and festooned with a potted fern. Wooden shutters at the windows were slatted against the afternoon sun, giving the parlor a faint air of oppression, but the shadowy coolness was almost a relief to Amy. Her knees trembling, she sat gratefully in the chair Lottie motioned her to, then watched while her stepmother—Amber's stepmother—assumed the seat across from her.

Again, Lottie wiped her hands on her apron, as if she couldn't quite still her fingers. But her gaze never left Amy's face. "The woman's name was Jessop, you say."

"Yes. Nona Jessop. She told me once her brother still lives around here. I need to find him if I can."

Lottie frowned. "I can't recall anyone by that name, and I've lived here most of my life."

"Jessop may have been her married name. She told me she was a widow. But I haven't been able to find out what her maiden name was. She didn't leave any papers or records, or anything."

Lottie shook her head in disbelief. "This is just so strange, you turning up like this, after all these years. We didn't even know if you were alive or dead—"

"*Strange* is the word for it, all right," said a voice from the doorway.

A thirtyish-looking woman, reed thin and well-groomed in a lime sundress, sauntered into the room, trailed by an almost mirror image of herself. Both women were redheads, both tall and pale and quietly attractive.

The only difference in the two that Amy initially discerned was the style of their hair. The first woman wore hers in fiery corkscrews that bounced against her shoulders, while the second woman had pulled hers straight back, highlighting the freckles that dappled her pale skin like tiny copper pennies. Amy knew at once that she was the shy, demure twin while the other tried to make the most of their wan coloring with thick mascara and bright red lipstick.

"These are my daughters," Lottie explained. "Your stepsisters, Phaedra and Philomena Darling."

The second twin, dressed in jeans and a white shirt tucked neatly into the waistband, stepped toward Amber and offered her hand. "Please call me Mena." Her smile was soft, hesitant. "Everyone does. Welcome home, Amber."

Amy returned her smile and took her hand. The redhead's grasp was surprisingly firm. She shook hands with Amy, then retreated into the background when her sister moved forward.

"You might as well call me Fay," she said. "I detest the stupid name, but I can't seem to shed myself of it." Her hand barely brushed Amy's fingertips as her gaze, cool and appraising, moved over her, taking in the soiled white dress and wilted, tangled hair. Her mouth twitched in amusement—or satisfaction, Amy couldn't tell which—as she turned and took a seat on the sofa, curling one leg underneath her.

"Please get your feet off the furniture," Lottie scolded.

Fay's expression soured, but she did as she was told. "Tell us more about your life in Houston, especially the part about that woman practically holding you prisoner all those years." She shuddered, but her blue eyes were bright and malicious. "How did she manage to brainwash you like that?"

"Phaedra!"

Fay shrugged and smiled. Her teeth were small and pearly white. "I'm just curious, Mama. You don't mind, do you?" she asked, turning back to Amy. "After all, that is why you're here, isn't it? To get everything out into the open? At least that's what you told our attorney."

"I'm here to learn the truth," Amy said, "About the night I disappeared and about why the woman I thought was my aunt lied to me."

Fay shuddered again. This time, her revulsion seemed quite genuine. "I can't imagine what it must be like to wake up one day and realize you aren't who you always thought you were. To look in the mirror and see a stranger staring back at you. To not even remember all the terrible things you might have done in your past..." Her voice trailed off as she gave Amy a knowing glance.

Unsettled, Amy let her gaze wander from Fay to Lottie, and then to Mena, seeing an uncanny resemblance in all of their faces, and yet they seemed so different: Lottie, with her kind eyes and mothering ways; Mena, with her lovely features and bookish demeanor; and Fay—Phaedra—a glamour girl trapped inside a rather plain-Jane body. How that must rankle, Amy thought, sizing her up.

The front door slammed and footsteps hurried across the foyer. A youthful voice called out, "Is she here yet?"

The girl stopped dead in the doorway, her question trailing away when she saw Amy.

The sight of her took Amy's breath away, and she found herself standing on wobbly legs to greet the newcomer. The girl looked about seventeen or eighteen, with long wheat-colored hair, tawny eyes that tilted at the corners and a smooth complexion that had been tanned to golden brown.

She wasn't tall—probably about five five or five six, like Amy—nor was she rail thin like the twins. Rather, the denim cutoffs and midriff top showed off a body that was lush and curvaceous, hinting at baby fat that would someday melt into more svelte and sedate lines. For now, however, she exuded a kind of raw magnetism that could only spell trouble in a girl her age.

And she looked exactly like the picture Amy had seen of herself at that age.

It was as if she were peering in a mirror that erased nine years from her face, and for the first time, Amy glimpsed in her sister's eyes, in the knowing curve of her lips, the "package" Darnell Henry had hinted that Amber Tremain had once been. A wild, headstrong young woman who might well have run off and married a man like Conner Sullivan.

The notion made her legs tremble even more, and Amy stepped to the side of her chair so that she could cling to the back as she greeted her sister. "You must be Jasmine."

Elegant brows arched sharply. "You recognize me? I thought you didn't remember anything."

"I just guessed. There's a family resemblance."

"Not much of one. Not anymore." The girl crossed the room to stand in front of Amy, her gaze drinking in Amy's disheveled appearance. A shadow moved over her features. "You don't look anything like you used to."

"Nine years is a long time," Amy said, her tone defensive though she wasn't sure why. "People change."

Jasmine gave her a sly look beneath thick lashes. "Daddy used to say a leopard can't change his spots, no matter how hard he tries."

The inference wasn't lost on Amy, and she felt a sinking sensation in her stomach. The day was not turning out at all as she'd hoped. She might have expected a fair amount of wariness from her stepfamily, or even Fay's snide antagonism and Conner Sullivan's dark accusations. But the open animosity in her sister's eyes—her own flesh and blood—was hard to understand.

Jasmine couldn't have been more than nine or ten when Amber disappeared. What could have happened between the two of them to make her sister so hostile now? Or was it, as Con had hinted, the fact that Amber's return challenged Jasmine's inheritance?

As if she could read Amy's thoughts, Jasmine abruptly turned away and went to stand at the window, staring toward the river. Her gaze took on a faraway look, and Amy wondered what her sister was thinking.

"Did you have any trouble finding the house?"

Lottie asked her. "Darnell said he gave you detailed directions."

"Yes, he did. He even drew me a map."

Lottie glanced at her. "We expected you some time ago. I don't mind telling you, we were all getting a little worried."

Somehow Amy doubted that. She hadn't exactly been welcomed with open arms. "I'm afraid I got sidetracked. I decided to take a drive along the river."

Lottie's hand crept up to finger a button at the neck of her blouse. "You...didn't go all the way to the old bridge, did you?" When Amy nodded, Lottie said, "Oh, honey, why? Why would you go there?"

Amy shrugged. "I'm not sure why. I just wanted to see it. Is there any reason why I shouldn't have gone?"

"That's where our mother killed herself," Jasmine said bluntly, still gazing out the window. "That's where we thought you'd drowned."

A shudder ripped through Amy. So that was why she'd felt so compelled to find the bridge, why she'd been so terrified standing on the edge, staring down into the water. She remembered the vision she'd had of the hand reaching out of the darkness, of a body falling into the water—

"Did you...see anyone there?" Mena's soft, anxious voice cut into Amy's thoughts.

She frowned, wondering if they knew about Con, if they were aware of his claim that he and Amber had gotten married the night she disappeared. Or was the elopement still a secret, after all these years?

She said hesitantly, "I saw a man there. He said his name was Conner Sullivan."

The room stilled with a tension that was almost electric. Lottie's face froze into unreadable lines, while Fay's expression twisted in contempt and Mena's cheeks flushed bright red.

But the most interesting reaction was Jasmine's. She turned slowly from the window, her eyes narrowed in what Amy could only call suspicion. "What did he say to you?"

Amy shrugged, still tentative in how much she wanted to reveal. "For some reason, he doesn't seem to like me. He doesn't believe I have amnesia."

Triumph flashed in Jasmine's eyes before she turned quickly back to the window.

Fay, after a moment's consideration, said slyly, "Well, I hate to admit it, but he does have a point." As if sensing the inevitable reprimand, she lifted a manicured hand to silence her mother. "Wait a minute, Mama, just hear me out. How do we really know she has amnesia?" Her gaze locked defiantly with Amy's.

"I guess you don't," Amy said. "But why would I lie about something like that?"

"It'd be a great cover for an impostor."

"Phaedra!"

"Oh, don't 'Phaedra' me," she chided her mother. "And don't tell me you haven't thought the same thing yourself. If squirrely ole Mr. Henry hadn't talked you into it, you never would have invited her here."

Lottie's face turned beet-red. She seemed at a loss for words, but Mena quickly came to her mother's rescue. "This isn't a novel, Fay. Things like that don't happen in real life, and besides—" she glanced shyly at Amy "—no one could look that much like Amber and not be her."

"Oh, please," Fay said in contempt. "No offense, but you don't even look that much like Amber to me. Even Jasmine said so. How do we know you're not some gold digger who has cooked up this wild scheme to try and bilk money from us?"

"You can't bilk blood from a turnip," Jasmine muttered at the window.

"Girls, please," Lottie said, wiping her hands rather urgently on her apron.

Ignoring her mother, Fay leaned toward Amy, scouring her features with a cold, appraising glare. "If you really believe you're Amber Tremain, then you wouldn't object to a DNA test, would you?"

"*DNA test?*" boomed yet another voice from the parlor doorway. "Why, you're out of your cotton-pickin' mind, Phaedra Sue Darling, if you think I'll fork over good money for some fancy smancy blood test. Y'all think I won't know my own kin just by looking at her? Let me see her. I can tell you in two shakes of a lamb's tail whether she's the real thing or not. And if she's not—" the voice turned ominous "—by gawd, we'll call out the Mississippi Highway Patrol to chase her clear back to Texas."

CHAPTER FIVE

AT THE SOUND of the strident voice, Jasmine, Fay and Mena all jumped, as if they were connected to an invisible string that had suddenly been yanked. A frown creased Lottie's brow as she gazed at the doorway. "Corliss! I thought you were in Yazoo City."

"I was," the woman confirmed unhappily. "And I'd still be there, too, if Merrily Tucker hadn't called to tell me what was going on around here. Which is more than any of y'all saw fit to do."

Tall and big boned, the woman sailed into the room on a draft of talcum powder, gardenias and a more pungent aroma that might have been liniment. "Where is she? I swear, I can't see a damn thing in here. You keep this place as dark as a mole's butt, Lottie, just so you can save a buck or two on the electric bill—"

Her tirade ended abruptly when she spotted Amy. Her hand flew to her heart where her chest visibly rose and fell beneath a chic lavender jacket as she struggled for breath. For a full ten seconds, she couldn't seem to move. Then, collecting herself, her gaze narrowed and she said sternly, "So, young lady. You're the one who's claiming to be my niece Amber, are you?''

"Not exactly," Amy said, nervous in spite of the fact she hadn't done anything wrong. "I'm just here to find out the truth. I don't remember anything before nine years ago."

"So I've been told. Amnesia, huh?'' The woman's tone implied she wouldn't easily fall for any such nonsense as that. "Well, don't just sit there like a knot on a log. Stand up, girl. Let me get a good look at you."

As Amy stood, she returned the woman's perusal. Like Lottie, she appeared to be in her fifties, with a long, handsome face, wide-set, hazel eyes and a smooth cap of dark brown hair. Her skin was lightly suntanned, her large hands smooth and bejeweled with two enormous amethyst rings. Her lavender pantsuit, exquisitely tailored and deceptively simple, made her at once one of the most stylish and most formidable-looking women Amy had ever seen.

For a long moment, no one said anything, but Amy sensed an undercurrent in the room she couldn't define. Out of the corner of her eye, she saw Lottie shift uneasily and wipe her hands on her apron before the larger woman, obviously satisfied with what she saw, swooped down on Amy and scooped her up in a smothering, fragrant embrace. "My gawd!" she cried, as if overcome with sudden emotion. "What's the matter with y'all, anyway? Any fool can see this child is Amber! Oh, my sweet girl, you've finally come home to us! My prayers have finally been answered!"

Over the woman's shoulder, Jasmine said dryly, "In case you haven't figured it out yet, this is Corliss Witherspoon. Our aunt."

At the sound of Jasmine's voice, Corliss released Amy long enough to pull a lace hankie from her sleeve and dab at her eyes. "Why, Jasmine Louise, I'm so glad you're here for this momentous occasion," she said in a suspiciously sweet voice. "You and I are going to have ourselves a little talk, dear heart."

"What about?" Jasmine pouted.

"As if you didn't know. About the company you've been keeping, that's what."

Jasmine rolled her eyes. "I'm not a kid anymore, Aunt Corliss. You can't tell me what to do."

Corliss arched a brow. "Oh, I can't, can I? We'll just see about that. And you—" She whirled on Lottie. "What in tarnation are you thinking, letting her traipse all over the county with that man? Emmett must be rolling over in his grave—"

"Corliss," Lottie said, her voice steely soft. "I don't think now is the proper time."

Corliss stiffened, as if readying herself for battle, then, like a balloon slowly deflating, she said to Jasmine, "I'll deal with you later, Miss Priss. But for now—" She turned back to Amy, giving her another once-over. "Lord a-mercy, girl. What've you been doing to yourself? You're as skinny as a fence post, and you're not nearly as pretty as I remembered you." And with that, her eyes teared again and she grabbed Amy, clutching her to her breast as if she were afraid to let her go.

Amy thought, in wry amusement, of the stranglehold the rosebush out front had on the persimmon tree.

Lottie rose and cleared her throat. "You'll stay to supper, won't you, Corliss?"

Reluctantly, Corliss released Amy and blew her nose noisily on the lace hankie. "What are you having? You know I can't eat beef. Or pork. And all that salt you put in your casseroles goes straight to my arteries."

"I'll fix you a salad," Lottie murmured, her mouth twitching in amusement or annoyance, Amy wasn't sure which.

"Bottled dressing gives me gas, but I reckon I can take an antacid," Corliss grumbled, somewhat appeased. "Besides, it'll give me a chance to visit with my niece. We've got a lot of catching up to do, don't we, dear heart?" She wrapped an arm around Amy's waist. "That goes for you, too," she added over her shoulder, and Amy glanced back to see Jasmine squirm under her aunt's accusing glare.

"That's settled, then." Lottie headed toward the doorway, as if anxious to escape. "Mena, will you give me a hand in the kitchen?"

Mena started to rise, but Corliss snapped, "Not so fast. I need to have a word with Philomena."

Mena paused, her face flushing a dark, guilty red. "Wh-what did I do?"

"I didn't see my ad in the *Journal* today."

Relief washed the color from Mena's cheeks. She said in a rush, "Oh, that. I told you it wouldn't run until Saturday, remember?"

"I want a full-page ad," Corliss warned. "In big enough letters so's even that fool Marcelus Beaucamp can't miss it. 'You keep that damn dog out of my flower beds, or I'll fill him full of buckshot and have him stuffed like a Christmas turkey!' I've got my 12-gauge pump loaded and ready."

Lottie turned at the doorway. "Oh, Corliss, you wouldn't. Marcelus loves that dog."

"I wouldn't, would I! You wait and see if I won't. And don't act so all-fired high and mighty with me, Lottie Mae. Who was it slipped Junior Crouch's favorite coon dog a little rat poison when he got into your prize tomato patch, hmm?"

LOTTIE SERVED DINNER that evening on the enclosed back porch, with ceiling fans slowly whirling overhead and moths clinging to the screen, trying to find a way into the light.

The food was delicious, succulent baked chicken seasoned with rosemary, sweet potato puffs, a bowl of fresh sliced tomatoes, and corn bread dripping with honey. Even Corliss had trouble finding fault with the meal, though she certainly didn't offer up any compliments. She cleaned her plate, wiped her lips daintily on a linen napkin, then announced she had to get home in time for *Wheel of Fortune.*

Likewise, Fay excused herself, muttering something about a phone call she had to make. Lottie and Mena stood and began clearing the table, but when Amy offered to help, Lottie wouldn't hear of it. "Not on your first night home. You and Jasmine need a little time together. Why don't you take a walk?''

Jasmine started to protest, then shrugged. ''Sure, why not?''

Hardly overwhelming enthusiasm, but Amy welcomed the chance to talk to her sister alone. They left the house through the back door. Darkness had fallen, and the evening was balmy and redolent with roses, honeysuckle and magnolia blooms. Lightning bugs darted through the trees as Jasmine led them through the garden gate.

''There's a path over here. Let's go down to the river,'' she suggested. The moon was up, full and round, crowning a sky studded with summer stars, and Amy could see clearly the mossy trail that led past the outbuildings.

''It's quiet out here tonight. Just you, me and the cicadas.'' Jasmine's voice sounded a bit ominous in the darkness. ''Sometimes at night, when I leave my bedroom window open, I can hear kids partying down by the bridge. I've been known to climb out my window and join them.''

Amy wasn't sure what role she should assume here. Big sister? Casual listener? She said tentatively, ''I hope you're careful.''

Jasmine laughed, a harsh sound that seemed far too old for someone her age. ''That's good, coming from you. Where do you think I got the idea? Daddy caught you crawling out your window once, and you told him you must have been sleepwalking, like you used to do when you were a little kid.''

''Did he believe me?''

"Of course. You were his little darling. He even took you to see a doctor to make sure you were all right. You played along without batting an eye." Jasmine's tone was half contemptuous, half admiring.

Amy frowned. The road to discovery was not proving to be as smooth as she'd hoped. She wondered fleetingly if she should have stayed in Houston, been content to live her life as Amy Calloway, because Amber Tremain was turning out to be a person she wasn't at all certain she wanted to know.

A whippoorwill sounded in the woods, the plaintive cry like a distant memory. "I don't have any idea what I was like back then," she said softly, almost to herself.

"I wouldn't worry about it." Jasmine stopped on the path, reaching down to rescue a magnolia blossom that had fallen from one of the trees. The petals looked milky soft in the moonlight. She held it to her cheek and closed her eyes. "Being a Tremain is like riding a bicycle. You never forget how."

"What do you mean?"

Jasmine shrugged. "You can do whatever you want, regardless of who you hurt. Like running off the way you did. You broke Daddy's heart." Her voice turned bitter, and she moved away from Amy, as if afraid of revealing more than she wanted to. "But, hey, I'm the last person to blame you for leaving this place. I can't wait to get away from here."

"I wouldn't do anything rash," Amy warned her. "It's not all that much fun out there in the real world."

"And you think it's been a party here, stuck in the same house with the wicked stepmother and her evil twin offspring?"

"Has it really been that bad?" Amy asked doubtfully. "Lottie seems really nice."

Jasmine glared at her in the moonlight. "Don't let that Betty Crocker act fool you. Lottie can be *cold* when she wants to be."

"Like poisoning a dog?"

"Among other things." The path narrowed, and Jasmine took the lead, saying over her shoulder, "I bet you didn't know she was seeing Daddy before our mother died, did you? Lottie's the reason Mama jumped off that bridge."

Amy sputtered in shock, "You mean...Lottie and our father—"

"Were doing the horizontal mambo. Hard to believe, isn't it?" Jasmine made a gagging sound.

Amy didn't know what to say. For a few moments, they both fell silent as she struggled to digest everything her sister had told her.

When they came to a fork in the path, Jasmine pointed to the right. "This way. The other trail leads down to a bog. You don't want to go there, especially at night, when the bobcats and water moccasins like to come out."

Amy wasn't sure whether to believe her sister or not, but chill bumps rose along her spine. "Is it safe for us to be out here like this?"

"Safe enough, if you know where to step." Jasmine smiled over her shoulder. "Don't worry. I know exactly what I'm doing."

Amy didn't doubt that. Jasmine appeared to be a young woman with a definite purpose, and her aim at the moment seemed to be in keeping Amy off balance, perhaps even in nudging her back to Houston.

They crested the top of the embankment and stood gazing down at the water. A fine mist hovered in patches over the river, subduing the moonlight as it danced upon the surface. The evening took on a hushed quality, the stillness only broken by the occasional plop of some night creature taking to the water.

Several yards from where they stood, the old river bridge loomed out of the haze, its girders like the bloody sails of some vast, ancient ship. "When I was here earlier, I had no idea I was so close to Amberly."

Amy thought she saw her sister shudder in the moonlight. "It's a good thing you didn't try to drive across the bridge. I don't think a car has been over it in years." She paused. "Come on. Let's go down to the water."

They took off their shoes and sat on the sandy bank. Jasmine still wore the cutoffs and top she'd had on earlier, but Amy had changed into a skirt and sleeveless blouse. She undid several of the buttons on the long skirt so that she could curl her legs underneath her. Jasmine stretched out on the sand, folding her arms beneath her head as she gazed up at the sky. She seemed more relaxed than she had all evening, but the river had the opposite effect on Amy. She sat, tense and waiting.

"I need to ask you something," Jasmine said after a bit.

Amy shrugged. "Go ahead."

Jasmine raised herself on her elbows, studying the water. "What did Con say to you earlier?"

"I told you. He doesn't believe I have amnesia. He seems...hostile toward me."

"He used to be crazy about you."

Something in Jasmine's tone made Amy turn and stare at her. Amy wondered if her sister knew about the marriage, if that was what this conversation was leading up to. Her heart started to pound. "You certainly couldn't tell it by his actions today."

Jasmine frowned at the water. "You didn't feel anything for him? Leftover sparks or something?"

"What are you getting at, Jasmine?" Amy drew up her legs, wrapping her arms around her knees as she watched her sister's face in the pale light.

Jasmine shrugged. "It's just that Con and I have become...friends."

An alarm sounded somewhere inside Amy. "He's...a bit older than you, isn't he?"

Her sister threw a handful of sand toward the water. "What difference does that make? I like older men. Besides, Daddy was almost ten years older than Mama, and he dated her big sister first, too."

"Corliss?"

Jasmine nodded. "She introduced them, and Mama was just about my age when she and Daddy got married."

Amy said carefully, "You're not thinking of getting married—"

"It would be my own business if I were," Jasmine retorted defiantly. "I'm eighteen and I can do what I want. But don't worry," she added grudgingly. "Like I said, Con and I are just friends."

She sounded almost disappointed, and as much as Amy wanted to believe her sister, she suspected Jasmine would like the relationship to become something more. Eighteen was a very vulnerable age, and a man like Conner Sullivan could be irresistible.

Amy toyed with the idea of relaying to Jasmine what Con had told her earlier, that he and Amber had been married the night she disappeared. But somehow Amy couldn't bring herself to do it, maybe because she wasn't quite ready to believe it herself. Instead, she said quietly, "How did the two of you get acquainted?"

Jasmine smiled, her features looking very youthful in the moonlight. She tucked a strand of hair behind one ear. "It was actually pretty dramatic. Some of us were having a party down here on the bridge one night. Things got a little out of hand, and one of the girls fell into the river. Most of the guys were too drunk to even notice, and the rest of us panicked. Tara would have drowned if it hadn't been for Con. He appeared out of nowhere, jumped into the river, pulled her out and then gave her CPR. The paramedics said he saved her life. After they took her away, he just…disappeared again."

"That's incredible." An image of the way Con had looked that afternoon flashed through Amy's mind. The dark eyes, the grim features…

Who would have thought such a man would turn out to be a hero?

"Ever since then, I've felt a...connection with him," Jasmine said. "I've gone to see him a few times, and I can tell by the way he looks at me that he feels something for me, too." Her eyes took on a dreamy quality. "Did you know he was in the service for a long time, and that he was almost killed down in South America?"

"He told you that?"

"Oh, no way. He'd never say anything like that. He's very private. But Mena wrote an article about him when he first moved back to Magnolia Bend last year, and there's been some talk around town. He has a snake tattoo on his arm, and someone told me that it meant he'd been in the special forces, one of those secret commando groups that are trained to kill with their bare hands."

Amy wasn't sure how much of what Jasmine had just told her she could believe. Gossip was rampant in small towns, but Conner Sullivan did have the look of a man who could very well be a trained killer.

She shivered, remembering his arms around her on the bridge. Remembering that if everything he'd told her was true, she was still married to him.

"Anyway," Jasmine was saying, "that's why I asked you if there were any sparks left when you saw him earlier. I don't want to see him get hurt again. Not by you."

Her bluntness stung Amy. "I don't intend to hurt anyone."

Jasmine met her gaze in the moonlight. Her eyes were like chips of topaz. "Maybe you don't intend to, but that's what always happens when you're around. People get hurt. Con and Daddy and—" She broke off, turning back to the water again.

"And you?" Amy asked with sudden insight.

Jasmine lifted her chin. "You didn't hurt me. I couldn't care less that you left. In case you haven't noticed, I turned out just fine."

"I'm glad." A deep sadness came over Amy for all the pain her leaving had caused, for all the years she'd lost. If she'd stayed, would she have been able to redeem herself by now? Would she and Jasmine have become close, like sisters should be? Would she and Con...have lived together as man and wife?

A thrill of excitement raced through her at the thought of sharing that man's bed.

Trying to block the image, she asked hesitantly, "So what did I do back then that was so terrible? How did I hurt people?"

"Among other things, you let us all think you were dead."

"You really think I did that on purpose?" Amy bit her lip. "No one really knows what happened the night I disappeared."

"So what? I know what happened *after* that. Daddy almost died, he was so worried. I can still see him standing on one side of the bridge and Con on the other while they dragged the river for your body."

Amy could almost see it, too. She felt chilled all

the way to her soul. "Why did they think I might have drowned?"

"Because they found your shoe floating in the water. And because you and Daddy had a terrible fight that night over Lottie. You hated her back then for what she did to Mama. You accused her of stealing some antiques or something, and then you told Daddy that if he didn't make her and the twins leave Amberly, he'd be sorry. When you didn't come home that night, he couldn't stop thinking about Mama."

"You mean he thought I might have killed myself?" Amy asked, the chill inside her deepening.

"Not exactly." Jasmine's voice grew cryptic. "He thought someone might have killed you."

Amy's heart thudded against her chest. "My God," she breathed, her voice hoarse with shock. "Who would have wanted to kill me?"

"Con, for one."

Amy gasped. "Con—"

Jasmine gave her an almost defiant look. "Daddy thought he'd killed you in a fit of jealous rage or something. Con always did have a wicked temper, and you'd been hanging around with him a lot that summer, leading him on. Everyone in town knew you were just seeing him to spite Daddy."

Amy couldn't speak. She sat helplessly watching her sister in the moonlight, feeling as if she were drowning for real this time.

Jasmine almost casually twirled a lock of tawny hair around one finger. "When you didn't come home, Daddy had the sheriff go out to Con's trailer and arrest him for your murder."

CHAPTER SIX

LONG AFTER JASMINE had gone back to the house, Amy sat on the bank and watched the fog thicken and curl over the water. The night was warm and humid, but the scattered mist drifting toward the bank was cool. Still shaken by what her sister had told her, Amy ran her hands up and down her arms, trying to chase away the black chill that had invaded her.

How had her quest taken such an unexpected turn? She'd been searching for her past, perhaps naively hoping to find home, hearth and, if she were honest with herself, love. What she'd uncovered instead was an insidious hostility that had not abated in nine long years. Amber Tremain had left behind a string of bad feelings, emotions that ran so deep, her own father had believed her the victim of murder.

Murder. The word was like an echo inside Amy's head. Con had been arrested for Amber's murder. *Her* murder.

Held on suspicion, Jasmine had finally clarified. After her father's accusations, the sheriff had gone out to Con's trailer, searched his belongings, then hauled him off to jail, where he'd remained all night.

In the morning, Con had been released without ever having been formally charged, but the damage had already been done. Everyone in town suspected he was a killer.

What had that done to him? Amy thought with a shiver. What kind of stigma would something like that leave on a nineteen-year-old boy?

He'd grow bitter. Hostile. He might even start to blame the person he'd been accused of killing.

Was that why Con was so angry with her? Or was it something more than that? Some deeper pain that hadn't healed in all this time?

Amy's thoughts raced as she tried to put together the meager puzzle pieces of her past. The night she'd disappeared, Amber and her father had gotten into a terrible argument about Lottie. Amber had threatened to make him sorry if he didn't kick Lottie out.

But her sister had been so young back then. How accurate was her memory? What if Amber had told her father about the elopement, and they'd been arguing about Con instead of Lottie? If her father had been upset about the marriage, he might even have ordered Amber to leave.

Then what? If she hadn't gone back to the bridge to meet Con, where *had* she gone? What had happened to cause her to lose her memory?

And how had she ended up in Houston with Nona?

It occurred to Amy, perhaps somewhat anticlimactically, that she no longer had any doubts about her real identity. She knew she was Amber Tremain, but the knowledge was far from comforting. In so many ways, Amber was still a stranger to her, a young woman who had been stubborn, spoiled and rebellious. A woman who was nothing like quiet, hardworking Amy Calloway.

But Amy Calloway's persona had not been a perfect fit, either, Amy suddenly realized. She'd always struggled with emotions and impulses that didn't seem to belong to the woman she was supposed to be. Now she understood those dark feelings, the intense longing that had been a part of her for as long as she could remember. Amber had been there all along, buried somewhere deep inside her, fighting to survive.

Amy wasn't sure how long she'd been sitting lost in contemplation when suddenly she noticed that the mist had begun to intensify. Low-hanging clouds moved in to obscure the moon, and the darkness became eerily silent. Even the cicadas had stopped singing.

Alarmed, Amy reached for her sandals. If the fog drifted to the banks, she might have a hard time finding the trail back to the house. She started to get up, but a sound in the woods behind her made her pause, listening.

A few seconds passed before she heard the noise again—a twig snapping underfoot, louder this time, as if someone, or something, was moving toward her. The hair on the back of her neck rose in warning.

Remembering Jasmine's omen about bobcats, Amy struggled to her feet and slipped on her sandals, then hurried to the top of the embankment. But as she started down the path toward Amberly, she heard the sound again, this time somewhere in front of her.

Something was in the woods, watching her, waiting for her. Amy could feel it.

The underbrush crunched again, louder and closer still, as if the stalker, in anticipation of the kill, was no longer making an effort for stealth.

Trying to still the sickening thud of her heart, Amy told herself she was letting her imagination get the better of her. But the nightscape had suddenly become menacing. The shrouded moon made vague shadows in the woods appear like monsters. One of the shadows moved, and Amy could have sworn she saw something— someone?—dart out of the woods toward her.

Her heart pounding, she whirled and ran back along the path toward the river. The bridge loomed before her, and Amy raced toward it, her footsteps echoing like gunshots on the wooden floorboards.

Halfway across the bridge, she paused, glancing over her shoulder, almost expecting to see the yellow eyes of some ferocious beast glowing in the dark as it chased her. But the way behind her was clear, and Amy realized in relief that she'd overreacted. The noise she'd heard in the woods had probably been made by a squirrel or a raccoon, the shadow she'd seen nothing more than a tree forced to life by her fear.

Even so, she didn't immediately retrace her steps, but stood at the railing of the bridge, staring down into the mist-shrouded water. After a few moments, when no apparent threat reared its ugly head, Amy told herself it was safe to go home. But she couldn't seem to tear herself away from the railing. It was almost as if some strange force had compelled her onto the bridge, and now that she was here, she couldn't leave. The lure was too powerful.

What had happened here? What was it about this place that drew her back time and again?

Her marriage to Con?

Her mother's suicide?

A wave of dizziness washed over Amy as the vision came back to her. The disembodied hand reaching out of the darkness. Someone falling—

Suddenly, a woman's scream shattered the quiet, and Amy's heart slammed into her chest. Terrified, she spun away from the railing just as someone reached out of the darkness to grab her—

A scream rose to her own throat a split second before she recognized Con. She still would have cried out if he hadn't said, quite calmly, "It was just a peacock."

"Wh-what…?"

"That noise you heard. It was one of Amberly's peacocks. They roost in the trees around here at night."

The adrenaline still pumped fiercely through Amy's veins. It took her a moment to comprehend Con's words. Then, when she finally managed to calm herself, she became aware of something else. How quietly he'd come upon her. The weight of his hand on her arm. The way he towered over her in the darkness.

The fact that he'd been suspected of killing her.

"What are you doing here?" she asked breathlessly, searching in the darkness for the snake tattoo on his arm.

He shrugged. "Just out for a stroll."

"Did you come through the woods just now?" Her tone was anxious, frightened.

He frowned down at her in the moonlight. "No, why?"

"I thought I heard something."

"Like what?"

"I'm…not sure." Amy drew a long breath. "It was probably nothing, but I thought I heard someone walking toward me."

Con's gaze scanned the darkness around them. After a moment, he glanced back at Amy, but she couldn't read his expression. "Probably just a coon hunter getting a jump on the season." But something in his voice made Amy shiver. "What are you doing out here alone anyway?"

"Jasmine and I came down to the river a little while ago."

His gaze narrowed as he glanced over her shoulder. His hand dropped from her arm. "Where is Jasmine?"

As acutely as Amy had been aware of his touch, she was even more conscious of the absence of it. Why had he released her the moment she'd mentioned her sister?

"She went back to the house." Then, hesitantly "I'm glad you're here, Con."

She sensed more than saw one dark brow rise in question, but he remained silent.

"I'd like to talk to you about Jasmine," she said.

"What about her?"

Amy paused again, not sure how to continue. Not sure she had any right to continue. "Look, I know this is going to sound strange coming from me. It's probably none of my business, but…Jasmine told me the two of you had become friends."

Was her imagination playing tricks on her again, or had he moved away from her in the darkness? Had he intentionally put a gulf between them? "We've talked a time or two." His voice was non committal. "Is that still taboo?"

Amy frowned. "What do you mean?"

"A Tremain associating with a Sullivan."

If there was bitterness in his voice, he managed to conceal it. He seemed different tonight, Amy thought. Not antagonistic as he'd been this afternoon, but restrained, controlled.

She thought again about the sound she'd heard in the woods. *Had* that been him?

Gooseflesh tickled her neck as she said, "I just thought you should know Jasmine may have a crush on you."

"Is that so?"

She couldn't tell by his tone if he was pleased or annoyed. She said hurriedly, "Like I said, it's probably none of my business, but—"

"Why wouldn't it be your business?" If he'd

moved away from her before, he was suddenly standing so close, Amy's breath left her in a swoosh. He stared down at her, his shadowy expression mocking her. "She's your sister, isn't she?"

"Yes," Amy murmured, although that wasn't at all what she thought he meant. "She's barely eighteen...."

"She's the same age you were back then."

Amy couldn't remember being eighteen. She didn't even remember Con. But something of that last summer rose within her, and the nostalgia and the bittersweet emotions that swept over her were so intense, they left her shaken, disoriented.

What had happened between them the night she'd disappeared?

"What is it you're so afraid of, Amber?" His voice was like the night—warm, dark and deeply mysterious.

Amy shivered, gazing up at him. She wasn't sure if he was still talking about Jasmine or not, but she preferred to believe that he was. "I don't want my sister to get hurt."

"Why would I hurt her?"

Because you're dangerous, Amy thought. *Because Jasmine's at an impressionable age, and God help me, so am I.* Aloud, she said, "Maybe because she's a Tremain."

"I see." His eyes were like dark pools in the moonlight. Deep. Dangerous. He cocked his head slightly. "Or maybe because she's the spitting image of you at that age."

She sensed his sudden tension, his awareness as

he stared down at her in the misty darkness. Just as she had this afternoon, she thought he was going to kiss her, wanted him to desperately, she realized, and the knowledge was almost as shocking as it was frightening.

What was happening to her? Yesterday, she'd been a quiet, unassuming person in search of her past, and now, less than twenty-four hours later, she'd become a woman who seemed daring, passionate, emotionally reckless. She was becoming Amber Tremain again.

As if reading her mind, Con swore under his breath. He took a step back from her, once again putting distance between them as if his very life depended on it. "No," he muttered before turning to stare down at the water.

"Wh-what?" She wasn't sure what he was saying no to.

He still didn't look at her. "You were talking about Jasmine."

Yes, she had been, hadn't she? Amy made a helpless gesture with her hand. "I don't think she knows about…us. About what you told me earlier. The…elopement."

"Then why didn't you tell her?"

His voice held a note of challenge, and Amy thought, *That's a good question. Why* didn't *I tell her?*

Con glanced at her. "What exactly is your concern here? Are you worried I'm going to take advantage of your sister? Do you think I'm the type of man who would try to seduce an eighteen-year-old girl?'' The bitterness had returned, along with the hostility. Amy wondered what she'd done to trigger his anger.

She said almost defensively, ''You've done it before, haven't you?''

She could have sworn she saw his eyes darken in the moonlight, and his expression assumed the angry scowl she'd sketched so often in the past. He glared down at her as if he would like nothing better than to strangle her and throw her body off the river bridge. ''What makes you so damn sure I'm the one who did the seducing that summer?''

''Are you saying *I* seduced *you?*'' Her eyes flashed in disbelief, her tone heavy with what he could only assume was scorn.

Amnesia or not, here was the Amber he remembered all too well, Con thought dryly. ''I'm saying you always found a way to get what you wanted, and you didn't let anything or anyone stand in your way.''

''And I wanted you?''

His laugh sounded harsh in the quiet darkness. ''Hard to believe, isn't it? Maybe you ought to figure out what your motive was that summer. It might all make a little more sense to you then.''

She hesitated. ''What do you mean?''

Whether she had meant to or not, she'd moved closer to him on the bridge, searching his face in the moonlight. Con felt a familiar tugging at his insides as he stared down at her, and he swore under his breath. Why the hell was he letting her get to him like this? A minute ago, he'd wanted nothing more than to haul her against him and kiss her, long and hard, until she either remembered the past or he forgot it.

But he'd been trained a long time ago to keep a cool head in the face of overwhelming danger. And make no mistake, he thought grimly, Amber Tremain was as hazardous to his mental well-being as she'd ever been.

He only had to look at her—those eyes, those lips, that face—to know she could put him through the emotional wringer once more, if he let her. But he wasn't about to go falling for her again—or, for that matter, for any woman. He'd finally gotten the upper hand around here, and he sure as hell wasn't about to lose it.

"You had your reasons for wanting to get close to me that summer," he told her, trying to keep his voice devoid of emotion. He shrugged. "You played me for a sucker."

Unconsciously, she put her hand on the railing, and Con heard the metal squeak in protest. He took her arm, pulling her back from the edge, even though they both knew she was in no danger of falling.

Her skin felt warm beneath his touch, as smooth and fragrant as the magnolia blossoms she'd always loved. He remembered how she'd worn one in her hair that night, how the scent had enveloped him when he'd leaned down to kiss her before she left him.

He remembered a lot of things about that night. The feel of her lips beneath his. The way her white dress had clung to her young curves, revealing just enough flesh to drive him wild. But most of all, he remembered the promise in her eyes when she'd cupped the back of his neck, drawing him to her, whispering to him that she would always be his.

He released her arm as if she'd burned him. For just a split second, he could have sworn he saw her eyes cloud with regret, but that had to be his imagination. An illusion created by the moonlight. Amber Tremain never had regrets.

"How did I play you for a sucker?"

He shrugged. "What better way to spite your old man than to marry a juvenile delinquent he despised?"

"You think I married you to get back at my father?"

"I know you did. I heard you tell him so."

"When?"

"I followed you up from the river that night. I heard the two of you fighting. He accused you of marrying me to spite him, and you said something like, 'So what if I did? Now you know exactly how I feel.'"

Amy turned away from Con, a wave of shame washing over her. Had she really been that careless with people's feelings? No wonder her return had not been met with open arms.

"You have to admit, it makes more sense than your having been swept away by passion." His tone mocked her, but Amy had a feeling that underneath the sarcasm lurked a deep, lingering hurt, a pain that had not gone away in all these years.

"I don't know what to say." She still couldn't quite meet his gaze.

"There's nothing to say. I'm not looking for an apology. I'm not looking for anything from you. I knew the score when I married you."

Amy glanced up at him. "Then why did you go through with it? If you knew I was using you, why marry me?"

He shrugged again, but Amy could sense the tension inside him, coiled like a spring waiting to snap. "I used to ask myself that a lot. I would sometimes lie in my bunk, in whatever foreign country I was stationed, and wonder what I'd do if I ever came face-to-face with you again. What I'd say to you."

"Even though you knew I might be dead?"

When he didn't answer, a coldness seeped over Amy that had very little to do with the rising mist and everything to do with the man—the stranger— who stood before her. If what he'd told her was true, he had every reason in the world to hate her, to want revenge against her.

Maybe even to murder her.

Amy was suddenly afraid of him, but it was a strange kind of fear, because she knew, deep down, he would never harm her physically. The pain he could inflict would be far more subtle and far more devastating.

As if reading her mind, he lifted his hand to cup the back of her neck, pulling her ever so slightly to him. Amy held her breath as his head lowered toward hers in the darkness. She should stop him, she knew. She should never allow this man, this stranger, her husband, to kiss her, but she felt almost powerless to stop him.

Except for his hand on her neck, Con wasn't touching her, but excitement tingled through every nerve ending in Amy's body. She'd never felt such a potent attraction, never experienced such a dangerous need, and when he brushed his lips against hers, her heart threatened to explode.

"It's getting late. I'd better go back," she said shakily.

He didn't argue with her, didn't even look annoyed. He merely straightened and said, "Running away again, Amber?"

"I'm not running away." She tried not to sound too defensive. "It *is* getting late. Lottie may be worried. She might send someone to look for me."

"And God forbid they should find you with me."

CHAPTER SEVEN

JAMES BIRDSONG WAS one of only two attorneys-at-law listed in the Magnolia Bend telephone directory. The other was Darnell Henry, the Tremain family lawyer, but Amy didn't think it a good idea to seek his advice on such a personal matter.

James had agreed to see her late that afternoon, and after having spent three days at Amberly going through photo albums and family heirlooms—none of which had elicited even a glimmer of memory—and three nights where the tension remained so thick around the dinner table that she could have cut it with a knife, Amy welcomed the opportunity to get out of the house and drive into town.

She hadn't seen Con since that first night, even though she'd taken nightly walks down to the river, once with Jasmine and twice with Mena. The bridge was the one place that seemed to stir something inside her, and Amy told herself she wasn't going there so much to look for Con as to search for memories. But it was hard to say which pull was stronger.

All this and more rolled through Amy's head as she pulled into a parking space in front of the Choppowah County Courthouse. James Birdsong's office was located across the street in a single-story brick building with an old-fashioned shingle hanging from the awning over the door. An attractive brunette greeted Amy in the reception area and ushered her into the inner office. James rose, dismissing the receptionist with a curt nod, then turned his full attention on Amy.

"Amber! My God, it really is you. I still can't believe it!" He came around the desk and took her hand, squeezing it warmly in both of his as his eager gaze moved over her features.

In his late twenties, he was a tall, wiry man with a receding hairline, a hesitant smile and truly beautiful gray eyes that were magnified by wire-rim glasses. Those gray eyes glinted with admiration as he stared down at her. "You haven't changed a bit."

"That's nice of you to say." Amy smiled, trying to alleviate the uneasiness his familiarity caused her. "I'm afraid there's one big change, though."

He sobered. "Right. The amnesia thing." Moving around his desk to sit, he motioned her to a comfortable, leather chair.

"You know about it, then." Amy settled herself in the chair.

"News travels fast in a small town. You can't keep anything a secret."

Except a marriage, she thought. Apparently, no one knew about her and Con's elopement.

James scratched his head. "To think you've been alive all these years, and none of us knew. It's hard to believe."

"I'm sure it is," Amy agreed.

"This must be especially difficult for you, meeting people who knew you so well, but of whom you have no recollection.'' His smile turned wry. ''Take our situation, for instance. Here I am talking to you as if we're old friends, which we are, but you don't remember a thing about our past, do you?''

''No, I'm afraid I don't.''

He looked oddly disappointed by her answer. ''When you called earlier, I was rather hoping it was because...'' He trailed off, as if unwilling to finish his thought. Then, clearing his throat, he sat back in his chair and studied her thoughtfully. ''I don't mind telling you, I was surprised to hear from you. Delighted, but surprised. Darnell Henry has always represented both the Tremains and the Witherspoons.''

''Yes, I know. I've met him, but under the circumstances, I didn't want to consult with him on this matter.'' She paused. ''Whatever I tell you will be held in confidence, won't it?''

His brows rose over the rims of his glasses. ''That goes without saying. Lawyer-client privilege aside, you've always been my friend. I would never betray your confidence.''

''Thank you.'' Amy took a long breath and released it. ''I learned recently that I may have been married on the day I disappeared.''

James stared at her, his expression frozen. ''But that's impossible...you weren't seeing anyone...not seriously...'' His gaze deepened on her. ''Who?''

''Conner Sullivan.''

His gray eyes, so compassionate moments before, now hardened with disbelief. He removed his glasses, wiping the lenses almost fiercely with a tissue. "That's preposterous. Who told you that?"

Amy bit her lip. "He did."

James seemed speechless for a moment, then he blurted, "I've never heard anything so ridiculous in my life! There were rumors about the two of you that summer, but I never believed them. And besides, your father would never have allowed you to marry—not at eighteen and especially not to someone like that. Sullivan was bad news. He was always into some kind of trouble. Judge Tremain even suspected he might have...been dangerous."

"I know all about my father's accusations." Lifting her hands palms up, Amy said, "But as you can see, he was wrong."

"Evidently," James agreed with a frown. "But the point is, the judge would never have given his permission for you to marry Conner Sullivan."

"According to Con, my father didn't know. We eloped. We were married by a justice of the peace in Memphis." Amy wove her fingers together in her lap, trying to appear calm and in control. "Anyway, I need to...verify his claim, and if it turns out to be true..." She paused. "What would be the legal standing of our marriage?"

James ran a hand through his thin hair. Without his glasses, his eyes looked slightly out of focus as he gazed at her. "Verification won't be a problem. My cousin's ex-wife is a supervisor in the county clerk's office in Memphis. I can give her a call right now. Everything is computerized these days, so with the exact date, it should only take a matter of minutes to call up the records. We can even have her fax us a copy of the marriage license. If it exists, of course.''

He slipped on his glasses, checked his Rolodex and placed the call. After politely inquiring about the woman's two sons and her mother's health, he repeated the names and date Amy had given him, explained what they needed and then hung up. ''She'll get back to us as soon as possible. Probably within the hour. But I don't mind telling you that this worries me.'' He glanced at Amy, his expression troubled. ''I can't help wondering what Sullivan may be up to.''

His tone alarmed Amy. She sat forward slightly in her chair. ''What do you mean?''

He picked up a pen, absently rubbing it between his thumb and forefinger. ''Property values along the river have been steadily going up for the last couple of years. A development company out of Memphis has a big project planned for the area—vacation homes, a golf course, you name it. Con sold them his mother's old place, and now I hear he's got some kind of arrangement with them. He finds property along the river, makes an offer well below market value, somehow gets a signature on a contract and then the development company swoops in and takes over before anyone can object, giving Con a sizeable finder's fee for his troubles.''

Somehow Amy had a hard time picturing Con as a ruthless businessman, although she wasn't sure why. The image Jasmine had created last night— that of dark soldier and trained killer—had seemed almost too plausible. "What does any of that have to do with me?" she asked doubtfully.

"Surely you know the terms of your mother's will? Amberly belonged to her. The house has been in the Witherspoon family for generations. She left Amberly and a considerable amount of river property to you and your sister jointly, to be held in trust until each of you turned eighteen. Neither of you could sell the property without the other's consent. In other words, once you turned eighteen, half of the inheritance became legally yours, but you couldn't dispose of the house or land until Jasmine's eighteenth birthday, and only then if she agreed. Now that Jasmine's come of age, she's received her half of the inheritance, and she's made no secret of her desire to sell. I've heard talk that Sullivan's been sniffing around, but, of course, now that you're back, Jasmine can't do anything without your permission."

Amy had been given an inkling of the situation by Darnell Henry, and by Con's insinuation that she'd returned to lay claim to Amberly. But until that moment, she wasn't sure she'd quite absorbed all the implications.

"Are you saying you think Con may try to buy Amberly?"

James shrugged. "All I'm saying is that you need to be careful. He's always been a bit…shady, if you ask me. It's in his blood, I guess. His father, Jude Sullivan, would have sold his own mother for a buck, and then spent it on a quart of moonshine whiskey."

Amy had the strongest impulse to defend Con, although she couldn't imagine why. Even if he turned out to be her husband, she didn't remember him. She didn't know anything about him. Maybe he *was* ruthless and cold. A trained killer, for all she knew.

"I haven't even talked to Jasmine about her plans," Amy told him. "If she wants to sell Amberly, I'm not sure I have the right to stop her." But even as she expressed her doubts, a feeling of resolve came over her, a fierce protectiveness of her ancestral home that she didn't understand. She didn't remember Amberly, either. The house meant nothing to her. So why did she feel so...possessive of it? Was it because, as Lottie told her yesterday, Amber had once loved the place as much as she did?

James watched her intently. "I'm glad to hear you say that, Amber, because we're talking about the potential for a great deal of money. With the Tremain sawmill and logging interests gone, Amberly is about all you and Jasmine have left. A house like that is a considerable financial drain, especially with the family's dwindling resources, but with the right buyer, you and your sister could both make a nice profit." He emphasized the word *right*. Another dig at Con, Amy thought. "In fact, I know of someone who may be interested."

Amy lifted a brow. "Who?"

The phone cut him off before he could answer. He gave Amy a quick, anxious glance as he picked up the receiver. After a moment, he hung up and sighed. "Everything Conner Sullivan told you is true. The two of you were married nine years ago."

Amy's head reeled suddenly. A myriad of emotions washed over her—disappointment, trepidation, fear and, oddly, relief. But why would she be relieved to know she and Con were married? It made no sense.

"So then...are we still married?"

"If neither of you filed for divorce or petitioned for an annulment, then yes."

Why *hadn't* he gotten a divorce? If he really believed she'd married him to spite her father, why stay married to her?

As if reading her mind, James said gravely, "This puts you in a precarious legal position, I'm afraid. As your husband, Conner Sullivan could have a claim against your inheritance."

His warning tone sent a chill up Amy's spine. "Do you think he'd really do that?"

James gave a sharp laugh. "Don't let his appearance fool you. Sullivan is a very shrewd businessman. It occurs to me that the reason he never made a claim before, or never even made public your marriage, was because he knew that while the judge was still alive, he wouldn't stand a chance in court. But now that your father's gone, the dynamics have changed. Sullivan will be looking out for his own best interests—you can count on that. What we have to do is look out for yours."

"Meaning?"

"As I said earlier, he's made some money recently, quite a lot of it, from what I understand. As his wife, you could be entitled to half.''

Amy stared at him in shock. ''But I wouldn't take his money. I don't have any right—''

He put up a quick hand, silencing her. ''Don't be too hasty in dismissing your options.''

''But I don't want anything from Con,'' Amy said quickly. ''I don't even remember being his wife.''

''In that case, maybe the best option for both of you would be anullment. It would be as if you were never married. I can start the paperwork immediately, if that's what you want.''

That *would* be the logical option, Amy thought, but something held her back from compliance. It wasn't as if she cared about Con, or anything like that. It was just that she was hardly in any position to make important decisions of any kind right now. She had to first get her bearings.

Or so she told herself.

''Thanks for your time.'' She rose. ''I'll let you know what I decide.''

''Amber.'' James stood and came around the desk to take her hand in his again. ''Whether you decide to sell Amberly, or whether you decide to divorce Conner Sullivan—those are your decisions. But my advice in either scenario is to proceed with extreme caution. Like I said, we're talking about the potential for a great deal of money here.''

''I understand.''

His grasp tightened on hers. ''I'm not sure you do. Somehow I don't think you realize how your coming back here changes things. For a lot of people.''

''What are you getting at, James?''

The door to his office burst open, and a feminine voice demanded, ''I have to see you, Jimmy. *Right now.* You won't believe what's happened—''

Fay stopped dead in the doorway, her expression one of shock when she saw Amy. James was still holding her hand, and he dropped it, almost guiltily, it seemed to Amy.

Fay's eyes narrowed on the two of them. ''Well, that didn't take long, did it?''

''Can you please wait outside for a moment?'' James's voice was plainly conciliatory, as if he didn't want to trigger Fay's anger. ''Amber and I are in the middle of something.''

Fay arched a brow. ''I can see that. What are the two of you doing anyway? Taking a little stroll down memory lane?''

''I needed some advice,'' Amy felt compelled to explain. To James, she said, ''I'll be in touch.''

James said, too softly for Fay to hear, ''I meant what I said. Take care, Amber.''

The words would have been innocent sounding, spoken under ordinary circumstances, but in James's hushed tones, and with Fay's eyes shooting daggers at her, the farewell seemed almost ominous. As she left the office and stepped outside into the late-afternoon sunshine, Amy shivered.

The warmth of the fading light did little to alleviate her growing chill. So she really was married to Conner Sullivan. The two of them had been husband and wife for nine years, during which time Amy hadn't even known he existed.

But that wasn't really true, was it? She'd drawn his face countless times, stared at his dark features over and over as she'd wondered who he was. If he was real or a fantasy.

In all those years, Con had been the one person, his the one face, she hadn't been able to get out of her head—

Her thoughts crashed to a halt as an uncanny feeling suddenly came over. An impression that someone was watching her.

It was the same sensation she'd experienced down by the river that first night, when she'd been sure someone was in the woods behind her. Had that same someone followed her into town?

Warily, Amy glanced around, as if to make sure no evil presence lurked behind a tree or in a shop doorway. The streets were sunlit, the town ordinary in appearance, but an undercurrent of something she couldn't name seemed to flow just beneath the surface.

Her gaze moved across the street, to the courthouse nestled in a circle of magnolia trees and water oaks dripping with Spanish moss. A huge, bearlike man rose from a bench underneath one of the trees and lumbered toward the street, pulling a red Radio Flyer wagon full of aluminium cans. When he got to the curb, he glanced up and spotted Amy across the street, then stopped so abruptly several of the cans tumbled from the wagon and rolled toward the gutter.

He wore a baseball cap pulled low over his face. Amy couldn't make out his features, but something about him struck her. She'd seen him before. She knew this man.

Her heart pounded in excitement. Her first thought was that she should cross the street and confront him, but something stopped her, an instinct buried deep inside her that warned he could be dangerous.

He could hurt her.

CHAPTER EIGHT

FOR THE LONGEST MOMENT, Amy stood motionless as they stared at one another across the street. She couldn't move, couldn't tear her gaze from his, and he appeared just as mesmerized by her. Who was he?

"Amber?"

A touch on her arm caused her to give a violent start. Amy's gaze flew upward, and for a moment, she couldn't disassociate the fear she felt for the man across the street from the one who stood before her. Without thinking, she took a step back from Con.

He studied her quizzically. "Are you all right?"

She finally found her voice. "That man across the street—who is he?"

Con glanced toward the courthouse, then back at Amy, frowning. "What man?"

Amy looked back. "He was there just a second ago. I thought I recognized him. He seemed to know me—"

"He probably did know you. Everyone in town knows you."

"Yes, but—" She wrapped her arms around her middle.

"Do you want me to go across the street and see if I can find him?" When she didn't answer right away, Con said, "Amber?"

She shook herself. "No. He's gone now. And I'm sure you're right. He was just someone who recognized me. I've gotten all kinds of strange looks today." And maybe that's all it had been. But she still couldn't explain why he'd seemed so familiar to her. Or why he'd frightened her.

Con took her arm. "You look as if you could use a drink."

This time, Amy didn't move away from his touch. There was something almost comforting about his presence.

She glanced back over her shoulder, but the man was nowhere in sight. For someone so big, he could certainly move fast, she thought with a shiver.

THE DECOR OF Jolene's Diner was typical of small-town eateries everywhere—formica-top tables and stainless-steel chairs arranged haphazardly in the center of a large, square room while red-vinyl booths lined the sides.

Con and Amy took a booth by the plate-glass window that looked out on the street. A woman glanced inside as she walked by, then did a double take when she saw Amy. She was still looking over her shoulder as she hurried down the street, no doubt eager to tell someone of the sighting.

Con muttered, "Maybe you'd like something a little more private."

"No, this is fine."

He saw her hands trembling and glanced up at her. "What really happened back there? You looked as if you'd seen a ghost."

"I'm not sure," she admitted. "Maybe I did. There was this man on the courthouse lawn. He was huge. I couldn't really see his face, but he wore a baseball cap and denim overalls, and he pulled a little red wagon full of aluminum cans. I thought for a moment that I recognized him."

She'd looked scared to death, although she was trying to cover it now. He wondered if something more had happened that she wasn't telling him. Amber always did have her secrets. He studied her curiously. "Frankie Bodine pulls around a wagon like that."

"Frankie Bodine?" A look of alarm flitted across her features, then was gone. She shook her head. "That name doesn't mean anything to me. Does he live around here?"

"Not in town. I think he has a place way back in the sticks somewhere."

"Did I used to know him?"

Con shrugged, still watching her. "You knew of him, I guess. But he's always kept to himself."

"Then why would I remember him?" she asked, almost to herself.

An uneasiness Con couldn't explain came over him. He leaned slightly toward her. "Did he bother you back there? Say something out of line to you? Because if he did, I'll go and have a talk with him."

But even as he said the words, Con was asking

himself, *What are you doing? What the hell are you doing?*

Amber had never asked for or wanted his protection in the past. Why would she do so now?

"That isn't necessary," she said, as if reading his mind, and Con swore under his breath as a waitress appeared at their booth.

"Evening, folks." She took a pencil from behind her ear. "What can I get for you?"

"A glass of iced tea, please," Amber told her.

"A beer for me. Whatever you have on tap." After the waitress left, Con said, "Sure you don't want something to eat?"

"No, tea is fine."

An awkward silence fell over the table, during which time a dozen thoughts flashed through Con's mind. What the hell was he doing here with her? Why couldn't he leave her alone? It wasn't as if they'd shared some great love affair back then. They weren't star-crossed lovers, forced apart by circumstances. He and Amber were never meant to be together. It was as simple as that.

But he couldn't deny she still had a powerful effect on him, even after everything she'd put him through. And now that she was back, without a memory of what had happened to her, without a memory of *him,* Con was torn by a myriad of conflicting emotions.

He still wanted to hurt her, as she'd hurt him, almost as much as he just plain wanted her.

As if sensing his dark thoughts, Amy said almost

tentatively, "I haven't seen you down by the river in a few days."

Had she been looking for him? Con tried not to read too much into her words. He shrugged. "I've been out of town on business."

"I heard you were working for a development company in Memphis."

Con frowned. "Who told you that?"

"James Birdsong." Something flickered in her eyes, a tiny little flare of doubt, as if maybe she'd said more than she meant to. As if maybe she didn't want him knowing she'd consulted an attorney.

He glanced at her coldly. "I wouldn't trust James Birdsong with my phone bill, let alone anything legally challenging."

Amy's brows raised. "Why? What's wrong with him?"

For one thing, he used to hang all over you, Con thought grimly. For another, he was the kind of lawyer, and suitor, that Judge Tremain had always relished—overly eager and easily controlled. "I think he may have an ethics problem."

Amy looked suddenly alarmed. "You mean he may be...indescreet?"

"Let's put it this way. I wouldn't trust him with my deepest, darkest secrets if I were you."

She looked as if she wanted to challenge him, then she shrugged. "I'll keep that in mind." As if eager herself to change the subject, she pointed to a flyer that had been tacked to the wall near their table. "Why are they having a Fourth of July barbecue on the third of July?"

Con barely glanced at the poster. "The fourth falls on a Sunday this year. Most people around here think that beer and fireworks are a little too unseemly for the Lord's day." A judgment call, he reckoned, but then, folks around here always had been big on judging.

"Is it a big event?" Amy asked him.

"By Magnolia Bend standards, I guess."

"Do you go?" Her voice sounded hesitant, almost shy.

Con frowned. "I usually skip it."

"Is that where we got the fireworks that year?"

And suddenly, without warning, the old memories flooded through him. The bright green fire of the roman candles against the night sky, the sparkle of moonlight on water and his arms around Amber, his lips nuzzling her neck as he whispered to her how much he loved her, how much he wanted her. What he wouldn't do if he couldn't have her...

The waitress returned with their drinks, and as she placed Amy's tea before her, she said, "Say, aren't you Jasmine Tremain's big sister? I heard you were coming back, but I never expected to see you in this dump. Wait'll I tell Cherée."

Amy gave a shaky little laugh once the waitress had departed. "Being back here is a little like waking up in Oz. All these people know who I am, but I don't have a clue."

Con took a drink of his beer, trying to clear his mind, but it was like walking through cobwebs. The memories clung to him. "So what was your life like down in Houston?"

"It was...quiet. Ordinary." She gave another little laugh, but her tawny eyes were clouded. "All those years, I thought I was Amy Calloway from Iowa. I lived my life accordingly. I did what was expected of me. I went to college, made good grades and after graduation, I got a job with an advertising firm where I did quite well, I guess. But looking back, I didn't...flourish. I never really threw myself into anything. My work. My friendships..." She paused, and something that might have been guilt flashed in her eyes. "There was always a part of me that I held back, and now I realize why. I think I was scared to find out about my past. All that time, I should have been trying to discover who I was and where I came from, but instead I was...hiding."

"From what?"

"Myself?"

He lifted a brow in skepticism. "Do you really believe that? Do you really think you stayed away all those years because you couldn't face being Amber Tremain?" She'd once relished the role. She'd been spoiled, impulsive and wild, getting away with a bad reputation because she was a Tremain. Whereas Con had never gotten away with much of anything, though God knows it wasn't for lack of trying. His old man used to beat him with his belt buckle at the slightest provocation, but rather than subduing Con, it had made him want to fight back. So he'd joined the army, where he could.

"So what about you?" Amy was saying. "What was your life like these last nine years?"

He shrugged. "Quiet. Ordinary."

She laughed at his imitation, and a soft glow lit her beautiful eyes. She looked very young, all of a sudden, as if the past nine years hadn't touched her. Con felt as though he'd crammed a hundred years of living in that space, and he knew it showed in his face. He would be thirty next month. He looked at least ten years older than that.

"Jasmine told me you were in the service," Amy said. "The special forces."

"I was in the army for a while. And then I got out and came back here." That was all she needed to know. All he intended on telling her.

"I heard your mother was sick for a long time. Is that what brought you back to Magnolia Bend?"

Another taboo subject. Con shrugged. "Partly, I guess. And partly because I had nowhere else to go. When I found out how sick she was, I decided to stick around for a while."

Until after she was gone, Amy thought. He didn't say the words, but she knew, instinctively, that he'd stayed in town to be with his mother, so she wouldn't be alone when she died.

Of all the things Amy had learned about Con—that she'd married him to spite her father, that he'd once been accused of murdering her, that he'd been a trained killer by profession and that he was now a ruthless businessman—none seemed as dangerous to her as the knowledge that he'd come home, wounded and changed, to be with his dying mother.

The other Con was cold, remote, almost untouchable, but this Con...

She lifted her gaze to his. "Why did you stay on,

after everything that happened? Why are you still here?''

''I guess I still don't have anyplace else to go.''

Amy realized suddenly, devastatingly, that she had nowhere else to go, either. She couldn't go back to Houston. The city seemed foreign to her now, the job she'd once enjoyed hardly more than a distant memory. Her friends and business associates—had she ever really known any of them? And Reece?

He was her one regret, not because she'd left him, but because she'd hurt him. But sitting across the table from Con, a man who was hardly more than a stranger to her, Amy had never been more certain of her decision.

The two of them had shared something once, something more than Con was willing to admit. Amy's amnesia didn't weaken the potency of those emotions, didn't dilute the power of the past, which hovered over them like a storm cloud waiting to burst.

''Can I ask you something else?'' she said.

He glanced at her.

''Why did you keep our elopement a secret all these years?''

''You were the one who wanted to keep it a secret. After you were gone, I didn't see the point in telling anyone.''

Even if it had helped clear the suspicions surrounding him? He'd been that willing to keep her secret? ''Why did you never divorce me? You would have had grounds. You probably could have even gotten an annulment.''

"There didn't seem much point in that, either." His tone was cool, measured. "I wasn't ever going to marry again."

Amy's heart turned over. "You could be that certain at nineteen?"

"Some things never change."

Their conversation seemed almost surreal. Amy couldn't believe she was sitting here talking about divorce and annulment, when a few days ago, she hadn't even known a man named Conner Sullivan existed.

She tore her gaze from his and studied her glass. "There must have been someone else. In nine years?"

When he didn't say anything, she glanced up to find him watching her with eyes that had seen too much of a dangerous world and now gazed upon her with a glimmer of emotion that might have been longing.

He reached across the table and took her left hand, holding it up. In the light from the window, Amy glimpsed the faint white circle left by her engagement ring, but it was too late to snatch her hand away.

"I guess there was someone for you." His voice was edged with something that made Amy tremble.

She removed her hand from his. "I was engaged for a while, but it didn't work out. I couldn't go through with it."

"Why not?" The glint in his eyes hardened. It didn't seem so much like longing now as...what? Anger? Resolve? Or just plain hurt?

Amy chose her words carefully. "We weren't right for each other. I knew that all along, I think, but once I found out about my past, I realized what a mistake marrying him would be. How could I expect to make a marriage work when I didn't even know who I was?"

"Not to mention the fact that you were already married," he said.

"But I didn't know that."

"Didn't you?"

Amy thought about the countless pictures she'd drawn of Con, the nights she'd lain awake, wondering about him. Had there been some ethereal bond, some spiritual communication with him that had told her she wasn't free to marry Reece? Was that why Con had invaded her dreams?

Or was she reading too much into a teenage marriage that would probably have ended long ago if she'd stayed in Magnolia Bend? Maybe James Birdsong was right. The real reason Con had never divorced her was purely monetary, and not some sort of fatal romanticism Amy wasn't even sure existed outside of storybooks.

"Maybe a part of me did remember," she said. "Maybe that's why I couldn't marry Reece. But I'll never be sure of that, or anything else, until I get my memory back."

"Then you'd better get it back, hadn't you?"

Amy stared up at him, surprised by the harshness of his words. "It isn't that easy. I've tried to remember."

"Have you?" He leaned toward her slightly. "Do you really want your memory back, Amber?"

"Of course. Why wouldn't I?"

"That's what I'd like to know."

Anger shot through Amy. "Are you saying you still don't believe I have amnesia?"

He shrugged. "No, I believe that, all right. What I don't believe is that you've tried as hard as you say you have to get your memory back."

"Oh, and you're an expert suddenly on amnesia?" She barely recognized the tone of her own voice. She sounded hard, aggressive, like Amber Tremain.

"I've done some reading," Con told her.

He surprised her again. She gazed at him almost resentfully. "And?"

"There may be something we can do to jolt your memory."

Amber's heart started pounding inside her. The way he was looking at her…the way he'd said "we." With one simple pronoun, he'd joined them together. Made them a pair.

Before she could comment, he said, "We could try to reconstruct that night."

Their wedding night.

How far was he suggesting they go?

She lifted her chin, gazing at him almost defiantly. "Why would you, of all people, want to help me?"

"Why wouldn't I?"

"Because of what you told me last night." She studied him for a moment, wondering if his motives were sincere. Could she trust him? Did she dare?

"You said the reason I married you was to get back at my father. If that's the case, I don't understand why you'd want to help me. Why would you even care what happened to me?"

"Because you're not the only one whose life was affected by that night." His jaw hardened as he turned to stare out the window. "I've spent all these years wondering if you were really dead, or if…"

"What?"

He still wasn't looking at her. His gaze, cold and remote, was focused on the street. "I'm sure you've heard about your old man's accusations."

And suddenly it hit her why Con was still angry with her after all this time. Why her return had generated such contempt in him. If she wasn't dead, then he'd been forced to believe she'd run off of her own free will, leaving him to face her father's allegations, a whole town's blackest suspicions. He'd even been arrested, and she still hadn't returned to set the record straight. She'd let everyone in Magnolia Bend believe him a murderer.

Or so he'd thought.

"I didn't know," she whispered, almost too herself. "I couldn't have known."

Con turned to face her, his features implacable. "Maybe you didn't know," he said. "I'm willing to give you that. But it still doesn't change what happened. I got away from here as fast as I could that summer, but my mother stayed on. This was her home, such as it was, and she had her pride. She wouldn't let them drive her away. But having a son suspected of murder did things to her. The whispers, the stares. All that took its toll.''

On him, as well, even if he wouldn't admit it. He had his pride, too.

Tears stung behind Amy's lids suddenly. She wanted to reach out and take his hand, but she didn't think he'd welcome her touch. Not now, maybe not ever.

"It's like this, Amber. Your disappearance changed a lot of lives, for better or for worse, and I don't think either of us will ever have any peace until we know the truth about that night.'' His dark gaze challenged her as his voice deepened. ''That's why I want to help you. That's the only reason why.''

AMY'S HEAD SPUN in confusion on her way home. She'd stayed in town far longer than she'd meant to, and now twilight had fallen. The sky deepened to purple, and the first star twinkled on the horizon as she followed the blacktop road through the cotton fields.

A sense of impending doom settled over her. Con had promised to help her unravel her past, but Amy knew she would have to be careful. She was vulnerable in a way she never had been before, and her feelings for Con were turning out to be far more complicated than she could ever have dreamed.

Shivering in the growing gloom, she tried to concentrate on her driving. A huge tractor loomed on the road in front of her, and she slowed, waiting for a chance to pass. When the double yellow lines vanished on a stretch of pavement, she pulled into the other lane and accelerated around the tractor, easing back into her own lane when she could see the vehicle's lights in her rearview mirror.

Glancing back again, she saw another set of headlights dart around the tractor. But instead of pulling into the lane behind Amy, the driver hit the gas, and a dark, four-wheel-drive truck, with huge tires and blacked-out windows, shot around her. Almost instantly, the vehicle's taillights disappeared from her view.

After a few moments, Amy could no longer see the tractor lights, either. There was no one in front of her, no one behind her. She was all alone on a dark, unfamiliar road, and as the strange scenery whipped past her, she began to grow uneasy. What if she had a flat tire or her car stalled? How long would she have to wait before help came along?

But then, as she rounded a curve, she saw the cherry glow of taillights ahead of her. Somehow the knowledge that she wasn't completely alone made her feel a little better, and Amy accelerated, trying to catch up to the lights.

She came upon the vehicle so quickly, she had to throw on her brakes. The truck crept along the two-lane highway, going no more than ten miles per hour.

The driver didn't speed up as she pulled up behind him. If anything, he slowed even more, and Amy had to apply the brakes again, coming almost to a stop. Somewhere ahead was the hairpin curve that would wind the road back toward the river, but

she knew she had plenty of time to get around the
slow-moving vehicle before the warning stripes appeared on the blacktop.

Signaling, she pulled into the other lane and accelerated. The truck immediately sped up.

Feeling slightly panicky, Amy shoved the gas
pedal all the way to the floor, and the car gathered
speed. When she was almost around and breathing
a sigh of relief, the other driver stomped on the gas
and the truck leaped forward, flying by Amy, but
then slowing until they were once again dead even
on the road. She couldn't get around him, and she
couldn't move in behind him.

Amy cursed under her breath. The double yellow
lines ahead glowed in the headlights. They were
nearing the dangerous curve, and she knew she had
to make a move quickly. Easing off the gas pedal,
she intended to slip into the lane behind the truck,
but the driver decelerated, blocking her path.

Cursing out loud this time, Amy slammed on her
brakes. The truck driver did the same, and for a
moment, they sat side by side on the road, Amy
fuming while the other driver gunned his engine.

Amy tried to get a look at him, but the windows
were tinted too darkly and he'd extinguished his
headlights. She couldn't see inside the truck,
couldn't even tell for sure what color the vehicle
was, but it seemed to have a lot of chrome. She
could see the metal shining in the early moonlight.

''What the hell are you doing?'' she yelled,
knowing the driver couldn't hear her. But she pic-

tured some yahoo inside, laughing his fool head off at her.

Or was he laughing?

A cold chill swept over her as she realized again how isolated she was out here. She glanced in her rearview mirror, but the tractor was still not in sight, and no other vehicle could be seen on the road. What if whoever was in that truck decided to get out? What if he had a gun or a knife? Way off out here, he could do whatever he wanted to her and then haul her body down to the river and throw it in. No telling how long it would be before anyone found her.

Making sure all the doors were locked, Amy glanced around, weighing her options. Then, her heart hammering, she let off the brake pedal and slammed her foot against the gas. Her rental vehicle was no race car and no match for the powerful engine throbbing beneath the hood of the truck, but Amy didn't let that stop her. She floored the accelerator, pressing the pedal as hard as she could as she raced toward the curve.

The truck was instantly beside her, lights still off and matching her speed as they headed into the turn. They were going way too fast. Amy wasn't sure she could maintain control. What if she met an oncoming car rounding the curve? She was in the wrong lane. They'd crash head-on.

Holding her breath, Amy leaned into the turn. She whipped the steering wheel as hard as she could to the right, but her rear tire slid off the pavement and sputtered uselessly on the gravel shoulder. She fought the wheel even harder, and for a moment, she thought she'd gotten control again. She thought she was going to make it. But then, terrifyingly, she saw the truck, like a giant, menacing shadow, slipping into her lane, crowding her toward the treacherous shoulder.

Amy lifted her foot from the gas and pressed her brakes, but the momentum of the car propelled her around the curve, still at a dangerous speed. The truck, towering on its huge tires, moved in for the kill. He bumped her fender, just nudged it really, but it was enough to send Amy's car careening out of control.

The wheel spun uselessly in her hand, almost snapping her wrist, but Amy fought it for all she was worth. She slammed on the brakes with both feet. Tires screamed as the car fishtailed, rotating a full circle before coming to an abrupt halt in the middle of the road, just on the other side of the curve.

She sat for a moment, ears buzzing, head swimming as she numbly tried to decide what to do next. Her windows were up and her doors were locked, but she doubted the precautions would keep her safe from a maniac.

Sick to her stomach with nerves and fear, Amy watched the truck's taillights flash as it stopped on the highway several yards ahead of her. Even with the windows up, she could hear the powerful engine gunning, as if the driver were daring her to continue their game.

Then the headlights came on, and the truck shot

forward. Within seconds, it rounded another bend and was lost from sight, but Amy couldn't be sure the driver wouldn't stop and wait for her again somewhere up the road.

She glanced in her mirror. The road behind her was dark and empty, but she knew she couldn't remain where she was. Someone could come barreling around the curve at any moment, and Amy's car wouldn't be visible until it was too late.

Her hands shaking on the steering wheel, she headed for home. But now there was yet another mystery to be solved. Who had been driving that truck?

And why had he—or she—tried to kill her?

CHAPTER NINE

STILL TREMBLING, Amy pulled into the driveway at Amberly and shut off the ignition, sitting for a moment as she tried to gather her poise. Maybe she'd overreacted, she finally decided. The driver's actions had been reckless and almost criminally stupid, but it wasn't likely he'd really tried to kill her. It had probably been some crazy kid out for a little sport, and she'd let herself be lured into a dangerous game.

Telling herself she'd allowed her imagination to run away with her, Amy got out of the car and let herself into the house. It was quiet inside. The foyer lights were on, but the parlor beyond was dark, as was the dining room.

"Anyone home?"

Getting no response, Amy walked out into the kitchen. A delicious aroma wafted on the air. Pots and pans littered the stove and sink, but there was no one in sight. It wasn't like Lottie to leave such a messy kitchen. In the little more than three days that Amy had been there, she'd observed how particular her stepmother was about cleaning, how fastidiously she kept the house. Amberly was her pride and joy.

So where was she? What had made her leave in such a hurry?

Amy started to withdraw from the kitchen, but a slight sound on the back porch drew her attention. A nervous thrill ran up her backbone. Had the truck driver followed her home?

She glanced around the cluttered kitchen, looking for a weapon. Grabbing a knife, she clutched it in her hand as a shadow moved outside, and then the doorknob slowly turned.

Almost paralyzed with fear, Amy watched the door open, and then recognizing Lottie, she let out a loud breath of relief. "Thank God it's you."

Lottie started at the sound of Amy's voice, and her head jerked up. As she glanced at the knife in Amy's hand, her gaze widened. "Oh, my heavens—"

Amy dropped the knife, and it clattered into the sink. "Sorry. I didn't mean to frighten you."

"I just…didn't expect to see you here." Lottie took a moment to catch her breath. Wisps of hair escaped the bun at the back of her head to coil at her nape and around her face. Her cheeks were bright red, as if she'd undergone extreme physical exertion. Or as if she were excited.

Again Amy wondered where she'd been.

"I had to go out for a little while," she explained breathlessly. "I hate to leave the kitchen in a mess like this, but it couldn't be helped. One of the neighbors called and needed—" She broke off with a nervous laugh, pushing the hair back from her face. "Oh, well, you don't care about all that. Dinner's running late, I'm afraid, which is just as well. It looks like you're just getting home, and I don't know where everyone else is."

She bustled about the kitchen, turning on burners and stacking pans into a sink of soapy water.

"May I help?" Amy asked.

"I've got everything under control now, but you might go upstairs and see if Jasmine's home. I hope she hasn't gone off with—" Lottie broke off again, glancing at Amy almost apologetically. "She's at that age, you know. Feeling rebellious. You were the same way."

Was that a touch of resentment Amy heard in her voice? "I'm sorry if I made things difficult for you."

Lottie looked surprised. "I didn't mean that. A lot of teenage girls go through that stage. Sometimes I think Fay has never quite grown out of it."

Her tone was edged with worry now, and Amy said carefully, "What about Mena?"

Lottie smiled, her face instantly transforming. "Mena's different. She's always been such a quiet, shy girl. Never given me any problems."

Amy would have expected that. Of all the family, Mena seemed to be the only one who didn't have an ax to grind with her. She'd been genuinely warm and friendly, and Amy had enjoyed their evening walks by the river. She'd even come to hope the two of them might be friends. *God knows I could use one here.* "I'll go and check on Jasmine."

"Bring her along if you find her," Lottie said,

bending to remove a foil-covered pan from the oven. "Dinner is almost ready."

IT WAS ANOTHER HOUR before everyone finally straggled in. Mena got home first, apologizing to her mother for being late and explaining about a problem she'd had at the paper. Fay came in next, offering no explanations or regrets, but glowering at Amy before breezing upstairs to freshen up.

Jasmine was the last to appear, dressed in hip-hugger jeans and a short, cropped T-shirt that revealed her young curves in a very provocative manner. As she sat down at the table, her expression was secretive and smug, like a cat who had swallowed the proverbial canary. Amy wondered what her sister had been up to.

They ate on the back porch again—one of Lottie's wonderful meals of spiced ham, black-eyed peas and homemade biscuits slathered with butter. Conversation drifted in and out, and finally, after Lottie had served her Coca-Cola cake, Amy said, "Do you know of anyone who owns a dark-colored truck?"

"Only about half the people in this county," Jasmine replied, licking icing from her fingers.

"What about a four-wheel drive with huge tires and a lot of chrome?"

Jasmine shrugged. "Why do you ask?"

"Someone almost forced me off the road earlier. I just wondered if you knew who it might be."

Lottie clucked her tongue in concern. "I swear, the kids around here get more reckless every year. They're all driving by the time they're ten because they have to help out with the crops. But when they get out on the streets, they're a real menace. Did you happen to get a license-plate number?''

"No," Amy admitted. "I should have, but there wasn't time. I was too busy trying to stay on the road, and besides, it was dark.''

Fay said, almost slyly, "Conner Sullivan has a four-wheel-drive truck, doesn't he? I thought I saw him in town earlier.''

Mena turned to her sister in surprise. "You were in town today?''

"You're not the only one who has business to take care of." Fay took a bite of her cake. "I had a job interview at the hospital, if you must know. Then I went to see Jimmy. He's taking me to the barbecue tomorrow tonight.'' Her gaze met Amy's almost defiantly.

"How did the interview go—?" Lottie began, but Jasmine interrupted her.

"Are you implying Con tried to run Amber off the road?" she demanded.

Fay shrugged. "She said he seemed hostile to her the other day.''

"Con wouldn't do such a thing," Jasmine insisted, her cheeks coloring in anger.

Fay just laughed. "Oh, and you know him that well, do you? What is it with the women in this family? Why do you all seem to find that man so irresistible? I don't even think he's attractive.''

"Like James Birdsong is God's gift to women,'' Jasmine mocked.

Fay's face hardened into unattractive lines.

"Well, at least he's my age," she retorted. "And he's not in love with my sister."

"No," Jasmine agreed with a smirk. "He's always been in love with mine."

AFTER THAT LITTLE BOMBSHELL, dinner ended abruptly. Fay threw down her napkin and flounced from the room, and Mena announced she had to get back to the paper. Jasmine left the house without a word to anyone.

After Amy helped Lottie clean up, she pleaded a headache and went upstairs early. She was exhausted, emotionally drained, and settling in underneath the folds of the mosquito net, she fell asleep almost at once. But dreams plagued her rest—dark visions of a hand reaching out of the darkness and a body falling into the river.

A woman—her mother she thought—floundered in the water, screaming for help as Amy stood on the bridge, unable to move, unable to save her.

Then suddenly, Amy was the one in the water, and it was Con who stood on the bridge. He laughed down at her, mocking her, telling her she was getting exactly what she deserved.

A parade of dark-colored trucks roared onto the bridge, and Jasmine got out of the first one. She went to Con's side, and they wrapped their arms around each other as they stood laughing down at Amy. Fay stepped out of the next truck, joining the laughter, and then Lottie and Mena. All of them stared down at her, watching her drown and laughing because none of them had wanted her to come back.

Amy woke up in a cold sweat, her heart pounding in terror. She bolted upright in bed, gazing around the strange room while she tried to tell herself it was only a nightmare. It meant nothing.

But the dream had seemed so real. And it had left her feeling so disoriented. So alone.

Parting the mosquito net, Amy struggled to her feet. Moving across the room, she stood at the window, staring out at the darkness. Magnolia trees cast eerie shadows in the moonlit backyard, their pearly blossoms hanging motionless in the still night air.

Amy started to turn away, but a movement on the river path caught her eye. She held her breath as she watched a figure move stealthily through the back gate.

Her first instinct was to scream for help, then call the police, but as she hesitated for just a split second, she realized there was something familiar about the person outside. The way he walked with a sort of concentrated effort made her think of Con.

Then, gasping, she realized the man outside *was* Con. Why on earth was he here?

Before Amy had time to analyze her actions, she stepped out of her room into the hallway, lit with moonlight. She could see her way without turning on a light. Which was good, she decided. No sense waking the whole household.

Letting herself out the back door, she hurried down the porch steps, and only when her bare feet touched the dew-sodden grass did she stop to examine her reaction. What was she doing, slipping out of the house at midnight, dressed in her night-gown, running off to meet a man she'd been secretly married to for nine years, but who also happened to be a stranger?

Might even be a killer, according to Jasmine.

Not very smart, Amy, she scolded herself as she slowed her pace to a walk. Moonlight rippled on dark green leaves, making the giant trees come alive in the darkness. She shivered, glancing around the shadowy yard, but Con was nowhere in sight.

Then, as suddenly and quietly as he'd appeared on the bridge that first night, he was beside her, and Amy's heart flip-flopped inside her.

"Do you always have to do that?"

"What?"

"Sneak up on me like that. I'm not the enemy, you know."

He stared down at her, his expression dark and wary. Amy could see the barest hint of a beard shad-ing his face, making him look almost sinister in the sterling light. "Sorry," he muttered. "Old habits die hard, I guess."

The habit of sneaking up on people or the habit of thinking of her as the enemy? Amy searched his face, wondering how, even without memories, she could still feel so drawn to him. A part of her was very deeply attracted to him, even while another part of her feared him. Feared what he could do to her.

In a flash of insight, she realized why she'd al-lowed herself to become engaged to Reece, knowing all the while something was missing from their relationship. He'd been safe. He'd never generated these dark and dangerous emotions in her. The fear. The attraction. The...*need*.

Overcome with the revelation, she turned away from Con and stared at the woods beyond. "What are you doing out here?"

"I saw Jasmine in town a little while ago. She told me something that worried me."

"You were with my sister tonight?"

"I didn't say that. I said I saw her." He paused. "You still think I'm trying to come on to her, don't you? For God's sakes, she's just a kid. What kind of man do you think I am?"

The kind who would make a woman behave foolishly and act impulsively, the way she had tonight by rushing out here. "I'm sorry. I shouldn't have implied there was anything wrong with your having spoken with Jasmine."

His eyes were unreadable, but Amy could sense his anger. "I know what people around here think of me. But I'd never do anything to hurt your sister. Or you."

He added the last so softly, Amy wondered if she'd really heard him. Her breath quickened, but she managed to ask casually, "What did she say that worried you so much?"

He cast a glance toward the house, as if concerned he might be overheard. "She told me someone tried to run you off the road tonight. Is that true?"

Amy shrugged. "It was probably just some kids horsing around. I'm surprised Jasmine even mentioned it to you."

"She said someone tried to kill you."

His words hung in the still air, like the echo of gunfire. After her initial shock, Amy forced a laugh. "Why on earth would she tell you that? I never said anything of the kind. I just asked if she knew of anyone who drove a dark-colored pickup."

"Which, of course, I do."

"A lot of people do. I never thought you were the one in that truck," Amy told him.

"No?" She saw one dark brow lift in the moonlight. "You never considered the possibility? Not even for a second?"

When she hesitated, he turned away from her. "That's what I figured."

"All right, maybe I did wonder for just a second," she admitted, remembering the dream. "But be fair—"

"Fair?" She could tell he was angry, furious maybe, but his control was almost more frightening than an outburst would have been. "I'm not exactly concerned with being fair here. I'm more worried about history repeating itself."

"Meaning, you think I'll let you take the blame again for something you didn't do," Amy retorted, her own anger building. "All these years, you've held that against me, haven't you? You blamed me for what happened to you. But you don't know what happened to *me* back then. No one does."

"You're wrong," he said darkly. "Someone knows."

Amy's breath stilled. Before she could stop herself, she reached out and took his arm. When he didn't resist, her grasp tightened on him almost desperately. "Who knows? What have you found out?"

He moved closer to her in the darkness, and Amy's breath caught in her throat. He didn't touch her, but she sensed he wanted to. The idea was not unappealing to her. Far from it.

But instead of taking her in his arms, he glanced over her shoulder, and Amy turned, almost expecting to see someone walking across the lawn toward them. But nothing stirred that she could detect. Amberly remained dark and silent, almost menacing in the moonlight.

"I think your disappearance had something to do with this house."

A shiver ran up Amy's backbone. "What do you mean?"

"This place has always evoked strong feelings. It makes people act irrationally. People develop... unnatural attachments to it. Your mother. You. And then she committed suicide, and you disappeared for nine years without a trace."

"God," Amy said, rubbing the goose bumps on her arms. "You make it sound almost cursed."

"I think it is in a way. I sometimes used to think it would be better if this place just burned to the ground. That way you wouldn't be—" He broke off, as if he'd said more than he meant to reveal.

"I wouldn't be what?" Amy pressed.

He shrugged. "You always loved this place more than anything. Or anyone." His voice was traced with bitterness, edged with regret, and suddenly Amy understood. It wasn't just this house Con had been threatened by, but everything it stood for. Everything he could never hope to have, including Amber.

It's just a house, she wanted to tell him, but as she stared at the shadowy silhouette, she felt an undeniable pull—an almost fierce sense of pride. Generations of her family had lived here, had fought and died here. Had loved here. Amberly *was* a part of her.

But so was Con, in a way. He, too, was a part of her past she wasn't yet ready to let go of. She wondered how she could have ever used him, why she hadn't wanted him for the man he must have been. She wanted him now, she realized, but it was too late. Or too soon. So much more than lost memories stood between them. His bitterness. Her uncertainty. And a marriage they'd entered into for all the wrong reasons.

She sighed deeply. "I do feel something for this house. I can't deny that. But for the last nine years, I didn't even know this place existed. I didn't remember it. But I never forgot you. Your face. I used to see you in my dreams. I must have drawn your features a thousand times over the years, because I…couldn't let go of you."

He was stunned into silence, and Amy sensed more than saw the dark scowl come over his expression. Then, without warning, he raised his hand to her face, outlining her jaw with his fingertip, as if he were memorizing her features the way she had his.

"You've changed," he murmured, his tone almost awed.

"So I keep hearing. Corliss tells me I've lost all my looks."

"I wouldn't say that." His gaze dropped from her face as his finger trailed down her throat, whispering against the rounded neckline of her white cotton nightgown. "I definitely wouldn't say that."

He grazed the tops of her breasts, and Amy drew in her breath, a warm excitement spiraling through her.

When she didn't object, he touched her more openly, more urgently, and Amy reached up quickly to put her hand over his. But instead of stopping him, she pressed his hand against her breast, closing her eyes as a storm of sensations swirled through her. She could feel the heat of him. His skin seared through the fabric of her nightgown as her heart beat a frenzied staccato against his hand.

He met her gaze in the moonlight, watching her while he touched her, almost daring her to turn him away.

She said in a voice she hardly recognized, "It's all right if you want to kiss me."

He laughed, the sound low and masculine, almost unbearably intimate in the dark. "Maybe you haven't changed as much as I thought."

But he didn't seem to object. He pulled her to him, fitting his body against hers, staring down at her for so long that Amy would have kissed *him* if he hadn't stopped her. He put a fingertip to her lips, tracing the contours until she trembled with excitement.

"Be still," he murmured against her mouth. He outlined her lips with his tongue, toying with her, making her ache for his kiss.

He knew what he was doing. The buildup was exquisite.

Finally, he pressed his mouth to hers, and his tongue slipped inside. Amy's heart went wild as she kissed him back, as she thrust her tongue inside his mouth and molded her body to his. She felt wanton and sensual, a woman who knew exactly what she wanted and how to get it.

When they finally broke apart, she said shakily, "I never expected that."

"I guess this is where the 'it never should have happened I made a mistake' routine begins." He was trying to be flip, but Amy didn't think he was as unaffected by the kiss as he would have her believe. His eyes were dark in the moonlight. Smoldering, Amy imagined, and her heart skipped a beat as she stared up at him.

"That's not what I meant. I guess I never thought—" She broke off and tried again. "Was it always like this between us?"

She saw him frown in the darkness. "We kissed a lot that summer, if that's what you're asking."

"Were we…?"

"Lovers?" He wasn't touching her, but they were still standing so close, she could feel the warmth of him. Her skin tingled with awareness.

"Were we?" Her voice sounded breathless, anxious, still excited.

Con hesitated. "Does it matter?"

"It matters to me," she tried to say lightly. "I wouldn't like to think I left behind a string of lovers I don't even remember."

She saw his body tense and knew immediately she'd said the wrong thing.

He turned away from her, facing the woods. "You were the most popular girl in school back then. You had a lot of boyfriends, but how many of them were your lovers…I'm not sure that's for me to answer."

There was only one lover that Amy really cared about, but she couldn't bring herself to ask again.

Con said, "It's late. You'd probably better go in." When he hesitated, Amy thought for a moment he meant to kiss her good-night. Instead, he said, "Promise me you'll be careful."

The edge of urgency in his voice alarmed Amy. She stared up at him, remembering the footsteps she'd heard in the woods. The man she'd seen in town. The truck that had almost forced her off the road. "You don't think I'm actually in danger, do you?"

He shrugged, as if uncertain how to explain his concerns. "Think about it. Something happened nine years ago to make you leave this place, to make you forget who you were and where you came from. You don't lose your memory because of an argument with your daddy."

A shiver of fear ran through her. "What are you getting at?"

His expression was unfathomable in the moonlight. "Like I told you, I've been doing some reading." He'd even consulted a psychiatrist while he'd been in Memphis, but he didn't tell her that. "The two most common causes of amnesia are head trauma and emotional shock. What did the doctors in Houston tell you?"

Amy frowned. "I had a mild concussion when Nona checked me into the hospital, but nothing too serious. They couldn't find a physical reason for my memory loss."

"Which leaves emotional shock," Con said. "Something must have traumatized you."

Amy sucked in a breath. "Are you saying...someone did something to me that night?"

His dark gaze flickered in the moonlight. "That's what we have to find out..."

He didn't finish his thought, but the echo of his unspoken words lingered on the air around them. *Before it's too late.*

THE DOOR TO Fay's room stood ajar when Amy slipped back down the hallway, and for a moment, she worried someone might have seen her and Con outside. She didn't relish the idea of having to explain herself, not to Lottie or Fay or Mena, but especially not to Jasmine.

Trying to be as quiet as possible, Amy started by Fay's door, then paused when she heard Lottie say in an urgent, hushed tone, "Calm down, Phaedra.

You'll wake up the whole house. Everything is going to be fine.''

"How can you say that, Mama? Everything is going to *hell* now that she's come back. I saw her in Jimmy's office today. She was asking about Miranda's will.''

"How do you know? Did he say she was?'' There was an odd, anxious note in Lottie's voice. "How do you know he didn't call and ask her to come?''

"Because he doesn't still care about her,'' Fay said angrily. "I know he doesn't.''

"He's never married in all these years,'' Lottie said softly. "And God knows, it wasn't for want of you trying.''

"Thank you for pointing that out, Mama. For your information, he was about to propose to me before she came back. I know he was.''

"And now?'' Lottie sighed. "Nine years is a long time, Phaedra. Don't you think it's time you moved on?''

"And let her have him?'' Her tone was so contemputous, a shiver of fear ran up Amy's backbone. "She hasn't changed, you know. That amnesia bit doesn't fool me. She still thinks she's the little princess, and can have any man she bats her eyes at. God, how I hate her!''

Amy stood outside Fay's door, knowing she shouldn't eavesdrop, but fearing she would be detected if she moved or even breathed. She knew they were talking about her, and the animosity, the *hatred,* in Fay's voice was startling.

"She'll never let us stay here. You know that as

well as I do. She's never thought we belonged here.''

"She'll go back to Houston soon," Lottie soothed. "And then everything will be fine."

"How can you believe that? We got lucky once, but now that she's back, Amber will never leave this place again. Not of her own free will anyway. You know how she felt about this house. She's starting to feel that way again. I can tell."

"I don't think so," Lottie murmured. "She *has* changed. There's nothing here for her anymore."

"Don't count on that. What about Conner Sullivan?"

Lottie gave an uncharacteristic snort. "He's nothing but trailer trash. She won't take up with him again."

"He's got money now, and besides, she was wild about him back then." Fay's voice became strangely subdued.

"Only because he was forbidden," Lottie insisted. "He'd have no appeal to her now that Emmett is dead."

"I don't know about that," Fay said slyly. "Maybe you ought to ask Mena about his appeal."

Silence. Then Lottie said in a shocked tone, "Mena and…Con?"

"I'm surprised she never told you. She was in love with him all through high school. Of course, he didn't look at her twice when Amber was around, but I don't think Mena has ever gotten over him. I've seen the way she looks at him since he's been back. I know she'd like to get in his pants, but whether or not they've actually done the dirty deed is anyone's guess.''

Amy's breath came in sharp little spurts, and her heart pounded so hard her chest hurt. She stood trembling in the hallway, not wanting to hear any more but unable to stop herself from listening.

Mena and Con. Mena and Con. The two linked names were like a mantra inside her head. She put a finger to her lips, remembering his kiss. Remembering his promise to help her.

Lottie said stiffly, ''There's no call for that kind of vulgarity, Phaedra. I'll speak with Mena when she gets home.''

''Don't tell her I said anything,'' Fay said, her voice suddenly anxious. ''You know how she feels about me.''

''That's ridiculous. Mena loves you. She's been a wonderful sister to you.''

''Oh, please. Spare me the litany of Mena's saintly attributes. I've heard them all my life, and, frankly, they're starting to bore me.''

''Phaedra—''

''I'm sorry to be the one to break this to you, Mama, but your dear, precious Philomena isn't quite as dear or as precious as you'd like to believe. One of these days, you're going to have to face up to the truth—about her and about this house. Mena's not the person you think she is, and there's no damn way this place is ever going to be ours.''

After a moment, Lottie said primly, ''Of course this house will be ours. Once Amber is gone, Jasmine won't be a problem. She hates it here. She can't wait to be rid of Amberly.''

''That may be true. But there's still one teeny tiny little problem. Even if we can somehow get rid of Amber, how are we going to come up with the money to buy this place from Jasmine?''

''I've got a little nest egg put away,'' Lottie said proudly.

''A nest egg?'' Amy could almost picture the redhead perking up with interest.

''I've been putting away a little something for years. Plus, I still have the money Emmett left me.''

''That's nowhere near enough to buy this house. Besides, if Amber gets wind of what's going on—''

Lottie's voice, usually so gentle, took on a dark tone. ''That girl will not mess things up for me this time. It took me years to repair the damage she caused between Emmett and me. There was a time when I thought he might actually ask me to leave Amberly. I don't know what I would have done if he had, but thank God it didn't come to that.'' She drew a long breath. ''Don't you worry, Phaedra. I haven't worked my fingers to the bone since his death to have Amberly ripped away from me now. This house belongs to me. To us. We're not leaving here again.''

Trembling, Amy backed away from Fay's door. She'd had no idea of the depth of Fay's hatred for her, or the strength of Lottie's obsession with Amberly.

She'd never once suspected Mena's feelings for Con.

Did he return those feelings? Were his words to Amy earlier just empty promises? Maybe he'd never had any intention of helping her. Maybe he was merely…toying with her.

The same way you toyed with him nine years ago, a little voice whispered inside her.

Because after all, that same voice taunted her, *isn't revenge a dish best served cold?*

CHAPTER TEN

WHEN AMY GOT UP the next morning, she had dark circles under her eyes. Sleep had eluded her after she'd overheard the conversation between Lottie and Fay. She'd lain awake thinking about the night's events, and wondering if James Birdsong had been right to warn her. Was there something sinister at work here?

Was there no one here she could trust?

For a moment, she considered calling Reece. She even went so far as to pick up the phone in her room and listen for the dial tone. He'd offered to help her two weeks ago, but that was before she'd broken their engagement. Could she swallow her pride and tell him he'd been right? She couldn't handle this alone. There were too many dark secrets in Amber Tremain's past. Too many people who had wanted her to leave and never come back.

But she *was* back, and Con had been right about one thing. She would never have any peace until she found out what had happened to her nine years ago.

Replacing the phone in the hook, Amy went into the bathroom to shower and dress. Emerging from her room a little while later in jeans and a blue sleeveless shell, she stood in the hallway, listening to the silence of the house. It was still early, but Lottie was usually up by dawn. Today, however, there were no sounds of clanking dishes, no vacuum cleaner running, no soft hum as she went about her household chores. Amberly was almost ominiously quiet.

Pausing on the second-floor gallery, Amy stared up at an oil painting she'd been told was of her mother. The woman was delicately beautiful, lovelier by far than either Amber or Jasmine, although both daughters bore a striking resemblance to her.

In the portrait, Miranda Tremain stood at the top of the stairs, her hands clasped around a magnolia blossom she cradled against the bosom of her misty green ball gown. Her blond hair was swept back and up, showcasing her exquisite features and a magnificent emerald pendant that nestled in the smooth hollow of her throat.

But it was her eyes that were her most arresting feature. They tilted at the corners, just as her daughters' did, but the color was a deep, mossy green. Dark and mysterious, her eyes seemed to hold untold secrets, a melancholy mixture of sorrow, longing and ennui.

What had made her so sad? Why had she felt desperate enough to believe her only recourse was to throw herself into the river? Did her suicide have something to do with this house? Or was it because of her husband's betrayal?

"I see you're staring at Mama's portrait again."

Amy jumped at the suddenness of Jasmine's voice. She turned as her sister walked up beside her at the top of the stairs. "I didn't hear you come down the hallway. You startled me."

"Sorry. Lottie says I'm like a cat. Personally, I think if she didn't have such a guilty conscience, she wouldn't startle so easily."

"I don't have a guilty conscience," Amy pointed out.

Jasmine's smile was cryptic. "How do you know? Maybe you just forgot." Before Amy could respond, her sister turned to stare up at their mother's portrait. "Wasn't Mama beautiful?" Jasmine looked very fresh and pretty this morning in her shorts and tank top.

"She was," Amy agreed. "I wish I could remember her."

Jasmine glanced at her with an expression that almost looked like sympathy in her eyes. "If I couldn't remember Mama, I don't know what I'd do."

"What was she like?" Amy asked softly.

"Kind. Gentle. She used to come into our rooms before bedtime and brush our hair, sometimes for hours, it seemed, while she'd tell us stories about this house, about growing up here. It was like a ritual every night. She brushed our hair on the night she died, I remember."

Amy's eyes filled with sudden tears. Something flickered between her and her sister, whether a shared memory or shared genes, she wasn't sure. But the connection was there, no matter how much Jasmine might wish to deny it.

"You never got over her death." She frowned up

at the portrait. "For the longest time, you wouldn't believe she'd killed herself."

Amy glanced at her sister. "What did I think happened to her?"

"I...don't know for sure." For the first time, Amy sensed an uncertainty in Jasmine. It made her seem very young and very vulnerable. "I remember after Daddy told us what happened, you became so hysterical, he had to get a doctor out here to sedate you. You kept insisting you heard Mama scream that night."

Shock shimmered through Amy. The vision appeared to her again. A hand reaching out of the darkness. A body falling into the water. She said hoarsely, "*Did* I hear her?"

"You couldn't have. You were asleep in your room. Daddy kept telling you that the scream you'd heard was a peacock. It was only after you found out Mama was dead that you became convinced you'd heard her."

Amy remembered the peacock's scream the other night and how frightened she'd been of it. It *had* sounded like a woman.

Beside her, Jasmine said, "The pendant was never found, you know."

"What?"

"Mama's emerald. It was Daddy's engagement present to her. She never took it off, but when they found her body, the necklace was missing."

"What happened to it?"

"The police said it probably came off her neck in the water and is still lying somewhere on the bottom of the river to this day. I used to think that if I could dive down there and find that necklace, somehow I'd be able to bring Mama back. Pretty lame, huh?''

''No. I can see how you might think that. You were so young when Mama died.''

Something flickered in Jasmine's eyes. She scowled slightly, as if displeased by what Amy had said. ''That necklace was worth a fortune. Nowadays, I think if I could find it, I'd be able to do something else with it.''

''Like what?''

Jasmine looked as if she wanted to say more, then thought better of it. She shrugged. ''What difference does it make? No one's ever going to find Mama's necklace. Not after all these years.'' She stared up at the portrait, fingering her own neck.

''Tell me about this house,'' Amy said. ''It was Mama's, too, wasn't it?''

Jasmine glanced at her warily. ''You've been doing some checking, I see.''

''It's not a secret, is it? Darnell Henry mentioned it when he came to see me in Houston. He said Amberly had been in the Witherspoon family for years. I guess Mama and Corliss were raised here. Just like you and me.''

Jasmine shrugged. ''So what? There's nothing special about this place. Antebellum homes are a dime a dozen in the South. If you really want to know about Amberly, you should ask Lottie. She can go on forever about the French-empire antiques and the Eli Terry clocks and the Zuber wallpaper, not to mention our status in the National Register. She gets off on that kind of stuff. You'd think this place was the White House or something. I don't know why she even cares. It's not like she's ever going to own it,'' she added a bit maliciously. ''Although she'd sure like to. But where would someone like her come up with that kind of money?''

I've been putting away a little something for years, Lottie had said last night. Enough to buy this house? Or had she come into money some other way? ''Is Amberly for sale?'' Amy asked, trying to keep her voice neutral.

Jasmine slanted her a glance. ''I'm sure Darnell told you about Mama's will. Now that you're back, I can't get rid of this place without your permission.''

''Do you really want to get rid of Amberly? I can't believe this place means nothing to you.'' Amy made a sweeping gesture with her hand. ''There's so much history here.''

''Yeah. Bad history. Look at everything that's happened here. Mama and Daddy both died here, and you—'' Jasmine broke off and shrugged again. ''I'd have to be out of my mind to want to stay here.''

At first, Amy thought Jasmine was being superstitious, but then she realized what her sister was really saying. Amberly held too many unhappy memories for her. For Jasmine, this house represented sorrow and loneliness.

''Leaving Amberly won't get rid of those memories,'' Amy said quietly.

"It worked for you, didn't it?"

Amy sighed. "You may not believe this, but I wish I'd never left here. I wish I'd never left…you."

She expected a smart retort, some quick sarcasm that would put her back in her place, but instead, Jasmine seemed on the verge of tears. She glanced away. "Then why *did* you leave me?" she blurted.

"I don't know. That's what I'm trying to find out."

Jasmine said angrily, "After Mama died, you took care of me. You were everything to me, and then you disappeared that night, just like Mama. You left me here with *them*."

"I'm sorry," Amy said helplessly. "I know what it's like to feel alone. I know what it's like to feel betrayed."

"You don't know anything." Jasmine glared at Amy, her eyes glinting with the same old resentment. The same old defiance. She lifted her chin. "You should never have come back here."

"Why not?"

Jasmine gave a bitter laugh. "Because I don't need you anymore, that's why."

"I'D LIKE TO HELP YOU, Con. I really would," Mona told him. "But I don't know what I can tell you. I don't remember seeing Amber the night she disappeared."

Con studied the woman before him. She was dressed in a soft blue blouse and black skirt that rose to mid thigh when she crossed her dark-stockinged legs. He'd never seen her dressed like that before.

It made him a little uneasy. He wondered if he'd made a mistake in coming here. They shared a past after all, he and Mena. And not a very pleasant one at that.

Still, she'd seemed the logical person to question. He barely knew Lottie, and he'd never trusted Fay, though he couldn't say why exactly. Call it instinct.

"You didn't hear the argument she and her father had that night?"

Mena smiled sadly. "No, but I probably wouldn't have thought anything about it if I had. They were always fighting, especially after he and Mama were married. Amber never approved of her, you know." Resentment flared in her eyes before she quickly glanced down at her desk. Con remembered how he'd always thought of Mena as shy and conservative, compared to Fay, but there was another side of her, a darker side that he suspected few people besides him even knew about.

Still waters run deep, his mother used to say about her.

"Did your mother and Amber ever have words?"

A frown flickered across her brow. "Why are you asking all these questions, Con?"

"I'm just trying to figure out what happened that summer—that's all."

"Why?"

He shrugged. "Aren't you curious?"

She looked as if she wanted to say more, then bit her lip. "You have to understand, that was a difficult time for all of us. Like I said, Amber resented Mama for marrying Emmett, and she and Fay never got along, even before we moved into the house. I guess everything just got worse that summer.''

''How?''

Mena's eyes looked very blue in the sunlight streaming in from her office window. They reminded Con of a pool he'd seen in the jungle once. Clear and blue, with dangerous depths. ''Amber started having nightmares about her mother's death. She started making accusations and innuendos that broke Mama's heart and very nearly destroyed her marriage.''

''What kind of accusations?''

Mena hesitated, as if it were a subject she didn't much care to talk about. ''She accused us of stealing things from the house, a set of antique silver combs, a music box....'' She shrugged. ''She even hinted that she thought Mama had something to do with Miranda's death.''

Con stared at her in surprise. ''But I'd always thought her death was a suicide.''

''Oh, it was. Everyone knew Miranda had been having...mental problems for years. She was very depressed. Amber seemed to think Emmett's friendship with Mama drove Miranda to kill herself.''

Friendship? Con had always heard the two of them were having an affair, but he knew better than anyone how destructive false rumors could be. ''What about Jasmine?'' he asked. ''How did all that tension affect her?''

''She took Amber's side, of course. She was only a child, but she followed Amber around like a shadow. She adored her. The house became sort of a war zone that summer. It was us against them, although Mama never wanted it that way.''

"What about Emmett?''

She glanced away, but not before Con saw a flash of anger in her eyes. "He never stood up for Mama the way he should have. She was his wife. There should have been no question of his loyalty. But if Amber hadn't disappeared, I'm not sure how much longer the marriage would have lasted. In some ways, her leaving was a blessing—''

Her words broke off as she gazed at the open doorway. From his vantage by the window, Con couldn't see anything, but Mena's face flushed a deep, dull red. She said in shock, "Amber! What are you doing here?''

"SORRY TO INTERRUPT, but the receptionist told me to come on back—'' Amy stopped short when she saw who was in Mena's office.

Con stood leaning against the windowsill, his arms folded, his ankles crossed, his demeanor one of total relaxation. He wore jeans and a dark cotton shirt, unbuttoned and untucked over a white undershirt.

Amy hadn't seen him since he'd kissed her last night, since she'd overheard the conversation between Lottie and Fay. ...*Whether or not they've done the dirty deed is anyone's guess.*

They both looked guilty as hell, Amy thought. At least Mena did. The blush that had bloomed when she first saw Amy in the doorway had yet to fade. What was going on here?

Amy's gaze almost reluctantly drifted to Con. He lifted a brow, almost as if he were daring her to think the worst of him.

Her pulse started to hammer in her ears. "I can come back later if you're busy—"

"We were finished anyway." Con straightened lazily, his gaze raking Amy, and her stomach fluttered in awareness.

She turned to Mena. "I wanted to ask you if I could go through some old copies of the *Journal*."

Mena nodded, but she had a distracted air about her. "How far back do you want to go?"

"Nine years, to start," Amy said, acutely aware of Con's gaze still on her. "But I also want to read about my mother's suicide."

Mena visibly started. Her gaze flew to Con's, as if the two of them were conspirators. What had they been talking about when she'd come in?

He said, "She died two years before you disappeared. It was in the spring, I think, but I don't remember the exact month."

"April," Mena said softly.

Suddenly, a line of poetry came back to Amy. "April is the cruellest month…"

She drew a long breath. "I have a feeling that if anything can help me get my memory back, it's my mother. I *do* want to remember her," she said, glancing at Con in challenge.

He didn't respond, but as their gazes met, an almost electrical awareness shot through Amy. She remembered the feel of his hand against her breast last night, his lips against her mouth. The attraction between them was very potent, almost scary, and Amy wondered if it had always been that way. If her feelings for Con had had anything to do with her leaving town.

Had she been running away from that attraction?

"I don't know how much was written about the suicide," Mena was saying. "Emmett always valued his privacy." She picked up the phone and punched a series of buttons. Amy could hear another phone buzzing somewhere in the building. After a moment, a young man appeared in Mena's doorway. "Todd, will you take Miss Tremain down to the archives and show her around?"

He gave Amy an appreciative once-over and a charming gap-toothed grin. "My pleasure."

Amy thought she heard Con mutter something as she turned and followed Todd from the office.

CHAPTER ELEVEN

AMY HAD ENVISIONED herself wading through mountains of yellowing newspapers, but to her pleasant surprise, everything had been transferred to microfiche and stored in long, narrow drawers labeled by years, months and even weeks. It took only a matter of minutes to find what she needed.

Going about her work, she tried not to wonder why Con was in Mena's office, or what they might be talking about. She tried to forget what she'd overheard the night before, that Mena had been in love with him all through high school, that she might still be in love with him now. *...whether or not they've actually done the dirty deed is anyone's guess.*

Feeling nervous and uneasy, Amy loaded the film into the machine and began scanning through the pages. The local accounts of her disappearance were no more informative than the articles she'd read in the Jackson papers, and the headlines were virtually the same. Judge's Daughter Still Missing. Authorities Haven't Ruled Out Foul Play.

There was still no mention of anyone named Nona Jessop.

Sighing, Amy paged through a series of older issues, trying to locate an article regarding her mother's suicide. But there was nothing to be found. Had her father somehow kept all mention of his wife's death from the paper? Why? Because he valued his privacy, as Mena had said, or because he'd been afraid Lottie's name might have been brought into it?

Stymied for a moment, Amy chewed her lip, trying to decide what to do. There was one other thing she wanted to check out.

It took a while, but when she finally found the article with Mena's byline, the headline almost jumped out at her. Decorated War Hero Returns Home.

The first paragraph below it read:

After nine years of service to his country, Conner Sullivan returned to Magnolia Bend last week as quietly as he'd left. No parades, no fanfare, no hero's welcome for a man who has been awarded the Silver Star for valor above and beyond the call of duty and a Purple Heart for wounds received in a South American skirmish few people here in Magnolia Bend even know about.

Con was a war hero. Somehow that didn't surprise Amy as much as it might have once. There was so much more to him than he allowed people to see. The troubled boy from the wrong side of the river, the "delinquent" who had been suspected of murder, was the same man who had gone off to defend his country "with valor above and beyond the call of duty," the same man who had rescued a young woman from drowning with apparently no thought to his own safety, the same man who had remained steadfastly at his dying mother's side.

The same man who was still Amy's husband.

Her heart thudding, she glanced over her shoulder. She wasn't sure why, but she felt like a guilty teenager reading something forbidden. Or as if she were intruding on Con's privacy. If he'd wanted her to know these things about him, he would have told her.

So how had Mena found out? Amy couldn't help wondering if her stepsister had kept track of Con all the time he'd been away. Had she been as obsessed with Con as her mother was with Amberly?

A shadow fell across the desk, and Amy jumped. As usual, he'd come into the room so quietly, she hadn't heard him. Before he could see what she was reading, she pressed the off button and the screen in front of her went black.

CON WALKED AROUND the desk and gazed down at Amy. "Find what you were looking for?" She had the appearence of a woman who had been caught red-handed in a compromising situtation.

"Not exactly." Her smile seemed nervous. "What are you doing here?"

"I thought you might need some help."

Amy said carefully, "I'm sorry I interrupted your meeting with Mena."

He shrugged. "No problem. We were finished."

She looked as if she wanted to say something else,

and it hit Con with almost a physical jolt that she seemed jealous. Her cheeks were flushed, and there was a tiny little flicker in her eyes he couldn't quite figure out.

"Is there a problem?"

"No, of course not." She got up to put the microfiche away, taking care not to brush him as she walked by. Changing the subject, she said over her shoulder, "I couldn't find anything on my mother's suicide. I don't know how my father managed to keep it out of the paper."

Con gave a bitter laugh. "Are you kidding? Judge Tremain could do whatever he wanted to around here." Like getting an innocent man arrested for the "murder" of a daughter who was still very much alive.

Con couldn't help himself. He let his gaze slip over her. She was wearing jeans today, and the way they molded to her hips and thighs gave him all sorts of ideas. Ideas he had no business entertaining. Not about Amber Tremain.

She turned to face him. "That's exactly what Nona told me once. She said her brother was accused of assaulting a girl. Nona was convinced he was innocent, but the girl's mother was a friend of my father's, so he sent Nona's brother away to a mental institution."

Something flared in Con's memory. "When was this?"

"More than ten years ago, I guess."

"What was the girl's name?"

Amy shrugged. "I don't know. Like I told you

before, I don't even know Nona's brother's name. She didn't leave behind any papers, any record of her maiden name, but there must be some way—''

She broke off as Con walked over to the file drawers, studied the labels, then finding the one he wanted, removed several sheets of film. He loaded the machine and began scanning through pages of newspaper. Amy went to stand over his shoulder. ''What are you doing?''

''I'm not sure.'' He frowned as the articles flashed by him. ''This could take a while. I don't remember when it happened.''

''When what happened?''

He glanced up at her. ''What you said about Nona's brother being sent to a mental institution – I think I remember something.''

''You know who he is?''

''Maybe.'' Maybe not. But if what he suspected was true, Amber was in for a big shock.

She grabbed his arm. ''Who is he? Tell me.''

It was a light touch, an innocent touch, but Con felt his stomach tighten. The kiss they'd shared last night had been on his mind all morning, and now he realized why. He wanted more.

He wanted much more than a kiss, which was stupid, considering their past. Her memory had haunted him all these years, had changed his life in ways she couldn't begin to understand. Making love to her wasn't the way to exorcise her ghost.

He'd always thought there was only one way to do that.

She wasn't the only one with secrets, and Con

wondered what she would do, what she would think of him, when she found out what he'd done.

He let his thoughts trail away as he found the article he was looking for. "Now it makes sense," he muttered.

"What does?" Amy had dropped his arm, but she was still standing very close to him.

"The reason you recognized Frankie Bodine yesterday is because he's Nona Jessop's brother."

AMY FELT AS IF the bottom had dropped out of her stomach. There was a strange buzzing sound in her ears, and the hair at the back of her neck stood on end.

"Then why didn't anyone *know* that he was Nona's brother?" She ran her hands up and down her arms, trying to get rid of the chill bumps. "This is a very small town."

Con shrugged. "Her real name was Winona. She was a lot older than Frankie, the best I remember. She left Magnolia Bend years ago. After a while, everyone around here forgot that Frankie even had a sister."

A cold sweat broke out on Amy's brow. This was what she wanted, wasn't it? To find Nona's brother? Why then, was she suddenly so afraid? Was her fear of Frankie, or of what he could tell her?

Trembling, Amy moved back around to read over Con's shoulder. As her gaze scanned the lines, another named leaped out at her. Phaedra Darling.

Fay had been the one to accuse Frankie of assault. Which meant Lottie had been the friend of Amy's father. Which meant that Jasmine's suspicions could be true—Lottie and Emmett Tremain could have been having an affair before his wife's suicide.

"My God," Amy breathed, still reading. "It says he held her at knife point. He threatened to kill her."

"That was her account," Con pointed out. "Frankie denied everything, but no one believed him. And why should they have? He was always an outcast here, not anyone who mattered."

Was he talking about Frankie or himself? Amy wondered fleetingly. "I have to find him," she said in an urgent tone. "I have to talk to him."

Con stood and faced her. "Look, we don't know if Fay's accusations were true or not. People have been wrongly accused before. But if she was telling the truth, if Frankie did try to kill her, then he could still be dangerous."

Amy shivered violently. "I know that. But what choice do I have? Frankie Bodine may be the one person who can tell me what happened that night."

Con's eyes darkened. "That's what worries me."

"What do you mean?"

"It's like I said last night. You don't get amnesia from an argument with your father. It had to have been something more traumatic."

Amy's stomach twisted as she got his meaning. "You mean, you think Frankie may have...done something to me?"

If possible, Con's eyes darkened even more. His jaw hardened as he stared down at her. "God help him if he did."

IT WAS LATE AFTERNOON by the time Amy returned home. The house was empty and so quiet it was more than a little spooky. She shivered as she climbed the stairs. Lottie had left a note on her bedroom door, reminding her of the Fourth of July barbecue that evening in Riverside Park. Lottie and the girls were all going, and she hoped Amy would join them.

"No, thanks," Amy muttered, wadding the note and tossing it into the wastebasket in her room. The crowd had already been gathering in town when she'd left, but Amy had had enough stares from total strangers for one day. All she wanted to do was take a quick shower and maybe hit the bed early. Last night's insomnia was taking its toll, and she hoped that sleep would obliterate, at least for a while, the turmoil raging inside her.

Con had asked her to do nothing about Frankie Bodine until he could check the man out for himself, and Amy had agreed. She didn't relish going to see Frankie alone anyway. Not after seeing him in town yesterday. But there was still a part of her—a tiny part—that didn't quite trust Con. Did he really have her best interests at heart?

Why had he gone to see Mena?

After she'd gotten out of the shower, Amy wandered around her room, too restless to climb immediately into bed. A strange uneasiness came over her, and she began to wonder if she was really alone in the house. She even went so far as to open her bedroom door and call down the hallway, "Hello? Anyone home?"

When no one answered, Amy closed the door of her room, and, on an afterthought, locked it. Instead of dressing in pajamas—her original plan—she put on a sundress and sandals. Fully dressed, she felt less vulnerable somehow.

But again that odd feeling invaded her, and this time she walked to the window to stare out into the fading twilight. She remembered seeing Con down by the gate the evening before, and for a moment, she watched a shadow, thinking her memory had conjured the movement.

Someone *was* down there! He—or she—didn't come through the gate, as Con had last night, but stood on the other side, gazing up at the house.

Amy's heart catapulted against her chest. One instinct told her to go down and see who was there, even as another instinct—the one of survival—screamed for her to run. Get out of the house. Get in the car and drive somewhere, *anywhere,* to safety. It was too dangerous to be here alone.

But in that split second of indecision, the shadow vanished, absorbed by the deep shade of the woods. It was almost as if the person had melted, so thoroughly did he blend with his surroundings.

So much for an early bedtime, Amy thought, grabbing her purse and car keys. Suddenly, the barbecue in town sounded very, very inviting.

CON HADN'T CELEBRATED the Fourth of July in years. He didn't like the memories associated with the holiday, nor the crowd that gathered every year in the park. Frowning, he watched the star bursts of color over the river and thought of other, deadlier explosions. The children's excited shrieks reminded him of other screams, horrifying screams.

Tearing his gaze from the night sky, he scanned the crowd for Amber. Where was she? She wasn't home, and she wasn't here. Where the hell had she gone off to? Surely she wouldn't go to see Frankie Bodine without him. Bodine lived so far back in the sticks, it wasn't likely she'd even be able to find his place. But if she did—

Tamping down a feeling of unease, Con turned as he heard his name being called.

James Birdsong walked toward him, wearing pressed khakis, a light blue oxford shirt and tassel loafers—a lawyer's idea of dressed down, Con reckoned.

"Birdsong." He took a swallow of his beer, gazing at the attorney over the rim of his plastic cup, remembering a fistfight the two of them had once gotten into after school. Over Amber, of course. He wondered if James remembered it, too. Con was pretty sure he did.

James cleared his throat. "I've been meaning to talk to you."

"What about?"

He hesitated, adjusting his glasses with his index finger. "Amber. She's my client now."

"Is that right?" Con studied the Japanese lanterns circling the park. The scent of barbecuing meat wafted on the night air, and he realized suddenly that he hadn't eaten all day.

"I want to talk to you about the annulment."

"Annulment?" Con felt as if the man had sucker punched him in the gut. He had to resist the urge to retaliate.

James gave him a triumphant smirk. "Amber and I agreed that was probably the best course of action to follow, considering the two of you never lived together." *Never consummated your marriage,* Con was almost sure the man wanted to add.

A bitter taste rose in his throat even as he told himself this wasn't a surprise. What else could he expect? He hadn't actually thought they'd take up housekeeping, had he, now that she was back?

"We're hoping you'll be sensible about this," James said smoothly. "There's no reason for you to contest it. An annulment is best for both of you."

Before Con could retort, Fay came slinking out of the shadows, laughing as she looped her arm through James's. "There you are! I thought for a minute I'd lost you."

James scowled down at her. "I need to finish my conversation with Con in private."

"In private?" She blinked up at him, then turned to glare at Con. "What could you possibly have to talk to *him* about? What are you doing here, anyway?"

Con shrugged. "It's a free country, last time I checked."

She staggered a bit, and James caught her arm.

"You've been drinking," he said, his tone disapproving.

She giggled. "A little. Alcohol lowers inhibitions. You should try it sometime."

Con almost laughed himself at the look on James's face. "We'll talk about this later," the attorney said. "Right now I need you to go back over there with your family."

"I don't want to go," she said obstinately. "I want to stay here and find out who's getting annulled."

"I'm not at liberty to talk about that."

"Oh, don't be so stuffy." She gave him a playful shove in the chest, then stopped abruptly. "Wait a minute." She turned back to Con. "Don't tell me *you're* married."

She made it sound a very doubtful prospect, and Con grinned suddenly. "Who would have thought I'd beat you to the altar, Fay?"

He could almost hear her inward hiss. She said scathingly, "Does Amber know?"

When James stiffened beside her, Fay turned back to him, her expression pensive. Sly. Con didn't think she was as drunk as she'd first let on. "Amber came to see you yesterday, didn't she? I wondered what that was about."

"Drop it, Fay," James warned.

But she'd already put it together. Con saw the revelation register on her face and her eyes widened. "Oh, my God! You and Amber are married! I should have known she'd pull something like that. That scheming little bit—"

James grabbed Fay's arm. "I said drop it."

"Why?" She glared up at him, daring him. "You're not still in love with her, are you?"

When he didn't answer, Fay jerked her arm from

his hand. "You idiot! You goddamn, stupid idiot! When has she ever looked at you twice?"

"Why don't you keep your voice down?" Con advised. People were starting to glance curiously in their direction. Another minute and a crowd would build.

"Why don't you mind your own business?" Fay snapped. "Why don't you go off and find your wife? I wish the two of you would leave town and never come back. I wish—"

"Phaedra, please!" Lottie came rushing up to her daughter. "What in the world is going on here? You're creating a scene."

"So what if I am?" Fay demanded, turning on her mother. Mena was standing a few feet away, and just behind her, Jasmine. "You two are going to love this," she said over her mother's shoulder.

"You're drunk," Lottie said in disgust. She cast a disparaging glance at Con, as if Fay's condition was all his fault. "We'd better get you home."

"Oh, I'm not going anywhere, Mama. Not until I tell Jasmine and Mena Con's dirty little secret."

"Why don't you just shut the hell up?" Con growled. "What business is this of yours?"

"None whatever," she agreed. "I've never been able to stand you, thank God. But Mena and Jasmine—they both think you're some kind of hero. They've both been pining away for you when all this time..." She gave a hard, unpleasant little laugh. "All this time, Con's been married to *Amber*," she said loudly.

THE FIRST FAMILIAR FACE Amy saw when she entered the park was her aunt Corliss. She was standing off to herself, wearing a starched, cotton print dress and watching the proceedings with a critical eye. A country-western band played on a makeshift stage, but Corliss didn't so much as tap her toe to the music. Her face was a mask of stern disapproval.

Even though Amy had been intimidated that first day by the woman's formidable appearance, she didn't hesitate to approach her. "Aunt Corliss!"

The big woman spun, sloshing red punch from a plastic cup over her hand. The sticky liquid dripped like blood to the ground. "Why, Amber Rochelle!" she said in surprise. "Lottie said she didn't think you were coming."

"I changed my mind." Amy glanced at her aunt's hand and said, "Sorry. I didn't mean to startle you."

"Don't you fret about it." She tossed the cup in a nearby barrel, then scrubbed her hand on a delicate white hankie she pulled from the pocket of her dress. "Let's go somewhere and sit down, away from all this infernal noise. I've got a pounding headache."

They found a deserted picnic table near the edge of the park, and Corliss eased herself down with a groan. "My arthritis is giving me fits tonight. When you get to be my age, it's just one thing after another."

She wasn't that old, and she looked to be in perfect health, strong and big boned, but Amy murmured the appropriate sympathy.

Corliss pursed her lips. "Would you look at that?" She nodded toward two long-haired boys heading rather stealthily toward the woods. "Up to no good, I'll wager. High as a cat's back, the pair of 'em. I'm just glad to see Jasmine Louise isn't with them. Although God knows where she is."

Amy watched the boys for a moment, then turned back to her aunt. "Could I talk to you about something?"

"Well, of course, dear heart. You can talk to me about anything. I know you don't remember, but you and I were very close once."

"I want to know about my mother."

Corliss, who had continued to scrub her hand with the hankie, paused. Her gaze looked wary. "What do you want to know about her?"

"Why she died."

Pain creased Corliss's brow. "What can I tell you? Miranda took the easy way out, and the rest of us had to deal with the consequences."

The bitterness in her voice surprised Amy. "Did you and my mother not get along?"

"Course we got along." Corliss scowled at someone in the nearby crowd. "She was my only sister, and I loved her. But I can't say I ever truly understood her. She was a beautiful child. I was Mama's favorite, but Daddy...he just thought the sun rose and set on Miranda Lee." She paused. "There was always a sadness inside her, even as a little girl."

"Is that why people assumed her death was a suicide?"

Corliss stared at her for a moment. "What else could it have been?"

Amy shrugged, not yet ready to voice the suspicion that had been lurking on the fringes of her mind. She asked instead, "Do you think her suicide had something to do with Lottie?"

Corliss's eyes narrowed on her. "You've been talking to your sister, I take it."

"Is it true? Did Lottie and my father have an affair? Is that what drove my mother to suicide?"

"I don't know." Corliss sighed. "I've always hated to think Lottie would do something like that. She, Miranda and I were all childhood friends. Lottie's mother was our housekeeper when Miranda and I were just girls. Lottie was our playmate."

"You mean Lottie lived at Amberly a long time ago, before she even married my father?" The revelation shocked and troubled Amy, because if it was true, it explained a lot. Namely, Lottie's obsession with the house.

Corliss nodded. "She and Miranda used to pretend that she was our long-lost sister, kidnapped at birth, and that she would someday grow up to become the mistress of Amberly. Miranda encouraged all that nonsense by giving Lottie some of our dresses and hair ribbons and such, so that she looked as if she really did belong there.

"After a while, I think we all started believing in the fantasy, especially Lottie. Then her mother died, and she had to leave Amberly to go live with some of her kinfolk in Greenville. They were dirt poor and already had too many mouths to feed. I suspect they didn't really want Lottie, poor thing."

"Did you keep in touch with her?"

Corliss grimaced. "I never was much of a letter

writer myself, but she and Miranda corresponded for a long time. Then when Lottie moved back here with her husband years later, I guess she probably figured they could pick up the friendship where they left off as kids. But Miranda had her own life by then. *She* was mistress of Amberly, and I don't think she was all that eager to have Lottie underfoot.''

"When did the affair with my father start?''

"While you girls were all still in high school. I sometimes wondered if that's why Fay resented you so much. You had everything she wanted. A mother and father who adored you, a beautiful home, more friends than you could shake a stick at. You got every bit of the attention she craved.''

Which brought another question to Amy's mind. "Did Frankie Bodine really assault her?''

"Why, how odd that you would ask about him. I just saw him not more than five minutes ago.''

Amy stared at her aunt in shock. "Frankie's *here?*''

"He always shows up for free food, then disappears into the woods again, although I expect he hangs around a bit longer than most of us think.'' Corliss gave her a sharp glance. "Why this interest in Frankie Bodine all of a sudden?''

Amy considered telling her aunt what she and Con had learned that afternoon, but they'd agreed to keep it quiet until they had a chance to talk with Frankie and find out what he knew. She said instead, "Could I ask you just one more question?''

"Shoot, dear heart.''

"Is there any chance Lottie could buy Amberly?''

Corliss gave a bark of laughter. "Where on earth did you get such a notion? Emmett left her a little something, I reckon, but I'm sure she and the girls have gone through most of that by now. Fay's never been one to hold down a job, you know, and Lottie's never done anything but keep house."

Amy said in a hushed tone, "What about Mama's emerald necklace?"

Something flashed in Corliss's eyes, something that might have been dread, as if Amy had touched on something Corliss had already thought of herself but tried to deny. She leaned across the table, lowering her voice to match Amy's. "You always did have a wild imagination, Amber Rochelle, but I think it would be best for everyone concerned if you keep those ravings to yourself."

AFTER SHE LEFT Corliss, Amy walked around the picnic area, wondering if Con was somewhere in the crowd. She wanted to talk to him about her and Corliss's conversation, but she didn't think he'd come to the barbecue. It didn't seem like his style.

Catching a glimpse of Jasmine, Amy called out to her. Jasmine glanced over her shoulder, saw Amy, then ducked into the crowd. Amy sighed. Obviously, her sister still harbored deep resentment toward her, but Amy wasn't going to give up trying. She hurried through the crowd in the direction she'd last seen Jasmine.

Twilight had turned into nightfall. Lightning bugs flitted through the trees, and the rising moon silvered the surface of the river. Amy walked along the water, letting the noise of the crowd and the music fade behind her as she looked for her sister. The putter of a boat engine sounded over the water, then was extinguished, leaving the night almost unnaturally quiet.

A few moments later, Amy decided she'd better head back. Her sister was nowhere in sight, and she didn't want to get too far from the park. But as she turned to head back, a noise in the trees behind her spooked her, and before she could glimpse over her shoulder, something hit her in the back of the head.

Stars exploded behind her eyes as Amy's knees collapsed and she fell to the ground. She wasn't sure how long she clung to consciousness before she sensed someone kneel beside her. A rough, anxious voice whispered, "You done been hurt?"

Amy tried to speak, tried to open her eyes and respond, but her head reeled dizzily, and she squeezed her lids closed, finally letting the darkness close over her. She dreamed that someone was lifting her, carrying her, and then, all she heard, was water lapping against a boat.

CHAPTER TWELVE

WHEN AMY CAME TO, her head throbbed and a wave of nausea washed over her. She lay perfectly still for several long minutes, breathing deeply, trying to remember what happened.

And then it all came back in a terrifying rush, and she glanced frantically around, wondering where she was and who had attacked her.

She was lying on an old sofa, and someone had covered her with a blue-and-white patchwork quilt. The tiny room was dimly lit by what looked to be a kerosene lantern, but Amy could make out the details. A cot had been shoved up against one wall and spread with another quilt. An empty rocking chair sat near a wood-burning stove, cold now because of summer.

Just beyond the stove was the kitchen, and Amy could see a sink equipped with an old-fashioned pump. The cabin was crude, but looked spotlessly clean and neat. As she gazed around, a feeling of foreboding stole over her.

She'd been here before! She knew this room. She'd lain on this very couch....

Panic exploded inside her. Ignoring the pain in her head and the nausea in her stomach, Amy swung her feet off the couch, shoving aside the quilt. She had to get out of here! She knew, without a doubt, that she was in very grave danger.

The front door stood open. Moonlight glimmered through the screen door, and as Amy struggled to her feet, a shadow fell across the porch beyond. Floorboards creaked, the screen door squealed in protest as it was drawn back and Frankie Bodine walked into the room.

Amy's heart flailed against her chest. She shrank back against the couch, terror clawing at her backbone. As if in protection, she grasped the quilt, pulling it over her like a shield.

"What do you want with me?"

He stood gazing down at her, his expression masked by the bill of his cap and the shadows flickering in the room. He wore denim overalls and a worn plaid shirt rolled up at the cuffs. His forearms looked massive. Powerful. Had he been the one to hit her earlier? He must have been. Who else could it have been?

Without answering her, he lumbered to the kitchen, his work boots rumbling on the bare wood floor. Amy thought about making a dash for the door, but she remembered how quickly he could move. He'd be on her before she could reach the porch.

Trying to think rationally, she gazed around for a weapon. A shotgun hung on a rack near the door. Even if she could manage to get it down before Frankie saw her, she didn't think she'd know how to use it. She might have better luck with the iron poker behind the stove—

Frankie came back into the room, carrying a mason jar of what looked to be iced tea in one hand and a white envelope in the other. When he shoved the jar at Amy, she shook her head.

"It won't hurt you none." His drawl was thick and crude. "Drink it."

He thrust it at her again, and this time Amy accepted it. While he stood staring down at her, she took a tentative sip. It was very sweet and very good. The cool liquid soothed the rawness of her throat. She took another drink, then handed him back the glass. "Thank you."

He nodded, took the tea from her, then handed her the envelope. Amy stared down at it in the gloom. She could see writing on the face, but she couldn't make it out.

Frankie, sensing her dilemma, retrieved the kerosene lamp from a tiny drop-leaf table and brought it over to the sofa. For the first time, Amy saw his face clearly, and her breath caught in her throat. He looked very much like his sister. He had the same soft gray eyes, the same gentle expression. He didn't look at all dangerous. Only his size was intimidating.

Amy glanced back down at the envelope. Her name was written across the front in Nona's neat, precise penmanship.

Her heart skipped a beat. "When did Nona give this to you?" she asked urgently. When he merely stared down at her, she said, "I mean Winona."

He shrugged, then turned and, taking the shotgun down off the wall, walked back out to the porch. His footsteps clattered on the steps, but Amy didn't think he'd gone far.

With trembling fingers, she tore open the envelope and removed the pages inside, controlling her desperate urge to scan through them. Instead, she forced herself to sit back against the shabby couch and begin at the top of the letter, reading slowly, digesting Nona's every word.

Dear Amy,

The fact that you are in possession of this letter can only mean you've somehow discovered who you really are and have managed to find your way home. But after I tell you what happened all those years ago, I pray you'll leave that place again and never, ever return.

It all began that hot summer night. I'd arrived from Houston that morning to visit my brother, but as usual, Frankie couldn't sit still inside. He had to be out on the river. I'd given him a new flashlight when I first got there, and he was just like a kid with a new toy. He couldn't wait to try it out.

After he left, I went on to bed. I knew he sometimes stayed on the water for hours, but just after midnight, I heard him hollering up from the woods. I knew by the sound of his voice something was wrong, and then he came bursting into the house, with you unconscious in in his arms. He'd carried you all the way up from the river.

You were the most pitiful little thing I'd ever seen. Your hair and clothing were soaked, and you were bleeding from a cut on your forehead.

As I tended to the wound and tried to figure out what other injuries you might have suffered, Frankie told me what had happened.

Someone tried to kill you that night, Amy.

The words blurred before Amy's eyes. She had to read the line twice, then once again to comprehend the full meaning. Someone had tried to kill her!

My God. Oh, my God.

Her heart pounded inside her as she looked up at the door. Frankie was still outside.

Trembling all over, Amy glanced back down at the letter, forcing herself to continue.

Someone tried to kill you that night, Amy.

Frankie's boat was tied off underneath the bridge when someone threw you into the water, then drove off. Frankie dived into the water and found you. There was no way it could have been an accident or suicide, like your mama, because a weight had been tied to your ankle. Frankie said the rope came undone real easy-like, as if maybe whoever had tied it had only wanted the knot to hold long enough for you to drown.

He managed to get you out of the water and into his boat, and he brought you back here to me. He was scared to death, bless his heart, and so was I. We were both worried Frankie would get blamed for what happened. I know that must sound strange, but your daddy already had it in for Frankie. He'd sent him to the state home once before for something Frankie didn't do.

Frankie never touched that girl, but Judge Tremain didn't believe him or me. There was no reason to think he'd believe us this time, especially with his own daugther. And Frankie was an adult. He would have gone to prison this time. He could never have survived that.

You can't imagine the terrible dilemma I faced, Amy. You were unconscious when Frankie first brought you home. I knew I should get you to a doctor, but he would have reported your injuries to the sheriff. How could I take a chance on Frankie getting sent away again for something he didn't do? I was all he had. The only person on this earth who cared what happened to him. He was always like a sweet, innocent child. I had to protect him.

I told myself you'd be okay. The cut wasn't deep, and I couldn't find anything else wrong with you. I knew you'd come around in a little while, and then you could tell your story to the sheriff. Frankie would be in the clear, and whoever had tried to kill you could be arrested.

But when you did come to a few minutes later, you didn't remember anything. Not even your own name. I thought it was temporary at first, brought on by the shock of everything that had happened. figured you'd remember in time, but until then, I couldn't risk having you found at Frankie's. I didn't know what else to do but take you back home to Houston with me. That way, no one would connect your disappearance with Frankie.

You slept most of the way, but when you roused a couple of times, I told you I was a friend, taking you to get help. You were pretty out of it, so you believed me, and there was no one around to tell you any different.

When we got to Houston, I took you to the hospital where I worked, and had a doctor friend of mine run some tests on you. I sat by your bedside and talked to you, tried to soothe your panic without telling you anything that might lead you back here. I couldn't let you come back until you could clear Frankie.

But days turned into weeks, weeks into months, and you never got your memory back. After a while, I had to tell you something. I couldn't let you linger in that terrible limbo.

So when the therapist I took you to see couldn't help you, I began making up a past for you. Once I had committed myself, and Frankie, to that terrible deception, there was no turning back. If he wasn't a suspect before, he most certainly would be after what I did. So I had to keep you away from Magnolia Bend— at any cost.

I convinced myself it was for the best that you never remembered. If the person who tried to kill you continued to think you were dead, then you'd be safe. You could lead a full, healthy life, and no one ever had to know that Amber Tremain was still alive. You and Frankie were both protected this way, and that's all that mattered to me. Because by this time, I'd come to think of you as the daughter I could never have. I began to pray your memory never returned....

The letter went on for several more pages, Nona explaining herself, begging Amy to forgive her and praying that Amy and Frankie would remain safe once the whole truth came out.

Her hands shaking, her insides trembling with everything she'd learned, Amy folded the letter and returned it to the envelope. She sat for a moment, her mind reeling. It was almost too much to comprehend, and yet it made a strange, perfect kind of sense. Someone had tried to kill her that night, and Nona had taken her away to protect her. And to protect Frankie.

Or had she? Could Amy trust the letter? Nona had lied to her about her past. What if she was lying to her about the events of that night? What if Nona was still trying to protect Frankie?

As quietly as she could, Amy rose to her feet. She slipped the letter into her dress pocket as she crossed the floor on tiptoes, glancing through the kitchen doorway. It was barely larger than a closet, with a two-burner stove, one sink and an old, rusted icebox. There was no back door.

She moved to the screen door, peering out. Frankie was nowhere in sight, but Amy still doubted that he'd gone far.

Pushing open the screen, she stepped gingerly onto the porch, which was several feet off the ground. The house sat on stilts, and she could see piles of mussel shells gleaming in the moonlight. So that was how Frankie made his living, she thought fleetingly.

She walked down the steps, almost expecting him to materialize at any moment. Her feet crunched against bits of shell as she took a few steps into the yard. The house had been built years ago in a small clearing surrounded on all sides by woods. There was no road that Amy could detect, but a series of footpaths led back into the trees. She had no idea which way to go.

As she stood contemplating her predicament, a shot rang out, shattering tree bark not ten feet from her. Another shot followed and, gasping in terror, Amy rushed into the woods in front of her. She raced through the trees and underbrush, unmindful of the limbs tearing at her hair, unaware of anything but the hard thumping of her heart.

Someone had shot at her, tried to kill her. Had it been Frankie? He had a shotgun, and he'd brought her to this isolated cabin. Amy wanted to believe Nona's letter, but how could she? Nona had lied to her about so many things, and she'd always tried to protect her brother.

After several minutes of blind panic, reason caught up with her, and she stopped to gaze around. She had no idea where she was, but she could glimpse a light through the trees. The tiny glimmer drew her toward a clearing, and as Amy stared at the back of the house, she realized she'd gone in a circle, had run straight back to Frankie's cabin, straight back into the arms of her would-be killer.

Terror mushroomed inside her. She stood helplessly looking around, not knowing which way to go in the darkened woods.

And as she stood there, the sound of hard, labored breathing came to her. The hair on the back of her neck stood on end. Slowly Amy turned.

CHAPTER THIRTEEN

HE LAY ON HIS BACK, not more than five feet from where she stood. In the moonlight, Amy could see the dark stain on the bib of his overalls, the trickle of blood at the corner of his mouth. He put out a hand toward her, and Amy's own hand flew to her mouth, suppressing a scream.

She realized with dawning horror that Frankie had been shot. He hadn't been shooting at her. Someone had shot him.

Everything in Nona's letter was true, then. Frankie had saved Amy's life that night. He'd probably saved it again tonight.

She fell to her knees beside him and took his huge hand in hers. "Frankie? Can you hear me?" she whispered urgently.

His eyes fluttered open, but Amy wasn't sure if he could see her or not. She squeezed his hand. "Who shot you?"

He struggled to speak, but nothing came out.

"You brought me here to protect me, didn't you?" Whoever had attacked her at the park was undoubtedly the same person who had shot Frankie. Who had tried to kill her nine years ago. The irony was, Amy couldn't remember his identity and Frankie couldn't tell her.

"We have to get you to a doctor," Amy whispered. But there was no way she could lift him, and she had nothing with which to staunch the flow of blood. Her only recourse was to head to Frankie's house, find something inside with which she could bind his wounds.

As if sensing her intention, he clutched her hand, pulling her toward him. Amy put her ear close to his lips, her heart pounding all the while. At first she couldn't make out what he was saying, but then, his voice grew stronger, as if he'd summoned every last ounce of his strength. "Get out of here! Run!"

Then Amy heard it, too. The crunch of underbrush nearby. If she ran for Frankie's house, she would be exposed in the clearing. She would be shot in the back, and she and Frankie would both die here in these woods.

The footsteps came crashing through the underbrush. The only thing Amy could do was lead the killer away from Frankie. If he was found alive—

She spun away from Frankie and plowed through the woods, ignoring the vines and brambles that tore at her arms and legs and face, and the mosquitoes that swarmed like a cloud around her head the deeper she ran into the woods.

The ground became increasingly wet, the footing more treacherous. A ground mist hovered over the area, hiding the muck that sucked at her feet and oozed over the straps of her sandals. With a new sense of terror, Amy realized she'd entered a bog of some sort, the kind Jasmine had warned her about. The kind where water moccasins and bobcats lived.

The insects were even more torturous here, and as Amy lifted her hand to swat a mosquito on the back of her neck, she heard the telltale sound of a twig snapping. A flock of blackbirds, disturbed from their twilight roosts, soared into the air, twittering frantically as they circled overhead, then disappeared into the gathering gloom.

Amy's pulse leaped against her throat as someone moved among the trees, not fifty yards from where she stood. Wearing dark clothing, the figure blended with the shadows, making it impossible to see features, to even determine whether it was a man or a woman.

But Amy knew it was the killer. Knew he—or she—was looking for her.

There was no time to run. The sudden movement would draw the killer's attention. Instead, as silently as a ghost, Amy sunk to the ground, letting the fog-shrouded underbrush hide her.

She lay facedown in the mud, shaken and terrified and fighting the nausea that rose inside her when she thought about the killer's identity. Whoever was out there was someone she'd known, maybe even someone she'd trusted. Someone she'd loved?

Another twig snapped to her right, so close Amy almost gasped. She held her breath, her heart thundering in her ears. Her muscles ached from remaining so still, and then, as if to test her will further, something slithered across her legs. A water moccasin. She was sure of it. She could almost see the snake's white mouth gaping, feel the razorlike fangs sinking into her skin, and then she would surely have to scream and the killer would see her and shoot her dead before the venom could taint her bloodstream.

Slime oozed between her fingers where she splayed them in the mud. After an eternity, the snake slid from her legs and glided away, and then, miraculously, the killer began to move way, too.

Amy listened to the crush of the underbrush subside. The killer had moved on, but how far and for how long, she had no idea.

Slowly, she rose from her hiding place, pushing away limbs that clawed at her arms. Kneeling in the fog, she gazed around. She had no idea which way the killer had gone, but she knew she couldn't remain here. There were too many other dangers, and if Frankie was still alive, he'd need help and fast.

Struggling to her feet, she stood listening for a moment. But all she could hear was the subtle rustle of leaves in a tree as one of the blackbirds came home to roost and the gurgle of mud settling back into place. Even the rhythm of her own heartbeat faded in her ears.

Gingerly, Amy began to pick her way out of the woods.

SHE HAD NO IDEA where she was or where she was going.

The woods went on forever. She was exhausted, her mind so numb that she no longer even feared her would-be killer. He might be a real killer now, if Frankie had died, but Amy wouldn't let herself think about that. She simply shoved the murderer and Frankie out of her head and concentrated on putting one foot in front of the other.

She ignored the scratches and insect bites that covered every exposed area of her body. The torment would have been too much to bear, so Amy blocked it out. She blocked it all out and kept walking.

She had no idea how long she'd been moving when something roused her from her daze. She glanced around. The woods were thinning. Moonlight fell in slanting rays against the trees, silvering the leaves and casting an unearthly glow on the ground beneath her, but anything was better than the gloom of the deep woods.

Pausing once again, Amy tried to get her bearings. She could smell the river, and the scent instantly buoyed her. Hurrying her steps, she burst out of the trees. The old river bridge rose over the water not a hundred yards away from where she stood.

Amy began to run toward it, so relived to see a familiar landmark she completely forgot that somewhere out there someone still wanted her dead. She was already on the bridge when she realized that the way home to Amberly might also lead her straight back to the killer.

And then, as if conjured by her terror, a dark silhouette appeared in front of her. He'd been standing by the railing, Amy realized, hidden by shadows until she was almost upon him. Now he stood directly in front of her, barring her way. At his side, he carried a high-powered rifle with a night-vision scope.

When he started toward her, Amy screamed and jumped back. She landed against the iron railing and hovered for a moment, trying to catch her balance. But the balustrade had already torn loose from the girders, and Amy screamed as she tumbled backward.

She grabbed air, frantic for a handhold. Blindly, she clutched the railing that had torn loose from the bridge, clinging desperately with both hands as she dangled over the river. The rusted iron squealed in protest against her weight, and another portion of the railing broke loose. She dropped another two feet before the metal caught. Scared to even breathe, she gazed around frantically for help. Then, over the edge of the bridge, she saw his face.

The face that had haunted her for nine years. Now she understood why.

CON'S HEART PLUMMETED when he saw Amber disappear over the side of the bridge. Her scream seemed to echo over and over through the darkness as he ran to the edge of the bridge and knelt.

She was there, hanging about five feet down, just out of his reach. When she saw him she started to struggle, but the iron railing groaned ominously.

"Don't move," he commanded. "Just hold on. Let me figure out a way to get you up."

Quickly, he lowered himself over the side of the bridge, hanging on to the edge with one hand as he reached for her with the other. His fingertips brushed hers on the broken railing, and he heard her gasp.

"Let go," he instructed. "Grab my hand."

"I...can't." She clung to the railing, her eyes wide and terrified in the moonlight.

Con said calmly, "Don't be scared. What's the worst that can happen if we fall? We get a little wet, that's all."

"I...can't swim."

"What are you talking about?" He inched his fingers nearer the edge of the bridge, trying to lower himself toward her. His hand closed over hers on the broken railing. "You could always swim like a fish."

"Not...anymore. I can't swim. I'll...drown if I fall."

The metal creaked again, and he heard her breath leave her in a panicked rush. The railing tore free from the support just as Con's hand closed over her wrist. Amy screamed, swinging from his grasp as the railing dropped thirty feet to the water.

Her slim form was like a deadweight pulling at Con's muscles. Taking a deep breath and straining with everything in him, he heaved her up until she could grab the edge of the bridge. She clung there for moment, trembling and frightened, until he gave her another boost, and she was finally over the side.

Somehow he managed to pull his own weight up, and the moment he collapsed on the floorboards, Amber gasped and scrambled away from him.

"What the hell—?" He rose shakily to his feet

and started toward her.

Amy cowered away from him. "Stop! Don't come near me."

"What's the matter with you?" Was she in shock?

She looked like a scared rabbit in the moonlight. She wrapped her arms around her middle, trembling from head to toe. "Someone tried to...kill me. How do I know it wasn't...you?" Her gaze dropped to the rifle he'd placed on the bridge.

For the first time, Con's gaze took in her appearance. Her hair was caked with mud, her skirt and blouse torn and filthy, her arms and legs scratched and bleeding. "Jesus Christ," he said on a breath. "What happened to you?"

She shoved a strand of matted hair from her face. "Do you know why Nona took me away that night? Because someone tried to kill me. Because someone tied a weight to my ankle and threw me off this bridge. How do I know it wasn't you?" she asked again.

Shock ripped through Con like a switchblade, followed by a hot dose of anger. "In case you missed it, I just saved your neck here. Why would I have done that if I'd tried to kill you back then?"

"I don't know." She looked defeated and her legs almost buckled. "I don't know what to think. Who to trust. Someone attacked me earlier at the park, and then just now, he was stalking me out in the woods. When I saw you standing there..." Her gaze dropped to his mud-caked boots.

She shook all over. Her teeth were chattering so badly, Con could hardly make heads or tails of what she was saying.

He took a step toward her, holding out his hand to her. "I've been out looking for you. You weren't home, you weren't at the barbecue…I didn't know what the hell had happened to you."

She blinked up at him. "What are you doing here at this bridge?"

"I thought you might show up here."

She glanced up at him, biting her lip. She wanted to believe him. He could see it in her eyes.

He said softly, "It's all right. Obviously, you've been through a lot tonight. Let's go back to my place and get you cleaned up. You can tell me what happened—"

"No!"

"For God's sake, I'm not going to hurt you!"

"I've got to get help for Frankie. He's been shot. We have to go back and find him."

Con stared at her in confusion. "Frankie Bodine? How do you know he's been shot?"

"Because I was there. I saw him. He took me to his house from the park. At least, I think it was him. Then he gave me a letter from Nona." She put her hands to her pocket, then her eyes grew frantic again. "It's gone! I must have lost it in the woods. She told me someone tried to kill me nine years ago. That's why she took me away. And whoever tried to kill me then tried to kill Frankie tonight. And me."

"Where's Frankie now?" Con demanded, trying

to make sense of her babbling. Trying to keep his own anger—and fear—at bay.

"He's still back there in the woods." She shivered. "I tried to lead the killer away from him—"

Con swore. She'd almost been killed tonight. She'd almost been killed, and he hadn't been there to protect her. Again. "Come on. You can tell me everything on the way to my place."

Something in his voice must have gotten through to her, for she stopped suddenly and gazed up at him. "Someone tried to kill me tonight. They tried to kill me nine years ago."

"So it would seem," he said grimly.

"But I got away from them." She almost smiled at that, but then, without warning, her knees collapsed, and Con caught her, slinging the rifle strap over his shoulder, then scooping her up into his arms. She gave only a token resistance before she wrapped her arms around his neck and laid her head against his chest.

How could something that hurt so much feel so good? Con wondered as he carried her off the bridge. He wished he could hold her like this forever, but his knee screamed in protest as he started down the embankment, and he stumbled a bit from the strain.

Against his neck, Amy murmured, "You can't carry me all the way home. You were wounded in South America."

He swore. "I've walked a lot farther carrying more than twice your weight. This is a piece of cake,'' he said as sweat popped out on his forehead.

"This is ridiculous, Con. Put me down. I'm perfectly capable of walking."

Her voice sounded almost back to normal. Con stopped and set her down. "You're right. You are capable of walking."

He limped beside her up the path, and Amy took his arm. "You should take better care of yourself."

"Look who's talking."

She shrugged. "I'm okay now. I was just...in shock, I guess. But we have to get help for Frankie."

Con glanced over his shoulder. "Let's get you safe inside first."

THE TRAILER WHERE Con grew up was almost hidden among the cypress trees and water oaks that grew along the river. He'd left an outside light on, and Amy noticed almost absently the beds of hollyhocks and larkspur that hid the underpinning of the trailer, and the four-o'clock bushes that sprang up around the tiny porch.

Once they were inside, Con leaned the rifle against the wall near the front door, then fetched her a blanket and a whiskey. Amy belted the drink right down.

The fiery liquid was instantly fortifying. She sat on the couch, gripping the blanket around her shoulders as Con knelt in front of her. He took one of her hands in both of his.

"Are you sure you're okay?"

She nodded. "Feeling much better."

"Good. When I come back, I want to know everything that happened tonight."

"When you come back...where are you going?"

"I have to go see about Frankie. I can't leave him out there."

Amy knew he was right, but she fought the idea of Con going out there in the darkness, back to those woods, back to the killer. She clutched at his hand. "You can't go out there alone. What if the killer is still out there? Con—"

"It's all right. You'll be fine here until I get back. No one knows you're here. Lock the door and don't open it to anyone but me, do you hear?"

Amy nodded. In spite of his knee, he rose swiftly and disappeared into the bedroom, leaving the door ajar. Amy could see him moving about inside the room. He took something from a bureau drawer, and in the silence, Amy heard a series of clicks. It came to her in a flash that he was checking the clip on a weapon. Her gaze went to the rifle by the front door. Why had he been carrying a weapon tonight?

The doubts started to assail her again, but Amy shoved them aside. She had to trust someone. She had to believe in someone, and Con was right. He saved her life on the bridge. She shivered as he came back out with a small handgun that looked only slightly less deadly than the rifle.

"I don't know how to use that," she protested when he tried to give it to her.

He took her hand and laid the weapon in her

palm. "It's loaded and the safety's off. Just point and pull the trigger."

Their eyes met, and Amy saw something in his dark brown gaze that made her start to tremble again. His expression was hard and coldly resolved, that of a trained soldier who relished the prospect of battle.

She started to tell him to be careful, but the adage seemed inane under the circumstances.

"Lock the door behind me," he said again, and then picking up the rifle, he was gone in an instant.

HER HAIR AND CLOTHING were caked with mud, and now that she was out of immediate danger, the scratches and mosquito bites tormented her. Carrying the loaded gun gingerly, Amy went into the bathroom to clean up. She tried to make do with a sponge bath, but the grime only smeared.

"You're safe," she murmured, trying to reassure herself. "You've got the gun, the doors are locked and you can be in and out of the shower in two minutes." Catching a glimpse of herself in the mirror, she muttered, "Make that five."

Locking the bathroom door and putting the gun on the sink within reach, Amy turned on the shower, climbed out of her filthy clothing and stepped under the steaming water. The shower felt wonderful at first, the hot water soothing to the dozens of bites and scratches.

But over the sound of running water, she began to hear noises. Someone rattling the doorknob. The tinkle of broken glass. Footsteps in the bedroom.

Her heart thudding, Amy turned off the water and stood listening. Nothing. All was quiet. But the moment she started the water again, the noises came back to her. Amy knew her imagination was conjuring the sounds, but even so, she lathered, shampooed and rinsed as quickly as she could, then stepped out of the shower to dry off.

But even with the water turned off, the occasional creak of the metal roof, the sound of a dog barking in the distance and a wind chime somewhere out in the yard made her heart skip a beat.

Finding one of Con's undershirts, Amy slipped it over her head, then wrapped the blanket around her shoulders and clutched it to her while she walked through the trailer, peering out windows.

The moon was still up, and through the trees, she could glimpse the sparkle of silver on water. Even inside, she could smell the river, and the scent reminded her of Nona's letter. No wonder Amy had had such an aversion to the bridge her first day back here. She'd thought it was because of her mother's suicide, but now she knew the truth. Someone had tried to kill her that night. Someone had tied a weight around her ankle and thrown her off that bridge.

You're safe, she tried to tell herself again. *No one knows you're here.*

But somewhere in the yard, the faint tinkle of the wind chime sounded again, and a chill washed over her. There wasn't so much as a breeze outside....

Grasping the gun, Amy turned and stared at the

front door. Had the knob turned? Were those foot-steps she heard?

Then, as if she'd almost willed it, a knock sounded on the door. She nearly jumped through her skin, and the gun fell clattering to the floor. Rescuing it, she crossed the floor as softly as she could and stood listening at the door.

The knock came again, and then she heard Con say, "Open the door, Amber. It's me."

She reached for the lock, then hesitated. "How do I know it's really you?"

A hesitation. Then, in a low voice, he said, "Because I'm your husband."

She turned the latch and let him in. He walked inside, then closed and locked the door. The gun trembled in her hand, and he reached down to remove it. "Better let me have that thing before you shoot a toe off. Or something worse."

There was a streak of blood on the front of his white undershirt, and his right forearm was wrapped with a white bandanna.

Amy gasped. "Oh, my God, what happened to you? Were you shot? Con—"

"Take it easy," he said. "I lost a fight with a thornbush, that's all."

Blood was seeping through the bandage. Amy put her hand to her chest, trying to still her racing heart. "It looks deep. Do you want me to clean it up?"

"Later," he said wearily.

He limped into the kitchen and poured them each a shot of whiskey. He downed his and poured another.

"Did you find Frankie?" she asked, following him into the kitchen.

"No, but I didn't find his body, either." The second drink disappeared. "I'll go back out there in the morning and look around. But in the meantime, I think you'd better tell me everything that was in Nona's letter."

Amy sat on the couch, huddled beneath the blanket as she recited to Con what she could remember from the letter. When she got to the part about a weight tied to her ankle, a dark chill came over him. The cold-bloodedness of the act filled him with rage, and it was all he could do to sit there and listen to Amy, instead of going out and tearing those woods apart until he found the person who had done that to her.

When she stopped speaking, she sat watching him, the tension between them almost unbearable.

Finally, she dropped her gaze, staring at the floor as she held the blanket around her. "I didn't run out on you that night, Con."

It was a moment before he could say anything. "I know."

Amy tucked a damp strand of hair behind one ear. "I've been sitting here trying to figure out who hated me enough to want to kill me."

"Maybe it was more than hate," Con said. "Maybe you were a threat to someone."

"But who?" Amy said desperately. "Lottie? Fay?" She paused. "Mena?"

When Con didn't respond, she said, "Mena's in love with you."

"I don't know about that. Maybe." He dragged his fingers through his hair. "I've never done anything to lead her on. I hope you believe that."

"She was in love with you even back then."

Con got up and strode to the window, staring out into the darkness, "I dated her a few times, but when I thought she was getting too serious, I broke it off. I knew there could never be anyone for me but..." He shrugged. "She didn't take it well. She started following me around at school and in town. Sometimes when I'd look out my bedroom window at night, I'd see her down by the river, just staring up at the trailer. Then some of my clothes started missing from the clothesline...." He glanced at Amy and saw her shiver.

"That sounds a little...creepy, if you ask me. But maybe no more so than Fay wanting to be popular so badly she accused Frankie of trying to kill her. She got him sent away, and I'd be willing to bet Frankie didn't lay a finger on her."

"I don't think he did, either," Con said, "Fay's always had a cruel streak."

"And then there's Lottie," Amy said. She worried her bottom lip in contemplation. "Amberly is...I don't know...symbolic to her. Corliss said Lottie lived there as a little girl, and she and my mother used to pretend they were sisters. Then Lottie had to go live with relatives who didn't want her, and I imagine that must have been pretty traumatic for her. Maybe Amberly represents stability to her, and she thought I was going to make her leave. You said yourself, that house has always evoked powerful emotions in people.''

''Yeah,'' he muttered, turning away from her face. ''Maybe more than you know.''

AMY AWAKENED WITH A start. She didn't remember dozing off, but as she gazed around, she saw that she was in a strange room, sleeping in a strange bed. Con's, she presumed.

She saw him standing by the window, staring out at the night sky. Getting up from bed, she padded across the room toward him.

''How long have I been sleeping?''

He glanced at her over his shoulder. ''Not long. You fell asleep on the couch, but I thought you'd rest better in here.''

Amy studied him in the moonlight. He wore only jeans, and he'd wrapped a fresh bandage around his arm. His hair looked damp, as if he'd just come from the shower. She could smell the faint scent of soap and shampoo, and the fragrance was uncommonly masculine. Virile.

''Have you gotten any sleep?''

He shrugged. ''I don't need much sleep.''

She moved beside him, staring out the window into the darkness. Several yards from the trailer, she could see the skeletal frame of a house. ''Are you building a home?''

He didn't say anything for a moment, then, ''It was going to be my mother's house.''

''I thought you sold all your property to that development company.''

"I started the house before my mother died, and once she was gone, there didn't seem much point in finishing it. I don't mind the trailer...not anymore."

"Con—"

"Amber—"

They both started to speak, but she said in a rush, "Let me go first. I may lose my nerve otherwise."

He looked as if he were going to protest, then he shrugged. "Go ahead, then."

She drew a long breath and released it. "You said I married you to spite my father."

"That's what I thought. That's what I heard."

"Is it possible you could have been mistaken about what you heard?"

He searched her face in the moonlight. "What are you getting at?"

She took another breath, her heart beating in long, painful strokes against her chest. "If that was the only reason I married you, how do you explain the way I feel about you now?"

She sensed more than saw him tense. His gaze darkened on her. "How *do* you feel about me?"

"I...think I'm in love with you."

CHAPTER FOURTEEN

HE GAZED AT HER for a long moment, as if he wasn't quite sure he could believe what she was saying. As if he might not *want* to believe what she was saying.

Amy held her breath. "Should I not have admitted that?"

He almost smiled. "You always did say what was on your mind."

"Then I guess there's no reason for me to stop now, is there?" She moved toward him, lifting her hands to cup his face. "I'd like for you to make love to me."

He inhaled sharply. "Amber—"

"I know," she said breathlessly. "I know all the reasons why we shouldn't. I've only been back here a few days. But it seems like an eternity and..." She trailed off, holding his face in her hands, staring up at him, wanting him. "Someone out there hates me enough to want me dead. Do you have any idea how that feels?"

Something flashed in her eyes. He did smile a little then. "I think I do."

"I'd like to believe there's also someone who cares about me. At least a little."

Con closed his eyes briefly. "I do care about you.

I've never stopped caring about you. No matter what I did or how hard I tried, I couldn't get you out of my head. You haunted me. That's why I've…done some things I've done.''

Amy's hands trembled as she let them slip to his shoulders, feeling the warmth of his skin beneath her fingers. "What have you done?"

When he opened his mouth to speak she put a fingertip to his lips. "No, don't tell me. I don't want the past in here with us now. I just want you."

His gaze made her melt. With one hand, he reached out and cupped the back of her neck, drawing her to him, then plowing both hands into her hair. He stared down at her for the longest moment before he lowered his head to hers.

The power of the moment was breathtaking. Amy's lips trembled beneath his, and then opened like a flower, drawing him inside. With a groan, Con ground his mouth against hers, tasting, savouring, pouring nine years of longing into the kiss.

He kissed her again and again, silently and intently, and when they broke apart, Amy's legs threatened to collapse right out from under her. But Con wasn't finished with her. He pulled the undershirt over her head and tossed it aside, so that she stood before him naked with desire.

His gaze worshiped her, ravished her, and then he did the same with his hands and his lips until Amy thought she would go mad from wanting him. He walked her back a few steps, and when she felt the bed against her legs, she lay back, watching him in the moonlight, ravishing him with her gaze as he stripped aside his jeans.

Then he moved over her and in her, and all Amy could do was whisper his name over and over.

AMY'S EYES WERE CLOSED, but she could feel Con's gaze on her, moving over her, and the sensation was incredible. When he circled her breast with his fingertip, she opened her eyes and stared up at him.

"Wow," she whispered.

"Thank you."

She grinned. "I've been lying here wondering about something."

"And?" His finger drew tighter and tighter circles. Amy shivered.

"Was it always this way between us?"

"You asked me that once before."

"And you never answered me."

When he didn't answer now, Amy demanded, *"Well?"*

He cocked a dark brow. "Do you think I'm the kind of guy who kisses and tells?"

"I'm serious. I want to know. Were we lovers?"

He hesitated, then rolled on his back, staring at the ceiling. "Once. The night we were married. It was down by the river. I guess that's why when you didn't come back, I thought I'd better go find you. I already had my suspicions about your motives. And then, too, I was a little worried I might have hurt you somehow."

Amy frowned. "Hurt me?" She turned over to

stare at him. propping her chin on his chest. "You mean physically?"

He shrugged.

"Why would you think you'd hurt me? From everything I've been able to gather, I wasn't exactly an innocent." When he still didn't say anything, Amy lifted her chin and stared at him in surprise. "Are you telling me I was a *virgin?*"

"Surprised the hell out of me, too."

Amy flopped back on the bed. "But I thought…I mean, everyone keeps telling me how wild I was back then."

"Apparently, neither one of us sowed as many wild oats as we led other people to believe."

She turned her head, staring at him. "You mean you were a—"

He grimaced. "Damn near it. But let's keep it to ourselves. No use spoiling our reputations after all these years."

Amy put her hands to her face and laughed.

"It's not that funny," he said, glowering at her.

"No, you're right. It's very…sweet." She sighed. "So what was our wedding night like?"

"Awkward. Fumbling." He paused. "Beautiful."

She sighed again. "I wish I could remember."

Con trailed a fingertip across her lips and Amy shivered. "Why don't you concentrate on the memories we just made?"

"I plan to," she said, kissing him. She kissed him lightly at first, and then more deeply, more confidently as she felt his body respond.

AMY LEANED ON HER ELBOW, watching him. His eyes were closed, but he could feel her gaze on him, moving over him. The sensation was powerful, and when she traced a finger down his stomach, he opened one eye and stared at her.

"What are you doing?" he asked gruffly.

"Just checking."

"On what?"

"On whether or not you were asleep," she said innocently, although her eyes told him something very different.

He captured her fingers, linking them with his, and then lifted her hand to his lips. "Sleep might not be a bad idea. We've got a lot of decisions to make in the morning."

"That's hours away." But a shadow passed briefly across her features. "And anyway, you said you didn't need much sleep."

"Good thing."

She smiled down at him. "I have another question for you?"

He sighed deeply.

She traced his tattoo with her fingertip. "What does this mean?"

There was an odd note in her voice. He gave her an amused glance. "It means I had too much to drink one night in Rio."

"That's all?" She looked vaguely disappointed.

He turned his head to stare at her. "What did you think it meant?"

She shrugged. "I don't know. Tell me about being in the service."

"What do you want to know?"

She paused, then said, "I heard you were almost killed in South America. Is that true?"

Con closed his eyes again. "You can hear a lot of things in this damn town. You should know that better than anyone."

"Were you in the special ops? When he opened his eyes and gave her a look, she said defensively, "Well, isn't that what they call it? And isn't that why you have that tattoo?"

"You've been watching too many Sylvester Stallone movies." Con stared at the ceiling for a moment, not wanting to remember. Not wanting her to know everything he'd seen and done in the past nine years. His service to his country had been honorable, and he wasn't ashamed of following orders, or giving them, but somehow even the bravest of acts didn't always translate well in the civilian world. "I was in the service. Period. I got my knee shot up in a third-world country no one has ever heard of, and if the State Department has their way, no one ever will. After that, Uncle Sam didn't have much use for me, so we parted company. Does that answer your question?"

"Why did you get the Silver Star?"

He tensed. Damn Mena for writing that article.

Amy said softly, "It's okay if you don't want to talk about it."

Con didn't, but maybe he should. He'd never told anyone what happened back then. It was part of his past, and he thought he could shove it into the shadows, along with Amber's ghost. But both had haunted him over the years. Both had changed his life in ways he was only now coming to understand. "We were fighting guerrillas in the jungle. We'd been told they were little more than peasants with outdated weaponry and an immoral cause, when in reality, they were professionals armed by Castro and well-trained by the KGB."

Amy frowned. "I didn't know the KGB existed anymore."

"A lot of people don't. And that's what's scary. We had no idea what we were getting into down there."

"What happened?"

Con drew another breath. "The rebels ambushed our unit one night. We were badly outnumbered, and some of our men were taken prisoner. After the smoke cleared, we couldn't find out where they were being held. It was almost as if they'd just disappeared into the jungle. The attempts we'd made to infiltrate the group hadn't worked, and we'd already learned that intelligence was unreliable. The only way we could find out where the men were being held was for someone to lead us in."

"Like who?"

"Another prisoner."

He sensed more than saw Amy's shock. "I think I understand. You allowed yourself to get captured so that you could lead your unit to the prison camp."

She was quick. He'd give her that. Con shrugged. "Someone had to do it. We had reason to believe the hostages would be tortured, and several of them had been given sensitive information. If I hadn't volunteered, we would have drawn straws. A lot of the other men had wives and families back home. It made more sense for me to go.''

Amy's arm slipped around him, hugging him, as if she could protect him from the memories. ''What happened?''

''We got the men out.'' He turned to meet her' gaze, saw a dark knowing in her eyes.

''How long did it take for your unit to come and rescue you?''

''Three days.'' That's enough, he told himself. Time to draw the shutters. He didn't want her knowing any more. He didn't want her looking at him with the same pity he'd seen in a medic's eyes when he'd tried to field dress Con's knee. He'd been luckier than a lot of guys in that hellhole.

Amy drew a tremulous breath. ''You've been through so much.''

He smoothed his hand down her hair. ''I guess neither of our lives has exactly been paradise.''

''Until tonight.''

CON WENT BACK OUT to look for Frankie the next morning. Amy stayed inside the trailer, with the doors and windows closed and locked. She felt like a prisoner of war herself.

Unfortunately, she didn't have many options. She could pack her bags and head back to Houston, but flight wouldn't necessarily guarantee her safety. Running away might even be more dangerous in the long run. Back in Houston, or anywhere else, she might become complacent, and who was to say her would-be killer wouldn't be waiting around the next corner when she got careless? Here at least she would be constantly on her guard.

There was also Jasmine to consider.

And Con.

She drew a deep breath, thinking of last night. How wonderful it had been. How deeply she loved him.

It seemed impossible. She hardly knew him, and yet there it was. She couldn't see her life without him now.

And stranger still, she didn't think she could leave Amberly. Not yet, at least. Her ancestral home was so much a part of who Amber Tremain had been, that leaving it now would be like leaving something of herself behind. Something she was just now coming to know.

So if she didn't want to leave and she was afraid to stay, what other option did she have? Go to the same sheriff who had arrested Con for her murder nine years ago? Without Winona's letter, why would he even believe her? And even if he did believe her, what if he blamed Frankie, as Winona had feared all those years ago? Or Con?

Amy's stomach tumbled at the thought. Con had told her once he didn't want history to repeat itself, but what if it came to that? What if he was once again blamed for something he didn't do? How would he feel about her then?

Her predicament was paralyzing. The only thing she could do at the moment was to stay locked inside Con's trailer. If he could somehow find Frankie, and if Frankie could tell Con who shot him, then Amy would know who had tried to kill her all those years ago. She'd be able to look her would-be murderer in the eye and ask, *Why?*

She sighed, not wanting to consider how important—and how remote—those ifs were.

AS THE MORNING CREPT BY, Amy's imagination went wild. The walls started closing in on her. She was sure something must have happened to Con, and it was all she could do not to go out and look for him.

Stay put, she ordered herself. *Don't get antsy.*

No one knew where she was, and she had to keep it that way for the moment.

But the need to be out there, looking for Con and for Frankie, was almost too great to bear.

By sundown, when she'd still had no word from Con, Amy couldn't stand it any longer. She knew if she didn't do something to relax, she'd start climbing the walls. Or worse, leave the trailer and put herself in danger.

Retrieving her skirt and blouse from the tiny laundry room built off the kitchen, she carried them into the bedroom, then went into the bathroom to take a shower, hoping the hot water would calm her. Like the night before, she had Con's loaded gun with her, and she laid it on the sink, within easy reach. Then she locked the bathroom door, turned on the shower and stepped under the water.

But also like the night before, noises invaded the

bathroom. This time Amy recognized the turning of the doorknob, the opening of a door, the footsteps somewhere in the trailer for what they were— products of her overtired and frightened mind.

Ignoring the sounds, she stood under the hot water and closed her eyes.

CON WALKED EVERY square inch of the woods, searching in thickets and bogs and behind every fallen tree he came across. There were dozens of hiding places, hundreds of nooks and crevices in which a wounded man could hole up and wait out the storm. Or wait to pick off his predator.

Frankie would know all the hideaways, but Con had grown up in these woods, too. And he was trained to track. Sooner or later, he'd find Frankie Bodine. It was just a matter of time. But the day was slipping away from him. How much time did he have?

He thought about Amy, back at the trailer, alone and frightened and vulnerable. Vulnerable in a way she'd never been before.

Someone wanted her dead. And now that Frankie could identify that someone, the killer would be getting desperate, reckless.

As the hours passed, Con tried to tamp down his growing sense of urgency. He couldn't afford to get careless. He had to find Frankie before anyone else did. He had to discover what Frankie had seen last night.

For the past thirty minutes or so, Con had been following a deer track through a particularly rugged bit of terrain. The underbrush here was mainly thornbushes and blackberry vines that ate through the denim of his jeans. The area was deeply shaded by hardwoods, almost as dark as night in places, and the mosquitoes that swarmed his neck and face and darted occasionally into his eyes, were only momentarily distracted by the insect repellent he'd used earlier.

But Con was in his element. He'd walked through South American jungles far deeper and darker than this, tracking a quarry much more agile and dangerous than Frankie Bodine. The trick was to not be lulled by the monotony of the terrain or the pursuit.

Something snapped in a grove of sycamores, just off to Con's right. He stopped dead still, listening, as the mosquitoes vectored in on the back of his neck and sweat tickled down his arms and back, stinging the myriad of scratches and cuts left by the thorns.

A lone hawk took flight, soaring from the top of a loblolly pine, and Con tracked it with his eyes, listening all the while for a whisper of sound, inhaling the faint, metallic scent of blood.

Someone else was here in the woods, close enough that he could almost smell fear. But whether it was Frankie, or someone else looking for Frankie, he couldn't yet tell.

Con pulled his weapon and thumbed off the safety. The soft click sounded like a cannon shot in the deathly quiet of the woods. He stood waiting, ready, his patience endless as his gaze scoured the underbrush.

And then, after minutes—or hours, for all Con could tell—he heard another sound, up ahead of him and to the left. A low groan, no more than a soft animal whimper, but the sound sent a chill up Con's backbone.

He started through the brush.

AMY CLIMED OUT of the shower, scolding herself for letting her imagination get the better of her. The doors were locked, she had a gun and the sounds she'd heard weren't real. Still, she dried off in a hurry and secured the towel around her, then picked up the gun, unlocked the bathroom door and peered cautiously down the hallway.

The trailer's windows were small, not letting in much light, but Amy could see well enough to tell that no one was lurking in the corridor. Just as she had the evening before, she'd let her fears produce noises that, when explored, had innocent origins.

She padded down the hallway to the bedroom to dress. As she pushed open the door, she saw someone sitting on the bed, and before she had time to even scream, her sister rose and faced her.

"Jasmine! You scared me half to death. How did you get in?"

"It wasn't hard." She held up a thin-bladed knife. "This place is little better than a tin can."

Amy came slowly into the room. "What are you doing here?"

Jasmine's expression was shuttered. Amy had no idea what her sister was thinking, but Amy realized, instantly, that wrapped in a towel, she didn't exactly look uncompromised.

"We've all been looking for you," Jasmine said. "You didn't come home last night."

"There's a lot going on here that you didn't know," Amy told her. "Let me get dressed. I'll explain everything to you."

"Oh, don't bother." Jasmine moved slowly toward her, and a frisson of fear crept over Amy. "I know about you and Con."

"You do?" What exactly did she know?

"The two of you are married. You've been married for nine years. You've both played me for a fool." Her face crumpled suddenly, and she looked like a wounded child.

"I'm sorry," Amy whispered. "I should have told you."

Jasmine's head jerked up. "Yes, you should have. But that's like you, isn't it? Only thinking of yourself."

"Jasmine—"

"You think you've won, don't you? You think you've got Con all to yourself, but you don't know him like I do. You don't know what he's after."

Amy frowned. "What are you talking about?"

"You'll have to find out for yourself." She stalked past Amy to the door, then paused in the hallway, glancing back at her. The knife blade gleamed in her hand. "You're dead, Amber. You just don't know it yet."

CHAPTER FIFTEEN

JASMINE'S OMINOUS WORDS hung in the air, and for a moment, Amy couldn't move. She watched her sister rush from the trailer, slamming the door with a loud, final bang.

That spurred Amy into action. She dressed quickly, and hurried out of the trailer. What had Jasmine meant—she was a dead woman, she just didn't know it yet? Did Jasmine know something about the night Amy disappeared? About last night?

Even as a shiver of fear raced up Amy's spine, her mind rejected the notion that Jasmine had tried to kill her. They were sisters. She wouldn't do such a thing. She was just upset, and at the very least, Amy owed her an explanation.

The twilight was warm. A light mist crept over the river, and where moonlight touched the surface, the water shimmered like an opal. Amy hurried across the bridge, resisting the temptation to constantly glance over her shoulder. Invisible eyes seemed to watch her from the gathering darkness, and she told herself she was a fool for venturing out.

In less than ten minutes, she was at Amberly, but Jasmine was nowhere in sight, and her car wasn't in the driveway.

Letting herself into the house, Amy started toward the stairs, hoping her sister might be in her bedroom. But as she crossed the foyer, she heard voices coming from the parlor. Stepping to the doorway, she glanced inside.

The room seemed crowded with people. James Birdsong and Fay sat side by side on the sofa, while Mena perched on the edge of Lottie's chair. All four expressions were almost identical masks of apprehension. A man wearing a brown uniform leaned against the fireplace, and another man stood at the window, his back to Amy.

When Amy moved into the room, they all turned to stare at her in stunned silence before Lottie jumped to her feet. She came toward Amy, her blue eyes clouded with worry. "Amber! Oh, my heavens, we've been so worried about you."

Amy stared at her stepmother in confusion. "I'm sorry for worrying you. I'll try to explain everything to you later, but right now, I need to find Jasmine. Have you seen her?"

Lottie blinked. "Jasmine? She's out looking for you."

"Looking for me—" Amy broke off abruptly as her gaze traveled over Lottie's shoulder. The man at the window turned to face her, and she gasped. *"Reece!"*

He hurried across the room to her side. "Amy! Thank God you're all right. I've been going out of my mind with worry."

"I'm...fine." Shaken, Amy glanced at the sheriff, then back up at Reece. "What are you doing here?"

His mouth tightened as he stared down at her. "Evidently, there's a lot going on around here. I can't believe I let you walk into this."

"Walk into what?"

"We'll get to all that later," the sheriff drawled, propping a booted foot on the hearth as he stared at Amy from across the room. His voice chilled her, but it was the cold gleam of triumph in his steely blue eyes that really frightened her.

It hit Amy in a flash that he was the same sheriff who had arrested Con all those years ago.

He pulled a grimy envelope from his pocket and held it up for her to see her name written across the front.

Amy said in shock, "That's Nona's letter. How did you get it?"

"Coon hunter found it in the woods last night, near Frankie Bodine's place. He brought it into my office a little while ago."

"We've all been so worried about you," James said, adjusting his glasses with his finger. Amy couldn't help comparing him to Reece. Both men were lawyers, but there was a world of difference in their demeanor. James was shy, hesitant, but Reece exuded confidence. Arrogance. Maybe even a streak of cruelty. Why had Amy never noticed that about him before?

Her gaze slowly moved around the room as she wondered if one of these people—Lottie, Mena, Fay, maybe even James Birdsong had tried to kill her last night.

"We need to talk to you for a few minutes

alone," the sheriff said grimly. "If you'll excuse us."

James rose to his feet. "I'm her attorney. I think I should stay."

"I'm her fiancé," Reece said coldly. "I can handle any legal question she may have."

James looked as if he wanted to argue, but Fay tugged on his arm. She gave Amy a killing look as she passed by her. Lottie was more reluctant to leave. "Sheriff Van Horn, what's this all about?" she asked anxiously.

Mena said softly, "Come on, Mama. Let's give them some privacy."

She shepherded Lottie out of the room, and then turned, her gaze meeting Amy's briefly before the parlor door closed between them. But a look Amy couldn't fathom flashed in Mena's eyes.

Reece grabbed Amy's shoulders and turned her to face him. "Are you sure you're okay? My God, when I heard you were missing again..."

"I'm fine," Amy said, stepping back from his grasp. "Would you please just tell me what's going on here?"

"It's pretty simple." Van Horn rested his hand on the butt of his holstered weapon. "This here letter proves I was right. Someone tried to murder you nine years ago, and I expect I had the right suspect all along."

Amy stared at him, appalled. "You think Con did that to me? You're wrong, Sheriff. Dead wrong."

"Am I?" His gaze narrowed on her. Beside her, Reece took her arm. Amy suddenly wanted to shake off his hand, but she stood rigid, returning the sheriff's cold glare. "Nearest I can figure, Frankie Bodine must have given this to you, probably sometime last night. Am I right?"

"Yes, but — "

"I drove out to Frankie's this afternoon after I read this letter. I just came from there. Couldn't find Frankie anywhere, but his place had been sacked pretty good and I found a lot of blood out in the woods." Van Horn took a pouch from his pocket, and pinched tobacco between his thumb and forefinger. Then he stuffed it in his jaw. "Someone got to Frankie. Maybe someone looking for this letter, or maybe someone who figured he knew more than he was telling."

"It wasn't Con," Amy said flatly, realizing suddenly how he must have felt all those years ago, trying to explain himself when no one would listen to him, least of all a thickheaded sheriff with a penchant for jumping to conclusions. "Frankie was shot last night. I saw him."

"Did you see who did it?"

"No, but I know it wasn't Con."

"The way I see it," Van Horn continued, as if Amy hadn't spoken, "Sullivan figured out that Frankie was the one to pull you out of the river that night. He was worried Frankie might have seen something. He followed you out there last night, Frankie surprised him and the two of them scuffled. I wouldn't be surprised if Frankie didn't inflict some damage himself before Sullivan shot him. We found

Frankie's hunting knife in the woods, and there was blood on it. Frankie always was good with a knife.''

Amy shook her head, pushing away doubts that started to burn inside her. But suddenly she had an image of Con on the bridge last night, waiting for her. The muddy boots. The high-powered rifle. And later, when he'd come home from looking for Frankie, his arm was bandaged.

She wouldn't listen to this. She wouldn't believe any of them. She wouldn't betray Con by turning on him. ''You're wrong about this. About everything. Why would Con want to hurt me? He—''

''Loves you?'' Reece asked softly.

Amy turned to face him. He looked down at her with a wounded gaze. ''I know all about the two of you, Amy. The way it was between you back then. You wanted to hurt your father that summer so you started running around with a hoodlum.''

''How would you know?'' Amy defended. ''You don't know anything about him.''

''And how much do you really know about him?'' Reece's voice hardened. ''He's been lying to you, Amy. He's deceived you ever since you came back here.''

A chill shivered up her backbone, but Amy refused to give in to it. She crossed her arms, glaring up at Reece. ''What are you talking about?''

''I'm talking about this.'' He pulled a document from his pocket and handed it to her.

She glanced at the paper doubtfully. ''What is this?''

''It's a copy of a court order presuming death.

Your death, Amy. Con's had you declared legally dead.''

You're dead, Amber. You just don't know it yet.

Amy gasped. Fear shot through her heart like an arrow. "I don't believe you. Why would he do—?''

"Because he wants something you've got,'' Reece said. "And the only way he can get it is for you to be dead.''

A tiny bubble of hysteria rose inside her. "What are you talking about? What does he want?''

Reece paused. "He wants Amberly. Evidently, Jasmine has been receptive to his offer. They've signed a contract.''

Amy gazed at the paper in her hand, trying to find something in the legal wording that would contradict Reece's claim. But the writing blurred before her eyes. Why hadn't Con told her?

She lifted trembling fingers to her lips. "He wouldn't do this. Not behind my back. He would have told me.'' When Reece remained silent, Amy cried, "Why didn't anyone else tell me, then?''

Reece shrugged. "Maybe they didn't know. Once the judge signed the order, all Con had to do was run an ad—a tiny ad—in a local newspaper, so that any interested party could come forward to object to the granting of the final order. It's a pretty forthright procedure.''

Like a strobe, another image flashed through Amy's mind. Con, in Mena's office yesterday. Mena had been so embarrassed and flustered to see Amy. It made sense now, if she knew what Con was up to. If she was a party to it somehow.

"Why?" she whispered, almost to herself.

Reece moved toward her, staring down at her urgently. "Don't you understand? Amberly is symbolic to him. Think about it, Amy. He thought he'd killed you nine years ago. Imagine how he must have been haunted by your memory. What better way to exorcise your ghost than to destroy the place he most associated with you?"

This place has always evoked strong feelings.

Con's own words came back to taunt her.

As if sensing her vulnerability, Reece said, "You were almost run off the road the other day, Amy. You could have been killed. Who do you think was in that truck?"

Amy gasped. "How did you know about that?"

Something flashed in Reece's eyes. A look of regret that he had to be the one to tell her. "The sheriff must have mentioned it to me."

"He didn't know. I never reported it."

"Lottie or one of the twins, then." Reece dismissed her question impatiently. "What does it matter? The point is, you can't trust Sullivan."

Amy didn't think she could trust anyone. A black suspicion took form inside her. How had Reece known about that truck?

She looked up at him. "How did you find out about all of this? How long have you been here?"

"I just got here this morning. When I found out you were missing—"

Amy cut him off with a look. "You've had a private investigator down here, haven't you? After I asked you not to."

"I couldn't let you come down here alone. My God, Amy, think about it. You disappeared that night without a trace. No one knew what happened to you. For all I knew, you could be walking into a dangerous situation."

"For all you knew," she said slowly. "And you knew a lot, didn't you, Reece? You knew the truth about my past, even before I did."

"You're not making any sense. I know you're frightened—"

"I'm making perfect sense," Amy said coldly. "You had me investigated months ago, didn't you? You knew I was Amber Tremain."

Guilt flickered in his eyes before he had time to conceal it. He reached for her, but Amy jerked away from him. "You set this all up, didn't you? The woman who approached me in the restaurant—that was your doing. There's no such thing as coincidence."

His jaw set in an angry line. "What was I supposed to do? Marry you without knowing what I might be getting?" As if realizing he'd said too much, he looked at her in supplication. "Please try to understand."

"Oh, I do understand," Amy told him. "You knew I was about to back out from our wedding. You thought if my past started coming back to haunt me, I'd rush to you for protection. I'd go through with the marriage, and you'd not only get me, but half of Amberly."

"Look, someone had to watch out for your interests," he defended.

"Don't," she said in contempt. "Don't try to make this anything other than it was. All this time, you've been manipulating me to get what you wanted. That's how you knew about the truck almost running me off the road, isn't it? You set that up, too, so I'd come running back to you in fear. What else have you done to me, Reece?" She stared at him in outrage, realizing there was so much more to him than she'd ever guessed. He had a dark side she wished she'd never seen.

He returned her stare, a tiny tic pulsing at his temple. "I've done some things I'm not proud of. I'll admit that. But you have to look past that now. Your life depends on it. Sullivan is the one who is a threat to you. He lied to you. He deceived you. And if the sheriff's suspicions are true, he even tried to kill you. More than once."

Amy shook her head, still in denial. "I don't believe any of this."

Reece grasped her arms, his grip tightening painfully. "There's something else. Sullivan has another reason for wanting Amberly. A more powerful reason. You accused me of being greedy, but so is he. His deal with the development company hinges on his ability to acquire property on this side of the river, as well. Namely, Amberly. This is where they want to build a marina. Your coming back here threatens the whole agreement, and from what I've been able to determine, Sullivan stands to lose everything if he can't deliver Amberly. The only way he can win is to get rid of you again. This time for good."

"And that kinda ties everything up real nice and neat, now, don't it?" Van Horn drawled from across the room, injecting himself back into the confrontation. "Means, motive and opportunity. All I have to do now is find him and haul him off to jail. Once Frankie's body turns up, that'll be all she wrote for Conner Sullivan."

CON'S TRAILER WAS DARK when Amy got there. She didn't see his truck, but she knew that he usually parked around back. Running breathlessly up the porch steps, she banged on the door. "Con! Are you in there? We have to talk."

When he didn't answer immediately, she tried the knob. The door was unlocked and she rushed inside, intent on warning him. No matter what he might have done in regard to Amberly, Amy knew he hadn't tried to kill her. He hadn't murdered Frankie, either, but the sheriff, and maybe Reece, too, were trying to frame him. "Con!

Amy paused, getting her bearings in the moonlight. She didn't want to turn on a light for fear someone had followed her across the bridge. She had the impression that Van Horn was definitely of the "shoot now and ask questions later" persuasion.

Water was running in the bathroom, and Amy realized Con must be in the shower.

Crossing the room, she called to him again. "Con?"

The sparse moonlight allowed in by the trailer's tiny windows didn't penetrate the hallway. The corridor was black, and Amy had to feel her way along.

The bathroom was dark, too, and she wondered if Con had turned off the light and gone into the bedroom. She knew from experience he could move without making a sound, but why would he leave the water running?

Amy started to call to him again, but something— a premonition that tickled the back of her neck— stopped her. Almost in slow motion, her hand reached up to turn on the bathroom light.

And then she screamed. Screamed in terror and horror and revulsion at the blood streaked across the mirror and the sink and trailing across the floor to the bathtub. The running water washed pink stains down the drain, while bloody fingerprints clutched at the shower curtain, as if someone had tried to strip it away. But it remained intact, hiding whatever— or whoever—was behind the plastic.

Gasping for breath, retching, Amy reached a trembling hand to the shower curtain. It couldn't be Con. Please God—

Trembling, praying, she pulled the curtain aside. Frankie Bodine sat hunkered in the tub, his clothes covered with blood and filth, his eyes closed, his expression frozen.

Sheriff Van Horn's words stabbed through Amy like a dagger. *Sullivan figured out that Frankie was the one to pull you out of the river that night. He was worried Frankie might have seen something.*

"Oh God, oh God, oh God," she whispered. For a moment, she couldn't do anything but stare at poor Frankie.

Then she backed out of the room, grabbing at

walls as she stumbled toward the living room. Opening the front door, she all but fell outside, dropping to her hands and knees, gulping in fresh air as her stomach rolled inside her.

Glancing up, she saw Con in the distance, limping up from the direction of the river. He stopped when he spotted her and gazed at her for a long moment before he started up the path toward her.

At that precise moment, with visions of blood and death still fresh in her mind and Reece's warning still ringing in her ears, Amy was beyond thinking, beyond reasoning. She reacted instantly, whirling away from Con to sprint for the woods behind his trailer.

He called her name once, but she still didn't turn back, didn't even glance over her shoulder until she'd reached the cover of trees. She tore through the woods with some vague notion of circling around to the road, somehow making it out to the main highway and finding a phone.

Trying not to let her panic and fear completely destroy her sense of direction, she widened her arc, and then headed back toward the river road.

If Con was pursuing her, somehow she'd managed to lose him. He'd been limping badly, no doubt from the strain of searching for Frankie all day, maybe even carrying him back to the trailer. She remembered he'd told her the night before that he could carry more than twice her weight—

No, she wouldn't think about last night. She wouldn't think about Con's muddy boots or the high-powered rifle he'd been carrying at the bridge.

Amy wouldn't allow herself to think about anything except getting help for Frankie. Then, and only then, would she try to sort through her feelings.

She came bursting out of the trees onto the gravel road. Headlights from an oncoming car caught her in the face, and like a frightened deer, Amy froze for just a split second.

The driver seemed to come right at her. Amy tried to get out of the way, but the front fender caught her hard, lifted her off her feet, and she came down on the hood with a crash that immediately knocked the breath out of her.

The driver threw on the brakes, spewing gravel and dirt from beneath the wheels. Amy tumbled from the car and landed in the middle of the road, the sharp edges of the gravel cutting like razors into her flesh. Dazed with pain, she rolled onto her back, groaning.

A door opened and footsteps crunched on the gravel road. A figure stood over her, but the headlights blinded Amy. She put up a hand to shield her eyes. "I think I'm hurt," she said weakly.

The figure bent over her, and as Amy reached up in supplication, a hand clapped over her mouth, and a rag was shoved against her nose. Almost instantly, the sweet, sickly fumes overtook her.

CHAPTER SIXTEEN

CON WASN'T SURE why he didn't immediately go after Amber. He couldn't imagine why she'd run away from him like that, but then, it was possible she hadn't seen him, or heard him call to her. She'd appeared to be in a state of agitation, and as Con looked up at the darkened trailer, the front door swinging wide open the way she'd left it, he realized in an instant that something inside had frightened her, had sent her running away into the night. From him.

Lifting the rifle, he entered the trailer, moving through the darkness as silently as a shadow. He smelled the blood almost immediately, and tracked the scent to the bathroom.

He's seen blood before, plenty of it, sometimes even his own. But he wasn't prepared for the sight that met his eyes. Somehow, in his own home, the violation seemed more perverse.

Entering the room, his gaze flew to the bathtub, and he drew in a sharp breath. He'd been searching for Frankie all day and had thought he'd found him at one point. But either the noise had been a false alarm, or Frankie was a lot more clever, and a lot more fleet, than Con had given him credit for.

How the hell had he gotten here?

Moving quickly across the floor, Con knelt beside the bloodied bathtub. One of Frankie's arms hung limply over the side, and Con picked up his wrist, feeling for a pulse, but not finding one.

He got up then and searched through the trailer, quietly, efficiently, looking for evidence of who had been there. Finding nothing, he walked back into the bathroom, trying to piece together a likely scenario. One thing was clear to him now. Amy had seen him outside. She'd heard him call to her. The reason she'd fled was that she thought he'd done this to Frankie.

She thought he was a murderer.

Anger tore through him like a bullet. How could she think that? How could she believe that of him after what they'd shared last night?

How could she be like everyone else in this god-forsaken town?

Con turned to go after her, but out of the corner of his eye, he saw a movement. He thought it was his imagination at first. He hadn't found a pulse. Frankie was dead. But as he stood there, one of Frankie's fingers moved.

AMY AWAKENED IN darkness. She was lying on her side, and for a moment, she thought she was back at Frankie's house. But vague silhouettes took shape, and she recognized the glimmer of moonlight on a mirror, the shadow of an armoire, the posters of the bed where she lay.

Her stomach lurched sickeningly, and as she tried

to get up, her arms screamed in pain. She realized her wrists were bound tightly behind her.

For a long moment, she struggled with the bindings. Sweat broke out on her forehead as the rope cut into her skin and the knot tightened. Forced to give up, she rolled to the edge of the bed, and swung her legs off.

Although she had only a vague impression of the room, a sense of recognition came over her. Like Frankie's house, Amy knew she'd been here before. Was she back at home?

She crossed softly to the door and put her back to it, turning the knob with her fingertips. To her surprise, the door was unlocked. The hallway beyond was lit, and Amy knew at once the house she was in wasn't Amberly. Where was she, then?

A door stood ajar across the corridor, and Amy peered inside. The recognition grew stronger. The room was another bedroom, decorated as if for a child. The pink canopied bed, ruffled curtains and collection of what Amy knew were antique dolls instilled a deep sense of dread in her.

Whose room was this?

Walking over to the bureau, she stared down at the collection of heirlooms assembled like offerings on the top. Silver antique combs, a French music box—

Suddenly, images bombarded her. As if she were floating free from her body, Amy saw herself—at eighteen this time—opening the lid of the music box and picking up the emerald necklace inside. And then, her voice cracking on a sob, "You killed my mother!"

It all still seemed so dreamlike to her. Almost calmly, Amy turned as a shadow moved in the corner of the room. She stared at the gun in Corliss Witherspoon's hand, and her aunt smiled. "You're up and about, I see. Time to take a little ride, Amber Rochelle."

THEY WERE IN CORLISS'S car, traveling along the highway. Amy sat in the back, tearing at the bindings on her wrist. "Where are you taking me?"

"Now, that would spoil the surprise if I told you that. And you always did love surprises."

"Why did you kill my mother?" Amy blurted.

Corliss glanced at her in the rearview mirror. "Because she deserved it. Emmett was mine and she took him from me." She lifted her fingers to her neck and touched the emerald lovingly. "This necklace was mine, too. He bought it for me. Everyone knew green was my color. He was going to give it to me for Christmas. It was going to be *my* engagement present."

She pulled down the vanity mirror, admiring the pendant as she turned one way and then the other to allow light to spark off the stone. And all the while, the car flew along the highway. Outside the tinted windows, the shadowy scenery passed by in a blur. Amy had no idea where they where.

"I saw the necklace that night, didn't I?" she whispered. "I came to your house the night I disappeared."

Corliss sighed. "You were always so worrisome back then, always whining about Lottie. As if I didn't have troubles of my own!"

"I came over after I had that fight with Daddy," Amy said slowly, letting the memories flow into her. There was still so much she couldn't remember, but the events of that night were starting to come back to her. "I'd gone down to meet Con at the bridge, only…he wasn't there. I didn't know what to do. Daddy had all but thrown me out, and Con had turned his back on me. Or so I thought. So I came to you."

"Lucky me," Corliss grumbled. "You just came barging in. I'll never forget it. I was sitting there in my green housecoat, enjoying a nice rerun of *Hart to Hart,* and you just appeared in my living room. You said you rang the bell, but I guess I didn't hear you over the TV."

"We talked for a long time," Amy recalled. "I sat there and told you all about eloping with Con, and you said you'd deal with Daddy for me in the morning. I went upstairs to bed and saw that the spare room was open. Something compelled me to go in. That's when I saw all the heirlooms you'd stolen from Amberly. And Mama's necklace."

Corliss shrugged. "I was never the careless type. Looking back, I think I must have wanted you to find that necklace. You'd always been so dang certain Miranda didn't kill herself, and I'd had to worry about that for so long. I guess I always knew I'd have to get rid of you sooner or later."

"So you took me out to the river, tied a weight

around my ankle and dumped me. You left me to drown, just like my mother.''

Corliss swerved to avoid hitting something in the road. Amy's head banged against the window. ''Damn rabbit,'' Corliss muttered.

Bruised and battered, Amy stared out the darkened window as she fought the ropes around her wrists. ''You were the one who stole the antiques, but you let me blame Lottie.''

Corliss shrugged. ''You despised her. I figured you'd get rid of her for me, save me the trouble.''

''The pink room in your house was like mother's room when she was a little girl. You wanted that, too.''

''She always got the best of everything,'' Corliss grumbled. ''Daddy said pink didn't suit me. He had my room done in green, because that was my color, but I always loved Miranda Lee's pink room the best.''

She coveted everything of her sister's, Amy thought. Because she had always been jealous. And that jealousy had finally consumed her.

Amy struggled even harder with the ropes, but it was no use. She tried to turn so that she could get her hands on the door handle.

''Don't bother with that,'' Corliss advised. ''I've got the child safety latch on.''

She turned on the river road, and after a few minutes, Amy could see the bridge in the distance, rising from the mist, and terror washed over her again. If she could somehow get her hands free...if she could climb over the seat...open the door...

What she had to do was distract Corliss, keep her talking while she worked loose the ropes. The element of surprise was crucial.

"How did you lure Mama down to the bridge that night?"

"It was almost too easy," Corliss said. "I made her think Emmett was meeting Lottie down there."

"You're the one who started those rumors." Her poor mother, Amy thought. Did she have even an inkling of what her sister was capable of?

They were at the bridge now. Amy could see the mist swirling over the water, curling like smoke around the cypress knees and swamp grass. She couldn't get loose. No matter how hard she tried, she couldn't get free.

Corliss pulled onto the bridge and stopped. The girders rose over them, dark and menacing in the moonlight.

Amy said, "Don't do this. You can't get away with it."

"Oh, I can't, can I? I've gotten away with it twice before, didn't I?"

"Corliss—" Amy was never sure what she was about to say, but suddenly, the boards beneath the car snapped, the sound as loud as a cannon shot. Almost instantly, the rear tires slipped through the cracks, and the front of the car pitched upward. Amy tumbled against the back glass, smacking her head on the window. She could feel blood streaming down her face, but she couldn't wipe it away. She couldn't do anything but lie there, breathless and waiting, as the car remained suspended, the broken boards creaking and groaning beneath them.

Corliss seemed stunned at first. Then, she started to panic, and her movements became frantic. Before she could open her door and escape, the bridge floor gave way with another loud crack, and the car slid backward into the abyss.

The car hit the water with a crash that pounded every bone in Amy's battered body. She shot forward, and then backward, blacking out momentarily. When she came to, the car was sinking. The darkness around her was almost as complete as her terror, the scene as surreal as any nightmare. Panic exploded inside her, and she struggled with the ropes, kicking and flailing, her only thought one of survival.

The floor filled rapidly with water, but the vacuum created inside the car allowed them to breathe. As the car settled to the bottom, Corliss rolled down her window and opened her door to escape. The river came rushing in.

Within seconds, Amy was underwater, fighting the ropes around her wrist, frantically trying to maneuver herself over the front seat. But the water was so cold and her fear so numbing, that after only a few seconds, she began to lose the fight.

This was what her mother had felt. This was what her last few moments had been like. The agony. The terror. The helpless feeling of betrayal.

As the precious seconds ticked by, Amy's struggles ceased. Her strength ebbed, and a strange lethargy slipped over her.

The water was warm now and welcoming. Her fear dissolved. She closed her eyes and visions came.

A soothing voice drifted through her head as the water carried her gently into her mother's waiting arms....

CON HAD NEVER KNOWN the kind of terror he experienced the moment he saw Corliss's car go crashing through the bridge. He knew Amber was inside. Frankie had gained consciousness in the hospital long enough to whisper who had shot him, and Con had known even then that Corliss would want to finish the job she'd started nine years ago.

Frantic with worry, Con had gone over to Corliss's house, but her car had been missing from the garage. And he knew then that she would bring Amy back to the bridge.

Back to the bridge where Con had been waiting nine years for Amber to come home.

Without a moment's hesitation, he dove from the bridge, sailing breathlessly through the air and then cutting through the water with his hands before plunging downward. The water was murky and cold, disorienting. But the moon was up, shimmering on the surface, and after a moment, Con saw the car, resting on the bottom, about fifteen feet down.

He swam toward it, and as he neared the submerged vehicle, an eerie feeling came over him, almost as if someone were watching him from those cloudy depths. Then he saw her.

The chill that coursed through him had nothing to

do with the frigid water, and everything to do with the woman hovering in the water.

Corliss stared at him through glassy, unseeing eyes. She'd become tangled in a fishing line, and the sturdy cord had somehow entwined itself with her necklace, trapping her. Even in the dusky light, the emerald seemed to flash with a life of its own. Shaken, Con turned away, propelling himself toward the car.

The door on the driver's side hung open, and he swam inside. Amy was lying in the back seat, her wrists bound behind her, her body lifeless and silent.

By this time, Con's lungs were screaming. His arms and legs were becoming numb. He knew he couldn't last much longer. He reached for Amy, pulling her easily over the seat in the water and then angling them both out of the car.

He didn't bother untying her. There wasn't time for that. Kicking with everything in him, Con pulled Amber upward, upward, to the gleaming moonbeams that seemed like beacons of safety in the dark and deadly night.

CHAPTER SEVENTEEN

AMY CAME OUT of the Choppowah County Courthouse, and paused on the steps to say a few words to James Birdsong. The two separated, and she started across the shady lawn toward the sidewalk.

It had been nearly a week since Corliss died. Amy had only been out of the hospital a couple of days. When Con had pulled her from the water, she'd been unconscious, coming to only when the emergency technicians were loading her into the ambulance. She'd tried to say something to him then, explain why she'd run from him, but he hadn't come to her. He'd kept his distance, standing alone, as he always had, while everyone rushed around her.

She hadn't seen him since that night.

A couple of times, she'd awakened in the hospital, still groggy from her medicated sleep, and thought she'd seen him, once standing at the window, and once hovering over her bed. But when she'd tried to speak to him, he'd vanished. Or perhaps she'd drifted off to sleep again.

Maybe he would never want to see her again, Amy thought as she headed back to her car. She'd turned against him, like everyone else in this town had. She'd blamed him for something he hadn't done, and it might be that he would never be able to forgive her.

Amy could understand that. There were some things she was having a hard time forgiving, too. Reece had finally admitted to her in the hospital that he'd been the one driving the black truck that had almost run her off the road. He'd wanted to scare her into coming back to him, but even more damning than that—at least in Amy's view—was the fact that he'd known for months who she was. He'd had her and Nona investigated long before he'd asked her to marry him, and he'd found out that Amber Tremain, if still alive, would inherit half of Amberly.

So many lies, Amy thought morosely, and so much deception. So much heartache, and all because Corliss Witherspoon had always hated her sister.

As Amy came off the shady lawn, the glaring sun on the street temporarily blinded her. She didn't see Con standing by her car until she was almost upon him. Then she stopped dead in her tracks, her heart pounding.

He wore jeans and a white undershirt that exposed his tanned muscles and the tiny snake tattoo that still fascinated her so.

Slowly, she lifted her gaze to his.

His eyes were dark and deep, his expression almost stern as he stared down at her, taking in the cuts and bruises, the bandage on her forehead.

"I was afraid I might not see you again."

He straightened from the car and came toward her, towering over her, making Amy's heart beat even harder. "I'm not going anywhere," he said. "Are you?"

"No." Then, almost defiantly, she said, "I'm taking steps to be declared legally alive again."

"Congratulations." His dark gaze swept over her. "I see you're wearing white."

"It's an important day." She drew a long breath. "Why did you do it, Con? Why did you have me declared legally dead? Did you really want Amberly that badly?"

Something flickered in his eyes. Regret. Pain. "Amberly was the least of it. I thought if you were legally dead, that would be the end of it. No more memories. No more ghosts."

"Instead, I came back." Another irony, she thought. She lifted her chin. "I'm warning you, Con. I'm going to fight to get Amberly back."

"I figured you would."

"I don't want it torn down to make room for a marina. I don't want my home destroyed."

"You don't have to fight for what has always been yours," he said. "I've torn up the contract with Jasmine."

"But Reece said you stood to lose everything if you didn't get Amberly."

He shrugged again. "I've been poor before. I always manage to get by. Besides, there's other property along the river." He paused. "So what about everyone else? Are they staying on at the house, too?"

"Under the circumstances, we thought it best if Lottie and the girls move out. There's been too much bad blood over the years...." She trailed off. "Maybe someday we can all work out our differences, but for now...I just want to concentrate on rebuilding a relationship with Jasmine." *And you*, she wanted to add.

"I've been to see Frankie," Con said. "He's going to be all right."

"I know. I've been to see him, too. He saved my life. I can never repay him for that, but I'm going to try somehow. Maybe I'll start by getting a confession out of Fay."

"Good luck," Con said grimly. "So how is Jasmine handling...everything?"

"Our marriage, you mean." Amy sighed. "I should have told her right from the first. She shouldn't have heard it from Fay. I'm not sure why I didn't tell her."

"Probably for the same reason I didn't tell you about my contract to buy Amberly. I was afraid."

Amy's heart fluttered at the way he was looking at her. "Jasmine and I have talked a lot in the last few days. She's put things in perspective since she found out about Corliss. And about our mother. She's done a lot of growing up."

"She nearly lost you again. I've never seen anyone more frightened than she was at the hospital that night."

Amy said carefully, "She still has a crush on you, you know."

"She'll get over it."

"You're not that easy to get over," Amy murmured.

They lapsed into silence, the thing that was most important still left unspoken. After a moment, Amy said, "I wish I hadn't run away from you that night. Con, I'm sorry. I never should have suspected you, even for a moment."

He glanced away. "I'd like to say it doesn't matter."

"But it does," Amy said. "I know it does. Everyone in this town has always thought the worst of you, and now I'm no different. But I thought I was."

He was standing silently in front of her, his expression shuttered by the sunlight. Although he was near enough Amy could reach out and touch him, he seemed a million miles away. Remote and unapproachable. A loner, not by choice, but by a town who had turned its back on him a long time ago, and by an eighteen-year-old girl who had married him to get back at her father.

Amy said quietly, "Why didn't you have our marriage dissolved?" When he glanced down at her, she said, "You petitioned to have me declared legally dead, but you didn't ask the court to dissolve our marriage. I can't help wondering why."

He lifted a hand and touched her hair, as if he still weren't quite sure she was real. "I told you once. I never intended to marry again. There was never going to be anyone else for me."

Amy's breath caught. She couldn't speak.

He buried both hands in her hair, holding her face still while he stared into her eyes. "We've both made mistakes, and we've both paid one hell of a big price. Nine years of our lives. But one thing has never changed. I've always loved you, and I always will.''

Amy's eyes flooded with tears. It was all she could do to hold them back. ''I'm in love with you, too. I still don't remember a lot of what happened back then, but—''

He silenced her with a kiss. When he lifted his head, his gaze was dark and intense. Smoldering, Amy thought. ''It doesn't matter, because I don't want to live with memories anymore. I want the real you, Amy.''

She brushed her lips against his. ''Amber,'' she whispered. ''My name is Amber.''

Every Man Has His Price!

HEART OF THE WEST

At the heart of the West there are a dozen rugged bachelors—up for auction!

This August 1999, look for *Courting Callie* by **Lynn Erickson**

If Mase Lebow testifies at a high-profile trial, he knows his six-year-old son, Joey, will pay. Mase decides to hide his son at Callie Thorpe's ranch, out of harm's way. Callie, of course, has no idea why Joey is really there, and falling in love with his tight-lipped father is a definite inconvenience.

Each book features a sexy new bachelor up for grabs—and a woman determined to rope him in!

Available August 1999 at your favorite retail outlet.

HARLEQUIN®

Makes any time special ™

*Amnesia...
an unknown danger...
a burning desire.*

With

HARLEQUIN®

I N T R I G U E ®

you're just

A MEMORY AWAY

from passion, danger...and love!

**Look for all the books in this
exciting miniseries:**

**#527 ONE TEXAS NIGHT
by Sylvie Kurtz**
August 1999

**#531 TO SAVE HIS BABY
by Judi Lind**
September 1999

**#536 UNDERCOVER DAD
by Charlotte Douglas**
October 1999

A MEMORY AWAY—where remembering
the truth becomes a matter of life,
death...and love!

Available wherever Harlequin books are sold.

HARLEQUIN®
Makes any time special ™

Starting in September 1999,
Harlequin Temptation®
will also be celebrating
an anniversary—15 years
of bringing you the
best in passion.

Look for these
Harlequin Temptation® titles
at your favorite retail stores
in September:

CLASS ACT
by Pamela Burford
BABY.COM
by Molly Liholm
NIGHT WHISPERS
by Leslie Kelly
THE SEDUCTION OF SYDNEY
by Jamie Denton

From *New York Times* bestselling author

Barbara Delinsky

Jenna McCue needs a favor—a very big favor—and Spencer Smith is her only hope. She's counting on his sense of adventure to give her something she wants more than anything: a baby.

But Spencer has a plan of his own. He just might give her that baby, but it will be the old-fashioned way! Since what Jenna doesn't realize is that he isn't willing to be *just*...

The Stud